A 'COP FOR CRIMINALS'

HUNT
— THE —
PREY

JACK GATLAND

Published by Hooded Man Media.
Cover photo by Paul Thomas Gooney

First Edition: June 2023

PRAISE FOR JACK GATLAND

'This is one of those books that will keep you up past your bedtime, as each chapter lures you into reading just one more.'

'This book was excellent! A great plot which kept you guessing until the end.'

'Couldn't put it down, fast paced with twists and turns.'

'The story was captivating, good plot, twists you never saw and really likeable characters. Can't wait for the next one!'

'I got sucked into this book from the very first page, thoroughly enjoyed it, can't wait for the next one.'

'Totally addictive. Thoroughly recommend.'

'Moves at a fast pace and carries you along with it.'

'Just couldn't put this book down, from the first page to the last one it kept you wondering what would happen next.'

There's a new Detective Inspector in town...

Before Ellie Reckless, there was DI Declan Walsh!

An EXCLUSIVE PREQUEL, completely free to anyone who joins the Jack Gatland Reader's Club!

Join at www.subscribepage.com/jackgatland

Also by Jack Gatland

DI DECLAN WALSH BOOKS
LETTER FROM THE DEAD
MURDER OF ANGELS
HUNTER HUNTED
WHISPER FOR THE REAPER
TO HUNT A MAGPIE
A RITUAL FOR THE DYING
KILLING THE MUSIC
A DINNER TO DIE FOR
BEHIND THE WIRE
HEAVY IS THE CROWN
STALKING THE RIPPER
A QUIVER OF SORROWS
MURDER BY MISTLETOE
BENEATH THE BODIES
KILL YOUR DARLINGS
KISSING A KILLER

ELLIE RECKLESS BOOKS
PAINT THE DEAD
STEAL THE GOLD
HUNT THE PREY
FIND THE LADY

TOM MARLOWE BOOKS
SLEEPING SOLDIERS
TARGET LOCKED
COVERT ACTION
COUNTER ATTACK

DAMIAN LUCAS BOOKS

THE LIONHEART CURSE

STANDALONE BOOKS

THE BOARDROOM

AS TONY LEE

DODGE & TWIST

For Mum, who inspired me to write.

For Tracy, who inspires me to write.

CONTENTS

1. Ding Boom   1
2. Bishop Takes Knight   13
3. Candid Shots   25
4. Job Interview   38
5. Fire Damage   49
6. Witness Statements   60
7. Offensive Play   70
8. Dead Men Scars   81
9. Sleep-Over   96
10. Graveside Confession   106
11. Eye Spy   120
12. Unwanted Visitors   131
13. Interrogation   142
14. No Vault Of Mine   154
15. Grandad, We Love You   166
16. Prodigal Sons   179
17. The Driver   189
18. Meet The New Boss   201
19. Hunt The Copper   212
20. Pull The Pin   227
21. Warehoused   240
22. Vigil   252
23. Pulling The Cords   264
24. Confrontations   274
25. Late Night Visitors   289
26. Mexican Waving   301
27. Burn The Favours   311
    Epilogue   318

    Acknowledgements   333
    About the Author   335

1

DING BOOM

NICKY SIMPSON HADN'T EXPECTED THE ATTACK.

Actually, that was a lie. Of course, he'd expected the attack; he'd been expecting it for weeks now, but he simply hadn't expected the direction it'd come from.

He'd been waiting for something to happen ever since Mama Lumetta and her gang of merry criminal sons and cousins had been either arrested, killed, or simply fled the country, as all hell broke loose around the stolen contents of an olive oil truck, and the subsequent collapse of her illegal empire.

The truck, the theft or any of the shit that followed it wasn't part of anything to do with Nicky himself, but he had been in business with the sons, looking to build some of his health clubs in Dublin and the surrounding areas, and the moment the shit had hit the fan, he was forced to reluctantly walk away from the deal. After all, he was a respected businessman and YouTuber; he couldn't hang around with identified criminals.

And yes, the irony of that statement wasn't wasted on him.

The deal hadn't been purely about the clubs, though. Nicky was looking to expand his other areas into Ireland, and the Lumettas had a very good and longstanding reputation on the eastern side, north of Dublin and up to the Mourne Mountains, where the border between North and South was a lesser, but nevertheless still visible, presence southwards down to Cork.

Expansion was good. Growth was good. And, if he had to admit it, he needed to grow before he stagnated. At almost thirty years old, Nicky Simpson was pretty much as high as he could be right now. His Simpson's Health Spas were going viral on TikTok because of some dance one of his personal trainers had done during a session – he'd almost fired them, but after he saw the video hit the millions, he actually invited her to work in his social media department. Which was a good deal, actually, because she was a shit personal trainer. Always going off and doing bloody TikTok videos, for a start.

He was muscled, recently detoxed, and his dirty blond hair gave the look of someone scruffy, but well maintained. He'd recently moved from Canary Wharf to a swish apartment in Battersea Power Station, near his new flagship health club empire HQ, and had gained great local press by this: the self-made South Londoner done good, returning to the "right" side of the river.

Personally, Nicky didn't care that much about the River Thames, London, or anything involving the city's tribal love of postcodes. He'd grown up just north of Camberwell, in South London; a third generation Simpson to live there, but he hadn't enjoyed it. He'd spent his childhood watching his father, Max Simpson, try to live up to the reputation Nicky's grandfather, Paddy Simpson, had left behind when he retired over twenty years earlier. Paddy had worked for the Richardson Brothers as some kind of self-taught accountant back in the sixties, stepping in to control their patch when they went down for three decades in Her Majesty's Prisons. He'd quickly shown himself to be just as vicious and psychotic as the pair of them in the seventies, and even in the nineties he was terrifying people, and was one of the people reported to have shot Pat Tate with a shotgun, in an assassination known as the Land Rover Killings.

Of course, that was a rumour, but Nicky had grown up hearing tales that "Granddad couldn't make his birthday because he had business," which matched, as his birthday was the same day as the killings.

He'd been a toddler at the time, but it'd followed him constantly.

After decades in the business, Paddy gave it up while he was ahead, feeling the change in the wind, and retired on the millennium, leaving the South of London under his son's care, and moving to Majorca, a giant villa on the cliffs looking out across the ocean, and part of the "Costa Del Crime," living a peaceful life mainly because of a lack of extradition agreements, and the knowledge that his capture wasn't really a priority for the Spanish authorities.

The problem was, Max Simpson wasn't the Michael Corleone to his father's Vito, and in fact actively lost respect and influence over the following decade. If it wasn't for a diagnosis of Parkinson's disease in 2014, Max would likely have carried on until the firm was dead, which would have likely been within a couple of years. As it was, Max was quietly ousted, while the then-nineteen-year-old Nicky was brought in, by Paddy, to become the heir apparent, while Max faded away on pain meds, eventually going to the Balearics to live with his dad and a few other South London "wrong'uns" to hang around with.

Nicky hadn't been an angel; he'd had his share of run-ins with the law as a kid, and had been caught multiple times in his childhood, usually nicking things in the Elephant and Castle, and always being bailed out, by proxy from the Balearics, rather than his own dad. In fact, for most of Nicky's teenage years, he'd classed Paddy as more of a father figure than Max. Which, over the years, became something he wasn't proud of. And, after Max showed symptoms, Nicky had realised how little time they'd actually spent together, as father and son.

But by then he'd been given three houses in Camberwell to sell – bought from illegal activities and now needing to be "washed" into clean money before the police inspected – took the millions in profit, and, after giving healthy percentages to his father and grandfather, he'd created Simpson's Health Spas.

It was a better way to launder the dirty money than with houses, you see. He'd taken the lead from East London's Johnny and Jackie Lucas, the "Twins" of the East End, who pushed their books through a boxing club, primarily at least. In a way, Nicky had started the health clubs to honour them, but at the same time it was to mock their club; why settle for a dingy boxing club in the arse end of nowhere, when you could take the same idea and place it into every city in the world?

Because Nicky Simpson had plans.

Every city he moved his criminal empire into had a Simpson's Health Spa appear. Every enforcer brought into the business found themselves in the club's PAYE system. He was making crime legit; a true "face", he was attending premieres and having television interviews, dubbed by the press as "the nation's personal trainer," even going so far as to have a meal prep book hit the Waterstones' top ten last Christmas. Christ, he was even in the early stages of getting an award from Princess Anne for his help with the elderly.

And then Ellie Reckless had brought it all crumbling around his head.

Actually, that was unfair; it wasn't Reckless who'd screwed him over; it was Matteo Lumetta, the idiot Italian son, over from Dublin and trying to take over the family, who, while thinking he had the winning hand against her on a rooftop face off, said one damning line, not realising he was being globally live streamed by the bloody woman.

'I came to London to meet with Nicky Simpson, and give my mother support. I decided I could use his criminal connections to help us into Boston. All I had to do in return was give him some land for his health club criminal fronts.'

These were the words broadcast out across the internet streams; carelessly thrown out, but aiming a spotlight on Simpson's Health Spas, and a crosshair directly on the forehead of Nicky Simpson himself.

He'd texted Reckless after the Lumettas had been arrested, expressing his annoyance at being called out as a criminal. Reckless had replied claiming she didn't know. In fact, he'd kept her last message as a keepsake.

> If you have a problem, you know where to find me. And what my office hours are.

At some point, he'd have to deal with Ellie Reckless once and for all, but right now, he had bigger problems. Even though there was no evidence, there was always the rumour mill. People started making YouTube videos about him, armchair forensic detectives started attacking his finances – with the same amount of diligence as the AI websites that tell you the net worth of a celebrity – with no basis to the numbers they gave out on their channels. He'd already had a few taken down legally, a couple taken down after he'd had some personal words, and in the process had neatly avoided the police, as they asked him about his father, and grandfather's dealings. As if this one comment by an overambitious Italian prick suddenly woke them up to the fact there was "crime, crime I say," in South London.

Which, to be honest, was laughable. After all, Nicky Simpson being connected to the criminal underworld wasn't exactly the best kept secret out there. It was just that usually the people weren't stupid enough to shout it from rooftops. And in Matteo's case, literally.

Nicky had gone into crisis mode after that. People had invariably knee-jerked; his Spa subscriptions had fallen, but not by that much. In a weird way, and echoing the celebs that would hang out in the Soho clubs owned by the Krays in the sixties, people kind of *liked* the idea of being a member of a club owned by a criminal. It made their workout sessions exciting. And Nicky had kept quiet, hadn't made any speeches outside his offices, even though the paparazzi would have loved that, simply stepping back and allowing the chatter to die down. There was no proof, as he'd made damn sure over the years to keep himself clean, even if others around him weren't. He'd had a couple of close calls during his reign, the worst of which was a few years earlier, when he realised his off-books accountant, Bryan Noyce, was informing on him to the police.

It was only after Noyce was killed that Nicky learnt the

extent of the betrayal, and it was only the fortuitous affair Noyce was having with the then-DI Reckless, that muddied the waters enough to escape the police's gaze.

Bloody Ellie Reckless again.

He knew Reckless was gunning for him; she had been ever since the trial. She knew he'd been involved somehow in the death of Bryan Noyce, but currently couldn't prove he did so. And that was for valid reasons he'd take to the grave.

But, pushing Ellie Reckless and her team of broken toys to the side, Nicky Simpson had carried on with business, while keeping away from anything too obviously criminal until the heat subsided.

And, with his eye taken off the prize, *that* was when they went for him.

His day had been like every other; he'd risen alone – he wasn't a monk or anything, but relationships exposed weaknesses, and he didn't need that in his life – showered and shaved, and then live-streamed a workout session for his followers. It seemed counter-productive to shower before working out, but he had to look good for the cameras. There was an image to be kept, after all. After that he showered again, skipped breakfast as he was intermittently fasting this week, checked his emails, replied to the more important ones and then went down to his offices. He'd moved to the Battersea club recently, after his Vauxhall offices had proven to be vulnerable to hacking, and when he said "down" he literally meant it, as the journey was a short walk and elevator ride to the offices in the same building, where he was able to plan his *real* day. He had a brand meeting, a discussion about licensing his smoothies to the UAE, and a weaselly scroat muscling in on his horse racing rackets to sort out; and that was just the morning.

Around now his driver, Saleh, would arrive; he'd been with the Simpsons since he was a teenager, and as a young child, Nicky would class Saleh, then more a "gopher" for the family as an older brother figure. Now in his late thirties, his bald head by choice rather than necessity, Saleh was the antithesis to Nicky; always in the shadows, always suited, and never caring about any kind of public reputation. Which made him good for certain "under the radar "tasks.

Today, however, Saleh hadn't turned up.

Nicky hadn't really noticed though, as he didn't need to drive anywhere soon, and he'd spent an hour working through his legal admin, checking on a few investments people around him didn't know about, and monitoring a private CCTV on his Macbook.

This was something he was a little ashamed of, as he'd found himself fixated on the new receptionist as of late, and had personally set up the feed from a secret camera facing the reception desk. One he'd placed himself a couple of weeks earlier, connected to his MacBook screen, so that now and then, he could check into it. He was aware this made him sound stalkerish, however he tried to justify it, no matter how he tried to phrase it with lies, about "ensuring she was happy in her new workplace" and all that, not really working in his head as to why he did this. He hadn't told Saleh, he hadn't told anyone, in fact. It was his little secret.

But he had a reason for this; there was something familiar about her – something he couldn't quite put his finger on. He *knew* he knew her from somewhere. He just didn't know where from.

He hadn't even looked into her personal life yet, mainly watching to see her habits, her quirks, hoping to get the closure he needed, the "oh, she was from *there*" remembrance that would surely come soon, before he really fell down the rabbit hole. And, alone in the office, he turned on the CCTV to see if she was working.

The image on the screen, however, froze him.

She was there, his unknowing obsession, and as he watched, she shouted out to the side, off camera as she started leading people out of the building. If he wasn't in the same building, he'd wonder if there was a fire alarm going on, but if there was one, he'd hear it here.

But there she was, leading people out.

Curious, he looked into this, and went to ask Saleh to check the main floor. It was here he realised he was still alone, and grabbing his state-of-the-art smartphone, he texted Saleh.

> Where are you?

Saleh not being there wasn't a major issue in the great scheme of things, but it was an irritation when he needed something done, and Nicky knew he'd need him to drive later – but at the same time Nicky could just drive his Tesla himself, and get Duncan the duty manager to tell him why all of his rich spa members were now being led out of the building.

The message that replied to this brought him to his feet.

> Sorry.

Nicky closed the MacBook, looking around the office.

Something was wrong.

He was being set up.

The building was being emptied, and he wasn't being

told. If there was a siren going off, he wasn't hearing it, and currently, he was all alone. He rarely had "muscle" with him; he wasn't a Lucas, a Tsang or a Lumetta, he was Nicky bloody Simpson, and he was always too many steps ahead to resort to violence. Well, usually.

And apparently, not this time.

Grabbing his backpack, a leather Osprey one that had pretty much everything he needed dumped inside, he threw his laptop into the back sleeve, grabbed a couple of macrobiotic smoothies from his fridge, and placed them into it as he walked quickly over to the elevator.

However, he slowed down, pausing as he reached across and pressed the button for it – if there *was* a problem, did he really want to be in an elevator as it happened? It was only a couple of floors by stairs. So, ignoring the elevator as it approached and instead opening the fire door with his key fob, he walked out into the stairwell and started down the stairs. He half-turned, however, as above him he heard the *ding* of the elevator doors opening.

He carried on down a couple of steps more, still looking up, and almost returned to the elevator, as it would save him time—

The blast of the explosion threw him down the first flight of stairs.

Now Nicky heard the alarms, as the sprinklers turned on, drenching the staircase, as smoke billowed out of the door he'd just left through, the door itself half-torn off its hinges by the force of the blast.

Nicky wanted to check the office, to see how bad it was, but his survival instinct kicked in. Someone wanted him dead, and there was every chance they'd be coming up right now to look for him, possibly up these same stairs.

Reaching into his pocket, Nicky pulled out a box-cutter knife. He'd fallen out of the habit of keeping a weapon on him; after all, when you have people who'd do violence for you, why worry about it yourself? But recently, he'd taken to keeping a flick-out box-cutter blade with him. A simple Stanley Blade razor blade with a handle, it was a slashing weapon more than a killing blade, and he could always claim he'd been doing some DIY earlier that day and forgot he had it if he was stopped, as the blade length was within legal parameters.

But, if anyone was coming up the stairs for him, they'd soon see what else could be done with such a weapon.

Luckily for Nicky Simpson, nobody intercepted him as he carried on down the stairs, past the main entrance and down into the basement where the car park was. They were either convinced he was dead; the bomb connected to the elevator he'd be standing outside of, or they wanted to let the flames die down.

Running into the car park he saw his Tesla against the back wall across the bays. It was a Type S, pretty new, and one of the few things he liked to drive himself. It wasn't charging right now, which was strange – but then usually Saleh would be the one linking it from the charger to top up before driving Nicky, and Saleh ... well, he was a conversation to have later.

Not wanting to be noticed, Nicky walked quickly to the car but stopped around twenty feet from the vehicle – as it started up, the lights from the headlamps hitting his face.

There was nobody inside it.

'Ah, shit,' he said, backing away as the Tesla revved. There was no bloody way he was going to be run over by his own sodding remote-controlled car so, sliding over the bonnet of the car beside him, he ran down the gaps between cars, heading for the side exit. He didn't know if the Tesla followed him; he didn't even know if the Tesla *could* follow him without a driver inside. All he knew, as he reached the external fire door, slamming through it and leaning against the outside wall gathering his breath, was that somehow he had a price on his head, and someone was trying to collect it. And, to make matters worse, following Saleh's response and the lack of anyone informing him of an issue in the Spa, he didn't know who in his organisation he could trust now.

He needed help, and he needed it from someone who had no reason to kill him. Someone he could trust to keep him safe, take him off grid until he could work out who was making their play right now.

After a moment, he screamed out into the street, his anger overpowering him.

He had a name.

He just really didn't want to use it.

So, as the chaos of the building's evacuation meant the crowds were filling up the courtyard beside him, Nick swallowed his pride, tossed his phone to the floor – stamping on it to make sure nobody could track him – and ran for the street beside the building, looking for a cab that'd take cash, and that'd take him across the bridge into the City.

2

BISHOP TAKES KNIGHT

AT THE TIME OF THE EXPLOSION, ELLIE RECKLESS WAS IN A basement bar, playing chess with a wizened old Chinese man; a gun to the back of her head.

'You know, Jimmy, this isn't the best way to focus me,' she said irritably, shifting in her seat as she tried to get comfortable. In her mid-to-late-thirties, her dark-brown – almost-black – hair, shoulder length and curly, she was wearing a more relaxed set of clothing today than her usual suited attire of cheap grey suit, and pale collared blouse, instead wearing a hoodie and jeans, but still with grey *Converse* 'ox' trainers she wore on her feet.

Jimmy Tsang smiled, leaning back on his chair, nodding at the young man behind her. He was dressed immaculately, his thinning white hair pulled back over his liver-spotted skull as he stared at her through his varifocal glasses with a sneer.

'If she complains about the gun again, shoot her in the head,' he said. 'But aim it away from me, as I like this suit, and brains are very difficult to remove.'

In response, Ellie flipped Jimmy a finger.

'I thought you were in Shanghai, anyway?' she asked, moving a Rook.

In response, Jimmy shrugged.

'My cousin died, my other is still wrapped in legal affairs, and my nephew was brutally murdered by a gangster,' he said as if rattling off a shopping list. 'Why *wouldn't* I come here?'

'So, it's revenge?'

Jimmy cackled as he took Ellie's Knight with a Bishop.

'Couldn't give a shit about them,' he said, waving the piece in the air. 'I came because I saw an opening. The same reason you came here.'

'Oh?' Ellie folded her arms as she leant back. 'You know why I came here?'

'Of course,' Jimmy Tsang nodded, the smile still on his face. 'You want a favour. You want the Tsangs in your pocket.'

'I don't know if you noticed, Jimmy, but I already have the Tsangs in my pocket,' Ellie's voice took on a darker tone. 'When I saved Kenneth's life.'

'And what has that got you?' Jimmy's eyes widened as he asked, almost mocking her. 'Nothing. Almost a year on and you're still no closer to where you were.'

'My plans aren't half-baked,' Ellie looked back over the chessboard, picking up a Pawn and moving it, but pausing, jerking back before she placed it, and returning it as she considered another move. 'I'm taking my time. Like in chess.'

'Back problems?' Jimmy had noted the jerk.

'Trapped nerve,' Ellie sighed. 'Not helped by anxiety.'

'You're lost. That's your problem, not your back,' Jimmy tutted. 'You don't know how to get where you need to go. That's why you came to me.'

'What, to have a gun aimed at my head while I play you at chess?'

Jimmy Tsang's mouth shrugged.

'To some, this is enjoyment,' he smiled. 'Russian Roulette, but you get to delay the bullet.'

'Yeah, you sick bastard, I suppose it is,' Ellie placed a Knight down. 'Check.'

Jimmy paused his reply and stared down at the board.

'No way,' he said. 'You cheated.'

'Your man has a gun at my head and you're both watching the board,' Ellie grinned as she sat back. 'So please, oh mighty Jimmy Tsang, tell me how I could do that?'

'I've beaten Grand Masters!' Jimmy moved his King out of check. 'You're nothing!'

'Let me talk to you a little about overconfidence,' Ellie replied calmly. 'You thought you had me. I come in, all innocent like, asking you to drop the hit you've placed on Alfie Kent. It's not important to you, it's a little thing. You don't even want him dead, or you'd have offered more money.'

'Maybe I don't think he's worth the money?'

'Exactly,' Ellie moved a Bishop on the board now. 'You put a high-cost hit on someone you *want* dead. You just wanted Alfie Kent scared, to come to me, as you knew I had a history with his mum, and you knew I'd come to you. Check.'

'So what are you saying?' Jimmy was concentrating now on the board as he spoke, sweat appearing at his temples as he moved his King again out of check.

'You wanted me here, in this room, having this chess match,' Ellie replied. 'You knew from the start what you wanted. But unfortunately, Jimmy, so did I.'

She slid the Bishop back a space, but Jimmy held up a hand to pause her.

'Check her ears for any kind of ear buds,' he growled. 'She's getting moves given to her. She has to be. If you see a bud, remove it with a goddamned bullet.'

Ellie leant back with a smile, allowing the gunman to check both ears.

'Nothing,' he said with a hint of reluctance. 'And we frisked her when she entered, and you took her phone away.'

Jimmy looked at the phone, placed on the table nearby.

'You win, you get your wish, and the hit is taken off,' he said. 'But I win, you owe *me*. Or, I have you shot in the head. Either way, my problem goes away.'

'That's what this is about?' Ellie almost laughed. 'You want Ellie Reckless to owe you a favour? There are easier ways to get that, Jimmy.'

'You don't know the favour,' Jimmy hissed. 'You lose, you burn every favour you've picked up over the years. And you return every gangster, criminal, whatever the hell they are, you return their lives to them.'

'And why would I do that?' Ellie moved the Bishop once more, this time not being stopped by Jimmy.

'Because if you don't, you'll die,' Jimmy nodded at the man behind her, gun now trained on her ear. 'You've pissed off powerful people, Reckless. And not just my family. There are others looking at taking you off the board more permanently. And, to be honest, the kudos I'd get for being the one who does that? It's intoxicating.'

'I'm close,' Ellie watched Jimmy as he tried to shore up his defences, before moving her Queen across the board. 'And I won't be denied my revenge against Nicky Simpson. Checkmate.'

She leant back.

'Overconfidence,' she said again. 'You decided before I even sat down that you'd won. You didn't consider for a moment I could win, that I could possibly beat you.'

Jimmy Tsang didn't reply, staring in abject horror at the chessboard.

'You drop the hit and let Alfie Kent live his life,' Ellie continued. 'Whatever issue you have with him is gone. You pack up and piss off back to Shanghai. If you do that? I'll burn Kenneth's favour, and the Tsangs won't owe me anything.'

'And if I say no to that?' Jimmy nodded to the gunman, but before he could do anything, Ellie moved her head to the side, sliding back so the gun now pointed past her, while grabbing and twisting the gun with both hands. As the gunman stumbled back, disarmed, Ellie rose, aiming the gun at Jimmy.

'Then you go back to Shanghai in a box,' she said coldly.

Jimmy laughed at this, waving his man back.

'You're a lawful woman, Reckless,' he said. 'You wouldn't shoot me.'

'Haven't you heard?' Ellie asked as she walked over to the door, unlocking it. 'The police reckon I'm a murderer. So maybe I would.'

Jimmy Tsang frowned, his eyebrows knotting.

'No, I am an excellent judge of character,' he smiled. 'I think you would not.'

'And how about *this* character?' Ellie asked as she opened the door, allowing Tinker Jones to walk in.

The same age, roughly, as Ellie, she wore her usual olive-coloured German Army coat, worn over an *Iron Maiden* tour T-shirt and tattered blue jeans, her curly blonde hair pulled back into a ponytail, pushed under a New York Mets baseball cap.

Tinker smiled at Ellie, took the gun from her, and aimed it at Jimmy.

'This must be your driver, Miss Jones,' Jimmy nodded. 'And yes, I do believe *she* would kill me. I thought my men would hold her back, but apparently I was wrong.'

Ellie walked back to Jimmy.

'Take a holiday,' she said. 'I know you're here to shore up the Tsang empire, and I'm sorry your family suffered in such a way. But I've heard of your tactics, and London isn't a chessboard for you to play your brutal and bloody chess game on. It's *my* town.'

Jimmy looked at the board and knocked over the King.

'I will drop the hit on Alfie and leave him alone, but only if he stops attacking my shipments.'

'Attacking? He stole a phone from one of your couriers as he drove past them on a moped!' Tinker exclaimed. 'That's hardly attacking.'

Jimmy shrugged noncommittally.

'Maybe this time.'

'Alfie will stop stealing phones from your couriers, but you need to tell them to stop being such easy bloody targets,' Ellie replied. 'The hit is off, you take a holiday, or at least promise to keep your affairs here within reason. No gang warfare.'

'Within reason I can do,' Jimmy said. 'And the favour?'

'You don't owe me one.'

'No, I meant Kenny's one,' Jimmy scowled. 'You said you'd burn it.'

'Yeah, but you're being a prick,' Ellie said. 'So, I think I'll hold on to it. But don't worry, I know exactly what the favour will be when I ask him.'

Quietly and with silent determination, Ellie leant close to Jimmy's ear, whispering the favour, stepping back and smiling as his eyes widened.

'He'll do it, too,' she said. 'Do I have your word?'

'I'll play by your rules,' he said. 'If you tell me how you won?'

'I already did,' Ellie replied as she walked out the door, Tinker emptying and tossing the gun back to the confused guard. 'Overconfidence.'

'THAT WAS BLOODY CLOSE,' TINKER GRUMBLED AS THEY WALKED back to their van, parked down a Chinatown side street. 'You could have lost more than you gained there.'

'Never,' Ellie patted Tinker on the arm. 'I always knew you were outside, and I knew Jimmy would be too arrogant to believe I could beat him.'

'Could you?' Tinker smiled. 'Beat him?'

'On my own? Not a hope,' Ellie grinned as she reached under her hoodie, pulling away a Velcro strap from her waist, and removing what looked to be a money belt, but worn back to front. 'But with this? I had a fighting chance.'

It had been Casey's idea, and at the start they'd thought he was mad.

They knew Jimmy Tsang was a wannabe chess Grand Master, and had played several over the years, winning many of the games. Of course, it was also known he'd find old, broken Grand Masters, who'd forgotten more about the game than they remembered, or he'd drug them before games, or even simply pay them a large fee to throw the game – anything that made him look great.

This was what Ellie had been banking on; that Jimmy's continual wins would give him an increased sense of grandeur. That he'd forget how he was winning and believe his own press. And that press laughed at the idea of a woman in her thirties, with no history of playing the game, defeating him for the prize of a hit being removed.

But it hadn't been just one woman. It had been an entire team.

Casey had been watching YouTube videos of chess Grand Master Hans Niemann, who'd been accused of cheating in dozens of online games, but also cheating somehow during an actual, televised face-to-face game. The rumours had been rife, but the leading opinion was that Niemann had somehow discovered how to use a Bluetooth sex toy, placed up – well, inserted somewhere private, and this was used, through vibrating morse code, or something similar, to give him moves from a high powered AI computer, working out all possible scenarios.

Of course, this had never been proven, but Casey had, as a computer genius, been enthralled by the idea it *could*. And, when Ellie mentioned the favour she'd receive if she could get Tsang to drop his guard, Casey explained his plan; a vibrating, 3D-printed device the size of a credit card, attached to the small of her back (there was never a chance of any "insertions" here) that connected to Casey in a van outside. It wouldn't need to be that well-hidden, as they expected nothing more than a vague frisk as she entered, so it'd be easily missed if worn on the back.

He would see the moves, and using chess software, the ones the best played against when training, tell her the best one to use. He didn't need to be playing at the top level, either, as Jimmy Tsang believed he was better than Grand Masters, but wasn't.

The problem was to have a way to see the board, and that had been Ramsey Allen, who, the night before, had broken into the warehouse Jimmy Tsang had been working from, and positioned four tiny web cameras around the main office, all so the board could be looked at from all angles. It was a tough job, but Ramsey wasn't a renowned cat burglar for nothing, even at his age.

This done, all Ellie had to do was make sure her phone was nearby, as the personal hotspot it gave off was enough to link the cameras – and the van – together.

As Casey saw a move, he'd enter it into the computer. The AI would respond, and he would use a form of morse code, giving the letter and number of the board the piece was on; so D4 would be four separate buzzes, twice, while C6 would be sets of three and six. He would then give the square to move to in the same way. Only once had Ellie miscounted, and he was able to buzz her while the piece was in her hand, so she could redo the move.

Jimmy Tsang never had a chance. And now there were four cameras still there, to be used in a future case if needed.

'Tell Sarah her son's safe,' Ellie opened the passenger door to the van and was instantly attacked with woofs of joy by a fuzzy brown lump of Cocker Spaniel as Millie, tired of being locked in the van, joyfully wagged her tail. 'Tsang will keep his word, although he'll need to be watched to make sure he keeps his other promises.'

She looked around the inside of the van.

'Where's Casey?' she asked. 'I was going to thank him for a job well done.'

'I sent him home after the checkmate,' Tinker replied, and Ellie narrowed her eyes at the way the comment was spoken.

'What don't I know?' she asked suspiciously.

'There was a new job that came up while you were in there,' Tinker was uncomfortable as she replied. 'A walk in of sorts. Asked for you by name. Robert called me to let me know.'

'Why didn't he call me?' Ellie asked, before shaking her head. 'Forget that. I was in there, wasn't I. So why send Casey home? What's the job?'

Tinker shook her own head.

'I don't think I want to tell you until we get there,' she said, starting the van.

'And why exactly is that?'

'Because I don't want you burning favours to get hold of a gun before we get there,' Tinker explained as she gunned the engine and the van left Chinatown.

ALTHOUGH SHE HAD A PLUSH, CHROME AND GLASS OFFICE ON the upper floors of The Finders' Corporation, Ellie's *other* office, *Caesars Diner*, was a small breakfast café amid the City of London, and also just south of Farringdon Station.

It was less than a block away from the Finders' offices and emulated a fifties diner; the floor was a chequered black and white design; the walls tiled white. There were tables in the middle and along the side were large, opulent red-leather booths, easily wide enough for six or seven people to sit and eat in.

On the wall were fifties advertising posters for milkshakes, burgers and soft drinks, and on each table was a small jukebox, where for a 20p piece you could change the fifties song to *another* fifties song.

It was a typical city diner, and its clientele were often rich, hungry, and nostalgic. And, as Ellie walked into the diner, Tinker a half step behind her as she looked across the chequered floor at her usual booth, she ignored the jump of anxiety at seeing the floor, probably connected to the recent chess match, and stared directly ahead.

There, sitting at the booth, facing both a scowling looking Ramsey Allen and a nervous-looking Robert Lewis, was Nicky Simpson.

It was Nicky who saw them first, his face moving quickly from resignation to mock enjoyment.

'Reckless,' he said. 'Thought I'd drop in, see how you are.'

Millie, usually a good judge of character, kept quiet as Ellie walked up to Simpson.

'What are you doing here?' she asked icily, resisting the urge to punch him in his annoying face.

'Funny situation, actually,' Simpson replied. 'I need your help.'

'You *what?*' Ellie wasn't sure she'd heard correctly, but Nicky Simpson nodded.

'I know,' he replied. 'It wasn't how I wanted to start my day either, but I need your help, Ellie Reckless. Your help and your team's help, in fact. And in return, I'm willing to offer whatever favour you want of me.'

Ellie stared at Simpson in a mix of abject anger and horror. The man she'd started her team, started these favours for, to take down and destroy, was sitting calmly in front of her, offering her everything.

It was Christmas and Halloween at the same time.

'And what exactly would we have to do to get this favour?' she asked suspiciously.

Nicky Simpson shrugged.

'Just keep me alive, Reckless,' he said. 'And find out who wants me dead.'

3

CANDID SHOTS

ELLIE RESISTED THE URGE TO LEAP ACROSS THE BOOTH AND throttle Nicky Simpson, to shout loudly that her life wasn't a joke, and how dare he make a mockery of it by asking for a favour job, but one look at the expressions on Robert and Ramsey's faces showed her this was deadly serious.

Robert Lewis was dressed in one of his usual suits, ever the solicitor, his dirty blond hair combed back and to the side, his temples silvering a little, the only sign on his youthful face that he was in his forties. He didn't wear a tie, his shirt open, but he still looked like he just walked out of a meeting.

Ramsey Allen, however, was wearing a black pinstripe suit with a dark charcoal-grey tie, over a white shirt – and looked more like he was almost attending a funeral, which, in a way with the sombre colour scheme he was wearing, made Ellie realise he probably felt he was. In his mid-to-late sixties with short white hair and moustache, usually Ramsey was in navy suits and colourful club ties; this was not the Ramsey she'd expected to see this morning, and it actually threw her a little.

'This isn't a joke, is it,' she said to them, a statement more than question, ignoring Simpson as he went to speak.

'No, Eleanor,' Ramsey shook his head. 'You'll want to hear this one out.'

Tinker stepped forward.

'I can take him out right now if you want,' she growled. 'Just say the word and he's toast.'

Ellie held a hand up to halt Tinker.

'Hold that thought for the moment,' she said calmly, her mind spinning through the possibilities here.

Nicky Simpson needed her help to stay alive.

If she said yes, and she managed it, he would owe her a favour. And she could skip to the end and simply force him to give up every piece of information he had on the death of Bryan Noyce, her onetime boyfriend.

Well, her onetime *something*. Affairs always made mockeries of such terms.

If she said no, there was every chance someone out there would kill him. Or, if she took the job and failed, he'd also be deceased by the end.

Neither of these were game changers either; she wouldn't be able to clear her name, but Simpson would be dead. And that wasn't a super bad position to be in, either.

Clear her name.

That was the phrase that niggled at her soul, though. If Nicky Simpson died, she'd never be able to prove he set her up. She'd never clear her name.

To do that, he had to live. And if he owed her, he could do so.

'I hate you,' she muttered softly.

Nicky Simpson didn't hear, or if he did, he chose not to understand.

'Sorry?' he asked innocently.

Ellie went to reply, but paused as she glanced at the corner of the diner. There, with a phone's camera aimed at them, were two teenage girls, one blonde and one red-headed, wide-eyed and giggling.

Ah shit, he has fans in here.

'We need to take this upstairs,' she said to Robert.

'You know the rules, Ellie,' he replied softly. 'We start up there, and then we come down here. It's a favour case. They're not done up in Finders.'

'Yeah, but this is a little different,' Ellie muttered, glancing at the girls briefly while making a plan. 'He's a celebrity, if you can call someone with a couple of thousand YouTube subscribers—'

'A couple of million, I think you'll find,' Simpson raised an eyebrow, his professional integrity pinched.

'Still not real TV though, is it?' Ellie mocked. 'Come back when you have an ITV show and we'll call you one properly. But—' and now she returned to Robert, '—there's too many eyes here.'

And, to make the point, she walked over to the two girls with a smile on her face.

'Hey,' she said. 'You fans of Nicky?'

The girls were nervous, no longer smiling, aware they'd been caught spying.

'Um, yeah,' one of them said uncertainly. 'It's not a problem, right?'

'No, not at all!' Ellie grinned. 'In fact, rather than sitting and watching from a distance, why don't you come and meet him? We'll get a proper photo for you.'

The girls looked at each other in a mixture of surprise and excitement.

'You sure?'

'Absolutely,' Ellie motioned for them to follow her. 'What are your names?'

'I'm Alaiya, that's Tina,' the redhead replied.

'Well come with me,' Ellie walked them over to Nicky Simpson who, unsure what was going on, watched Ellie cautiously.

'Nicky, these are Alaiya and Tina, and they're massive fans,' Ellie explained. 'Can you take a photo with them?'

'Sure?' Simpson said uncertainly, standing up, but in full "YouTuber" mode now.

Ellie pointed at a spot of blank wall behind him.

'Let's do it there,' she said. 'Light's good.'

She looked back at Tina, who'd been the one filming.

'Pass me your phone, I'll take the shot,' she said.

The two girls were over the moon, standing on either side of Simpson as Ellie took the camera phone and snapped off a couple of photos, both portrait and land-scape. Then, when she'd finished, she looked up from the phone.

'Now, we're happy for you to put these up on your socials, but only if you don't mention where you saw Nicky,' she explained. 'He's got a very important, secret meeting today and if people know he's in the City, it'll screw things up. Yeah?'

Tina frowned, and Ellie knew she was about to get some kind of "free speech" response.

'Yeah, but my mates won't believe it's true—' she started.

Ellie held up a hand.

'Write your social media handle down on a napkin and

I'll ensure my client "likes" it once it's up,' she said. 'That'll prove it, yeah?'

The two girls nodded. And Ellie's face darkened.

'But here's the other side of this,' she said. 'You filmed my client without his consent. I've deleted the video and removed it completely from your phone, and the cloud server it backs up to.'

'You can't do that!' Tina exclaimed. 'I got rights—'

'What you "got" is a photo with Nicky Simpson,' Ellie continued. 'And, in the time I've had your phone, I've cloned the data and sent it off to my computer expert. And, if you comment anywhere that you saw Nicky here in Caesar's, or in the City today, no matter where it is, we'll see it – and we'll know you broke our agreement. If that happens, we'll hack your phone, your contacts, your social media pages—'

'How would you …' Tina started, but trailed off in realisation.

'Ask yourself this,' Ellie passed the phone back. 'How many important passwords do you keep in your phone's data chain? Passwords I now have?'

She leant in.

'I own you, Tina Marshall,' she said. 'You get your photo, and good for you. And now you get a secret to keep to your grave.'

'You know my surname …' Tina whispered.

'I know *everything*,' Ellie hissed. 'Now go get your things, pay Sandra for your breakfast, leave the diner and have an enjoyable life.'

'Who's Sandra?'

Ellie blinked.

'Oh, sorry, she's the waitress,' she said, the dark booming voice gone. 'You both have a good day now.'

'And remember to like and subscribe,' Simpson winked, and the two girls, forgetting the terrifying woman in front of them, giggled and left.

Simpson grinned at Ellie.

'What?' Irritated, Ellie took Millie's lead back from Tinker as she glared at him.

'You called me your client,' Simpson replied. 'You took my case on.'

'Shut up,' embarrassed, Ellie snapped back.

Simpson looked back at the napkin.

'I never really realised how good your team is,' he said. 'I mean, when the twelve-year-old hacked my system a few months back I should have guessed, but to do all that from one play with a phone ... that's terrifying.'

'It's also bullshit,' Ramsey grinned. 'No way she managed all that without Casey being here.'

Ellie shrugged apologetically.

'I deleted the videos, but there wasn't anything else I could do apart from putting the fear of God into them,' she explained. 'Make them think we were Big Brother.'

'But how did you know the surname?' Tinker asked.

At this, Ellie nodded at the napkin.

@TMarshall2006

'Her username has the surname,' she said. 'And probably her year of birth. Not the best sort of thing to have out there, but I made a calculated guess. And if it all went wrong?'

She looked back at Nicky Simpson.

'Well, then everyone out there would know where you were right now, and your day would end real quick. Win win, I say.'

If Simpson wanted to argue, he instead wisely kept his mouth shut.

'Right then,' Ellie smiled. 'Let's relocate back to the boardroom.'

'But I just ordered breakfast!' Ramsey wailed.

'He did,' Simpson nodded. 'I think he deliberately found the greasiest, most artery-hardening food he could find just to piss me off.'

'We'll get it to go,' Ellie, tired of all this banter, nodded over at Sandra. 'We can't let another random photo pop up.'

Sandra the waitress, seeing the motion, walked over.

'He's already paid for it,' she said. 'Did you want anything else?'

'Can we get it to go?' Ellie asked, nodding back at the others. 'We're late for a meeting.'

'Who do you think we are, sodding Uber Eats?' Sandra, as world-weary as ever, sighed. 'You come in here with your dog and your celebrity friends, causing us hassle and work, and now you don't even want to stay?'

She shook her head, looking back at the kitchen area.

'Ali, did you hear this?' she muttered.

Ali, a middle-aged Turkish man in a white T-shirt and apron, currently working behind the hot plate grinned.

'Give her a break,' he said, passing a Styrofoam box over. 'She's obviously having a bad day. Just look at her.'

Ellie raised her eyebrows.

'What do you mean?' she looked around. 'Do I look that bad?'

'You've had better days,' Tinker admitted. 'Probably because you spent half the night preparing for a chess game.'

Irritatedly, taking the Styrofoam box and passing it across

to Ramsey, Ellie glared back at Sandra who was currently smiling triumphantly.

'You should have recyclable boxes,' she muttered.

'They are,' Ali said from the back. 'Once you finish them, you can recycle them into a Styrofoam hat.'

As the group left the diner Nicky Simpson looked bereft.

'And what's your problem?' Tinker asked.

'I thought being hunted was bad enough,' he bemoaned. 'But being seen with greasy food and non-recyclable packaging? *That's* what's going to kill me.'

'Poor dear,' Tinker mocked as they walked down the street. 'Don't worry, maybe you'll be lucky and get a bullet to the head before Greenpeace comes for you.'

THE FINDERS' OFFICES WERE NEW, AND SPORTED AN AESTHETIC of chrome and glass, which pretty much looked as if an Apple store and Wall Street had married and had babies. Open-plan offices with glass-walled boardrooms passed by, as Sara the receptionist walked them to the back offices and the boardroom.

Ellie was amused at this; there was no need for such formality, as everyone apart from Nicky Simpson had been there multiple times, and even Nicky Simpson had started his day there, in the first of his meetings. But from her face, it was obvious Sara was a viewer, a "like and subscriber" of Nicky's YouTube channel.

When they arrived at the boardroom door, Simpson even gave her one of his macrobiotic smoothies, from what seemed to be a small collection in his backpack, telling her to "chill it before drinking," and Sara's face beamed, as if she'd just been given the Ark of the Covenant, or something equally epic.

Now in the boardroom, Ellie motioned for Simpson to sit down, the window outside behind him. The table was oblong, with a TV at one end, and Simpson was obviously concerned about the seating arrangement.

'You think someone's going to shoot you through the window?' Ellie half-mocked.

'Didn't you hear about Wrentham in New York?' Simpson nervously muttered.

'That was the US,' Tinker scolded. 'This is the UK. We'd find better ways to kill you.'

Sitting down around the table, Ellie unclipped Millie's lead so she could lie down, and was a little disappointed to see the Cocker Spaniel walk over to Simpson, sniffing his hand before sitting near him.

'She's a terrible judge of character,' she muttered. 'So, Mister Simpson, how about you tell us what's going on? And I suggest, unlike usual, you tell us the truth, the whole truth, and nothing but the truth.'

Nicky Simpson smiled at the comment.

'Always a copper, eh, Reckless?' he asked.

'You can be as jokey as you like,' Ellie replied calmly. 'You're the one who came to me.'

'Yeah, fair point,' Simpson shifted in his chair, uncomfortable to be having such a conversation. 'Do you remember a few weeks back, when you had one of the Lumetta brothers on top of a roof, telling everybody the secrets about his criminal activities?'

Ellie did, and she also remembered this was the point where Nicky Simpson had been effectively outed as the criminal Underlord of the south of London.

'I do,' she said. 'I seem to recall you had a supporting role, you could say, in Matteo Lumetta's confession.'

Simpson nodded.

'To be honest, it wasn't that much of a problem,' he admitted. 'Because I had good lawyers and superb publicists. And, through them, I could point out publicly that I'd pulled out of a deal with the Lumettas for a series of health spas in Ireland, once I'd realised they had criminal connections, and this was a gangster being pissy.'

'Good on you for being so civic-minded,' Ramsey said, and he spoke so earnestly Ellie couldn't quite make out if he was joking or not.

Amusingly, from his conflicted expression, neither could Nicky Simpson.

'Anyway,' he continued. 'I pointed out this was probably Matteo Lumetta using this as a chance to get me back for my business withdrawal, and that in some twisted way, he thought he was getting some kind of "tit for tat" revenge.'

Ellie observed Simpson as she spoke.

'And you believe this?' she asked.

'Oh, hell no,' Simpson said. 'The problem is, even though the press were looking into it, and I had interviews and people wanting to talk to me about all this, my criminal past isn't exactly the best kept secret out there, shall we say? Anyone who's lived in Vauxhall or Camberwell, anywhere south of the Thames, to be honest, is pretty much aware of my family's history, even if they can't prove a lot of it.'

'And you can't keep editing a Wikipedia page, hoping it'll go away,' Tinker smiled darkly.

Simpson ignored the jibe.

'And so I decided I needed to make a comment about this,

perhaps do a vlog on it, talk about my family's gangster past while getting myself out of the issues that you've put me in—'

'Hold on,' Ellie held a hand up. '*We* didn't do anything to you. If you watch that live stream, we didn't in any way lead Matteo towards you. He did it all on his own.'

'I know,' Simpson said reluctantly. 'For once, you weren't the bane of my existence. Even if Ramsey there is nothing more than a tick on a shaggy dog.'

'I resent that,' Ramsey snapped. 'That implies I'm a parasite.'

'And you're not?' Simpson asked innocently.

'Only when it helps the team,' Ramsey gave a smile and turned away.

Simpson, surprised at the response, also smiled.

'Yeah, okay, I apologise, you weren't the one who screwed me. None of you were. Still, it didn't exactly help.'

He leant back in the chair, relaxing a little, regardless of the hostile audience in front of him.

'For years, I'd kept it quiet, although people out there knew what was going on. I had levels of plausible deniability, and suddenly they disappeared – as people I'd had close relations with for years suddenly weren't too sure about working with me anymore.'

'Criminals were spooked by a live stream? That's a first,' Robert noted.

'It wasn't just that. They were concerned the press information that was coming out – the renewed interest from the news stations of "Nicky Simpson YouTube sensation suddenly being some kind of criminal overlord" – were bringing a lot of unwelcome interest into our dealings. And there's the slightest concern someone was pulling the strings, you know, choreographing them to leave me. So, rather than going through all the hassle of finding out who that was and sorting them, I started considering whether or not I needed to be in it.'

'You were going to retire?'

'It's one thing having a criminal enterprise that makes you a few million a year, but when you have your own YouTube channel, macrobiotic drink label, a couple of book deals and even a TV show deal, I was making more as "Nicky Simpson YouTube guru" than I was as the son of Max Simpson.'

He sighed audibly.

'The problem is, all my life I've had remnants from my childhood coming at me left, right, and centre,' Simpson explained. 'There are people out there who loved my grand-dad. He was admired and feared as any gangland lord should be. He took over from the Richardsons, for God's sake. That wasn't no simple task. And then when my dad took over, he tried his best to mimic Granddad, but he was more of a blunt object than a precision tool. Then when he got Parkinson's, people began moving in. Bad people. The wrong people. The Turk, the Twins. Everyone who'd been waiting to kick in. And, when I took over, I had to come in hard and fast, which I did.'

'And thus the legend began,' Ramsey spoke, and this time Ellie could hear the scorn in his tone.

'Legends are stories, old man,' Simpson snapped, a little of his arrogance returning. 'And *anyone* can tell a story. Anyway, I took the money that I'd made from selling the houses and shored up the enterprise—'

Ellie put her hand up, halting him.

'I said to tell us the truth,' she said. 'Not give us your bull-shit revisionist history.'

'The whole story of how you sold three houses to build your health spa empire was purely a way to explain how you had millions in your bank account,' Ramsey added. 'I know for a fact you didn't sell those houses. I know for a fact those houses are still under your name.'

Simpson chuckled, almost sheepishly.

'You tell a lie so long it becomes the truth in your head,' he said. 'I'm believing it myself.'

'Well, perhaps you don't, and instead tell us the truth for a change,' Ellie leant forward, placing her arms on the table. 'Start from the beginning, Mister Simpson. Why are people trying to kill you, and how do you need us to react to them?'

4

JOB INTERVIEW

'ALMOST A YEAR AGO, THERE WAS A BIG FIGHT IN LONDON,' Nicky Simpson straightened in his chair. 'You know this because you were there. Seven Sisters. The Tsangs. The Twins. Everybody was fighting with each other.'

Ellie nodded. She did remember this. The previous summer, Jackie Lucas, the imaginary brother of Johnny Lucas, had seemingly come to life, killing the heir to the Tsang Empire. Eventually, after bouncing backwards and forwards for a while, it came out this was actually Johnny Lucas's estranged sister, pretending to be Jackie, purely to get Johnny arrested and placed in prison for a hideous murder, so she could destroy her rivals and not only take over the East End of London, but most of the other areas as well.

In the end, thanks to her old boss, DCI Alex Monroe, as well as DI Declan Walsh and their City of London squad, it'd turned out to be nothing more than a squabble over land rights; a corporation started during the 2012 Olympics. However, there was a suspicion the whole thing had been bankrolled by Nicky Simpson.

'It came out during that time that I'd been playing in the background, doing my best to be a puppeteer,' Simpson said, his hand mimicking a puppet. 'And when the fallout hit, I was barely touched. Nobody really wanted to come south of the river. The Sisters were having family issues. The Tsangs were falling apart – although I understand Jimmy Tsang has now come back into the scene.'

'He's going home soon,' Ellie replied coldly.

Simpson nodded at this, as if expecting the answer.

'Anyway, Johnny Lucas throws *all* his bad shit history onto his sister, claiming retroactively she was *always* Jackie, and now reborn, so to speak, from sin goes into politics. And the Lumettas, who up to this point had been quiet, nothing more than creepy spectators with an olive oil fetish, start showing up for their own interests ... well, before they shit the bed spectacularly and everything went wrong.'

Ellie nodded.

'Again, things we already know,' she said.

'But when the Lumettas imploded, they took everything with them in that bloody confession,' Simpson grumbled, staring at the table. 'And people started asking questions about me. As I said, I lost work, and we lost contacts. People started to think that maybe I was weak enough for a takeover.'

'That's what's happening, isn't it?' Ramsey asked.

In response, Simpson shrugged.

'No idea,' he replied honestly.

'So when did you know things were going wrong?' Tinker asked sweetly. 'And please give us all the details. We'd like to hear all about the bad things that happened to you.'

Simpson shifted again in his chair, once more uncomfortable to be in the room.

'This morning,' he said. 'Saleh wasn't there.'

'Your driver?' Tinker frowned. 'You're basing this on Saleh? Maybe he had a day off.'

'You've not been checking the news, have you?' Simpson asked. 'If you had, you would have known someone blew up my offices today.'

'Actually, the official story is it was a gas leak on your floor,' Robert interjected. 'And at the moment, the only person who's missing is you.'

'And I'm happy to keep it like that for the moment,' Simpson said. 'I know that it's gonna get out I'm alive.'

'Probably has already,' Ellie replied. 'Those two girls won't have wasted time putting the picture up there.'

'How did you get to the office if Saleh wasn't there?' Tinker asked.

'I live a couple of floors above,' Simpson explained.

'Of course you do.'

There was a moment of uncomfortable silence.

'Well, go on, rich boy,' Tinker mocked.

Simpson's face darkened, and Ellie realised Tinker's goading was really getting to him, and this mask he was wearing, that of the light-hearted banter-man from YouTube, was slipping.

Good. Let's see your true face, you bastard.

'I knew something was wrong when he sent me a message,' Simpson said, pulling himself back. 'A single word. "Sorry." I realised something was going on at that point, so I decided to get out.'

'Why?' Ellie asked. 'That could have meant anything. He could have informed on you. Crashed the car. Why did you think this was more immediate?'

I could see on the CCTV that the staff in my health club

were escorting every single guest out. I couldn't hear any sirens or warnings, but it looked like there was some kind of fire alarm going on,' Simpson explained. 'And, at that point, I realised someone had stopped the fire alarm hitting my offices. They didn't want me knowing or leaving.'

'So, what did you do?'

'Now I knew, I left,' Simpson shrugged. 'I grabbed my laptop, grabbed a bag, some supplies. I went to the elevator and pressed the button. And then I started thinking "maybe I didn't want to be in an elevator if there was a fire," so I went to the stairs. It's only a couple of floors, and you know, I *am* a fitness guru.'

'You're seriously claiming two floors is a challenge?' Ellie mocked. 'Or are you contractually obligated to continually remind us you're a fitness guy?'

Simpson looked away, sulking.

'Oh, stop bloody mithering. And then?'

'And as I was going down the flight of stairs, I heard the *ding* of the elevator, followed a few seconds later by an explosion. Blew the door off its hinges and sent me flying down a floor's worth of stairs. Got a bruised elbow if you'd like to see it?'

'Not really,' Ellie replied, stroking her chin. 'Sounds to me like the elevator was primed, with something inside. As soon as the door opened; boom. They expected you to be standing in front of that door as it exploded outwards – and if you had you'd be dead right now.'

She looked across at Robert.

'I don't know whether to hunt them down or give them a prize.'

'Not funny,' Simpson snapped. 'This is my life we're talking about.'

'Oh, what a shame,' Ramsey mocked. 'Because we've all *really* cared about your life for many, many months.'

Simpson ignored the jibe.

'How's your mum?' he asked in return.

At this, Ramsey's demeanour crumbled slightly.

'She's good,' he replied reluctantly, and Ellie understood why he was conflicted. Nicky Simpson had paid for Ramsey's mother's care in an old people's home when Ramsey couldn't afford it. And when the care prices had gone up, Nicky had covered these costs. But it wasn't because Simpson was a nice man, or a "guardian angel" or anything, it was purely so that Ramsey would spy on Ellie Reckless for him.

Ramsey knew that.

Ellie knew that.

And Nicky Simpson had recently dropped the conflict for Ramsey, letting him off the hook, effectively closing the debt, once he knew Ramsey had let Ellie know.

He had, however, kept paying the bills, which was a surprise.

'So, with the explosion, you now know somebody wants to kill you, and you want to find out who?' Tinker took command of the conversation once more. 'This is the case?'

'Yes and no,' Simpson replied. 'Somebody's trying to kill me and I'd like to know who it is. But until you find out who it is, and I'm able to shut it down, I need you to keep me alive.'

'This is a police job,' Ellie shook her head. 'We find things – the company's called Finders for a reason.'

'Yeah. Find who's trying to kill me.'

'We're not called "Keep Alivers," when there's no reason we need to try to keep you alive.'

'I'd owe you that favour you always ask for.'

Ellie stared at Nicky Simpson for a long, hard moment, weighing up her options.

'You should go chat to Vauxhall police: DI Mark Whitehouse and DS Kate Delgado,' Ellie suggested, unable to keep the implied suggestion out of her voice. 'As much as I dislike them I'm sure you have a good connection with them.'

Nicky Simpson smiled.

'Which one of them do you think it is?' he asked. 'You know, who I obviously have in my pocket?'

'I have my suspicions,' Ellie said. 'But I'm not going to say them to you right now.'

'Can't go to the police,' Simpson replied. 'If I go there I'm going as legit Nicky, and they'll come up with some kind of mad stalker idea. They'll go into my systems, hunt around, and they'll get nowhere while I'm still being targeted. We all know this isn't a mad stalker for Nicky Simpson. This is someone making a play to kill me, to remove me. This is something in my life that I don't want the police to really know about.'

He sighed, calming himself for the moment.

'This is more a "Reckless" kind of case. So for right now, I would like you to work on my behalf while I hide in the shadows. I would like you to find out who is trying to kill me, and provide me the details so I can fix it.'

'Kill them, you mean.'

'Fix it,' Simpson replied, his face cold and hard.

'That's not part of our deal, and you don't need to worry about it,' Ellie held a hand to stop Simpson from continuing, a gesture that still felt weird. As much as Nicky Simpson was playing the grateful client, the character he was playing here was that of his YouTube persona. She knew very well that Simpson was a cold bastard who had a pile of dead bodies behind him. Ones that were stretched all the way back to his grandfather Paddy in the sixties.

'If we do this, you owe me a favour,' she said. 'You're aware of this?'

'A favour freely given at a time of your choosing,' Simpson nodded. 'I know. It'll be one I can give and I understand that—'

'I don't think you do,' Ramsey spoke suddenly. 'You know why we've been doing what we're doing. You've known for ages.'

And with that, the elephant in the room was out.

The one thing Ellie had been trying to do for years now – gain enough favours to discover the truth behind Bryan Noyce's death, to bring Nicky Simpson to justice and regain her position in the police – was now out there for everyone to see.

Simpson nodded.

'I have,' he said simply. 'But let me just say this. Whatever you ask, I *will* provide as my favour payment. I want this attack on my life sorted, and I know you're one of the best – I know you can do it. So, if you keep me alive and you sort this out, I will answer the question you have.'

Ramsey looked shocked at this, and Ellie didn't blame him. She also didn't understand why Ramsey had said such a thing – if Nicky Simpson hadn't known, then he would by now.

Who are you kidding, she thought to herself. *There was a reason he wanted Ramsey as a spy. He knew something was happening. He always has.*

Ellie nodded.

'Okay,' she said, looking at Robert. 'Let me think about it.

We'll have to see if Casey is on board, so we can get the footage from the club—'

She stopped, staring at Simpson, who was now looking incredibly guilty.

'What aren't you telling me?'

Simpson shifted in his seat.

'I might have placed a personal camera on reception, to keep an eye on people,' he said. 'That was the camera I saw the people being led out on, and it didn't record.'

'Keep an eye on people? Or someone?'

'I'd rather not say.'

Ellie sighed, rising.

'Everybody stay here. I need to have a chat with my partner.'

Robert nodded, rising from his chair, following Ellie out of the office.

'You sure we should leave him in there with Ramsey and Tinker?' Robert asked, the door now closed.

'As long as it's not Casey, I think it's safe,' Ellie replied as they walked down the corridor. 'Thoughts?'

'You keep him alive, it'll end your crusade real quick if you can get to a point where he'll admit everything,' Robert suggested. 'However, your favour is going to be a tough one.'

'How so?'

'Because I don't think he's going to allow you to save his life, *and* find a person trying to kill him, before clearing everything up so he can continue along as he has done – and then allow a favour that makes him surrender to the police for the murder of Bryan Noyce,' Robert admitted. 'The best you'll get is him verbally admitting he did it, but you'll still have to prove it.'

'I can cross that bridge when I get to it,' Ellie folded her arms. 'Maybe I can get something out of him I can then use the other favours for, maybe to confirm or deny?'

'Possibly,' Robert nodded. 'But this needs to be watertight. We need to get paperwork from him saying we're allowed to work on his behalf.'

'And then we need to get Rajesh Khanna down to Vauxhall, to look at his office, root about the fire debris,' Ellie suggested. 'We need to know what kind of explosive or accelerant it was, maybe look to see if we recognise any of the ingredients. If it's the method of an arsonist, or is some kind of detonator we recognise, then there's every chance we can at least start aiming towards somebody—'

'Sorry, but no Rajesh this time,' Robert shook his head. 'He's being watched by Mile End now. When we used him during the Lumetta case, he popped up on too many police watch lists because he was skirting pretty much to the edge of what he could get away with.'

Ellie went to reply, but then nodded. Robert was right. Rajesh Khanna's forensic evidence a few years earlier was what eventually kicked Ellie off the force, and his sense of justice, after realising his evidence had been corrupted in the case, had made Rajesh offer his services for any cases Ellie had. However, if they kept using him, the police would simply end up kicking him out, just like they had Ellie.

'Well, that causes us a problem then,' she replied. 'Because we're going to need some kind of forensics expert to help us here, and although Tinker's very good with guns and bombs, she's not very good with all that technical stuff – and

Ramsey's only really good at stealing, and finding things that were stolen.'

'Don't worry, I found you someone,' Robert smiled. 'Someone you've met before. A walk in; they said they were told to come and have a chat with us if they found themselves at a loose end.'

He nodded across the hall at a glass wall.

'And they're in your office right now, waiting to speak to you, actually.'

Ellie looked into her office through the full-length glass windows. And for the first time that morning, she realised there was somebody sitting in there, facing away from them. She couldn't see the face, but she recognised the red curly hair.

Entering the office as she closed the door behind her, she smiled as DC Joanna Davey, previously of the City of London's "Last Chance Saloon," looked around, standing up as she saw Ellie.

'DC Davey,' Ellie said. 'I haven't seen you for a while.'

'It's just Joanna now,' Davey replied. 'I haven't been a DC for quite a while.'

'That's not what I've heard. I heard you were still an active serving member, on leave and helping the team out in December.'

'I was there helping Billy Fitzwarren as an independent contractor,' Davey replied calmly. 'Basically, I was helping a friend. I wasn't there as police, and I've not worked as police since, well, since the Justice case.'

Ellie nodded at this. She had met Davey last summer, during the whole London crime world debacle Nicky Simpson had been mentioning earlier, when DI Declan Walsh and the Mile End unit had been investigating Johnny

Lucas, crossing Ellie's path when her old mentor, DCI Alex Monroe had appeared on her doorstep.

Davey had been good at her job, but even then Ellie could see she seemed to have her own demons. And then a couple of months later, it came out that Davey's sister had been murdered by a serial killer years earlier, a serial killer that she gained revenge on, with other victims, under the name "Justice." Shortly afterwards, she'd been fired, but after some shenanigans in Whitehall and Westminster, she was brought back due to lack of evidence against her. But, at the same time, there was no smoke without fire, and Davey had eventually quit the force.

Officially, it was a sabbatical, but Ellie recognised the look in Davey's eyes. The look of a damned good copper who now couldn't do her job. Who was innocent in the eyes of the law, but damned by her fellow officers.

The same look *she'd* had several years earlier.

'We need a forensics expert,' she said. 'Starting now.'

'I can do that,' Davey replied. 'Client?'

Ellie grinned.

'Come and meet him,' she said. 'You won't bloody believe it. And you can help me work out if he's been stalking employees on a webcam, too, while we're at it.'

5

FIRE DAMAGE

SURPRISINGLY, RAMSEY ALLEN HAD BEEN EAGER TO GO WITH Davey to the fire-damaged offices above the Battersea Power Station Simpson's Health Spa, and so the two of them, leaving Ellie and Tinker to deal with Nicky himself, travelled south of the river in Ramsey's battered old Rover.

'So, how are you finding the commercial sector?' Ramsey smiled as they pulled into the car park that led to the Power Station itself.

The building was still closed, with fire engines and police cars blocking the way, and Ramsey nodded at a few of the first responders as he pulled his battered car to the side.

Davey shrugged.

'If you mean "how's being unemployed and broke," it's pretty shitty,' she smiled. 'Monroe has me held on a retainer, so I can take a percentage of my salary while on leave, but I haven't been touching it, in case I have to pay it all back at some point.'

'But you're still an active copper, right?' Ramsey asked as

they climbed out of the car. 'I mean, you still have your warrant card and all that?'

'Sure, I think,' Davey patted her coat. 'I haven't really needed it recently. Why?'

'Having someone who can get past copper cordons is always good,' Ramsey smiled. 'And Ellie's pretty much gone as far as she can with her old DCI badge.'

'Gotcha,' Davey nodded. 'Although I don't know how much good it'll do here.'

Ramsey shrugged, as they started towards the main entrance. At the front, there was a police "do not pass" cordon, with what looked to be a bored officer hiding a yawn as he saw them approach.

'Now's your chance to find out,' Ramsey grinned, looking back at the officer. 'All right, mate?'

'We're closed,' the officer replied, eyeing up the two newcomers. 'Come back this afternoon.'

'By then forensics will have destroyed the bloody place, and your clod-hopping shoes will have scuffed any clues we could find,' Davey said, reaching into her pocket, but to Ramsey's dismay, she didn't pull out a police warrant card. 'Joanne Davey. Mister Ramsey and I have been hired by Nicholas Simpson to look into this apparent "gas explosion," which, let's face it, wasn't one, yeah?'

The officer took the sheet, reading it.

'Yeah, he said you'd be coming,' he said as he folded the sheet back up, passing it to Davey.

'Who did?' Davey looked confused at this.

In response, the officer nodded over to one of the squad cars where, leaning against the bonnet, was a sixteen-year-old boy. Shaggy black hair over a hoodie, hiding an obviously skinny body, Casey was tapping on a Steam Deck console, a recent purchase following the Lumetta case; his backpack and skateboard beside him.

Ramsey smiled, but Davey could tell it was forced as, under his breath, he made the smallest of expletives.

'Friend?' Davey asked.

'Colleague,' Ramsey nodded at the officer and walked over to Casey, Davey following. 'One who was sent home the moment we heard the client was Simpson.'

'Why?'

'His father was Bryan Noyce.'

'Oh.' Davey was clued up enough to know the story about Ellie's fall from grace, and the name Bryan Noyce was plastered all over it.

Seeing the newcomer, Casey's face flashed an expression of concern as he straightened up, moving away from the car.

'Who's the fresh blood?' he asked.

At this, Ramsey smiled, looking back at Davey. It wasn't so long ago the same line, or similar at least, had been said about Casey.

'Hark, the voice of the veteran,' he said. 'Casey, meet Joanne Davey. She's our new Rajesh Khanna.'

'What happened to the old one?'

'We realised he was one more caution away from being fired, so we're holding him in stock,' Ramsey replied. 'Joanne here—'

'I prefer Davey.'

'Davey here is a serving DC and worked under Doctor Rosanna Marcos,' Ramsey continued. 'When Raj realised he was being watched, both he and DCI Monroe suggested Miss Davey have a chat with us. Apparently she's very good.'

'Serving Detective Constable,' Casey repeated. 'Surely you're in the same boat, with cautions? Should you be walking around with this old reprobate?'

'Difference between me and Raj Khanna is that I don't give a monkey's if they fire me,' Davey shrugged. 'You must be the shit-hot wunderkind they have here.'

At Casey's blank expression, Davey sighed.

'You're the tech expert who fixes everything,' she said.

At this, Casey's face brightened, but then darkened when he looked at Ramsey.

'I was, until they benched me,' he said. 'Did you think I wouldn't work out the client?'

'We wanted to keep you at a distance,' Ramsey's mouth shrugged. 'In case you tried to kill him.'

'I wouldn't have *tried* anything,' Casey sulked. 'I would have *succeeded*.'

'Shouldn't you be at school?' Davey asked.

'I'm on revision,' Casey replied. 'I'd be in the library, but there's also school strikes this week, so I'm making the best of it.'

'You think hanging around gutted health spas is making the best?'

Casey gave a thin-lipped, humourless smile.

'When it's Nicky Simpson, yeah,' he said, turning his attention back to Ramsey. 'So, we can have a look around, but you're not going to like it, as two of your favourite coppers are here.'

'Delgado and Whitehouse,' Ramsey didn't need to ask. 'Thought they might be. Another reason Ellie isn't here.'

'And where exactly is she?' Casey squared his shoulders.

Ramsey, in return, took a long, hard look at the entrance.

'Let's talk about it on the way up,' he smiled. However, that smile faded quickly as two figures, currently talking to some first responders, peeled away from the crowd and started walking towards them.

'Shit,' Ramsey grumbled. 'I hoped they'd been sent on another case.'

'Of course not,' Casey shook his head. 'We ain't that lucky.'

As DS Kate Delgado and DI Mark Whitehouse of the Vauxhall Crime Unit walked towards them, Ramsey side-spoke to Davey.

'I hope you've got your badge, because you're probably going to need it,' he whispered as the two detectives arrived, stopping in front of them – not actually blocking the way, but doing enough to pause them on their journey.

'Mister Allen,' Whitehouse said, with the slightest hint of a smile on his face. 'What brings you here?'

'Come to gloat?' Delgado added. 'We know you don't really have much love for Mister Simpson.'

'Actually, we're here on behalf of Mister Simpson,' Ramsey smiled, passing across the note they'd shown to the officer on the cordon a minute earlier. 'We're working on behalf of Simpson's Health Spas to find out what happened here today.'

Delgado looked back at the building behind her.

'It was a gas leak, nothing more,' she replied. 'Big explosion – terrible thing. Lots of shops gained water damage. There you go, all done, you can piss off now.'

Ignoring the command, Ramsey kept the smile on his face, refusing to give any other emotion.

'I'm sure you're intelligent people,' he said, lowering his

voice. 'I mean, you've not really shown me this in the past, but Ellie has spoken highly of both of you.'

He made an apologetic face at Delgado.

'Well, one of you, anyway,' he added, giving a look of mock shock as Delgado flipped him the finger, turning back to Whitehouse.

'We both know this wasn't a gas explosion,' he continued. 'And we, as The Finders' Corporation, are here to find out what's going on.'

'And you've brought the child and a new person, I see,' Delgado replied. 'One I know.'

'Delgado, Whitehouse,' Davey nodded amenably.

'I think you'll find it's Detective Sergeant Delgado, Detective *Constable* Davey,' Delgado snapped. 'Remember your rankings in the force, yeah? You might be one of Monroe's screw ups, but here in Vauxhall, we do things by the book.'

Davey gave a small, knowing smile at this.

'Yeah, I've seen the "books" you guys use down here,' she said. 'And for your information, *Kate*, I'm not a serving member of the police anymore, which means I can call you what I want, and you can call me *Miss* Davey.'

If Delgado was surprised at this, she hid it very well.

'So you're working for Simpson now?' she asked.

'Well, from what I've understood, it's a bit of a police tradition around here,' Davey looked at Casey to confirm this. 'Am I right?'

'Yeah,' Casey nodded. 'Lots of Vauxhall coppers like to work for Nicky Simpson.'

'Be careful, kid, that's fighting talk,' Delgado snapped. 'You're trashing the reputation of a lot of officers with a throwaway line like that.'

'Did I name names?' Casey asked. 'It was a generalisation.'

Whitehouse touched Delgado's arm, a subtle hint to let it go, but Delgado didn't get the message.

'Well, if you're making such a generalisation, I'm glad you've finally acknowledged your boss was one of his people,' she finished with a smug smile.

Whitehouse shook his head.

'This isn't why we're here,' he said, speaking before Delgado could continue, looking back at Ramsey as he spoke. 'I don't know what your plans are, but I know you're not happy with Simpson. If you're working for him, there's obviously some kind of plan going on.'

He leant in, lowering his voice.

'Be careful.'

'I appreciate the heads up,' Ramsey replied, 'but we're just here to check the explosion, nothing more.'

And, with the paperwork examined, Whitehouse reluctantly stepped aside and allowed the team in.

'Your funeral,' he said sadly as the three members of Finders passed him, Davey taking one last glance at the glowering Delgado as they did.

'Wow, Kate really hates you,' she said to Ramsey as they walked up to the main entrance.

'She hates everyone,' Casey replied, shifting his backpack as they walked. 'Ellie thinks she's the dirty copper in the team.'

'Could be,' Davey mused. 'Could well be.'

THE POLICE HAD BLOCKED OFF THE MAIN ENTRANCE TO THE building, but once through, they could see there wasn't much damage in the gym itself.

If anything, the health spa seemed to have gained more water damage from the sprinkler system turning on than from any explosion.

Walking through the disaster scene, Casey examined the walls, frowning as he paused in the main lobby.

'Webcams,' he said, pointing up near the reception desk. 'They weren't on the plans.'

'You've seen the plans?' Davey asked, before replying to her own question. 'Of course you have.'

'Maybe Nicky Simpson decided to have more security?' Ramsey suggested.

'Well, if he did, he's picked a stupid one to use,' the professional air of disdain in Casey's tone made Ramsey smile. 'These are cheap Wi-Fi ones. They're not going to a server. These are going to one computer.'

'But whose computer?' Ramsey mused aloud.

'Simpson, maybe, the arsonist, possibly, if they're his or hers,' Casey nodded. 'Hey, do me a favour? Give me a bunk up—'

'A what?' Ramsey was confused by the term, but Davey understood, clasping her hands together and allowing Casey to move his foot onto them, boosting him upwards to have a closer look at the camera.

'Don't touch anything,' she said.

'I'm not stupid,' Casey said, carefully taking close-up photos with his phone. 'I just needed to know the serial. I can come back down now.'

This done, they carried on through the waterlogged health spa to a set of stairs at the side.

'So, this is the stairwell that he escaped down,' Ramsey said as he opened the door, sniffing. 'You can smell the cordite in the air.'

Walking up the stairs they found the doors had been blown inwards on the second floor and slipped past them as they walked into the office.

The damage here, however, was a far cry from the health spa two floors below. The fire had burned most of the walls, and scorch marks were across the windows, leaving a trail of smoke and soot. And, as they looked around, they could see the furniture had been set on fire.

'Nicky needs to learn about fire safety,' Ramsey said, looking at the remains of what was once some kind of leather sofa. 'Those bloody things will have gone up like a Christmas candle.'

The elevator doors, or what was left of them, were still open, and the blast radius was visible for all to see, burnt forever into the carpet tiles that led to it. Casey carefully walked back to it.

'Can you see anything?' he asked, noting that Davey had already pulled on a pair of blue booties and latex gloves. 'Hey, should we have those?'

'If you're going to walk anywhere in this crime scene, I'd prefer if you did,' Davey said, tossing over a pair to him, and a second pair to Ramsey. 'Raj might not do these sorts of things, but where I come from, this is given.'

'In fairness, Raj rarely allows us to attend crime scenes,' Casey smiled. 'And the last one I went to was outside, and I got to fly a drone around.'

'Do you have the drone on you?' Davey asked, straightening.

'Yeah, why?'

'How big is it?'

Casey reached into his backpack and pulled out a small camera drone.

'Not that large,' he said, showing it off. 'It's a DJI Mavic 3, what the YouTubers use. Fifty frames per second, forty-five minutes flight time, does slow motion—'

'Yeah, I don't care about any of that crap,' Davey said, taking it and examining it. 'Do me a favour, film the place. Go into every corner. And then when you're done, I want you to have a really good look in this elevator.'

'Why aren't we looking in it, anyway?'

'Because I've got a feeling that the moment you step foot in it, the damn thing's going to crash down,' Davey replied matter-of-factly. 'I think the explosion came from inside, but if the blast went up, it'll have caught the cables holding it. And I don't know about you, but I'd rather not die on my first day.'

So, as Casey set up his drone, using his remote to fly it around the entire burnt-out offices, Davey looked back at the wreckage.

'What do you need me to do?' Ramsey asked, feeling a little out of place for a change.

'Honestly, I'm not sure,' Davey replied. 'I know you're a thief. And I know you're good at stealing stuff. But apart from that, I don't really know yet what your skill set is.'

She stretched her back, looking about the destroyed offices.

'What would you usually be doing around now?'

'Talking to people,' Ramsey smiled. 'I think, maybe, I'll go do that. We know there's a receptionist we need to have a chat with downstairs who was taking people out. So, while you scrabble in the soot, I'll go see if I can find anybody.'

He nodded over at Casey.

'You okay with the boy?'

'I've worked with worse,' Davey grinned. 'You've met the Last Chance Saloon, right?'

And so, leaving Casey to play with his drone, and Davey to examine the wreckage on the floor, Ramsey Allen returned to the stairs and the health club below.

6

WITNESS STATEMENTS

EVEN THOUGH THE BOMB HAD GONE OFF OVER AN HOUR OR TWO earlier, there was still a crowd outside, many of whom had come for the shops, but also several who were still waiting to be allowed back into the gym to pick up their items from the lockers, standing around in their gym kits and looking very pissed off.

Ramsey didn't want those witnesses; all they could tell him was how their personal bests were quashed because of a fire alarm. He wanted to start off with a particular witness, someone from what Ramsey could work out, Nicky Simpson had been quietly stalking. He hadn't wanted to tell Casey that the webcam was Simpson's, apparently purely for staring at the receptionist, as Casey already had enough reasons not to like the man, and quite importantly, not work for him.

Standing at the side, looking nervous and in Health Club uniform, was a young, dark-haired woman, no older than nineteen, maybe twenty. She matched the description Nicky had given of the woman he'd seen escorting people out, the one they knew he'd been watching – and so Ramsey decided that *she* would be a good opportunity to start his questioning.

'Morning,' he said, smiling. 'How's it going?'

'Not great,' the girl said. 'This is my second week.'

'Well, at least you get the morning off,' Ramsey kept the smile on his face. 'Can I ask what happened?'

'Are you police?'

'No, we're the insurance investigators,' Ramsey lied. Well, it wasn't *really* a lie. They didn't investigate insurance fraud, but technically, the insurance they were investigating was their client's life. 'We've got to make a report about the fire, and things like that. I'm guessing you were one of the people who got the members out of the building?'

The woman nodded.

'The sirens went off. We knew we had to leave.'

'The sirens went off ...' Ramsey started taking notes. 'Tell me more.'

'Well, I was on the front desk. Duncan, he's the duty manager – he's around somewhere – and when this alarm started ringing I'd never heard it before, Duncan comes over, tells me it's the fire alarm. Says it's often a drill, and it'll cut off within thirty seconds, but then a minute later it hasn't. People are getting worried. And we notice that the coffee shop next door is evacuating their people.'

'So you started evacuating people from here? I'm sorry, I never asked your name,' Ramsey asked. 'I'm Ramsey.'

'Carrie,' the woman, now known as Carrie, gave a faint half-smile.

'So, Duncan told you to get people out?'

'Oh, no,' Carrie shook her head. 'He's bloody useless. I took it on my own initiative to do that. I knew something was wrong. That we had to get people out. And so I started moving people towards the doors. I didn't know at the time that there was a gas leak.'

'You couldn't smell anything?'

'No. All I know is that we've got pretty much everybody out, and then there was a massive explosion from upstairs and the sprinklers all went off. Bloody soaked me to the skin, it did.'

'But it could have been worse,' Ramsey mused, still writing in the notebook. 'You got yourself out just in time, and you saved a lot of people.'

'Saved a lot of people from getting wet,' Carrie smiled. 'But thank you for the compliment. I appreciate it.'

Looking up from the notes, Ramsey turned as he glanced around the location.

'Did you see anything strange before the sirens went off?' he asked.

'What do you mean by strange?'

Ramsey shrugged and then pointed his pen over at the cordoned-off elevators.

'The elevators that go to the offices. Did you see anybody go there?'

At this, Carrie's expression changed, and suddenly Ramsey realised she was incredibly uncomfortable about the question being asked.

'No,' she said. 'There was nobody – I saw nobody. Nothing happened with the elevators. Why would something happen with the elevators?'

'You didn't notice anybody go over to those elevators?' Ramsey doubled down, leaning closer. 'You didn't see anybody place anything in the elevators—'

'Look, I don't know who you are, but I really don't know what you're talking about,' Carrie stepped back, looking around, her face pale with what Ramsey took as abject fear. 'I'm thinking I'd like to speak to the police, or a solicitor, if there's a problem here.'

'Why would you need to speak to your lawyer about someone walking into an elevator?' Ramsey replied innocently. 'Unless you know something you're not telling us, Carrie. Unless you know *exactly* who placed the explosive device in the elevator, that was supposed to take out Nicky Simpson.'

At this, Carrie's expression changed again, and Ramsey instantly recognised the expression. It was one Ellie had worn on her face frequently when talking about Nicky Simpson. It was also one he'd worn now and then; one of utter distaste, with a modicum of hatred.

'Nicky Simpson is scum,' Carrie whispered now, no longer caring about a solicitor, it seemed. 'He hurt my brother years ago. But he's the only job in town. If someone wants to kill him, I got no problem with that.'

She looked around nervously, maybe worried she was being watched, possibly by Duncan, the duty manager.

'We all know what he really is,' she continued. 'That FaceTime live stream thing that went out a couple of months back? Remember that? The Italian grassing him up? It told everybody the truth. And I thought "good."'

'If you feel so strongly, then why would you work for Nicky Simpson?'

Carrie didn't reply, instead looking away.

'I already told you why. I got my reasons. The alarms went off. There was an explosion. The sprinklers came on. That's all you're getting from me, Mister Allen, and I suggest you take what you can.'

And, this said, Carrie walked off, hugging her still damp sides for warmth as she headed for the outside air.

Ramsey watched her, and a smile slowly appeared on his lips.

She'd called him Mister Allen.

He hadn't given his surname. She knew who he was. Which meant that Carrie the receptionist knew far more about what was happening than she was letting on.

'Curiouser and curiouser,' he said, placing away his notepad. He hadn't needed to read from it, as he'd made no notes. He'd spent years learning not to leave a paper trail of any kind, and in fact the words he'd been writing were a hastily scribbled shopping list for later.

Nodding to himself he started looking around for Duncan, the duty manager.

UPSTAIRS, JOANNE DAVEY HAD MADE HER OWN SURPRISE revelation.

They had gone through the room; Davey by foot, Casey with his drone, and he'd explained more than once that the camera he had, when put through an app would give an outstanding 3D rendering of the crime scene. Davey had told him he reminded her of someone called "Billy" at her old job, and pointed out that he was an annoying little scroat as well. Nevertheless, the examination had been thorough, and unfortunately for them, the fire damage was quite extensive. There wasn't much that could be worked from.

And, at the end, Casey's drone had flown into the back of the elevator, hovering in the middle as Casey and Davey zoomed in on the screen. There had been a device that had detonated; that much was obvious, and Davey had done her best to get as many of the materials used noted down, in the hope there was a mad bomber who used the same mixture, and there were several items that were still scattered around the elevator carriage's floor that hadn't been destroyed. Casey had marked them down, on the basis that Davey might be able to use them.

There was one piece at the back, however, that confused Davey, a small piece of half-melted plastic that Casey couldn't get a clear view of on his drone's screen.

Davey was tapping the side of the elevator with her latex glove, staring into it, deep in thought.

'How much do you weigh?' she eventually asked.

'Less than you ... why?'

Davey pointed into the elevator.

'I need you to grab me that piece of plastic at the back,' she explained.

'I thought we weren't going in because it could collapse?'

'I think we're safe,' Davey shrugged.

'*We're* not anything,' Casey shook his head. 'You're not thinking of going in there, you're thinking of sending me alone.'

'You won't do it?' Davey rose from her crouched position. 'Let me know, kid. Because otherwise I'm going to get it. And I'll make sure everybody knows you made a woman go in when you could have—'

'I'll do it,' Casey interrupted, sighing as he focused on the black piece of melted plastic at the back. 'You're worse than bloody Tinker at guilt trips.'

Quickly stepping in, pausing as the elevator shook, eventually gathering his composure once the carriage settled, Casey gingerly stepped to the back of the blast area, and, picking up the small piece of melted black plastic case with his blue latex glove, he moved back as quickly as he could, exiting the elevator at speed as it made an ominous creaking noise.

'What is it?' he asked, passing it back. 'It looks like the CCTV things Nicky stuck up downstairs.'

Davey nodded.

'You might be right,' she said, turning it over in her hands. 'It's the outer casing of a webcam. Not the same ones from downstairs, but this is a small one you'd place on a laptop screen, connected by USB. You know, when you're having a Zoom meeting or something like that?'

'I know what a webcam is, Mum,' Casey mocked. 'So why hasn't it been utterly wiped out like the other things? It's just melted.'

Davey peered closely at the melted plastic.

'I think it was because this little thing was behind the blast, which was angled at the door. You know, like a Claymore mine says on it "front towards enemy."'

Casey shuddered at the comment.

'So, basically, whoever set this bomb up had a webcam watching the door,' he intoned, the realisation of his words hitting him as he spoke them. 'They wanted to see Nicky Simpson die. They were probably watching it live.'

Davey nodded.

'But if they were watching, then they'd know he's not dead, as they'd have seen he wasn't in the doorway. So why detonate anyway?'

'Well, I think the world knows he's not dead now,' Casey said, showing his phone. On it was a social media page, with an image of two girls with Nicky Simpson between them. 'I'm guessing this was Caesar's. Good to see he's making light of his assassination attempt. Idiot's even liked it.'

'If it's a webcam, there needs to be something to connect to,' Davey was thinking aloud. 'We need to work out how they were watching and what it connected to.'

Casey stared down at the elevator debris.

'The bomb could have been a remote detonator,' he said, working out the angles. 'Usually it's a cheap phone, and it detonates when a call comes through, or a message is received, but maybe it's a smart phone, an Android, perhaps, and they hacked the webcam into it?'

'Possible,' Davey said, straightening up. 'I think we've done all we can up here for the moment. What's the rules about leaving the old man alone?'

'Don't?' Casey grinned.

'Then I suppose we'd better go find him,' Davey sighed, pulling off the blue latex gloves. 'Come on, let's go see if we can have a rematch with Whitehouse and the Witch Queen.'

RAMSEY WAS WAITING FOR THEM AS THEY EXITED THE BUILDING, standing by the battered Rover just outside the cordon.

'Find anything?' he asked.

'They were watching when the bomb went off,' Casey said, packing his drone away into the backpack. 'We don't know how yet, but it looks like they wanted to see his expression when he died. You?'

Ramsey looked across the police and fire vehicles still outside the shopping arcade.

'The woman at reception, Carrie, she knows more than she let on,' he said.

'How'd you work that out?' Casey opened the back door to the Rover, tossing his bag and skateboard into it.

'She knew my surname when I hadn't given it to her, and she hates Simpson. Said something about her brother and Simpson having issues.'

'So why work for him?' Davey frowned.

'Apparently, the job market isn't that great.'

'No, there's something else here,' Davey shook her head. 'Trust me, I'm an expert on the job market right now. And it's not so bad you'd grab a reception job for your mortal enemy.'

'I agree,' Ramsey tapped his pen against his chin. 'But it's a great job to allow people in, especially giving them access to elevators.'

'You writing shopping lists again?' Casey went to snatch the pen from Ramsey, but as ever, the thief's reflexes were too fast.

'No, just your eulogy,' Ramsey said as he opened the driver's door. 'Okay then. We have some clues, and a hell of a lot more questions than before we started. Let's just hope the others are doing better—'

He stopped, staring across the car park.

'Hold that thought,' he said, walking away from the car, and over to the right-hand side of the building. There were still some ambulances and vans in the area, and he used the cover from these to his advantage as he slowly made his way to the edge of the car park, continually keeping his eyes on the two people in deep conversation.

One of them was DS Kate Delgado, arguing, her hands waving as she tried to explain a point to the older man watching her.

It was the older man Ramsey recognised, and he unconsciously reached for the side of an ambulance to steady himself.

Because Ramsey knew the old man.

Ramsey *feared* the old man.

And, more relevant to the case in hand, Ramsey knew without a doubt – because he'd been to his funeral – that the man currently talking to DS Kate Delgado was dead.

7

OFFENSIVE PLAY

'So, what's the plan, boss?' Nicky Simpson said, relaxing back on the chair in the boardroom.

'Well, first, we don't stay here,' Ellie said, snatching away the laptop that Simpson had borrowed from Robert, with the VPN on and hiding the IP address, when liking the social media photo, as agreed. 'We've done what we said we'd do, so now those girls will keep quiet, with a bit of luck.'

'But it does out you as alive,' Tinker shrugged. 'Which starts the clock towards the next attempt.'

'So, now we need to work out what to do next,' Ellie added, looking around. 'Ramsey will talk to the staff at your club, including the girl you have the hots for—'

'I don't have the hots for her,' Simpson objected. 'There's something about her. Something familiar. Like I went to school with her or something, even if she's a bloody teenager.'

'Whatever, voyeur,' Tinker mocked, backing down at a glare from Ellie.

'Let's just get this over, yeah?' Ellie asked politely. 'I, for one, would like this all finished quickly.'

'Said the actress to the bishop,' Simpson muttered, before holding his hands up to divert away any more arguments. 'Carry on, please.'

'Ramsey texted, and told me Casey's at the crime scene, so that's not ideal, but at least this means Casey and Davey will work out what's going on with the explosion. Now we just need to work out why someone wants you dead.'

'There's a list, most likely,' Tinker suggested. 'Who's at the top of it?'

Simpson rubbed at his chin as he considered this.

'The Lumettas aren't happy with me after I pulled out of the deal, but they have their own issues right now, and I can't see them going on a killing spree to get back at me,' he started. 'The Tsangs are in the middle of their own family drama with Kenny in prison and Jimmy trying to bring things back under his umbrella, the Seven Sisters are all over the place after Janelle's daughter screwed her over—'

'With the help of you,' Ellie reminded him.

'I was in the background, sure, but I didn't need to do anything,' Simpson shook his head. 'I just let them aim at each other.'

'The problem is that everyone you screwed over in London has their own issues to deal with first,' Tinker mused. 'Maybe it's someone from your past?'

Simpson grinned.

'Well, that opens up a much bigger list,' he said. 'But believe me, Tinkerbelle Jones, when I tell you that anyone who came for me in the past ... well, they're not around anymore.'

He looked back at Ellie.

'Just ask Bryan Noyce.'

Ellie's hands gripped into fists as she stared furiously at the man at the table.

'I'd tread very carefully around that,' she hissed. 'Before I throw you out of that window.'

'I didn't mean I *did* it,' Simpson held his hands up defensively. 'I meant the past isn't able to be spoken to. I don't know who went for me, because half the time it was sorted on my behalf, or they simply had … accidents.'

There was a moment of silence as Ellie stared daggers at Nicky Simpson, before turning away, her hands unclenching as she forced herself to back down.

'Well, apart from the obvious list of hundreds, I think we need to speak to your driver,' Tinker replied. 'He knew something was going on. The text proves it.'

'No, I can't believe that,' Simpson shook his head. 'Saleh's been with my family for years. He worked for my dad. I think he even started under Granddad. I mean, he wasn't a driver back then. He was a teenager, but he's been in the family since then. He's trustworthy. Always has been.'

'Then we need to work out who it would be that could turn him in such a way,' Ellie suggested. 'Do you have an address for him?'

'Yeah, I do,' Simpson said with a furrowed brow. 'But I thought we were hiding?'

'Yeah, that's the problem with being hunted,' Tinker replied. 'They expect you to go on the defensive. They expect you to find a nice place to hide. And they *really* get surprised when you turn up on their doorstep.'

'And if somebody tries to take you out, I'm still not losing here,' Ellie smiled. 'But he tried to take you out with an explosive device. This is somebody who's looking for shock and awe with your death – or he could have taken you out easily at any point with a sniper rifle.'

'Oh, so that's fine then,' Simpson looked queasy, which for someone used to such violence was a little surprising to Ellie.

I suppose he's never really had it aimed at him before, she thought to herself as she picked up her phone, checking it.

'I reckon they wanted you to escape so they could hunt you,' she continued.

'Oh, that doesn't sound creepy in any way,' Simpson said, rising from the chair. 'Come on then, let's go see my driver and find out why the hell he decided to betray me, and everything we've ever stood for.'

'Maybe he's learnt how to be a grade-A prick from the best,' Tinker suggested as they left the room.

ELLIE HADN'T BEEN SURE WHAT TO EXPECT FROM SALEH'S living arrangements, but the one thing she hadn't expected was a million pounds, semi-detached house in Bermondsey.

'This is what a driver makes these days?' she asked, both impressed and appalled. 'I have a flat in Shoreditch.'

'Which probably isn't that far off this,' Simpson sniffed as he stared from the back seat of Ellie's Ford Focus. 'I thought this was written off?'

'Had it fixed. Owed a favour,' Ellie said, staring across the road from where they were now parked. 'Being owed favours is nice.'

She looked back at Simpson, her face emotionless.

'I can't wait until you owe me one,' she said ominously. 'Oh, the things I'm going to make you do.'

Simpson decided, wisely, not to answer this, leaning back into the back seat.

Across the street, Tinker was pressing the door buzzer on the front gate, and had been for a couple of minutes now. Eventually, she sighed, loosened her shoulders and walked back to the car, climbing in.

'Where's he park?' she asked. 'I'm guessing he keeps a car to drive Little Lord Fauntleroy in the back about?'

'He drives my Tesla when I'm not driving it,' Nicky replied. 'But he drives to and from work in a BMW.'

'I can't see one.'

'He has it in a garage out back.'

Ellie started the engine.

'Then let's go see if he's left it there,' she said. 'If it's gone, we know he's out. If it's there, he's either inside, or he's gone for a local walk.'

Driving around to the back, however, was easier said than done, and in the end Ellie parked up as close as she could to the small lane that led to the garages at the rear of the row of houses, and walked briefly down it, returning quickly.

'Garage doors are closed,' she said. 'Which means Saleh might or might not still be in the house.'

Tinker looked over at Simpson.

'You said he texted you, right? Said he was sorry?'

'Yeah,' Simpson's face was dark. 'I have it right here—'

'Whoa!' Tinker almost jumped back as Simpson pulled out the phone. 'You're seriously travelling around with a phone people can track you on?'

'No, it's a burner,' Ellie said as she looked at the phone in Nicky Simpson's hand. 'It's not expensive or showy enough to be his actual day to-day one.'

Simpson made a face at Ellie, but nodded.

'I cloned the details,' he said. 'Always good to keep things on hand if you need to dump it.'

'Basically, you mean you had a cloud-saved backup,' Tinker shook her head. 'All this "I cloned my phone," like you're some kind of badass spy. So where's the original?'

'I stepped on it before I left the building,' Simpson replied. 'Felt quite cathartic, to be honest. I might do it more often.'

There was a silence that came over the interior of the car at this strange comment.

'So, what exactly do you want me to text?' Simpson asked, deciding to change the subject.

'I don't know, something that would get Saleh out of the house,' Ellie suggested. 'Maybe reminding him you're alive, that you know it was him ... something like that.'

'You think he's genuinely going to come out and talk to us if I say that?'

'Oh, no, I don't want him to come and talk to us,' Ellie replied. 'I want him to go on the run. I want him to run out the back, leave in his car, and drive off to whoever told him to keep out of your way today.'

Simpson nodded, typing in a message.

'Here, is this good enough?' he asked after he'd sent it.

> I know what you did. I'm coming for you.
> Wait there.

'Oh, that's perfect,' Ellie smiled. And quietly, the three of them sat in the car, waiting to see what happened.

It didn't take long.

After about ten minutes, a gunmetal grey BMW drove out of the side road at speed.

'Is that his car?' Tinker asked, revving the Ford Focus, having taken the driver's seat.

'Yeah,' Simpson replied. 'He'd usually drive it to the offices and then take over the Tesla if I needed him to.'

'Alright, then,' Ellie said. 'Let's see where he goes.'

As it was, where he went seemed to be more towards Vauxhall and Kennington, and, keeping a couple of cars away at all times, Tinker kept on his tail, watching to see where he went.

'Be careful,' Ellie said, watching the car in front. 'The last thing we want is for him to know we're following him.'

'Trust me,' Simpson said. 'If he knows, he knows already. He's not stupid.'

He shifted nervously in the seat.

'Also, he's gonna be on hyper alert after the text.'

'Good,' Ellie replied, keeping her eyes on the car. 'I want him to be alert. I want him to be nervous—'

'Why are you doing this?' Simpson interrupted.

'Because you came to us, you needed help,' Ellie turned her attention from the car, looking back over the chair at Nicky Simpson.

'Yeah, I get that. But let's be honest, Reckless. You haven't exactly been one of my cheerleaders for the last couple of years.'

'You came to me in need,' Ellie repeated. 'And as much as I dislike you, I realised I had to help you. I became a copper because I wanted to help people. You might have taken that from me, but it doesn't stop me from doing the job.'

She glanced at Tinker before continuing.

'That's why I helped Danny Flynn, why I helped Maureen Lumetta—'

'You did those for favours,' Simpson said, the smile now

gone. 'Don't tell me you're some kind of Robin Hood character. You did those because you wanted favours to take me down and we both know it.'

'Well, luckily for you, I don't need to use those favours anymore, do I?' Ellie smiled. 'All I need to do is keep you alive. And then you can tell me everything.'

Simpson went to reply, but then smiled, weakly raising an imaginary glass in a "Touché" toast.

'We lost him,' Tinker interrupted the moment with a curse. 'He must have seen us, and then turned down a side alley.'

She moved to the left of the road as she spoke.

'He did it at the last moment, like he changed his mind,' she said, indicating left, and turning onto the side road at speed. 'I'm going to cut down the next left parallel up, come out behind him.'

'He saw us,' Simpson spoke ominously. 'He knew we were following, so made sure we couldn't continue.'

'Well, we'll fix that real soon,' Tinker snapped back as she pulled back onto the road where the BMW had recently turned down.

The BMW had already pulled ahead, as it hadn't needed to do the road backtracking that Tinker had, but after two streets, they saw it under a bridge, parked up on the side of the road. The bridge was level with the street, the road under it a dip down as a turnoff to the side led up to the T-junction, and, as they approached slowly, they could see there was a figure in the driver's seat.

'Pull over,' Ellie said, frowning as she looked at the car ahead. 'Something feels off.'

They pulled over on the other side of the road about fifty metres from the car. Ellie had almost considered suggesting they follow the slip road up and over, coming down the other side, but this would leave them with another moment where no eyes were on the car, and they'd had one of those already. Where they were right now was close enough to see that Saleh was still in the car – although they didn't have a clear view of his face, they could see the baldness of his head.

'Why is he waiting there?' Ellie asked aloud, although it was a more rhetorical question.

'Should I send another text?' Simpson suggested.

'No, there's something going on,' Ellie shook her head, looking around the street, peering carefully at the other vehicles around them. 'I think this is a setup of some kind. Look at him. We're in an abandoned industrial part of Kennington, there's a bridge blocking any lights or any security cameras.'

She tapped at her teeth with a pen she'd pulled out of her pocket, seemingly for this very task, as she mulled the situation over.

'Okay, so we follow Saleh,' she said. 'We find him parked up. What are we expected to do in this situation?'

'Go speak to him,' Tinker replied cautiously. 'He's pulled over, so we would walk over, and then maybe knock on the window. And if they don't know we're working with Nicky here, they might expect him to do it.'

Ellie unclipped the seatbelt.

'Yeah. I think you're right – they want Nicky to walk over. That's the play here,' she said, but then paused, as down the street, an old man started hurriedly walking towards the car.

He was wearing a battered old overcoat that had seen better years, and held a small bottle of Evian water – a well-used one, that definitely didn't hold the original pure water inside it, with a squeeze-bottle sports cap – and some kind of wiper in his hands.

'Shit,' Ellie whispered. 'Not now.'

The old man walked up to the car, waving the wiper in a way of suggesting that he would happily clean the window of the BMW for a small donation. However, there seemed to be no response from inside the BMW, and as the man reached the car, still waving his wiper, he then stopped, staring into the car before he started tapping on the window, his body partially blocking Ellie's view, as he tried to gain the driver's attention.

'Something's wrong,' Ellie said, opening the passenger door. 'I need to get him out of there.'

Once out of the car and closing the door, she walked towards the BMW and the old man.

'Hey!' she called out. 'Back away!'

Before the old man could reply, however, there was a buzz from Ellie's phone. Pulling it out as she stopped on the road, she looked down at a new text from Ramsey.

Get out. It's a trap.

Ellie frowned as she looked around. *How did Ramsey know where she was, or even what she was about to do?*

She was about to text back, but the old man, seeing her close by, shouted out.

'He's not well! He looks like he's dead! You should call an ambulance!'

'Then get away!' Ellie replied angrily, starting towards the car.

The old man didn't listen, however, and instead turned and opened the driver's door by the side handle—

The force of the explosion pretty much killed him instantly.

And, forty yards away, it sent Ellie slamming back into the Ford Focus, hitting it bodily as the force of the blast knocked her backwards, pieces of broken and burnt BMW landing around her.

Scrambling to her feet, she looked around. There was nobody within visibility, but that didn't mean someone wasn't watching,

'Ellie!' there was the slightest of sounds above the ringing in her ears from the explosion, and Ellie looked to see Tinker, half out of the car, staring at her in concern. 'Are you okay?'

Ellie managed a weak nod as she gathered her bearings. But Tinker wasn't finished, running over to her, leading Ellie back to the car.

'You're bleeding,' Tinker said, and Ellie touched her forehead, wiping away a small trickle of blood from the side of her scalp, likely from when a piece of BMW had clipped her.

'I'm fine,' she said, climbing back into the car, noting the broken passenger window from where she had impacted against it. 'Get out of here now, this is a kill zone.'

'You got Ramsey's text?' Tinker said, showing her own phone with the message.

'Yeah,' Ellie nodded, wincing as pain raced through her head. 'Just a little too late, though.'

'Looks like he was right,' Tinker said as she gunned the engine, turning the car around and heading away from the explosion at speed. 'But how did he know?'

'That's a question I want to ask him,' Ellie held a tissue to her head. 'Just as soon as we find a place with no explosions.'

8

DEAD MEN SCARS

AFTER SEEING HIM AT THE BATTERSEA POWER STATION'S CAR park, Ramsey had followed the old man with the burn scars on his cheek. And, once Delgado had finished the conversation she was having with him, Ramsey had watched as the old man climbed into a Range Rover Discovery and driven out of the Nine Elms area.

With Casey and Davey in his battered Rover, both confused as to why they were doing this exactly, Ramsey had followed the same rules as Tinker had followed in her own car pursuit, keeping far enough away to make sure the man in the Range Rover hadn't noticed him.

But as they drove, Ramsey had convinced Casey to use his computer skills to try to find out whose car it actually was, using the licence plate and anything he could find.

Because the man driving it right now was dead.

Casey found the car was owned by a company, *Ferdia Holdings* – it wasn't familiar to Ramsey, and when Casey mentioned it, the name wasn't one known to either him or Davey. All they knew was it had been created in Dublin, was an EU-based holding, and had a main office in Dundalk, just south of Ireland's north and south border.

The Land Rover had carried on to Kennington, staying south of the river, not bothering to cross back into London itself. And after a while, Ramsey had pulled up at the side of the road, watching as the Range Rover drove under a bridge in a dip in the road, parking up and waiting.

Climbing out of the car, asking Casey and Davey to wait for him while he "played a hunch," Ramsey walked to the top of the slip road, looking down from the bridge over the road below, as the man he'd been following – the man who was dead – sat in his car and waited.

After a moment, a gunmetal grey BMW drove along the street, pulling up on the other side of the road. Ramsey couldn't see clearly without moving down the slip road, a walk which would definitely make him visible to the people below, and so he tried to sneak down the best he could, gaining an unobstructed view of the road below, as the man he'd been following walked to the BMW, and started talking to the driver.

A driver Ramsey couldn't see as the angle was wrong.

Deciding to move around to get a better view, he lost sight for a moment as he stepped back across the road to follow the path, doing his best to keep himself from the scarred man's gaze. No more than ten maybe twenty seconds had passed by, but when he gained a fresh view, he realised the lost time had been enough to change everything.

The man he was following was gone, the Range Rover driving off, and the BMW now alone in the street. Frowning, Ramsey had turned to go back, but saw Casey waving at him and pointing at a blue Ford Focus that had just parked down the street.

Ramsey immediately realised what Casey had seen here; that was Ellie's car, here for some kind of meeting, one the dead man with the burn scar had just left.

Oh, Jesus, she's following the BMW.

Ramsey looked back at the car, but couldn't see any movement. And, as he looked down at Ellie's car, he saw her release her seatbelt, as if preparing to leave the car and walk over.

'No, no, no,' he muttered as he pulled out his phone, typing a message, telling Ellie it was likely a trap. He didn't want to call out, in case his target was watching, and instead sent the message to Ellie and Tinker while moving around, trying to gain a better angle on the BMW from the bridge.

Now at a run, passing Casey and Davey, he hurried down the other slip road, moving out in front of the BMW as he crossed the bridge at speed, swearing at a car that dared to beep at him, and when there, found himself with a slightly better view of the man inside the car. It was instinctive, and the windscreen was reflecting the sun, but he had a couple of scant moments to pull his phone up and take a couple of quick photos. But, before he could check the quality, he saw an old man walk towards the car waving some kind of squeezy bottle and wiper.

Meanwhile, Ellie, now out of the car, was walking towards the BMW, but paused as a message, probably Ramsey's, appeared on her phone.

'He's not well! He looks like he's dead! You should call an ambulance!' The old man now shouted across at Ellie.

'Then get away!' Ellie replied angrily as she continued walking, as the man went to open the door. Ramsey went to shout, to stop the man, but before he could say anything, the explosion ripped the street apart – and Ramsey staggered back, grateful in a way he was on a different street looking down, and therefore not connected to the blast area itself – but at the same time worried for Ellie.

With the flames licking the underside of the bridge and a dozen car alarms now going off, Ramsey stumbled back to the car and Davey, who was already moving over to the driver's seat.

'Get going now!' he cried out, opening the passenger door. 'We don't want to be here when the police turn up!'

'What about Ellie?' Casey said, and Ramsey looked back from the car, seeing Ellie beside the Ford Focus, staring in horror at the flames as Tinker ran over to her, pulling her to the car door.

'She's fine,' he said. 'We need to get out of here now.'

And, this command given, Davey spurred the old Rover into life and slowly drove up the slip road and off into London as, on the lower road, Ramsey hoped to hell the Focus was doing the same.

———

ON A DIFFERENT STREET, LESS THAN HALF A MILE AWAY, AND watching a feed on his phone, footage taken through a webcam that had been connected to the side of a street lamp, the old man scratched at the burn scars on his cheek, frowning as he watched Ramsey clamber back into his crappy, battered Rover.

He knew he'd been followed. He expected it, even. Back in Nine Elms, he'd seen Ramsey and his friends as they walked around the police cordon, and he had followed them as they headed up into the offices above. It was the reason he had gone to speak to the copper, Delgado – he wanted Ramsey to see him. To recognise him.

After all, how could you send a message when they didn't know who it was from?

'YOU ARE BLOODY KIDDING ME,' NICKY SIMPSON SAID AS THEY pulled up outside the Globe Town Boxing Club. 'You're leaving me with Johnny sodding Lucas?'

'Let me guess, he's not on your Christmas list?' Tinker replied with a mocking pout. 'Or are you still hiding after you tried to help his sister destroy his entire empire?'

'Can't be proven, so I'd appreciate it if you stopped spreading lies,' Simpson's lips thinned as he glared across at her, before returning his gaze out the window. 'Bloody marvellous.'

'No, we're coming here for somewhere to stay for the moment,' Ellie replied, checking her phone for new messages. 'And I'm guessing right now that the Finders' offices, Caesar's Diner, my apartment, Tinker's – well, wherever Tinker lives nowadays, all of these places are compromised.'

She looked back at Simpson with a sardonic smile.

'Even your houses will be, let's be honest,' she said. 'Your offices are nothing but a charred mess, your apartment water-logged, and any other property you spend time in is probably being watched as well. Johnny is the only one at the moment without skin in the game.'

'Of course he's got skin in the game,' Simpson grumbled uncomfortably. 'He's a bloody gangster. His family and my family have hated each other for decades.'

'Yeah, but now Johnny's different. He's new and improved,' Tinker said, turning off the engine as she did so. 'He's an MP now, a Member of Parliament. Has to keep everything legitimate, which means he hasn't been spending much time here.'

'Which means we can use his back offices,' Ellie smiled. 'You know, for keeping you alive and all that.'

She had sent a text to Ramsey, thanking him for the timely message and suggested they meet here. She hadn't said the name outright, in case anyone hacked the message and work out the location, but instead she just said "where the bottles were kept," knowing that Ramsey would remember how Johnny Lucas had held the Lumetta bottles under his boxing ring.

Entering the gym itself, Ellie saw Pete, one of Johnny Lucas's bodyguards – and part-time boxing trainer – heading over to her.

'Heard you needed a place to hide out,' he said.

'If it's no bother?'

Pete smiled, saying nothing, but nodding over to a back room at the side.

'I didn't tell the boss who you were bringing,' he said, glancing at Simpson, his hoodie's hood currently over his head vaguely to disguise himself, even though it was branded with his health club's logo. 'He has a dicky heart. Didn't want to cause issues.'

'Thanks,' Ellie said, walking Simpson through the gym, keeping between him and any of the boxers, to lower the chances of any accidental meetings.

'He's done the place up, I see,' Simpson said with a slight hint of admiration. 'It's got some good weight machines here now. And the cardio's on point, too. You know, if it wasn't that

I didn't like the guy, I'd actually say he's making a nice little club here.'

'It's all about the look though, isn't it?' Tinker said. 'Because we both know that nobody comes into here to play with the weights.'

'No?' Simpson replied, raising an eyebrow.

Tinker grinned.

'Nah, they come in here to batter the shit out of each other in that ring,' she said. 'You should give it a go sometime. I'll spar with you.'

'And by "spar," you mean—'

'Take your head off your shoulders and remove your smug smile forever,' Tinker said conversationally. 'I know, I know, you're our client. Doesn't stop me from wanting to punch you in the face.'

Simpson actually chuckled at this.

'You know, I think I like you more when you're being honest,' he said.

'Really?' Tinker stopped at the door. 'Then maybe I should tell you how I've wanted to break your—'

'Give it a rest,' Ellie snapped, and Tinker stopped instantly. 'I have a stinking headache and at least two men are dead so far – so maybe calm it with the jokes.'

'They weren't jokes,' Tinker grumbled as they entered the back room, finding Casey, Ramsey, and Davey waiting for them.

At the first sight of Nicky Simpson, however, Casey started forward.

'This wanker needs to be removed—' he started, but Ellie held her hand up.

'We didn't put you on this case, Casey, because we knew you'd be like this,' she said. 'But as you've got onto it anyway, I need you to take a step back emotionally. Mister Simpson is our client, and when we save his life, and find out who's doing this to him, he's promised to owe us a favour.'

'Yeah? Then I want that favour to be "bring my dad back to life,"' Casey snapped.

Simpson wisely kept his mouth shut.

There was a buzz, and Tinker glanced at her phone.

'We've just had a call for you come through from the Finders' office,' she said, looking up. 'Robert sent it to me as he wasn't sure if you were using yours while in hiding.'

Ellie frowned.

'People usually call me on my mobile,' she said. 'I don't think I've had a call come through to the office in my life.'

'Well, you have this time,' Tinker showed her the number. 'Danny Flynn called you today.'

'Well, that can't be a coincidence,' Ellie took the number, dialling it into her own phone, Leaving it on speakerphone for everyone to hear.

After a couple of rings, the phone was answered.

'Flynn. Talk.'

'Danny—' Ellie said, and she didn't get any further, because Danny Flynn instantly responded.

'Ellie Reckless,' he laughed. 'You got my message. Excellent. Sorry to call you this way. I don't seem to have your number on my contacts list.'

'That's because I never gave you my number, Danny.' Ellie looked around the room as she spoke. Danny Flynn had been one of her recent clients; a wannabe East End tough boy, who, like many others, had a legacy to live up to; in Danny's case, it was his father, a known thief and gang lord who leapfrogged between east and south London regularly during his time. Ellie had been brought in when Danny owed a substantial amount to Nicky Simpson, trying to sell a painting to cover the debt, one that had been stolen before he could do so. Ellie had solved the crime, found the painting and arranged for Danny to pay Simpson, something that later on, she found had actually enraged him, because he'd wanted Danny to fail – because he had a clause in their agreement that gave him Danny's Boston resources if Flynn couldn't pay.

Still, the fact Danny was phoning up the day that Nicky Simpson was in trouble seemed too good to be true.

'What can I do for you, Danny?' Ellie asked.

'Actually, for once it's more of a case of what can I do for you,' Danny laughed down the line. 'I understand Nicky Simpson has a problem.'

'And what would you know about that?' Ellie looked at Simpson, waving at him to keep quiet. She knew that if Simpson spoke, this conversation could end real quick.

Danny's voice stayed light hearted as he continued.

'Well, I've got a lot of people out there who I still talk to; my men – and women, I'm an equal opportunities criminal – keep their eyes and ears peeled for me. And I can tell you now, there's currently two million reasons to kill Nicky Simpson.'

'Two million?' Ellie replied. 'Do you mean as a hit on him?'

There was a pause. And Danny replied again.

'Let's just say somebody's put the word out, if Nicky was to suddenly expire, the person who helped him along would suddenly become incredibly rich.'

Ellie's lips thinned as she looked across the room at Simpson, and she saw in his expression he'd heard this. It wasn't a look of anger that someone would do such a thing. It wasn't even a look of surprise, as if he hadn't expected such a thing.

It was more of a look of sad resignation; that Nicky Simpson knew that finally, his time had come.

'So what do you want, Danny?' Ellie continued. 'Are you here to gloat?'

'Actually,' Danny said, 'I'm here to offer you a chance to repay my favour to you. You know, I live in London now, right?'

Ellie hadn't known, but Tinker nodded.

'He sold his house in Chipping Norton after Chantelle, and now owns some warehouse or something.'

'It's more than a warehouse,' Danny replied. 'Since Chantelle, let's just say I've had a bit of a security issue.'

'What you mean is paranoia.'

'Call it what you want, but let's just say I now effectively have Fort Knox in the middle of Islington, a bolthole where you can lock yourselves in, and no one will get to you. And if push comes to shove, I've got weapons – if needed.'

Ellie considered this for a moment.

'I thought you'd be going for the two million,' she said.

'Oh, I'd love to, don't get me wrong,' Danny laughed down the phone. 'I still think Nicky Simpson is a prick. And I'd love to see him go down. And in fact, I'm loving what I'm hearing about him right now. But at the same time, a favour is a favour. I was stupid enough to allow you to have a second one. This, as far as I'm concerned, is a win win situation. I burn a favour from you, which means I'm no longer in your debt. And Nicky Simpson owes me his life.'

Ellie nodded, understanding the logic here.

'Can I come back to you on this?'

'Oh absolutely. I'm having a day off today, doing my

accounts. So don't worry, whatever time you call, I'll be able to sort it. You take care now – bye, Nicky.'

At that point, the call disconnected, as Ellie looked back at the others.

'He's got a point,' she said.

'You have to be kidding me!' Simpson exploded, finally able to make a noise. 'There's no bloody way I'm staying with Danny Flynn!'

'Nobody would expect it, but I don't trust him as much as any of you do,' Ellie admitted. 'We might have saved his life once, but that doesn't necessarily mean he's going to be all good and altruistic towards us. We'll hold him as a last resort. And we'll see what happens next.'

This said, Ellie looked at Ramsey.

'Who is he?' she asked. 'The bomber?'

'His name was Lawrence Flanagan,' Ramsey replied. 'He was IRA – terrorist, soldier, freedom fighter, whatever you want to call them – during the Troubles.'

He straightened, clicking his neck as he continued.

'After the Good Friday Agreement killed his mojo, he came over to London,' he explained, looking at Simpson. 'He was very good at creating explosives from tiny things, and he was the go-to guy for your granddad Paddy.'

He shrugged, though, continuing before Simpson could reply.

'And Johnny and Jackie Lucas, and the Sisters – I think even the Turk used him a couple of times.'

'Are you sure about this?' Ellie asked, and with a nod from Ramsey, Casey passed over his iPad. On it were the photos Ramsey had taken earlier on.

Ellie opened the first one, and was greeted with a slightly

blurry, camera phone image of Kate Delgado talking to a man with burn scars on his face.

'That's him all right,' Ramsey said as she looked back at him. 'I wouldn't forget that face. I knew him back in the day – until he died.'

'No offence, Ramsey, but this guy does not look dead to me,' Tinker suggested.

In return, Ramsey gave her a look as if to say "oh, really? I hadn't thought of that," and Tinker wisely didn't carry on.

'I went to his funeral,' Ramsey continued. 'He was working on a job for Paddy Simpson. It went wrong, and according to the reports, he got caught in a blast.'

He looked away.

'There was a body,' he said. 'We're talking over ten years ago, but I remember it like yesterday.'

'Did he have the burns back then?'

Ramsey shook his head.

'Look, I get this is a little weird, but that's definitely Flanagan, somehow, and this is definitely his wheelhouse. Although the webcams are something new.'

He shrugged.

'He always liked to watch, though. He would always find himself a viewing spot to watch his "art" come to life.'

'Going on the basis that he somehow didn't die, and is the person you think he is, you believe this is the man we're looking for?' Ellie looked back at the image.

'Yes, Eleanor, I do,' Ramsey continued. 'I genuinely think he did this. He was definitely at the offices, standing around, watching, probably working out who was looking into it. And then we followed him to Kennington, where I saw him talking to someone in a BMW.'

He looked back at Casey.

'On the way here, we learnt the BMW was owned by Saleh, your driver.'

'It was. That's why we were following him,' Ellie nodded. 'We were hoping he'd lead us to whoever told him to keep away today, but now it's a bit too late.'

'Why's that?' Casey asked.

'I don't know if you noticed, little boy, but my driver just blew up,' Simpson replied angrily.

However at this, Ramsey shook his head.

'No, he didn't,' he said. 'You were supposed to believe that. I'm guessing there was a point where you lost them?'

Tinker nodded.

'Last minute turn, took us off his tail for a minute, tops.'

'In that time, Lawrence went to the car once it'd parked,' Ramsey explained. 'I saw it, but couldn't get a good view. He spoke to the driver of the car, and then walked away. After a couple of seconds, you guys arrived. And then we know what happened.'

'However, Saleh wasn't in the car,' Casey added. 'I met him in this prick's office that time. I know what he looks like—'

'We could see him—'

'No, you saw what you *thought* was him,' Davey spoke now for the first time, nodding to Casey. 'Show them the other photos.'

Leaning over, Casey swiped forward on the iPad Ellie held, passing the ones showing Delgado in her meeting with the scarred man, and now, changing to a more recognisable scene of a BMW under a bridge, taken by Ramsey from the other side's slip road.

On it, and taken from a slight angle, was the driver of the BMW.

He was bald, like Saleh. And he looked passingly familiar to Saleh ...

But he wasn't the same man.

Davey now took over the conversation as Ellie looked up from the image.

'Did you see Saleh leave?'

'Yes,' Ellie, confused, nodded as she looked at Tinker for support. 'We texted him, a warning message to scare him, he came out, and we followed him.'

'No,' Davey shook her head. 'Sorry, I know that this is my first day and all that, but I come from a background where you check every angle first.'

She tapped the image.

'Yes, you saw the BMW leave. But did you see Saleh get into it?'

'No,' Ellie admitted, thinking back to the moment. 'We saw the car leave the garage with a bald man inside. We just assumed it was him.'

'The window reflected the light, and we couldn't get a good view of the face,' Tinker added.

'So all you actually know is that you followed a bald man away from the house,' Davey spoke slowly, letting every piece sink in. 'And you were with him all the way until he pulled up under a bridge and exploded.'

Ellie felt a shiver down her spine.

'A set up,' she said. 'Purely to have you walk up and confront him, and in the process ...'

'Boom,' Tinker muttered, more for dramatic intent than explanation.

'The old man shouted out to me,' Ellie spoke softly now. 'He went to ask if Saleh wanted his windows done, and then told me he was dead. And then the car exploded.'

Ramsey considered this.

'Lawrence Flanagan,' he replied. 'Must have walked to the car and set this up somehow. The driver might not even have been dead – he might have just been told to park up there, and somehow Flanagan knocked him out. And if Flanagan was watching, he saw his booby trap about to be set off, so he detonated anyway.'

Ellie's expression darkened.

'Either way, if you're correct about the guy, this Lawrence Flanagan guy has blood on his hands and needs to be brought in.'

She looked back at Nicky Simpson.

'You know, for someone so bloody cocky, you're being remarkably tight-lipped right now,' she said.

Simpson nodded.

'I met Flanagan,' he said. 'I know he faked his death.'

'And how do you know that?' Ramsey asked, his voice icy cold.

'Because after he did it, he's spent the last ten years as my dad's carer in Majorca,' Simpson replied, his voice emotionless, but with the tone of a man who's forcing such a measured response.

'And if he's here trying to kill me, it means my dad probably sent him.'

9

SLEEP-OVER

AFTER NICKY SIMPSON'S BOMBSHELL REVELATION, ELLIE HAD
decided to shake things up. For a start, they now had two
leads; the bomber now had a name, and a chance to be
found, and the possible mastermind behind this attack was
perhaps now in the open, which was unfortunate for Nicky
Simpson, as it was his dad.

The problem was, however, finding them.

Ellie, of course, had a plan. And so, with Ramsey having a
plan on finding out whether Flanagan really was dead or not,
and leaving Nicky at the Boxing Club with Casey and Davey,
she went alone to Vauxhall, heading for a meeting with an
old colleague.

If she was being brutally honest, she'd really tried not to
attend the Vauxhall crime unit as much as she could. After
all, this was a place she had spent years of her life in when
she was a copper. She had transferred across from Mile End
with DCI Alexander Monroe, and over two or three years, she
had built up a solid reputation south of the river.

Unfortunately, during the time, she'd also built up a

longstanding relationship with a confidential informer, Bryan Noyce, which then turned into an affair, a fight and then an accusation of murder – although Robert, then her defence solicitor, had managed to prove that she didn't do it, and the case itself was dismissed due to lack of evidence.

But there lay the problem – although free, she was never found to be fully innocent of all charges. And as ever, the other officers decided that where there was smoke, there was also a hell of a lot of fire. And, even though she was officially welcomed back to the police force, she knew her role would never be the same, not helped by the fact that she knew someone in the unit had been the one that gave her up to the higher ups, something that meant she couldn't truly be secure in her returned to role, constantly waiting to be betrayed again.

But that didn't really matter, as it was only a matter of days before Ellie was subtly reminded that perhaps it was time for her to find a new job.

She was never fired, for that would have been an accusation of guilt, but she was greatly encouraged to leave. And, although she'd followed Robert into insurance investigation, she felt she'd lost, that she'd given in to administrational bullying, a feeling that echoed with her, even now.

And now, finding herself outside this large brutalist building just south of Vauxhall Station, and to the east of Nine Elms, Ellie had never felt more exposed and uncomfortable.

This building was where she had partnered with Mark Whitehouse.

This was where she first met Kate Delgado, then just a Detective Constable.

And this was where she'd been told to leave by the latter, claiming her to be *murderous scum.*

But now she was back, standing across the road, doing her best not to be noticed by any of the officers entering or exiting the building. It had been a year or two since she lost her job, more since the court case had started, and this meant that many of the newer officers didn't recognise her – although, that said, you didn't have to *know* Ellie Reckless to know who she was.

She'd been plastered across enough newspapers and television screens at the time, and this was shown by a couple of officers she didn't recognise who, as they entered the unit had glanced over to her, and gave her a couple of nods of acknowledgment. But there were also the glares from the officers that *didn't* believe her, that felt she shouldn't even be near the building. These were the ones who believed the lies about her, and after five uncomfortable minutes of standing outside, the doors opened and a familiar face walked over.

Mark Whitehouse had been Ellie's partner from the moment she arrived at Vauxhall. Alex Monroe had placed them together, saying they were a good fit, and, in the main, Monroe was a good judge of character. Whitehouse had been there for her throughout the trial, never believing she could have done the things that were accused of her. But when she left, he was partnered up with the now-promoted-to-DS Kate Delgado.

And over the time that followed, now and then, Ellie had bumped into him. Their relationship had soured, become more icy as the suspicions grew, and his loyalty to Delgado, believing her to be honest while Ellie had her concerns, had driven a wedge between them.

Walking across the street, he looked around as well, as if uncomfortable being seen in Ellie's presence.

'Would you prefer going somewhere more private?' Ellie said as she saw this, almost mockingly.

'It depends,' Whitehouse replied coldly. 'I got your message. Why am I here?'

'I wanted to speak to you about your partner—'

'Oh, for God's sake, Ellie, not again.'

Holding a hand up to pause him, Ellie reached into a pocket, pulling out her phone.

'I also want to know if you recognise somebody,' she continued.

Whitehouse shook his head, however.

'No,' he replied. 'Before we get into anything, I need to ask what the hell is going on, Ellie? You're working for Nicky Simpson? When did this start?'

Ellie understood Whitehouse's concern, and let out a pent-up sigh. She'd been expecting the question; it'd been one she was still asking herself.

'Since someone tried to blow him up this morning,' she said. 'Believe it or not, he reckoned we were the better choice in sorting this than you were.'

Whitehouse chuckled.

'That's because he might be this YouTube guru, but we all know he's corrupt as hell,' he said. 'You in particular.'

He stopped as a thought crossed his mind.

'Jesus, it's a bloody *favour*, isn't it?'

'Yeah,' Ellie admitted. 'And I'll be honest, considering the fact I've spent the last year gathering favours against the man, to have the opportunity to have one favour owed to me that could explain everything? It's too good to miss, Mark. No matter what I think of the prick.'

She smiled ruefully.

'And if I fail, he dies. Which again? isn't that bad.'

'If Simpson dies without proving that you're innocent, though, you never gain your innocence,' Whitehouse replied. 'There's no way you'll be able to find out, or prove to anybody that he set you up.'

'I know,' Ellie nodded. 'But this could be the case, Mark. This could be the thing that frees me from this nightmare.'

Whitehouse shook his head sadly.

'So, where's the team?' he eventually asked.

'Ramsey's checking if someone's really dead, Tinker and Casey are watching over Nicky,' Ellie replied. 'I don't think they're happy about this.'

'You think the son of Bryan Noyce might not be happy about harbouring Nicky Simpson,' Whitehouse looked across the street at the concrete building. 'You are the queen of the understatement.'

There was a long pause, before Whitehouse turned to face her again.

'You can't just walk back in, Ellie,' he said. 'Hypothetical situation. You save Nicky Simpson, whatever this thing that you're doing ends, and he gives you a favour. You demand the proof that he killed Bryan Noyce, and he gives it. He goes to prison. You're cleared of everything.'

He shook his head.

'You can't just walk back into the office,' he continued. 'Everybody who believed in you will be happy to see you, myself included. But everybody who believed that you were a killer, a criminal, every single one of them, will find it harder to relate to you. There'd be the element of admitting they were wrong about you. And coppers never do that. They'd always believe they were right, somehow, and they'd always look for reasons to prove this.'

Ellie nodded. She knew what Whitehouse meant. The side-eyed stares, and the knowledge she'd never know whether or not somebody had her back, were something she already expected, no matter what happened.

'I don't want to be back here,' she said. 'You guys showed me very bluntly that you thought I was scum—'

'Now that's unfair,' Whitehouse interrupted.

'What I meant to say was all I want is my freedom,' Ellie shrugged. 'I want to be a police officer again, Mark. It's what I trained for, to help *people*, not bloody criminals. I don't want to do these bloody favour missions. I want to be able to get up in the morning and not worry about this thing over my head. I want Casey to know I didn't kill his father, because even though he works for me, he still has his suspicions; I still see it in his eyes every time his dad is mentioned.'

She leant against the wall, sighing.

'I don't want that anymore,' she whispered. 'And yeah, if I get my life back, I wouldn't stay here. I'll transfer up north, go to some God-forsaken Scotland station, or maybe Ireland. You know, join the Garda. I don't care where I'm a copper – just as long as I *am* a copper.'

Mark Whitehouse watched Ellie for a long moment before nodding, his anger dissipating.

'So what do you need?'

Ellie opened the phone, revealing the photo Ramsey had taken earlier, of Delgado and the scarred old man.

'This guy,' she said. 'He was at Nine Elms this morning. Kate had a very interesting conversation with him, apparently.'

Whitehouse's eyes darkened.

'You're following my partner?'

'Oh, come on Mark, let's be honest,' Ellie forced a smile. 'She's been following me, and we both know it. Ramsey was returning from checking out the apartment. You know that because you saw him there. As he walked back to his car, he saw them talking, and he recognised the man with the scar. The fact Kate was talking to him was completely coincidental, but also really interesting.'

'Why?'

'Well, that's the question I wanted to ask to you,' Ellie replied. 'Do you recognise him?'

'No,' Whitehouse replied, closely zooming in on the face. 'And I think I would, as the scar is pretty telling. Who is he?'

'Ramsey's convinced he's a bomb maker,' Ellie said, zooming back out so the full picture could be seen again. 'Ex-IRA, and used to work for the Simpson family. But he stopped a few years ago when he died.'

Whitehouse chuckled.

'So we're now looking at ghosts.'

'You know how this goes,' Ellie replied. 'It's very easy to fake a death, to disappear – go somewhere where the police aren't looking for you. At the time, people believed he was dead, and he was obviously happy to keep it that way. The problem we've got is *if* Ramsey is correct, then this is a man who wasn't on the side of the Angels and was known for his expertise in explosives.'

'Seen at a location where an explosive had just been detonated,' Whitehouse nodded. 'I see where you're going with this.'

'Do you? Because currently I have a man who has a history of explosives, who might have been involved in a

BMW explosion as well today, and who's conversing with your partner as if they're old mates.'

'You can't tell that,' Whitehouse looked back at Ellie. 'We don't know the context of this conversation. He might have asked her for the time. He might have done this knowing you were watching—'

'Or he did this because he knew Delgado was dirty,' Ellie replied. 'Come on Mark. You know I was ratted out by somebody inside the building. There were only two or three people who knew I'd had the fight with Bryan. Only one or two of you that knew I had blood on my clothing.'

'We've had this conversation before, and I've told you I don't think it was Kate,' Whitehouse argued. 'She might not be the nicest of people, but she's loyal to the force. She's not corrupt ...'

He trailed off.

'Like me?' Ellie replied, smiling. 'Finish what you were gonna say.'

'Ellie, you might not have killed Bryan Noyce,' Whitehouse said, leaning closer, 'but that doesn't mean you weren't involved in the situation. Christ, you were having an affair with an informant! And here you are, years later, telling me Kate Delgado is the person who destroyed your life, purely based on a photo! Why are you even here? Ellie? What did you even think you'd gain from this conversation? You think she's a buddy of Flanagan? That she's texting him or something?'

Ellie slumped a little as she leant against the wall.

'I think I hoped to gain an ally,' she said. 'I think I hoped to gain an old friend back.'

'I *am* still your old friend, Reckless. And I'm still an ally. But this photo alone isn't going to help you,' Whitehouse straightened, looking around the street, as if paranoid he was being watched. 'You need to find this guy and prove he's alive. And then work it—'

Ellie grabbed his lapel, stopping him from continuing.

'How do you know his name?' she hissed.

'You told me. Bomb maker, ex-IRA—'

'I never said Flanagan,' Ellie shook her head. 'I just said he was an old IRA bomber.'

There was a long moment of silence, and then, as he pulled away from her grip, Mark Whitehouse shrugged.

'Well, I must have known the name from the past,' he replied. 'There aren't that many ex-IRA members who worked for the Simpsons.'

'Did Kate give you the name?' Ellie pressed. 'Did she ever mention him before today?'

'I don't know, and I'm sorry to add to your conspiracy,' Whitehouse shook his head, now uncomfortable. 'But it's not a secret there used to be a bomber named Flanagan around here, who worked for Paddy, and then Max. My uncle used to be a copper, and he dealt with him and Paddy back in the day.'

Ellie softened, looking down the street.

'Look, it's clear Nicky Simpson is being targeted, but he doesn't know by who,' she said. 'My job is to find out who wants him dead, and make sure they don't succeed.'

'And what do you do when you find out?' Whitehouse asked. 'He'll want them dead. Will you be fulfilling that part too?'

Ellie straightened, her professionalism insulted.

'When we find out, we'll be coming straight to you,' she snapped. 'And then you can deal with that. After all, it's been pointed out to me many times – *you're* the police.'

And with that, and without a farewell, Ellie spun on her heel, storming off away from the perplexed Whitehouse, who watched after her, scratching his head.

'You're playing with fire, Ellie,' he whispered, more to himself than anybody else.

'And it's going to burn you worse than anything you've ever felt.'

10

GRAVESIDE CONFESSION

RAMSEY WASN'T A FAN OF CEMETERIES. AT HIS AGE, HE'D BURIED a lot more people of late, and the running joke was always "when he bought his next suit, to make sure it was one that can be used for funerals."

And to be honest, people weren't wrong. Old criminals didn't seem to last into their nineties, mainly because of their lifestyles and the excesses that they'd had during them always caught up.

For Ramsey, however, his excesses hadn't been that bad. He'd never been a drug user, he'd only dabbled with alcoholism in the nineties; in fact, his only big vice was gambling – although that had almost got him killed in the past. But, over the years, he'd done his best to keep himself in shape, a habit he'd picked up while in prison.

However, now, standing in Streatham cemetery, he stared down at the gravestone in front of him, wondering why exactly he was there.

Looking at it, even the simplest of glances showed he

wasn't the only person attending this area of the graveyard these days.

The grave had been maintained recently; the surrounding grave plots were overgrown with weeds and a couple of wild-flowers poking out here and there, whereas this grave had been obviously tended to. This was a puzzle though, as there wasn't anybody in the area who had such a connection to Flanagan; he had no family in London, and more importantly, there weren't many people would admit to knowing him.

So such tenderness on a grave was quite surprising.

The grave was very simple; it had a Celtic cross engraved onto the front of the headstone, and underneath the name "LAWRENCE FLANAGAN". There was a quote underneath, one that Ramsey didn't recognise but assumed it was some-thing to do with the IRA or Michael Collins.

"HE WAS AN IRISH PATRIOT TRUE AND FEARLESS."

You can take the man out of the freedom fighting, but you can't take the freedom fighter out of the man, Ramsey thought to himself with a little smile. No matter what you thought of Flanagan, he had beliefs he kept to until the very end.

'Are you in there, old man?' Ramsey asked, his voice soft and reverent. 'Or are you somewhere else?'

After a moment, Ramsey straightened. He wasn't super-stitious, and he wasn't a firm believer in ghosts, but he couldn't help having the distinct impression that he was being watched.

Without moving or looking away from the grave, he spoke gently, but loud enough to be heard.

'I know you're there,' he said. 'I'm guessing you've been following me since Kennington.'

There was a pause, and out of the corner of his eye, Ramsey noticed a figure break away from a large tree.

Lawrence Flanagan was slim, almost bald, tanned and scarred. He had a wiry, athletic look to him, the kind of man that would do ultra marathons – and if Ramsey had thought that he looked good for his age, then Lawrence Flanagan put him to shame. He looked fitter and stronger than he had when Ramsey had last seen him two decades earlier, with a glowing tan, and there wasn't an ounce of fat on his body.

'Actually, I guessed you'd come here,' Flanagan said, the Irish twang in his accent still audible, despite his years away. 'I didn't need to follow you, that's amateur work. It's all about knowing your foe.'

He tapped his head to emphasise the point.

'I knew the moment you recognised me, you'd come here, if only to see if there was a hole in the grave where I burst out, clawing my way back to life.'

'Perhaps,' Ramsey slowly and carefully turned to face Flanagan, making sure to make no quick movements. After all, there were two dead bodies already today, and Ramsey didn't want to make it three. There was a nervousness in the air, possibly because Ramsey knew the lengths and depths that this man would go to in keeping himself safe. 'You called me a foe. I'm no enemy of yours, Lawrence. I never have been. You know that as much as I do.'

'Do I?' Flanagan shrugged. 'Forgive me, Ramsey, but although we've worked together here and there, especially for the Twins, or whoever it was, there's still the fact I've seen you twice today, both times connected to Nicky Simpson.'

Ramsey nodded.

'I get why you'd be curious about that,' he said. 'But it's not what you think.'

'Well, I think you're working for Nicky Simpson,' Lawrence smiled. 'Either that or you're trying to kill him.'

'And what I think is that you're trying to kill Nicky Simpson,' Ramsey shrugged, ignoring the second part of the comment. 'And don't get me wrong. I've never been the killing type, Lawrence, and I don't owe him anything.'

'You sure about that?' Flanagan asked, raising an eyebrow. 'Last I heard, he was looking after your mum in a rather nice resting home.'

'There's a long story to that, and it started off with blackmail,' Ramsey replied, with the fact that Flanagan knew of this supposedly secret arrangement niggling at the back of his mind, Nobody outside of the Simpson top tier, or Ellie and her team knew about this. For Flanagan to know it meant there were loose lips somewhere, or there was a mole higher up in Nicky's team. 'And again, it's not what you think.'

'What I think,' Flanagan said, his posture changing, becoming more confrontational, 'is you believe I've been paid to kill a man you're trying to keep alive.'

Ramsey nodded.

'Yes, but are you?' he asked. 'I mean, are you really trying to kill him? Because the Lawrence Flanagan I knew of old wouldn't have failed twice.'

There was a long, quiet moment in the graveyard, the wind rustling through the gravestones.

Lawrence stared daggers at Ramsey before his face changed, softening. And then, relaxing, he chuckled.

'Yeah, I'll admit I've lost my spark a little,' he said. 'That's the problem with spending so much time away from the job you love.'

'So it's true then?' Ramsey asked. 'You've been Max Simpson's carer?'

'More "day-to-day buddy," really,' Flanagan suggested. 'I don't wipe his ass or anything. Max isn't actually that far gone with Parkinson's. He has the shakes, but he's not drooling or anything like that. In fact, there's been some remarkable recoveries of late, although he likes the CBD sweeties a little too much.'

He looked away.

'But yeah, I spend time with him. We hang out together. I drive him places. It's quite a nice, relaxed life. I don't blow people up.'

'So why return to the job?'

'Haven't you heard?' Flanagan smiled. 'Brexit managed to destroy the Good Friday Agreement. It's the Wild West out there again, and someone with my skills and abilities—'

'Cut the crap,' Ramsey interrupted. 'This isn't a freedom fighter thing. This is you coming into London and trying to kill Nicky Simpson – possibly for his own father. But you haven't, have you?'

Flanagan went to snap back a reply, but then stopped.

'You think I failed deliberately,' he said, curious.

'You had a camera watching,' Ramsey replied. 'We found it. Well, bits of it, anyway. When that door opened, you saw Nicky wasn't there, but you still blew the place up. And then you had some kind of decoy in a car, who you blew up randomly.'

Flanagan was silent for a moment, looking down at the grave that bore his name.

'I really did die in an explosion,' he said. 'I just didn't realise it when they pulled me out. Fifteen seconds I was dead for; long enough for me to realise it was time to change my world.'

He looked back up at Ramsey now, and for the first time, the thief saw genuine regret in the bomb maker's eyes.

'And there were so many bodies in that explosion,' he continued. 'People didn't know who was who – some of them were even vaporised. It was easy enough just to walk away.'

'How?' Ramsey asked. 'How did you leave that life behind?'

'Really easily,' Flanagan grinned. 'I had a couple of other identities I'd been using, and I caught a Ryanair flight over to Majorca … and stayed there.'

'Then why are you back?'

'Same as you. A favour to someone I can't say no to.'

Ramsey frowned at this. Flanagan owing someone would explain a lot, and if he was reluctantly doing this, it'd also explain the errors.

'Do you need help getting out of it?' he whispered now, slowly, making sure Flanagan knew exactly what he was offering. But instead, Flanagan simply smiled and shook his head.

'I owe them, and I'm happy to do this,' he said.

Ramsey considered the comment, and his eyes widened as he realised a second, more plausible option.

'You're not trying to kill Nicky Simpson,' he said in revelation. 'You're trying to save him by blowing him up. But why? How can that help unless …'

He trailed off as a second thought came to mind.

'How much is the hit worth?' he asked. 'The one on Nicky Simpson?'

'There you go,' Flanagan pointed at Ramsey. 'There's the cunning, devious bastard Ramsey Allen I remember.'

He looked out across the graveyard.

'Two million,' he replied. 'That's how much Paddy said.'

'Paddy?'

'He's the more coherent one out there,' Flanagan puffed out his cheeks. 'And nobody knows who placed it, but the bloody thing has everyone coming out of the sodding wood-work, all looking for a crack at the "YouTube prick." And he's got a lot of people out there with scores to settle against him, all thinking this gives them a chance to do it, and walk away with a nice nest egg in the process.'

'You know, if you told Nicky about this, you could have saved a ton of hassle,' Ramsey said irritably. 'For a start, he would probably have worked with you, and second, we wouldn't have two deaths in Kennington to work out.'

Flanagan nodded.

'Problem was, Nicky don't take his pa's calls no more,' he said. 'Max has been trying for a couple of days to contact him. Managed to get hold of Saleh, but by then Nicky was off on some influencer bash, and the hit was already out there. They dispatched me to fake a death, get him out, and drag him back to the Balearic Isles fast. The idea was to see him in the webcam, explain through a speaker that he needed to get to a particular safe house, some industrial place Paddy had sorted in North London, and then blow it when he left. That was why the camera was there.'

'But he didn't take the elevator,' Ramsey nodded, under-standing. 'He was already in the stairwell. But you didn't know that.'

'I worked out later that Saleh had sent a text, saying he was sorry for not being there. But the lad's a bit dim with words, yeah? Just said "sorry," so poor bloody Nicky thinks he's been set up, and heads for the safer option, making my life harder. I knew he'd been in the office, and the fire door opening had triggered an alert, so I decided it was safe enough to detonate.'

'But why, if he was gone?'

'The plan was changing by the second. I thought I'd do the job anyway, get Nicky out and work out the rest later. But he'd already split before I could get to him.'

He pointed a bony finger at Ramsey.

'Straight to you and your boss,' he said. 'One thing I can tell you is that his dear darling dad was the one who sent me in to try to divert the killers, but Nicky turned to you instead. What does that say?'

He spat onto the grass, almost as if disgusted.

'So when you go and speak to Ellie Reckless and all your other new friends, remember it's that part of his past that saved his life – and you.'

'And how'd you work that out?' Ramsey furrowed his brows. 'Sure, you faked Simpson's death, but you killed people, Lawrence. You didn't save anyone's lives.'

There was a moment of silence, the atmosphere so thick you could slice through it.

'How much did you see? Of the BMW?' Flanagan eventually asked.

'I saw you waiting for Saleh, I saw it wasn't Saleh, and I saw it exploding,' Ramsey replied icily. 'So I think I saw enough.'

Lawrence shook his head.

'Bloody toddlers, that's what I'm dealing with here,' he grumbled. 'This was where everything went wrong, Allen. Saleh was told to stay still after we failed to grab Nicky. So, when Nicky messaged to say he was coming for him, he started making alternate plans. And then the text message came.'

'Text message?'

Flanagan nodded, showing Ramsey his phone. On it was a simple message, an address in Kennington, with the instructions "Saleh's parking under the bridge," the letters "G-S-D" ending it.

'Who sent it?'

'I don't know,' Flanagan shrugged. 'I drove to the address, and after a few minutes Saleh arrived in his BMW. I walked over, asking if he'd had the same message. But then I realised the problem.'

'He sent a double.'

'He sent a bloody double,' Flanagan nodded. 'I mean, who does that? Saleh was supposed to be the trusted aide who linked us together. But with the double knowing nothing, all he did was confirm the message, and screw things up.'

'Deliberately?'

'Who knows,' Flanagan sighed. 'All I know is when I saw him pull up, I realised he wasn't the same man, and he had no clue. Apparently Saleh paid him a grand to shave his head and go to the pickup. He thought it was a drugs exchange.'

'I saw you drive off,' Ramsey added.

'There was no point being there, the bloke was useless,' Flanagan spat. 'I'd stuck up a webcam on a street lamp, and I drove down the road, parked up and watched the BMW on my phone.'

He sighed, looking away.

'I thought he'd drive off, but he waited there. Probably for another message to tell him to come home, poor bastard.'

Ramsey raised an eyebrow at this.

'Funny way to talk about the man you killed.'

'You think *I* killed him?' Flanagan almost laughed. 'Oh no, there were other players there.'

'You mean the homeless guy you killed? Yes, I saw that.'

'I didn't bloody kill him!' Lawrence Flanagan exploded. 'You saw the guy the second time, right? I watched from the shadows the first time he approached the car, Allen. It was shortly after I left, and I was watching on the phone by then. I saw him walk up, waving the screen wiper. The fake Saleh put his window down, telling him to piss off, and the window washer squirted the bloody bottle into the fake's face. I watched, horrified, as he started choking, collapsing back into the seat. This done, the homeless window washer walked off.'

'He was an assassin?'

'I think so,' Flanagan nodded. 'Whatever he was, the shit he sprayed into the poor bastard who was doubling for Saleh killed him within seconds. I think he was tracking the car somehow, and thought it was Saleh and Nicky making a run for it.'

'Or he was connected to the message sent.'

'No, Max sent the message.' Flanagan shook his head.

'You sure?' Ramsey asked. 'What if it was someone playing you? I mean, why would you believe a random text message?'

'The "GSD" in it,' Flanagan showed the message again. 'It was Max's code for "get shit done," and when he wrote it in messages, you knew things were important. But there were only a small amount of people who knew Max, who knew the code. Saleh knew it from when he worked for him as a teenager, and I ... well, I've had it a lot over the last ten years. It seems Parkinson's makes you very impatient.'

'So how did this killer know to go to the bridge?'

Flanagan couldn't answer this.

'Okay then, what happened next?'

'Well, I wasn't there to avenge some nameless dead man, so I did nothing,' Flanagan shrugged. 'But this fake homeless man, this killer, was waiting, and I realised he'd worked out what was going on here. But he'd been careless. He'd left the window down when fake Saleh had spoken to him. And when your boss arrived, and walked towards him, he ran back, pretending to be the same window washer, using this to raise the window, and toss a package into the car. He shielded himself from your boss, but not from the camera, you see. He didn't want Ellie close, but he needed to know where Nicky was; he had the bottle, too – the one that killed the fella in the car, so Christ knows what he intended to do. But I didn't want a woman dying, and so, I blew him up.'

He held up a finger, pausing Ramsey.

'The package he threw into the car was some kind of remote detonation device,' he explained. 'I didn't see it close, but I recognised what it was. They have a particular design, you see. And I realised his plan was to take out Nicky. But, when he made a point of closing the window, I understood he was looking to take out whoever turned up.'

'Basically, what we believed *you'd* been intending to do,' Ramsey nodded. 'But how did you blow him up with his own bomb?'

'There's only a minimal amount of frequencies he could have used,' Flanagan replied with the slightest hint of pride. 'I just went through them all until *boom*. Hit him as he went to open the door. Or, more likely, pretend he couldn't open it, so someone would come to help.'

His momentary good mood disappeared.

'I don't care he's dead, he probably deserved it,' he continued. 'Anyway, I'm getting out of here, back to Majorca. Things are too hot. And there are too many unanswered questions. Those, I leave to you.'

Ramsey understood; no matter what really happened on that Kennington street, the two things that weren't clear were why Saleh, nothing more than a driver, had sent a body double out in his place, and who actually sent the text message.

'I can get Simpson to you,' he suggested. 'If you truly want to save him—'

'Too late now,' Flanagan smiled. 'Max has sent bigger people than me to fix this.'

'How do you mean, "fix?"'

Flanagan scowled.

'What the feckin' hell do you think I mean?' he snapped, looking around, the nervousness in his body language obvious for anyone to see. 'The Simpsons are going to war. You need to get out of the way of the bullets.'

'One thing I don't get,' Ramsey placed a hand on Flanagan's arm, returning him to the conversation. 'Why talk to Kate Delgado?'

Flanagan went to reply, but then stopped, a confused expression on his face.

'Wait,' he said, carefully. 'You *know* her?'

'We think she's the one who screwed Ellie Reckless over, so yeah,' Ramsey replied.

At this thought, Flanagan chuckled, shaking his head.

'Oh, man, you have no idea who she is,' he said. 'Christ on a cross, Ramsey, how did you get so stupid—'

He stopped as he looked at Ramsey's tie.

Ramsey didn't need to look down to see what had caught

Flanagan's attention; it was a red laser dot from a rifle's laser sight.

And he knew this because he could see three on Flanagan's chest as well.

But it wasn't a sniper, as there was suddenly an explosion of action as multiple armed police officers came running from their places of concealment, aiming their assault rifles at Ramsey and Flanagan.

'Armed Police!' the leader shouted, his cap more baseball than peaked, but with the black and white chequerboard running around the rim. 'Give yourselves up!'

'Did you do this?' Flanagan asked, furious now, looking back at Ramsey.

'Of course I bloody didn't!' Ramsey replied, astonished and even insulted Lawrence Flanagan would even consider such a thing. But as he spoke this, his voice trailed away as Flanagan pulled out a pistol, holding it up.

'Drop the gun or we will shoot!' the lead Armed Response officer shouted once more.

'They'll nail me for everything I ever did,' Lawrence Flanagan said sadly as he looked around the churchyard. 'I'll never see daylight again. I'll probably get shivved up in prison by guards for the innocent people I've killed. I can't do that, Allen. I just can't.'

'Lawrence, don't be a fool—' Ramsey started, but it was too late as, stepping away from Ramsey, Flanagan raised his pistol.

'Bury me in Glasnevin with the boys—' he said, tears glistening his eyes, but he didn't get to say anything else as the churchyard suddenly filled with gunshots, and Lawrence Flanagan fell to the floor, his eyes wide and glassy in death.

Ramsey stared down in horror as the police charged in, tackling him, throwing him to the ground.

'You're under arrest, mate,' the officer cuffing him said. 'Your day is about to turn real bad.'

But Ramsey, staring at the cold, dead eyes of Lawrence Flanagan, didn't reply.

———

11

EYE SPY

'I SPY WITH MY LITTLE EYE, SOMETHING BEGINNING WITH "B."'

Tinker looked around the boxing gym before sighing and turning back to Nicky Simpson.

'Is it a boxing ring?' she asked.

'Well done, your go,' Simpson replied with the slightest of smiles, as Tinker leaned back against the wall.

They'd been sitting there for the last half an hour, watching two of the boxers as they trained, since Ellie had wandered off to speak to her friends in Vauxhall, and Casey had stayed in the back office working on his laptop.

'Shouldn't be allowed, it's the same thing you've picked every other time,' Tinker muttered, looking around the gym. 'Okay then. I spy with my little eye, something beginning with "P."'

Simpson sighed in response.

'Prick,' he said.

Tinker stared directly at him.

'Got it in one,' she said. 'I'm spying right now. At a prick.'

'Apart from the fact it's incorrect, it also shouldn't be allowed – as it too is the same thing you've picked every other time,' Simpson parroted.

But, in response, Tinker shrugged.

'Well, you do take up the room,' she said. 'Class it as your amazing YouTube persona.'

Simpson rested his head against the wall.

'Do you think she'll do it?' he asked.

'What, keep you alive?' Tinker chuckled. 'Against her better judgement, yeah, I think she will. The question I've got for you, though, is why are *you* here, Nicky? It's not like you don't have people who owe you favours, who could have taken you in, found out who did this. You could have gone to war. But instead, you use this as an opportunity to ...'

She trailed off, her eyes widening.

'Oh, you son of a bitch,' she said. 'You've taken someone trying to kill you, and used it as an opportunity to get in close to Reckless.'

'I don't know what you mean.'

'You lied.'

'Why would I?'

Tinker considered the question.

'An established YouTube guru and alleged gang land boss puts himself in a position where he owes a favour to someone he'll know wants him dead. That's not normal, and stinks of setup.'

Simpson spent a long moment waiting, as he considered his answer.

'You know, you always seemed to have the wrong idea about me,' he said. 'I'm not my granddad. And I'm sure as hell not my dad. Paddy Simpson was the last of a dying breed of sixties gangsters. People who shook hands with the Krays and if you shake hands with the Krays, there's a Brotherhood, an agreement you make—'

Tinker chuckled.

'What?' Simpson asked irritably.

'*When you shake hands with the Krays, you enter some kind of brotherhood*,' she laughed. 'Change the name to "Sinatra" and that's bloody *Ocean's Thirteen.* That's not even real life.'

Nicky Simpson was taken aback for a second.

'I didn't know that,' he muttered, genuinely surprised. 'It's something I've always been told. Maybe the screenwriter of the film you're talking about had it told to him, too.'

'Sure,' Tinker snarked. 'Maybe Sinatra shook hands with the Krays as well.'

'Actually, he did, you know,' Simpson replied, staring across the gym once more, watching the boxers as they trained. 'Ronnie and Reggie went to meet Vegas Mafia bosses in the sixties, and Ronnie was introduced to Frank Sinatra on the visit. And years later, Sinatra asked Ronnie to provide bodyguards to protect his son, Frank Junior, who was planning on a trip to London to play the Palladium. They even reckoned they arranged security for him, even though they were behind bars.'

'Of course you'd know that,' Tinker shook her head. 'Granddad was probably involved, right?'

'Nah, wasn't his thing at the time,' Simpson gave a faint smile, still watching the boxers.

'You okay?' Tinker asked, curious. 'Did you want to have a sparring session or something? Or are you jonesing for another workout session or "feel that burn" high intensity whatever the hell you peddle on your channel?'

Simpson didn't smile, but his posture relaxed a little.

'I could do with a workout, yeah,' he said. 'Usually by now I've done a second hour long lunch time YouTube session for my followers. And that didn't happen today because, well, my office got blown up for a start.'

Tinker looked out across the gym.

'Don't suppose anybody would stop you if you wanted to have a session,' she suggested. 'We're here until Ellie comes back. You could get on the treadmill, do some cardio, find some weights?'

She smiled.

'I would argue against putting it online, or maybe live streaming it.'

Simpson didn't reply to this.

'I'm sure there's kit you can borrow in the locker room, or maybe the back office has a "lost and found" box?' Tinker continued.

'Yeah, I don't think I'll be going into the back office,' Simpson said.

'Why?' Tinker replied, but then paused. 'You're genuinely telling me that Nicky Simpson, gangster overlord of the south of London, is keeping away from a sixteen-year-old boy?'

'There's a lot about me you don't know, Tinkerbelle,' Simpson said.

'Well, if you knew a lot about me, you know I can't stand people calling me Tinkerbelle.'

'No, I know that,' Simpson smiled. 'I just find it amusing to say.'

Rising, he straightened, stretching out his muscles.

'Right then,' he said. 'I'm gonna see if I can find myself some shorts.'

IN THE BACK, CASEY WAS ON HIS LAPTOP, WORKING THROUGH folders and files as Nicky Simpson walked into the room. As he did so, the temperature dropped significantly as Casey turned and faced him.

'You know I'm doing this for Ellie, right?' he asked. 'I'm not helping you. I'd rather you died.'

Simpson, already rummaging through the shelves for some kind of box with discarded gym kit inside it, nodded.

'I get that,' he said. 'If someone killed my family, I'd do the same.'

'No,' Casey replied. 'The difference is I *want* you dead, and I'd *dream* about it, whereas you'd actually do it, wouldn't you? You'd call people in to fix your problem. Like you did with Dad.'

Simpson paused his search, turning to face the teenager.

'And why would you think that?' he asked.

'Because the first time I met you, you took a selfie with me, gave me one of your bloody smoothies, and then tried to have us killed.'

Simpson nodded, chuckling.

'Yeah, good times,' he said mockingly.

'You might think it's a joke, but—'

'I don't think it's a joke,' Simpson interrupted. 'But I want to ask you to think back to that moment. You're supposed to be shit hot with a great memory.'

'You said "Break some limbs, dump them in some foundations, or something, I don't care," word for word,' Casey replied. 'I don't need a photographic memory. It was the first time someone ever threatened my life. It kinda burnt in deep.'

'Thank you,' Simpson smiled. 'The important part there was "or something, I don't care," yeah?'

He pulled out a branded pair of running shorts with "Johnny Lucas – fighting for London" emblazoned on them. He tutted to himself as he placed them against his hips, checking them for size.

'I told Saleh I didn't care, Saleh who I trust better than anyone else, who I knew would get what I was saying. I didn't want you dead. I wanted you scared, humbled,' he explained. 'He would have taken you somewhere out of the way and then done something that'd allow you to escape; to get away. You'd think you'd missed a close call, and you'd definitely think twice about crossing me in the future. I didn't even know who you were. Why the hell would I kill an unknown kid?'

At this, Casey paused. As much as he hated Nicky Simpson, the story he'd just given him was plausible.

'Bullshit,' he shook his head.

'Should a twelve-year-old be saying such words?'

'I'm not twelve, I'm sixteen, and I'm sure you were saying worse at my age.'

Simpson chuckled.

'Mate, I was *doing* worse at your age, let alone saying. There was a time, me and a couple of friends—'

'No,' Casey said, holding his hand up. 'I don't want to hear this.'

'I was just—'

'What you were doing was trying to get some kind of common ground between us,' Casey snapped. 'Banter. This is the YouTube persona coming out, the one who wants people to "like, click, and subscribe." The bullshit one that's not real.'

Nicky Simpson was surprised at the outburst, but, accepting it, leant back against a bench staring at Casey.

'Do you read comics?' he asked.

'Who doesn't?' Casey replied. 'I'm a big fan of *Jujutsu Kaisen*. I'm learning to read it in the original Japanese.'

'Yeah, I've never read manga,' Simpson admitted. 'I was talking more about the American comics, spandex super-heroes, Vertigo, DC, Marvel, that sort of stuff.'

'I know them,' Casey grumbled. 'Why?'

'Batman,' Simpson replied. 'Is Bruce Wayne Batman, or is Batman Bruce Wayne?'

'They're one and the same,' Casey stated, almost as if Nicky Simpson was an idiot. 'Anyone who says otherwise is stupid.'

'Yeah, but what I mean is, which one's the mask?' Simpson leant closer now. 'Is Batman the real person, pretending by day to be Bruce Wayne? Or is Bruce Wayne the real person, pretending at night to be Batman?'

'Batman pretends to be Bruce Wayne,' Casey answered. 'It's been done in the comics, and in the films as well.'

Simpson nodded.

'Exactly,' he said. 'If you killed Batman, removed everything *about* Batman, and left Bruce Wayne, he'd have nothing in his life anymore. He would fade away, possibly even become the villain he was fighting. But if you killed Bruce Wayne, then Batman wouldn't give a shit. It'd mean he could hide in his cave and have no alternate identity. He'd still do Batman stuff; he'd still fight crime, save the world, all that, because he's Batman – and as you said, we all know he pretends to be Bruce Wayne when he needs a break from *being* Batman.'

'So what,' Casey laughed. 'You're telling me you're Batman?'

'I'm nowhere near rich enough,' Simpson smiled. 'Although I do have the abs. What I'm trying to say is often someone will have two sides. On one side is the true persona, and the other side is what they have to do to *make* that persona. Is my YouTuber persona me, or is it the way I legitimise the true me, the son of Max Simpson, heir to the Paddy Simpson empire? Am I the vicious bastard people know, or am I the chap who "does the banter," as you said? The YouTuber who just wants to be liked and subscribed to?'

Casey watched Nicky Simpson for a long, long moment.

'I don't think it's a case of which one you are,' he said. 'I think it's more a case of which one you *believe* you are.'

He leant back in the chair, turning to fully face Simpson now.

'Every villain in every story doesn't think they're the villain,' he said. 'It's storytelling 101. Lex Luthor hates Superman, but not because he's a villain. He sees Superman as an alien threat and he thinks he's helping humanity by getting rid of him. But as far as Luthor is concerned, he's never been the villain. He's always been the hero. And even if he does hideous horrible things, it's because he believes that's the best thing to do. The Empire had the Death Star to bring peace and order to the galaxy—'

'Are you telling me you support the Empire?' Simpson smiled.

'Nah, I'm rebellion all the way,' Casey grinned back in response. 'You're the Empire. And all this right now? This is your Death Star exploding around you.'

Casey was gaining some arrogance in his tone at this point, feeling stronger, speaking louder. 'Your empire's gone, and you had such a good thing going, being Bruce Wayne and Batman, as you said. But you got complacent, and you made deals with idiots. And those idiots got caught on social media talking about you.'

'Accusations that can't be proven. Especially as I was able to—'

'I don't care,' Casey interrupted. 'Nobody does. All that matters is you were *seen.* Cancel culture doesn't give a shit about due process. It's instantaneous. You're the worst kept secret in South London. Everybody knew who you were. My dad knew who you were. And then what happened? You got found out, and your little bubble of a world was removed.'

Casey rose from the chair now, his fists clenching.

'And now you're on the run because people don't think you're *strong* enough. Even the members of your health clubs don't think you're strong enough.'

'How would you know that?'

'Because for the last six months, I've been pretending to be a member of your club,' Casey explained. 'I'm on all the forums. And today, after the explosion, you've got a ton of people saying there's no smoke without fire, and they're looking to cancel their memberships. Even the ones who said it was exciting when it first came out, that they felt cool hanging out where genuine gangsters could be bench-pressing weights.'

Casey took a deep breath and forced a smile.

'All this, the comics and the hero villain shit? That's your banter again, trying to change your narrative. But I see your narrative, Simpson. I see it changing in real time as you free fall to Hell. I just wish my dad was here to see you fall, as well.'

'Stop,' Simpson's face was twisted, angry now as the

barrage of insults continued to strike at him. 'You want real talk? Fine. Ask the question.'

'What do you mean?' Casey paused, thrown by the sudden shift in the conversation.

'You've got a question you want to ask, so ask it.'

Casey nodded.

'I've got two,' he said. 'Two questions that are burned in my head and missing answers—'

'So ask me them.'

Casey took a deep breath, looking around the room before returning his attention to Nicky Simpson.

'Really?'

Simpson kept his gaze locked on Casey.

'Really.'

'No diverting the question? No bantering yourself out of answering?'

Nicky Simpson made an over-theatrical sigh, rolling his eyes as he looked around the back room, as if looking for some imaginary audience to smile at.

'Just ask the sodding questions,' he said. 'Before I change my mind and go hit things out there.'

Casey nodded, clearing his throat nervously.

'First question. Did you kill my dad? Second question. Why?'

There was a long, drawn out moment of silence in the back room as Casey kept his gaze locked on Nicky Simpson. And, after a few quiet seconds, Simpson turned away, staring at the shelving.

'Your dad was informing on me to the police. You know that, don't you?'

'Yeah.'

'And he was having an affair with Ellie Reckless.'

'I know that too, but you haven't answered the question,' Casey said. 'Did you kill my father?'

Nicky Simpson considered the question, formed an answer, and looked back at Casey.

'I—'

And then all hell broke loose.

UNWANTED VISITORS

AFTER NICKY HAD WALKED BACK INTO THE BACK ROOM, TINKER had stayed out in the gym, watching the sparring. She'd been here many times over the years, and her own ability in the ring had Pete the trainer use her a couple of times as a sparring partner at a pinch – but it wasn't often, as half the time she went into the ring, she usually knocked out the opponents. Now she was used more as a "lesson" to be learnt if the trainee boxer was getting a little too big for his or her boots.

She found it relaxing, weirdly; the sound of boxing glove hitting heavy bag, the rhythmic *thump thump thump* almost sending her to sleep, but a commotion at the door brought her back to the present.

'Oi, Tinks,' Leroy, one of the boxers, and part-time enforcer for Johnny Lucas shouted out. 'You expecting backup?'

'Only Ellie and Ramsey,' Tinker clambered to her feet. 'And one of them *really* can't be classed as that now. Why?'

'Because a shit ton of cars just pulled up outside,' Leroy

replied, hurrying through the gym. 'And this is a legit place now, so I know it ain't for the boss.'

'Unless the Lib Dems are really pissed he beat them in the by-election,' Pete muttered.

Ignoring the joke, Tinker walked towards the main door, exiting the boxing club, and walking out onto the Globe Town street.

There wasn't the "shit ton" Leroy had said, but she could count three new cars, each with two or three people inside, all waiting for something to happen. As she emerged, however, one of the car doors opened, and a middle-aged man with a suntan climbed out.

'We're looking for Nicky Simpson,' he stated. 'Be a good girl and get him to come out?'

Tinker didn't recognise the man, but from his positioning, his well-maintained hair, expensive clothes, bronzed skin and his designer stubble, she assumed he was pretty much the Alpha of the team, well off, and the leader. However, the fact she didn't recognise him meant there was a strong chance he didn't know who she was, either. A chance made more solid with the "good girl" line.

'Who?' she asked, deciding to play it dumb. 'You mean Nicky from the butchers?'

The man gave a smile.

'No, love,' he replied. 'The YouTuber. Fitness guy, shaggy hair, probably in there with a couple of bodyguards.'

'Nobody in there like that,' Tinker frowned. 'Leroy has a squad, though. Hang around with him all the time. You mean like a squad?'

'Look,' the man closed the car door as he now faced Tinker. 'We know he's in there. So do me a favour and get him out here.'

'What's in it for me?' Tinker asked now, narrowing her eyes. 'I mean, group of lads, all wanting this Ricky—'

'Nicky.'

'This Nicky to come out – you gonna give him a battering?' Tinker sniffed. 'No skin off my nose if you beat the shit out of someone, but what do I get for it?'

The question seemed to throw the man, and he looked around, confused.

'You want something?'

'Sure, for getting this Nicky guy out here.'

The man considered this and then nodded.

'Ten grand,' he said. 'I'll give you ten grand if you bring him out.'

Tinker whistled.

'Shit, man, you serious?' she replied. 'Ten G's for this guy? It is a guy, right? I mean, Nicky could be a woman, Nicola—'

'I said it's a guy already,' the man growled. 'And yeah. Ten G's if you get him out here, with or without his "squad," or whatever you want to call it.'

'Yeah, man, I can do that for you,' Tinker grinned.

'I'm sure you could,' the man, tiring of this, replied. 'You could buy a better coat for a start. But know this. If you screw us around, I'll pull your spine out through your neck and do terrible things into the hole.'

Tinker didn't need to pretend to be scared; there was a tone to the statement that suggested this wasn't the first time the man had done something similar.

'I'll find him,' she said, backing into the building. 'You wait here in case you spook him. I want that finder's fee.'

Once the door shut, though, she was all business as she walked up to Pete.

'Where's the back entrance?' she asked.

'You brought trouble to my door, girl?' Pete asked, concerned. 'Johnny better not hear.'

'He won't if we're long gone,' Tinker replied. 'Back entrance?'

'What makes you think we have one?'

'Because your boss is Johnny Lucas,' Tinker shrugged.

Pete looked over at Leroy.

'Move the lockers, let them through and then put them back,' he said, turning back to Tinker. 'There's a fire door behind the lockers. And don't give me shit about fire safety, yeah? Takes you down some stairs and out into the estate. Easy to get away from there.'

'Cool,' Tinker said. 'Do me a favour, yeah? Pop outside and delay them? They offered me ten grand for Nicky.'

'For ten grand I'll let them in myself,' Pete grinned as he walked to the boxing gym's main entrance.

Now in a run, Tinker pushed past the back door and into the office, the door slamming open as she did so.

'Grab your things! Now!' she cried out. 'We got company and they're armed.'

Casey and Simpson looked as if they'd been deep in conversation, and Casey looked pissed that they'd been interrupted.

Probably having a slanging match, Tinker considered as she typed out a quick text to Ellie.

> Compromised. Plan B.

'How did they find me?' Simpson asked as they now ran down the side corridor to the changing rooms, where, already having pulled the lockers out, Leroy was waiting.

'No idea,' Tinker said, giving Leroy a wink as she passed

through the fire door. 'We'll work that one out once we're far away and alive.'

OUTSIDE, PETE OPENED THE DOOR, PEERING OUT AT THE MEN waiting.

'My daughter says you offered ten grand for someone called Nick?'

'Yes,' the lead man straightened in anticipation.

'I got a nephew called Nick—'

'Ten grand for Nicky Simpson,' the man growled. 'Don't screw us about, mate. We know he's in there.'

Pete bit his bottom lip.

'Show me the money,' he said.

'What?'

'The ten grand,' Pete folded his arms. 'Cash.'

'I don't have the cash to hand—'

'Then how are you paying it?'

The man looked at his companions.

'I can send it by bank transfer, or by PayPal?'

'Friends and family?'

'Sure.'

Pete nodded.

'Twelve.'

'Twelve? I offered ten!'

'Yeah, but you're now putting the money through the system,' Pete explained. 'I can't hide it, can I? I'll be taxed.'

The man had finally reached his breaking point, and pulled his gun out, aiming it at Pete's face.

'New deal,' he hissed. 'Get out of the bloody way or I shoot you in the balls.'

Pete grinned, stepping to the side.

'All you had to do was bloody ask, mate,' he said.

———

NOW OUT ON THE STREET, TINKER WATCHED FROM THE CORNER as the contingent of men in the cars ran into the boxing club, Pete politely standing to the side.

'How do we get out of here?' Simpson asked. 'You had two cars, and Ramsey and Reckless took them both.'

'We get another,' Tinker said, motioning for the others to follow her as she walked over to the rear car, a black Audi. The driver was standing beside it, watching the door, and only realised someone was approaching at the last moment, looking around, his eyes widening as he saw Nicky Simpson.

'Hi,' Tinker smiled as she slammed a solid left hook against the driver's jaw, and he collapsed to the ground, eyes rolling into the back of his head.

'Get in,' she said, pulling him out of the way. 'We'll use this one.'

Simpson and Casey didn't need to be told twice, as they clambered into the back, Tinker sliding into the driver's seat and revving the engine.

As the car sped off down the street, Tinker saw several of the men running out of the boxing club, angrily pointing after them.

'Buckle up, this'll be a bumpy ride,' she said, hoping Pete and the others were okay.

———

THE JOURNEY ITSELF WAS UNEVENTFUL; TINKER AND THE AUDI had a good distance before the other cars could even follow, and she knew the Mile End streets well, using the rat-run of back roads to her advantage, turning randomly, avoiding intersections as the two passengers on the back seat, even though they were secured in, grabbed onto the side handles for dear life.

However, as they hit the A13 Ratcliffe Highway, another car sped out of the side road, immediately following them. A black Lexus, the driver's face was obscured by a balaclava.

That's not concerning in any way, Tinker considered as, her instincts kicking in, she swerved around a corner and pressed down on the accelerator. However, the Lexus followed close behind, its engine roaring.

'How the hell did they find us?' Casey cried out. 'There's no way they could intercept!'

'Is the car tracked?' Tinker looked down at her dashboard as she weaved through the traffic, the Lexus gaining on them. Gritting her teeth, she sped up, shooting through a red light, the Lexus hot on their tail.

It won't be me that gets the ticket, she thought to herself as she pushed the Audi to its limits, speeding towards the City of London.

'No tracker,' Casey replied, checking his computer. 'I mean, there probably is, as it's a new Audi and all that, but it's not real time like this.'

As Tinker approached a crossroads intersection, she slammed on the brakes, causing the Audi to screech to a halt. Quickly surveying the area, she spotted a narrow alleyway to her right, and, without hesitation, slammed her foot down on the accelerator, hurtling down the alley, causing the cars on the other side of the road to force themselves to an emergency stop, and narrowly avoiding a row of green recycling bins on the side of the alley as she carried on through.

The Lexus followed close behind, but wasn't as lucky as Tinker, and clipped the bins, sending them flying everywhere, as they pulled to a stop.

'Good,' she muttered to herself as she retraced her steps, making sure this time the Lexus wouldn't find them. But, after a couple of random turns, she swore to herself; she'd glimpsed the Lexus in her rear-view mirror, and it was gaining on them fast.

'It might not be the car, but there's definitely something here. We're being tracked,' she said. 'Find the bloody thing.'

'What am I, the TSA?' Casey said, rummaging in his bag. 'Hold on, I might actually be able to do this.'

Pulling out his iPhone, he clicked on an app.

'It uses the phone's Magnetometer,' he said, running it around the doors. 'It picks up metal, but also electromagnetic fields.'

'You can do that?' Tinker asked, surprised.

'You can with the sort of apps I have,' Casey grinned.

'Great,' Tinker gritted her teeth. 'Just find the bloody thing.'

Wrenching the wheel, she veered off down a side street, then made a sudden turn onto a pedestrianised zone, accelerating down the walkway, honking the horn at startled pedestrians as she raced towards the end. Now back out onto another main road, she weaved in and out of traffic, muttering to herself.

'We've lost them, but not for long if there's—'

'Got something!' Casey said as his phone squealed, passing over Nicky Simpson's wrist. 'It's his watch!'

'This is a classic!' Simpson looked horrified. 'It's a gift!'

'It's screaming like a bitch, that's what it's doing,' Casey looked back at Tinker. 'Want me to take it apart?'

'The hell he is—'

'Shut up!' Tinker yelled, slamming on the brakes as she made a sharp turn down a side street. 'Just let him look!'

Reluctantly, Simpson undid the leather strap and passed the watch across to Casey, who pulled out a jeweller's screwdriver to pop the backplate.

'Try to give me a smooth ride,' he ordered as he examined the back.

'You just happen to have those tools with you?' Simpson asked.

'I open up PC's,' Casey's tongue was out and to the side as he concentrated on the back plate. 'How expensive is the watch?'

'It's a Bremont, and probably worth about five grand.'

Casey grinned evilly.

'So it'd be real bad if I scratched it, then?'

'For God's sake, stop being a dick and just do something!' Tinker yelled as Casey twisted and popped the backplate, leaning back as he looked inside.

'It's got a tracker,' he said, gingerly prising away a small circuit board, attached by two prongs.

'Then toss the watch out the window!'

'No you don't!' Simpson leant over and plucked the small board away with two fingers, yanking it out. 'Just disconnect it.'

Casey flinched, as if the watch would explode, but then checked the underside.

'You could have broken your watch,' he complained at Simpson.

'My other option was watching you toss it onto the street,' Simpson grumbled back. 'How did this get in there?'

'That's the question I was about to ask you,' Tinker said, now slowing as she turned into a car park. With the tracker now removed, she felt a little safer as she drove the car up the levels.

At this, Simpson narrowed his eyes, shaking his head.

'I wear it all the time,' he said. 'My granddad gave it to me shortly after I – well, I took over from Dad.'

He paused.

'Actually, that's not true,' he said. 'I'd take it off when I did my videos. You can't do cardio in a Bremont. I'd swap it for a Garmin or an Apple Watch.'

'And what happened to it then?'

Nicky Simpson went to reply, but all that occurred was a rapid opening and shutting of his mouth as he considered the options.

'I'd give it to Saleh,' he whispered. 'He was always there. He'd hold it, I'd do the video, have a shower and then take it back.'

Tinker pulled into a parking bay, turning to look back at Simpson.

'So Saleh had every opportunity to do this?' she said. 'Saleh, who told you he was sorry, and who sent a double out to divert us away?'

'Well, when you say it like that, it sounds bad,' Simpson stared at the tracker. 'Maybe it was done to keep me safe? So if I was kidnapped, he could find me?'

'Maybe, but why give the location details to a group of angry hitmen who want you dead?' Tinker was already checking through the glove compartment, pulling out a chocolate protein bar. 'Awesome. I'm starving.'

Nicky Simpson looked sick, and Tinker knew exactly why. He'd finally realised his location had been passed to killers via a tracking chip he didn't even know he was wearing.

'Someone's been planning this a very long time,' he muttered.

'It's a great idea, though,' Casey was still staring down at the watch. 'It makes me think you could ...'

He looked up, realising he was speaking aloud.

'Sorry,' he said. 'Tech geek inside me speaking.'

Tinker climbed out of the car, leaning back in.

'Come on, before they work out where we are again,' she said. 'With luck, Ellie and Ramsey will have found something out.'

And, this said, Tinker started across the car park as Casey passed Simpson back the watch, the backplate screwed back on.

'Nice watch,' he said. 'When it's not, like, trying to kill us, that is,' he said.

13

INTERROGATION

RAMSEY WASN'T SURE HOW LONG HE'D BEEN IN THE CELL; THAT was the problem with time.

When busy, it would go fast, and when bored, it would become infinitesimally slow – meaning without any kind of timekeeping accessory, you could never know how long things had taken.

When the armed police had taken him, they'd cuffed him and stuck him in the back of a van, driving him for about half an hour before removing him, setting him down in a car park at the back of a tall, grey brick building. He didn't recognise it, but at the same time it screamed "police," so he guessed he was being held somewhere until questioning. And, as it was, he was processed quickly by a disinterested police sergeant, placed in a cell, his tie removed in case he was some kind of suicide risk – they'd taken his belt as well, although for some reason they left his laces in his brogues, which he found quite amusing.

And then, after what felt like an hour – but could have been ten minutes – they took him out of the cell and moved him into an interview room. Where, twiddling his thumbs, he'd been waiting since.

And again, he wasn't sure how long he'd been here. It could have been another half an hour, or it could have been half a day. All he had was a table, a chair, the recording device at the end and his memories, currently reliving the moment he stared down at the dead, glassy eyes of Lawrence Flanagan, his throat pumping out blood from a bullet wound he had taken from the armed police—

Ramsey shut his eyes, trying to ignore the image, shaking it away, trying to think of something else.

What was he saying about Delgado? What was the connection they had?

His thoughts, however, were stopped when the door to the interview room opened, and two familiar police detectives walked into the room.

'DS Delgado, DI Whitehouse,' Ramsey said, a slight tinge of relief in his voice at seeing familiar, if confrontational, faces. 'Well, that explains where I am. I'm guessing it's Vauxhall?'

Delgado said nothing, instead sitting down opposite him, staring at him constantly. Whitehouse, however, was a little more conversational.

'Ramsey Allen,' he said, sitting down. 'Looks like you got yourself in a little trouble.'

'Really?' Ramsey asked with the smallest of fake yawns, looking around. 'I didn't notice.'

If Whitehouse was in a jovial mood, however, he didn't show it. Instead, he leant across the table, turning on the recording device.

'Interview with Ramsey Allen, beginning—' he looked at

his watch, '—two-fifty-two pm, DI Whitehouse, DS Delgado in attendance.'

He turned back to Ramsey.

'Tough day,' he said. 'Are you dealing with it all okay?'

Ramsey was surprised by the first question, but guessed this was some kind of "good cop bad cop" attempt by Whitehouse. He didn't know him as well as Ellie did, but the impression he'd always got was that Whitehouse was the more empathic of the two.

'I've had better,' he said, playing along.

Delgado made some kind of guttural noise; Ramsey assumed it was some kind of laugh.

'So, Mister Allen,' she said, 'why don't you tell us about your day?'

'What would you like to know?' Ramsey asked. 'I mean, I started with breakfast, scrambled eggs and a little avocado—'

'I want you to tell us your movements.'

'Oh, well,' Ramsey looked confused at the question. 'If you're sure. I've been having a lot of fibre, so they've been quite—'

'Don't piss around!' Delgado snapped, stopping the smiling Ramsey. 'We have you at two terrorist bomb sites. We also have you standing with a known terrorist when he was taken down, so at the moment, Mister Allen, you're looking at a really shitty day.'

It was as if the humour was sucked out of the room as Ramsey glared back at Delgado.

'I *was* at a bomb site,' he confirmed. 'An hour and a half *after* the bomb went off. I was there on behalf of my company's client, as well you know, because I spoke to *you* when we arrived.'

'Your client is Nicholas Simpson,' Delgado nodded, a statement more than a question. 'Where is he, exactly?'

'I have no idea,' Ramsey said. 'How could I? You've had me stuck in a cell for the last couple of hours.'

He felt comfortable saying this, knowing what the time was now.

'Look, Nicky Simpson had someone try to kill him today,' he continued. 'We were hired to find out. We arrived at Nine Elms, at Battersea Power Station, and we examined the scene while there. We spoke to you.'

'Then what did you do?'

Ramsey shifted in his seat.

'I saw a man I believed dead, talking to you,' he said to Delgado, before looking at the recorder. 'For the record, Mister Allen is looking at DS Delgado as he says that. Isn't that what you're supposed to say?'

Delgado looked uncomfortable at this.

'Lawrence Flanagan?' Whitehouse asked.

'Yes,' Ramsey replied. 'I knew him back in the day. Not close, but you know, when you work for the same people, you walk in the same circles.'

'And you believed Flanagan was dead?'

'I knew he was dead,' Ramsey replied. 'I went to his funeral. But then today I saw him talking to Miss Delgado here, purely by chance. That is, it was purely by chance I saw him, I don't know yet whether their conversation was purely by chance, or deliberate, you see.'

Delgado continued to glower across the table at him.

'And let me guess, you decided valiantly to follow him,' she said icily. 'Which is interesting, because we've been checking your phone records, and you've seemed to have a very busy day so far. You drove to the City of London. Then you drove to Nine Elms—'

'Where I met you.'

'Then you drove to Kennington. Then you drove *back* to the City of London. And then, just to finish the trilogy, you drove back across the Thames to Streatham.'

'Sounds about right,' unconcerned, Ramsey nodded.

'So you followed Flanagan to Kennington?'

'Yes.'

'Where you called 999 after a bomb had exploded?'

'Yes.'

'Were you aware there was a bomb?'

'I wasn't even aware there was a car to explode,' Ramsey replied. 'We were following Flanagan. We didn't know what was going on.'

'Tell me what happened,' Whitehouse took over now.

'We lost him,' Ramsey shrugged. 'We eventually worked out where he was, and there was a BMW at the location. We assumed it was a meeting, maybe with the person who'd hired him, so I walked down to see who it was as it exploded.'

'And that was it?'

'That was it. I called the emergency services—'

'And then you left the scene of the crime, after texting your boss.'

'Actually, I texted her before the explosion.'

'We know. We checked your phone records,' Delgado said, reading from her notes. 'You texted "get out, it's a trap." That's a little suspicious, wouldn't you say? Especially with all your travelling around?'

Ramsey nodded, knowing this was the bit that looked bad.

'We were trying to find where he was,' he argued. 'At this

point, we believed he'd tried to kill Nicky Simpson with an explosive device, and now he'd killed somebody else with one.'

'You were hunting a killer,' Delgado said mockingly. 'How brave of you.'

'Stupid, really,' Ramsey replied.

'So you went to hunt this killer, but instead drove back to what, the Finders' offices? Or were you fleeing for your safety, running from the scene of a crime?'

'You can think what you want,' Ramsey said coldly.

'Oh, I am thinking,' Delgado replied. 'I'm thinking you were working with Flanagan. I'm thinking you tried to kill Nicky Simpson, but it didn't work. And then you followed Flanagan to Kennington, where you helped him kill two random people, before meeting him again at Streatham Cemetery to discuss what happens next.'

'That's not true!' Ramsey snapped.

Whitehouse leant forward, resting his elbows on the table.

'Then tell me why you were there,' he said calmly. 'Because I'll be honest, Ramsey, that last part's the bit that's confusing me.'

'I wasn't meeting Flanagan,' Ramsey admitted. 'I was actually going to check whether his grave was still there. Or, you know, if there was a hole in the middle where he clawed his way out of. After all, this was a man I thought was dead for a good decade or more.'

'So, how did you initiate conversations with him?'

'I didn't. He was there waiting for someone to come along and check his grave, and it happened to be me,' Ramsey replied. 'He turned up, started explaining to me what was going on—'

'Like what?' Delgado interrupted.

'Like there's a hit out on Nicky Simpson,' Ramsey said, watching the faces of the two police detectives, and noting there was no surprise at the statement. 'But you already knew that, didn't you?'

'My contact informed us there was a substantial open reward for Nicky's expiration,' Delgado said.

'That's a polite way of saying "murder," isn't it?' Ramsey smiled. 'Who's your contact?'

'None of your business.'

'Do you know?' Ramsey smiled at Whitehouse, who shrugged.

'No, but I heard it too, and I confirmed it.'

Sighing, Ramsey returned to the topic at hand.

'Anyway, he also told me he wasn't there to kill Nicky, he was there to help fake Nicky's death. He'd been working with other people, trying to keep Nicky alive.'

'He's showing a funny way of doing that. What with killing his driver and a homeless man?'

Ramsey shook his head.

'He said the two people in Kennington weren't by him,' he explained. 'The homeless man who died? Apparently, he was an assassin.'

Delgado chuckled at this.

'And you believe this? God, Allen, do you believe in Santa Claus as well?'

'No,' Ramsey said. 'Because in this country we call him Father Christmas.'

He shifted once more, leaning forward, now staring at Delgado.

'He also said something else to me as well,' he said. 'Just

before he was conveniently shot, by the way. He started talking about *you*.'

He noted with a little pleasure the paling of Delgado's face as he continued.

'He was quite surprised I didn't know who you were,' he smiled. 'And it made me wonder, Miss Delgado, who you really are.'

Delgado straightened in her seat, glancing at White-house, who, in return, leant across and turned off the recorder.

'Recording paused,' he said before clicking the button, looking back at Ramsey. 'I don't know what your game is, but accusing officers of whatever the hell you're accusing isn't going to help you here. And I don't think you realise how serious this is. You're linked to two bomb sites, Ramsey. Granted, you arrived late to one, but it doesn't matter. The second one you were *definitely* at, when two people were killed by an ex-IRA terrorist who you then happen to meet up with in a cemetery.'

He let the statement sink in before continuing.

'Ramsey, this isn't just prison time,' he breathed. 'This is "MI5 turning up and locking you away in a black site" time. This is you "never getting a chance to wear a suit again" time. This is you "dying in prison" time. If you've got anything you can tell me ...'

Ramsey sighed.

'We're both trying to keep Nicky Simpson alive,' he said. 'The man in the car was supposed to be Saleh, his driver, but it turned out to be a double. Saleh had paid him to go to the meeting, and Flanagan and this double both received a text giving the location, and Flanagan believed this was from Max Simpson, who was trying to save his son before hitmen got to him. But somehow, everything that Max and Flanagan had planned had been changed. That's all I know.'

'Convenient.'

'Yes, it is,' Ramsey snapped. 'Doesn't mean it's not true, though, does it?'

'And where's Ellie?' Delgado barked. 'Where's Nicky Simpson?'

'Honestly, I don't know,' Ramsey admitted, turning to Whitehouse. 'The last I heard from Ellie, she was coming to speak to you.'

At this, Delgado started visibly, looking at Whitehouse, who flushed.

'She came to speak to me earlier today, talking of conspiracies,' he replied awkwardly. 'I ignored her, shut her down. After that, she stormed off.'

'Then this is on you,' Ramsey said. 'Whatever happens from now on. You had the opportunity to stop it – and you didn't.'

Whitehouse went to speak again, but stopped as the door opened, and Robert Lewis stood in the doorway.

'My client will stop talking to you now,' he said.

'Your client?' Delgado muttered, rising from her chair. 'This isn't "bring your thief to work day," Lewis. This is a police interview.'

'In which the recorder seems to be turned off, so I contest the validity of your claim.' Ignoring Delgado, Robert entered the room, nodding to Ramsey. 'Come on, Mister Allen, we need to have a conversation.'

As the two officers went to protest, Robert raised his hand, looking back at Whitehouse. 'I've spoken to your superiors, and Mister Allen here will not be answering any more questions until we've had counsel and a conversation about his immediate release.'

'His release?'

'He was standing in a cemetery, paying his respects to somebody long dead. And then the police turned up and shot someone who, by *happenstance,* was next to him, giving Mister Allen intense emotional trauma.'

He split his attention between Whitehouse and Delgado now, glaring angrily at them both.

'I don't see any support here for that,' he said. 'I don't see any help given to him, while you locked him in a cell like a criminal for the mental pain he's had, watching a man he believed was long dead killed once more in front of his eyes.'

Delgado sighed.

'I didn't think you were a solicitor anymore—'

'I'm always a solicitor,' Robert spoke over her now, the hand back in the air to stop any further conversation. 'I walk in here to see you interrogating my client with no recording, which not only makes me uncomfortable on whether his rights are being ignored, but also makes me suspicious you don't want any of this on record. So, my client will be leaving now. You have nothing on him.'

'We have—'

'He was not at the scene of the first explosion,' Robert cut Delgado off. 'He called the ambulance for the second, and yes, you can have a conversation with them later. But that makes him a witness, and doesn't require him to be placed in a cell. And third, he was standing alone in a cemetery, when a man you decided to hunt came to him.'

He looked at Whitehouse now.

'I've spoken to the armed police unit that came in, and they told me they were sent to the cemetery on an anony-mous tip,' he explained, his voice cold and slow now, ensuring every syllable was understood. 'That tip came from a mobile phone, of which I've asked for the number to be provided, and had a police requisition number, which means a serving officer called it in, and I'm more than happy to check deeper into this, because I know one of you two called it in.'

He smiled.

'Or you can let my client go, and we'll be at your disposal down the line.'

'We really are on the same side,' Whitehouse said softly.

'Good. Then prove it,' Robert replied. 'Because currently, we're the ones trying to save someone's life, and you're trying to get them killed.'

There was a long, incredibly uncomfortable moment, which ended when Whitehouse waved dismissively at Ramsey.

'Go on, piss off,' he said. 'Tell Ellie this isn't over.'

'Oh, we know,' Robert replied on Ramsey's behalf. 'And we have questions for the two of you as well. But unlike this clown car of an interview, I'll be doing it through the official channels.'

And, this ominous warning given, Robert waved for Ramsey to follow him out of the room.

'You have blood on your collar,' he whispered as they walked down the corridor. 'You okay?'

'It's not mine, and no, I am definitely not okay,' Ramsey hissed. 'Delgado is dirty, I know it.'

'Well, let's all go have a nice chat and see what's turned up,' Robert replied. 'Just as soon as Tinker and Casey work out who's been bugging Nicky Simpson, the assassins that are hunting them around London piss off, and Davey finds out more about the homeless killer.'

Ramsey stopped.

'More assassins?'

'Yeah, but not intelligent ones,' Robert continued as they walked out of the building. 'For a start, they went against Tinker.'

'Where's Ellie now?' Ramsey asked.

'Meeting Tinker,' Robert walked to his car, opening the door. 'She's burning a favour to get an answer. Come on, I'll drive you back to Streatham and your car.'

'And then back to Finders?'

Robert pushed the barking Millie, now trying to escape the back seat of his car, back onto it.

'God no,' he said. 'That's burnt, as are Caesar's and the boxing ring. No, we have a new place to stay.'

He grinned.

'And you're going to love it,' he finished as he started the engine. 'Now do me a favour and pass Millie a treat. I don't want her scratching up the leather.'

14

NO VAULT OF MINE

As Ramsey pulled up to the outside of the warehouse near London Fields, on the Blackstone Estate, and surrounded by Screwfix stores, courier warehouses and the "Lolita Pole Dancing School," he began to chuckle.

'I see what you mean by "safe" and all that,' he said as he climbed out of his Rover, now parked next to Robert's car, the solicitor pulling Millie out with a lead. The building was a familiar one: an enormous, three-storey-high, red-bricked building, somewhere between ten to fifteen years old, with a large roller door to the side, large enough to drive a medium-sized van into, a door built into the brickwork at the side. The door had an A4 sign on the other side of the wired glass stating the location was "Open 24 Hours" but was closed. There was a buzzer on the side, and apart from that small message to any visitors, there was no other signage on it.

But Ramsey didn't need to have signage to know the location, as this was the storage centre for criminals, or those who didn't want the authorities knowing what they were storing, known as "the Vaults." Inside were corridors of garage doors, each one locked and rising when opened, no questions asked to the contents inside. The people who hired these paid a yearly fee, and could come in and out as they needed. There was no CCTV, either, for obvious reasons.

It was the perfect place to hide out; a place that required complete secrecy.

Buzzing the doorbell, Ramsey shook his head, as if to shake away a bad thought.

'You okay?' Robert, concerned, asked.

'Fine,' Ramsey waved a dismissive hand as the buzzer intercom burst into life.

'Yes?'

'Squeaky, it's Ramsey and Robert. We're here to see Ellie.'

'Don't know any Ellie.'

Ramsey sighed.

'Come on, Squeaky,' he muttered. 'It's been a long bloody day, and I'm really not in the mood.'

There was a muttering the intercom couldn't quite pick up, and the door buzzed open. Walking through it, they entered the Vaults' bare white reception room. There was a small, no bigger than A2-sized bulletproof window at the other end, with a high table in front of it that looked through into another office, just as bare. Usually Willy James, known as "Squeaky," would be the other side of it. Instead, the window was empty, probably because Squeaky James knew exactly why they were there, and where they were heading.

Ramsey looked at Robert.

'Which lockup?' he asked. 'I'm guessing it's not the entire floor Nicky Simpson has here, as people would look there.'

'Danny Martin's one,' Robert replied as they walked through a side door, down some black-painted metal stairs, and through another grey fire door at the end, following the almost garage-width roller shutter doors along one corridor, and then turning right to continue on down a second, until they reached a black roller shutter with the number "62" written on it. 'He's not using it right now, and we still had a key.'

The shutter was down, so Ramsey crouched, pulling it up. On the other side were Ellie, Tinker, Casey and Nicky Simpson, with Tinker aiming a gun at the door before lowering it in relief.

'Must be bad if the weapons are out,' Ramsey said, pulling down the shutters after entering. It was almost a double garage-sized area, with covered paintings and shelves along the east wall. A fluorescent light strip illuminated the room, and a selection of chairs and boxes had been arranged as seats. 'Anyone know we're here?'

'No, so no nicking the paintings,' Ellie grumbled.

Ramsey smiled, walking to the wall, peeking under a cloth.

'I wouldn't do such a thing,' he said, pulling at his collar. 'Bloody hot in here, though.'

Ellie looked worriedly at Robert before replying.

'Hey, are you okay?' she asked. 'I heard what happened.'

'Sure,' Ramsey turned, forcing a smile. 'Honestly, I'm fine.'

The dead, glassy eyes of Lawrence Flanagan, his throat pumping out blood from a bullet wound he had taken from the armed police—

'RAMSEY?'

Ellie knelt beside the prone form of Ramsey Allen as he slowly opened his eyes.

'What happened?' he croaked weakly.

'You passed out,' Ellie said, helping him to a sitting position against a shelving unit. 'Right after you told us you were fine.'

Ramsey grimaced.

'Guess I'm not,' he said, resting his head against the cool metal, looking up at the light. 'He was right beside me, Eleanor. I barely knew the guy, but to see him ...'

He trailed off, paling.

'I'm okay,' he said. 'Just let me sit for a bit.'

Tinker passed him a bottle of water as Ellie rose, looking around the lockup at the other members of her team.

'Okay, we need to make a plan,' she said.

'A plan, yeah,' Nicky Simpson muttered. 'Because it's been a great plan so far.'

Ellie spun, fury in her eyes.

'Are you dead?' she snapped.

'What?'

'I said, *are you dead*?' Ellie stalked towards Simpson. 'Because it looks to me like you're not, even though you were *wearing a bloody tracker that led the assassins straight to our door.*'

'He did what?' Ramsey stopped sipping the water.

'We'll get to it in a moment, after Mister Simpson here admits we're in the shit because of him. *Again.*'

Admonished, Simpson looked at the floor.

'Sorry,' he said. 'This one was on me. Not you.'

'Damn right it's on you,' Ellie relaxed a little, looking around. 'Okay, we're on the back foot here and I bloody hate that. What do we have?'

'The tracker's not new, but I can't tell you how old it is,' Casey grumbled, tapping on his laptop's keys.

'Don't worry about that, I've called in a favour,' Ellie said, glancing at Simpson, who looked as if he was about to make a snarky comment, but then thought better about it. 'They should be here soon.'

'Where's Davey?' Ramsey asked while holding his head between his legs.

'With an ex-colleague at the forensics lab in Lambeth,' Tinker replied. 'They're checking the homeless man. Or, rather, according to what you texted us after your release, an assassin?'

Ramsey nodded weakly.

'Apparently so,' he said.

'Your text was quite brief, so tell us what you know,' Ellie asked. 'If it's not too traumatic?'

'I met Flanagan in a cemetery, wasn't expecting it, he said he was paid by the boy's dad to fake his death and get him out, but Saleh was supposed to alert him of this.'

'Well Saleh sodding well didn't,' Simpson muttered.

'Saleh did more than that,' Ramsey continued. 'He paid someone to shave his head and drive out, pretending they were him. There was a text message, and they met with Flanagan at an agreed location, as he'd had the message as well—'

'Who sent the message?'

'He thought it was Max Simpson.'

'He thought?' Simpson looked up. 'He didn't know?'

'I'd ask him, but that's a little hard right now,' Ramsey snapped. 'Anyway, he gets the message and waits, the BMW arrives, but Flanagan sees it's not Saleh and drives off. But this homeless assassin guy was there too, and killed the double with some kind of acid water or something, he wasn't too sure about that.'

'How did he see—' Tinker stopped herself. 'A webcam?'

'On a street lamp. So he watched from around the corner as they tossed an explosive into the car. When you arrived, they tried to cover it over, but Flanagan found the frequency and detonated the bomb before you could get there.'

'In the process destroying all evidence of this,' Ellie sighed.

'Maybe not,' Tinker replied. 'There might be clues we can grab from the car.'

'I could give you the details,' Simpson said. 'But I'd have to log into the company server.'

Casey passed over the laptop.

'It's on a multiple VPN network, so go wild,' he said. 'Nobody will see you.'

'Okay, so there's a hit placed on Simpson; Dad sends Flanagan to save him ... that doesn't explain the attackers or the tracker.'

'I think we need to speak to Saleh about that,' Tinker answered Ellie's question. 'He had the opportunity to put the tracker in. But also, he might be able to tell us when they did it. Anything else?'

'Delgado has a connection to the Simpsons,' Ramsey looked up from the floor. 'Flanagan was surprised we didn't know it.'

Ellie looked across at Nicky Simpson, who was now hitting the keys angrily.

'I've been locked out!' he hissed. 'Someone changed my password!'

He looked back at Ellie at this.

'Kate Delgado is the god-daughter of Richard Smith,' he

said, frowning. 'You didn't know that? I thought everyone did.'

Ellie shook her head. Ricky Smith was an enforcer back in the eighties, who worked primarily south of the river. The only reason she knew this was because of the work she'd done looking into Nicky Simpson's past. Ricky Smith was part of that past, having primarily worked for Paddy Simpson during his heyday.

'Well, that keeps her on my list of suspects,' she said. 'Unless you want to confirm or deny anything?'

Simpson was still glaring at the laptop, but Casey smiled, taking it from him.

'Here, let me get you in,' he said, tapping on the keyboard. 'I have a corporate account.'

'You have a what—' Simpson started, but then sat back, chuckling. 'Of course you do. Of course you bloody well do.'

Millie started growling, and Ellie nodded to Tinker to open the shutter.

Squeaky, rubbing his hands with a cloth, having obviously been working on an engine of some kind, stood there.

'Your visitor is here,' he said. 'He ain't coming in. I don't know him.'

'That's fine,' Ellie nodded to Tinker. 'I'll go show him the watch.'

As Tinker passed the watch and tracker to Ellie, she looked back at the group.

'We're still on the back foot,' she said. 'I don't like that.'

Following Squeaky down the corridor, Ellie heard the shutter close behind her. She knew they couldn't stay here for long; they needed another bolthole, but this couldn't keep continuing like that. Soon, they'd need a place to bed down for the night, and she needed to get food for Millie. They still needed to work out who'd placed the hit on Nicky Simpson and work out how to stop it.

You're probably going to have to burn a favour for that.

Ellie groaned as the thought crossed her mind; was a favour from Simpson worth more than the other favours she had? Probably. He had the opportunity to give her closure at worst, regain her life at best. And, as she walked up the metal steps to the reception, she started mentally going through the list of favours owed, working out who had enough sway to help them here.

In the reception was a mousey old man with a black leather doctor's bag in his hand, likely in his late seventies or even early eighties. He wore a shirt, tie and blue jeans under a tweed jacket, and his hair was almost non-existent.

'This had better be important, Reckless,' he said. 'And I'd better be free of you by the end.'

Ellie nodded, walking to the high table at the end, placing the watch and tracker down on it.

'All debts are paid after this, Charles,' she said, stepping back as Charles Bally, aka "Charley the Beak," wandered over, pulling on a pair of thick reading glasses to look at it.

Charley had been one of Ellie's first gained favours. He was a known electrician and engineer for the criminal classes, with an expertise in bank vault circuitry. He couldn't open a padlock if he had the key, but with a few wires, a soldering iron and a voltmeter, he could open the Royal Mint.

Amusingly, the favour had been gained because he'd lost his "work" bag, the doctor's briefcase filled with the tools of his trade that he held currently, many of which were irreplaceable, from a time before computers truly took over. He'd misplaced it on a bus in Penge. Ellie had tracked it down to a gang of teenagers who, after Tinker had scared the living hell out of them, gave it back.

Ellie wasn't sure if it was the fact she did something he couldn't, or because *she* did something he couldn't, so *easily*, that had pissed him off, but a favour was a favour.

'The tracker was attached to the watch,' she said. 'Obviously I'd prefer if you didn't attach it again. But I need to know when it was put in.'

Charley leant closer, peering at the circuit board.

'The solder isn't new,' he said. 'Duller than usual. I have forty-year-old plumbing solder that looks similar, but the watch ain't that old.'

Pulling on a pair of latex gloves, Charley reached into his doctor's bag and pulled out some kind of anti-static mat, unrolling it onto the table before placing the two items on it. He then pulled out a slim pair of pliers and held the tip of the board with them, turning it around.

'It's basic, but it's not that old,' he said. 'I'd say about ten years.'

'And can you tell when it was attached?' Ellie asked. 'Was it this week? Last week? Last month?'

Charley looked back at Ellie.

'You don't understand,' he said. 'This tech is a good decade old, yeah? And the solder is old. They put this in brand new, about ten years back.'

'You're sure?'

Charley nodded.

'Watch like this is a keeper,' he said. 'But the issue isn't when it was put in, it's why people didn't notice this before.'

He opened the back of the watch case, carefully pulling out the battery and looking at it.

'Yeah, this is five years old, tops,' he said, placing it back in. 'Someone changed the battery while the circuit was there and was visible. Maybe they thought it was part of the watch, though. Who knows?'

Ellie stared at the watch. Charley's analysis meant that someone had not only been following Nicky Simpson since he effectively took over the South London "family business," but that others had to know, because they changed the battery in the meantime.

'Thanks,' she said as Charley closed up the watch. 'Your debt is cleared.'

'Good,' Charley replied, tossing his equipment back into the bag and closing it. 'Lose my number.'

'Until the next time you need me,' Ellie winked, grabbing the items and leaving the room, heading back to the lockup. As she did so, her phone buzzed: a message from Davey.

> Can't talk – in morgue

> Old man was Seth Taylor. Get Casey to look into him as he had expensive dental work done recently, no way was homeless.

> Looking into car remains too. And these texts.

Sending a quick reply of thanks, Ellie carried on to the lockup, raising the shutter.

'Check into Seth Taylor—' she said to Casey, but paused. The atmosphere was off, somehow. 'What did I miss?'

'Nicky's been frozen out of his company,' Tinker said, doing her best to hide the glee emanating from her tone. 'More than just the password. Someone's taking it over and is closing off his access.'

'It has to be someone close,' Simpson was pacing as he spoke. 'Nobody else has a way to get in.'

'I got in,' Casey replied. 'And I'm a teenager.'

'A supervillain teenager,' Ramsey added.

Ellie held up the Bremont.

'Your grandfather gave you this, right?' she asked. 'When?'

'When I took—' Simpson started, before changing the line to '—when my father retired.'

'So, when you became kingpin of the south of London,' Ellie nodded, tossing him the watch. 'Your grandfather gave you this, and you've worn it ever since. What about when the battery needed to be changed?'

'Saleh did it,' Simpson was defensive now, crossing his arms as he did so. 'What do you know, Reckless?'

Ellie sighed, looking around the room.

'The tracker was placed in the watch about ten years back,' she said. 'Which sounds like it's shortly before you took over the family empire. If it was given to you by Paddy Simpson, it stands to reason he put it in to keep an eye on you. And, when Saleh had the battery replaced, he must have seen it too.'

She paused, letting this sink in.

'The hit that was put out on you gave the tracker data out as a way to find you,' she said. 'That's how the assassins arrived so fast, or kept finding the car. That's why Flanagan failed – the tracker said you were in the office, just not in the stairwell – and why he and Seth Taylor both knew you were in my car in Kennington. Everyone had it, Nicky. The tracker your grandfather placed in your watch was given out to anyone who wanted to execute you. What does that say to you?'

Nicky Simpson stared at the watch for a long moment, before hurling it violently against the wall of the lockup, where the splintering sound of the glass breaking echoed around the lockup.

'It means my bloody granddad is trying to kill me,' he muttered.

15

GRANDAD, WE LOVE YOU

FOLLOWING THE REVELATION OF NICKY SIMPSON'S grandfather potentially wanting to send him to the choir eternal, Ellie had decided to split up once more. The only reason they'd come to the Vaults was so that Charley could check on the trackers, but now this was done, there was no more reason to stay.

But, before they went their separate ways, there were things that needed to be discussed.

'Why exactly would your grandfather want you dead?' Tinker asked, confused.

'Because Nicky was outed,' Casey said, looking up from the laptop. 'It weakened him. He couldn't do what he'd done in the past, as the shadows were now gone.'

'Listen to you. "The shadows were now gone." You need to get laid, kid. Or stop reading bad fantasy novels,' Simpson grumbled. 'I was outed, and I didn't retaliate is more like it. Paddy Simpson would have gone to war with the Lumettas. He'd have killed them in the streets. I, meanwhile, grabbed a team of crisis PR experts and solicitors and sent out a ton of cease and desist letters.'

'And that works with criminals?' Ellie asked, half-amused.

'I didn't bother sending these to *them*,' Simpson replied darkly. 'These were to papers, bloggers, YouTubers doing attack videos, anything that was legally thrown against me.'

'So what did you do to the …' Casey trailed off. 'Forget that. I don't want to know.'

'I treated them in kind,' Simpson replied, and there was a darker tone to his voice now. 'Some of them thought that with the world knowing my secrets, they could bad mouth me and I wouldn't do anything. So instead, I *did* something.'

'You probably don't want to tell us things like that,' Robert said, looking a little queasy at the comment.

'Why?' Simpson genuinely looked surprised. 'You work for me now. Client-Reckless privilege and all that.'

'Yeah, it really doesn't work that way,' Robert replied, almost regretfully.

'Okay,' Ellie said, crouching down to stroke Millie, who, using her dog abilities, had realised it was feeding time, and was mithering a little. 'Casey, follow up on Davey's message about Taylor. And keep on with the accounts. Find out who's trying to overthrow Nicky here.'

'It's his granddad,' Casey said. 'Has to be.'

'Not really,' Tinker shook her head. 'He might have had the tracker for other reasons. Someone else could have bastardised its use.'

Casey nodded, typing code into a window.

'On it,' he said.

'The Lumettas have a lot to answer for,' Simpson muttered.

At this, though, Ellie frowned.

'One thing I never understood,' she said. 'Why Ireland?'

'What do you mean?'

Ellie paced as she spoke.

'Well, you're talking about building the Simpson empire, and having health clubs in Ireland, right? That's the deal you were making with the Lumettas, getting in with them to build a base in Dublin.'

'So?'

'It seems a little ... well, small,' Ellie replied. 'You're already reaching out into America through Boston. You've got connections in Europe. You're moving into Asia, but you got taken down and outed, because of a deal you were making, to get a couple of clubs in Dublin, of all places. It's not exactly where I saw you pushing financially, that's all. It felt personal.'

Simpson shrugged.

'The Irish deal wasn't about making money,' he said. 'It was about fulfilling a promise to my granddad.'

Ramsey nodded.

'He started there, didn't he?'

Nicky Simpson nodded at this.

'Paddy Simpson grew up in County Louth,' he explained. 'Started off in the fifties as the gopher for a small group of smugglers.'

'Smugglers?' Tinker coughed, hiding a laugh. 'Like Han Solo?'

Simpson didn't even glare at her, simply ignoring the glib comment.

'They pretty much used the Troubles to their advantage, smuggling items from the south to Northern Ireland, and vice versa. There was a lot of money to be made back then. You could take a hundred punt's worth of livestock north of the border, where suddenly you're making three times the profit, trade it for sugar and bring it back to Dundalk, where you'd sell it to a confectionery company. And again, for major profits. By the time you came back, the hundred punts that you would have spent are now worth six hundred. A solid return on your investments.'

'So why leave?'

'He fell out with the leader of the gang,' Simpson replied. 'While in Ireland, he'd found he was good with figures, mainly because of growing up in the smuggling world. He was best friends with the guy who'd started the gang, who was only a few years older, and they made the decision to put him through an accountancy course – primarily to see how else they could maximise profits. But this also made Paddy vital in any conversations with bigger gangs when they came to visit the area, as he could explain profit and loss. And over the years, he gained prominence in the firm, and gained job offers.'

He smiled as he thought about this.

'One of the offers led to him going to London and taking his family with him. To be honest, as the accountant he'd seen where some of the money they'd been making was going, and realised he was doing all the work, but making a pittance of what his so-called "best friend" was making. So, the first opportunity he had, he got out. Best thing he ever did, even if the company they created to launder the profits had them both as partners.'

His face took on a wistful appearance.

'He always claimed Ireland, and Dundalk, was a spiritual home, especially as Cú Chulainn came from there. He was some kind of mighty hero or something from legend, but I thought it was all fairy stories for kids, so I never bothered looking into it. But this legendary hero had been betrayed by his best friend in the stories, and Granddad had always likened his betrayal to that. I wanted to get back into Ireland, start building places in Dublin, just to show Granddad we could return and make money from it.'

'And what about his friend, the leader of the smugglers?' Casey, enrapt with the legend, asked.

'Oh, he disappeared in the mists of time,' Simpson shrugged. 'Once the Good Friday Agreement came in, the border was pretty non-existent. There was no need for smugglers anymore. I believe he moved to England with what remaining money he had left, and lived his life being normal, while my granddad became a legend like Cú Chulainn.'

There was a moment of awkward silence as Simpson finished; nobody in the lockup, apart from Nicky Simpson himself, seemed to believe Paddy Simpson was in any way a legendary Irish hero.

'What was the other guy's name?' Ellie asked.

'No idea,' Simpson shrugged, 'He never told me it, always changed the subject. I assumed it was a bad split, and didn't want to remember it.'

'Okay then, changing the subject from legends and mythology, let's make a plan. Davey's looking into the car, the dead double and the dead assassin,' Ellie counted them off on her fingers. 'Ramsey, if you're up for it, I need you and Tinker to go find Saleh and learn what's really going on.'

'Why me?' Ramsey paled.

'Because you're a burglar and you might need to break in,' Tinker smiled before looking back at Ellie. 'I'm not happy about leaving you alone with him.'

'You can use my toy,' Casey smiled, as Ramsey made a subtle motion for him to shut up.

'Now the tracker's gone, we'll be fine.' Ignoring Casey and Ramsey, Ellie waved Tinker off. 'Robert, look into Delgado, do it under the guise of freedom of information for your client, Ramsey, or something.'

'No, please, tell me how to do my job,' Robert grumbled.

'We're still no closer to working out who put the hit out, so what are you planning?' Tinker asked.

'I think we need to look at speaking to Nicky's family, but not about bloody legends,' Ellie said. 'Ramsey, did you mention something about Max earlier in the text?'

Ramsey nodded.

'Before he died, Flanagan said Max was sending bigger people in. His exact words were "The Simpsons are going to war. You need to get out of the way of the bullets."'

'And you're sure about that?' Simpson asked. 'Not "*Max* is going," he named the family?'

'A minute later he was pumping blood out of his throat, so yes, the entire bloody conversation is burned into my head,' Ramsey snapped.

Simpson held up his hands.

'There's someone else I want to check into,' he said. 'Sure, Flanagan could be the one who set the bomb off, but does he know electronics?'

'Depends on what you mean.'

'My Tesla was hacked and the bloody thing almost charged at me, remember?' Simpson continued. 'I need to know who had access. Also, there's the girl.'

'Girl?'

'The one on the counter who I was watching,' Simpson shook his head. 'Not like that. She's ... there was something off. I didn't hire her for a start.'

'Do you hire all your staff?'

'The pretty ones, yes.'

Ellie shook her head.

'Of course you do.'

'He's right,' Ramsey looked up. 'She's definitely part of this.'

He climbed to his feet.

'Carrie,' he said to Simpson. 'Not "the girl," her name was Carrie. And she bloody well hated you when I spoke to her.'

He leant against a covered painting frame trying to remember what she'd said.

'She got the people out on her own initiative, which was applaudable, but when I mentioned the elevators, and whether anyone had been seen going to them, she clammed up, started talking about solicitors, and then told me Nicky there was scum.'

'Harsh,' Simpson muttered, and Ellie almost believed she saw hurt in his eyes.

'Apparently you hurt her brother years ago. But Carrie said you were the only job in town. Her line was "if someone wants to kill him, I got no problem with that," and I believed her,' Ramsey said. 'But then something interesting happened. When I got her name, I gave her mine, said I was Ramsey. But when we finished, she clammed up again and walked off, and her last lines to me were "that's all you're getting from me, Mister Allen, and I suggest you take what you can."'

'You never said your surname,' Ellie looked up from Millie.

'No, I didn't,' Ramsey shook his head. 'But she knew me. And I'll swear on a stack of bibles I've never met her in my life.'

'They'd just burst into flames,' Casey muttered from the corner of the lockup. 'Want me to look into her?'

Ellie watched Casey as he awkwardly returned to the centre of the room.

'What were you doing?' she asked.

'Just looking around,' Casey reddened. 'Never been in a real criminal's treasure den before.'

'Well, don't steal any of the treasure,' Ellie said. 'And yeah, look into that. Maybe she can explain the Tesla, too.'

Casey nodded, picking up his laptop and typing into the window. After a moment, it pinged.

'Carrie Holden,' he said. 'Ring any bells?'

Simpson shook his head.

'I'll dig deeper,' Casey replied, glued to the laptop.

'Right then,' Ellie looked back at Nicky Simpson. 'Let's get you hidden again.'

'No,' Simpson folded his arms, his face tight. 'I'm sick of running, sick of hiding. I'm Nicky bloody Simpson, grandson of Paddy Simpson—'

'Who we think wants you dead,' Tinker mumbled.

'And I'm not running anymore,' ignoring her, Simpson continued. 'They want me? Let them come.'

'This isn't a good plan,' Ellie said.

'Your job was to keep me alive, not keep me in bubble wrap,' Simpson replied, looking over at her. 'Your team does all the dangerous shit while we hide? That's not how I work.'

'No offence, Nicky, but having others do your dirty work while you sit in your office is exactly how you work,' Ellie snapped. 'But, if you want to do something—'

'Oh shit,' Casey spoke aloud, before blushing. 'Sorry.'

'What?' Ellie looked up.

'So SCO19 sent Davey the number from the anonymous tip,' Casey explained. 'She's just sent me phone records for Saleh's phone – it was blown up, but the records still stand. If

Flanagan had the message too, as he showed Ramsey, then the same number texted both of them.'

'We know that,' Simpson frowned.

'Yeah, but what you don't know is the phone that called the armed police on you, that had a police reference number? It also called your health club, ten minutes or so before the boom. Davey said she tried it, the line's dead, likely a burner phone.'

'Max wouldn't have been able to do the reference number,' Ellie said. 'Who would he have spoken to at the club?'

'He would have gone through to reception,' Casey replied. 'And we all know who was there.'

'So our mysterious woman knows this person, too. Okay, anything else?'

Casey nodded.

'She checked phone towers. When the first two messages were sent, the phone was near Nine Elms. And the calls were made near Vauxhall.'

'Goddamn!' Ellie exclaimed. 'Bloody Delgado!'

'We don't know that,' Robert warned.

'It's Mark or Kate, Robert,' Ellie replied. 'And Kate's the god-daughter or great niece or whatever.'

She looked back at Casey.

'Get everything you can on it,' she said. 'Pass it to Robert. I want that bitch nailed to the wall.'

She stopped as Casey yelped again.

'What now?' Ellie asked, exasperated.

'Max Simpson is in town,' Casey looked up from the laptop. 'A "Maxwell Simpson" landed in Gatwick an hour ago on an EasyJet flight.'

'You said Flanagan mentioned new heavy hitters sent by

Max,' Tinker looked at Ramsey now, who was texting on his phone. 'You think he's taking a personal interest in this?'

'Looks like it,' Ramsey looked back at Nicky. 'Serious question. When you took over, how pissed was Daddy?'

'My "daddy," as you so eloquently put it, was fine with this,' Simpson replied. 'He knew he was losing power the moment people heard about his Parkinson's. People want a strong leader, not someone who could have an attack at any moment.'

'Did he ever deal with the watch?' Ramsey continued, nodding over at the broken timepiece on the floor.

Simpson went to reply, his face one of amusement, but then the expression changed to one of concern, as a silent thought crossed his mind.

'Granddad sent it from Majorca via Dad,' he said. 'So yeah. He flew back with it.'

'Plenty of time to place a tracker in it,' Ellie replied. 'Maybe Paddy isn't the issue here.'

'Yes, but why try to save him then?' Ramsey frowned.

'Hypothetical, if I may,' Robert suggested. 'Paddy gives a watch, a congratulatory present, to Mister Simpson here. Max takes it, but sticks a tracker in it. Maybe it's parental concern, maybe he still wants to be involved. Then, nine years or so later, someone gets hold of the tracker frequency and uses it to make sure a hit on Mister Simpson can happen. Maybe Max, realising he's the reason the frequency is now out there, tries to save his son.'

'Then why not just call him and tell him not to wear the watch?'

'Maybe if he does that, Nicky here realises Daddy's had an eye on him,' Ramsey walked over to the remains of the Bremont watch. 'Maybe he thinks he can use the frequency himself to find Nicky first, fake the death before anyone else attends. An explosion would take hours, days even before conclusive proof of Nicky surviving would be out there. Plenty of time to get the watch off him, stick him on a plane and get him to Majorca. Or a safe house, whatever.'

Ellie looked at Simpson, pursing her lips as she did so.

'You don't want to hide? Fine,' she said eventually. 'Let's go speak to your father. Do you know where he'll be?'

'It'll be one of three places, and your hacker will be able to narrow that down,' Simpson nodded at Casey.

'I'll need the three places first,' Casey muttered.

As Nicky Simpson gave Casey three locations, Ramsey walked off to the back of the room, pulling out his phone, googling and dialling a number then waited. After a minute, he walked back.

'Is one of the three the Red Lion pub on the Walworth Road?' he asked.

'Yes,' Simpson straightened.

'That's where he is then,' Ramsey smiled. 'They closed out the function room today and they don't know how long it'll be closed for.'

He looked back at Ellie.

'It's between Camberwell and the Elephant, and near where the Richardsons held court,' he said. 'Paddy used it back in the day, saying places had power. I know Max used it a couple of times. He's making a statement.'

'Or there's a water leak,' Tinker offered.

'No, it makes sense,' Simpson nodded. 'Well done, Ramsey. Your analogue ways beat technology.'

'Isn't hard when your opponent is twelve,' Ramsey winked at Casey, before looking at Ellie. 'You'll find him there.'

'Okay then,' Ellie nodded slowly. 'Looks like it's date night. They'd better be dog friendly.'

'I'll babysit Millie,' Robert offered, reaching for the lead. 'I'll be returning to the office and I know she has food there. And I'll walk her, too.'

'Do it an hour after food,' Ellie passed the lead over, standing up. 'And give her attention every hour.'

'Like I don't anyway,' Robert chuckled.

And with that, the team prepared to split off, pausing as Ellie received a new text.

'It's Davey,' she said, reading it. 'They've got more information on the BMW and the victim inside.'

She read the note, and then looked up, surprised.

'Bomb residue didn't match the office explosion, so it wasn't Flanagan, unless he changed his MO in the middle of the day,' she said. 'Explosion came from the passenger seat—'

'Which it would have, if someone had tossed the bomb through the window,' Tinker added.

'The driver was badly burnt, but they confirmed he died of poisoning, something literally burning through his throat lining, rather than the explosion.'

'Could they have been targeting Saleh?' Ellie asked Simpson. 'Could this be more than just an attack on you?'

'Why him? He's just my driver.'

'He's more than that,' Ramsey snapped. 'He's your dirty work. Your black bag man. You point, he clicks. What if he's also the target?'

'The hit's on Nicky.'

'Do we know that for sure?' Ellie asked. 'We have that from unreliable narrators. We should check into this.'

Casey nodded.

'I'll add it to my ever-growing list,' he smiled. 'Oh, one thing, I found Carrie's social media, based on a face search. She's not Carrie Holden on there, she's Carrie Mullen. Ring any bells?'

If Nicky Simpson recognised the name, he did a damned good job of hiding it. However, this time, he didn't confirm, deny, or make any glib comment, which put Ellie on alert.

'Right then, let's go speak to your daddy,' she said to him.

But rather than reply, he simply glowered at her.

'I need to pop upstairs first,' he said.

'What, to your lockup?' Ellie asked. 'Isn't anything there you need, Nicky. We're not tooling up.'

'No, if I'm seeing Dad, I have to bring a gift – it's tradition,' Simpson replied. 'Also, I need to check something.'

Ellie sighed.

'Fine,' she said. 'But people will probably be checking the lockup, now they can't follow on their phones ...'

She trailed off.

'Casey, how easy would it be to get the tracker working again?'

Casey shrugged.

'Attach the prongs to a power source and they should work,' he said. 'Why?'

'Let's take the fight to the hitmen,' Ellie smiled. 'Let's set up an ambush. Put the tracker somewhere, turn it on, see who turns up, find out who gave them the frequency.'

'Could work,' Ramsey nodded. 'But where and when?'

'I'll decide that after I speak to Max Simpson,' Ellie grinned. 'Come on then, sport. Let's go upstairs and look in your toy box.'

16

PRODIGAL SONS

ONCE IN THE UPSTAIRS LOCKUP, NICKY SIMPSON HAD TRIED TO slip a Glock into his pocket, but Ellie had been expecting it, and slapped his hand away as he reached into the drawer.

'No guns,' she snapped.

'They're trying to kill me!' he replied angrily. 'And you work for me right now, so piss off and leave me be.'

Ellie accepted the outburst, as they were reaching the end of a very stressful day for Nicky. His office had been bombed, his driver possibly a traitor, people had tried to kill him and it looked like it could have been set up by his grandfather or his father, or even both, the latter of whom he was now about to go and speak to.

'You walk in with a gun, it'll be used,' she said. 'That's your career as a YouTuber, an entrepreneur, a business owner, all gone in a second.'

'You don't think that's gone already?' Simpson muttered.

'Passive income,' Ellie shrugged. 'I reckon if you check your YouTube pay algorithm things, you'll see thousands of new views. Hundreds of thousands, even. You're on the news,

Nicky. Someone tried to blow you up, and you went dark. Nobody knows where you are. You'll feed the news cycle for a good couple of days.'

She smiled.

'And when you get to the Red Lion, you can put up a post.'

'I'm probably demonetised by YouTube – that means no money for Nicky, and posting something will make me a target,' Simpson frowned. 'Oh, wait, you think my dad being there will stop people trying to kill me?'

'If he's brought these heavy hitters, then yeah,' Ellie smiled. 'Make use of them. Give your dad the gift he wants, let him take you home. You'll be safe.'

'And your job will be over,' Simpson snapped. 'I see what you're doing here, Reckless.'

'Not what you think I'm doing, that's for sure,' Ellie replied. 'You hired us to keep you alive *and* find out who did this. I can't claim the favour if I haven't done both.'

Simpson considered this, and then nodded.

'Fair point,' he accepted. 'So you can stay by my side until it's done.'

'Your father—'

'He can be there too.'

Ellie shook her head.

'I had run-ins with him when I started in the force,' she said. 'I'd rather not.'

Before Simpson could reply, however, she carried on.

'So who's Carrie?' she asked. 'You seemed to know more when you heard the surname.'

'I don't know her, but I knew her brother, Mark,' Simpson reluctantly admitted.

'Go on then, who is he?'

Simpson thought about this for a moment.

'When I started out, I had to go hard,' he explained. 'My dad had been weak. Granddad was a legend. And so when I started, and remember this was at nineteen years old, I had to make sure that people were scared of me.'

'And Mark?'

'I knew him as a kid,' Simpson replied. 'You know, somebody on the scene. Always around, and his family knew us for generations. He was a small time player, so to speak – stole things, fenced things, kind of like your Ramsey Allen if he was part of the TikTok generation. But over time, he started to get arrogant, cocky.'

'Can't imagine where he got that from.'

Simpson gave a wry smile.

'Yeah, he'd grown up with me, and my dad liked him, said he was a good influence on me, which showed how much attention he was paying. And Mark thought because of that, he had some kind of "get out of jail free" card where I wouldn't kick off against him if he did something stupid. And over time he was right, you know – he was a friend, and I let him get away with murder. Almost literally.'

He stared across his lockup, deep in thought.

'He cost me big one day, back when I was just taking over, when his small criminal enterprise crossed over with something I was planning—'

'Small criminal enterprise?' Ellie interrupted. 'What is this, some kind of court case deposition?'

'I don't want to give you the details,' Simpson replied. 'You might be helping me stay alive, but you're an ex-cop and I don't really want anything else coming out.'

Ellie nodded, accepting this, as Simpson continued.

'I'm telling you this because it's relevant to our situation right now. But don't think for one second we're friends.'

Ellie chuckled at this.

'Nicky, with the best will in the world, we're never going to be friends,' she said. 'And you know damn well why.'

Simpson thought about this for a moment and shrugged, giving the impression of a man unbothered by the comment.

'Anyway,' he said, changing the subject back to the original topic, 'he stepped out of line, and when I castigated him for it he took offence, started bad-mouthing me, telling people I was weak. At this point I'm something like twenty-two years old. I'd managed to start the health clubs by then, and the YouTube site was growing slowly. I was straddling both worlds and doing my best, but I was still the new boy in town, and I still wasn't anywhere near Paddy Simpson.'

He chuckled as he idly wiped some dust from a surface.

'Although I like to think I'd slipped past Max Simpson in the rankings.'

'So, what happened?'

He badmouthed me; I kicked off. Simple as that,' Simpson replied matter-of-factly. But at this, Ellie shook her head.

'You've got a woman here who changed her name and joined your company, purely to do something to you – something we still don't know what yet. This isn't simple. This is detailed. You don't do that if your brother just got a beating.'

Simpson nodded, letting out a pent-up breath.

'Earlier on, we talked about how I'm all about stepping back and letting others do my dirty work,' he said.

'I've seen it first-hand,' Ellie replied. 'Or had you forgotten when you had Saleh punch me in the gut in your office back in Vauxhall?'

Simpson nodded, the slightest of smiles on his face.

'No, I remember,' he said. 'Sometimes when I can't sleep,

I think of it to keep me warm at night. But at the same time, it's all about the branding. "Nicky Simpson, YouTuber" has a particular branding that "Nicky Simpson, gang lord" doesn't. And yeah, I don't get my hands dirty. I let Saleh do it, or others. And the reason I do that is because Mark Mullen was the last time I did it myself.'

Ellie paused from replying to this, watching Nicky Simpson as he stared at the wall, seemingly reliving the moment in his head.

'I invited him over to the Red Lion, funnily enough, upstairs – where we're going right now. Dad had it as one of his haunts, Paddy had done the same. The Richardsons had visited it over the time, even the Kray Twins had some kind of peace meeting there. It's got history, you know, most of the pubs in our area have, but this was near Charlie Richardson's scrapyard, so, you know, I was keeping the brand going, keeping the image seen of me on script, so to speak.'

'Go on.'

'Well, Mark turned up full of piss and vinegar, claiming that I had belittled him, that I'd been treating him like shit, when I should be putting him next to the king,' Simpson's voice was more bitter now as he spoke. 'As far as he was concerned, Mark seriously believed he should have been my advisor, my consigliere. When, to be perfectly honest, he wasn't really the advisory type.'

'More a Fredo in *the Godfather?*'

'No, he wasn't Fredo, but he was definitely Sonny.'

Ellie nodded.

'You still haven't told me what you did,' she noted.

'I'm getting to it,' Simpson replied. 'Give me time.'

He sighed again, looking around the room again before

walking over to a corner, where he opened up a drawer, pulling out a wicked-looking blade.

'You know what this is?' he asked, as Ellie watched him carefully.

'A knife?'

'It's more than that.' Simpson was staring at it now, turning it in his hand as the blade glinted in the fluorescent light. 'It's a skinning knife, used by hunters to separate the skin from the meat.'

'And you have this why?'

Simpson looked up at Ellie, his eyes piercing into her.

'Because I used it on him,' he said, simply, his voice emotionless. 'When Mark came into the room, I told him he'd crossed the line and that he needed to apologise and back the hell down.'

'How did he take that?' Ellie asked, eyes glued to the blade in Simpson's hand.

'He'd been with me since we were teenagers, thought he was untouchable, and thought I was joking,' Simpson said, his voice darkening. 'He took the piss and carried on. I remember he brought a couple of friends with him, people who I didn't really know, but I guess they were following him because he'd made out he was the big whatever. And *they* were mocking me.'

His eyes flashed, and Ellie had to force herself from taking an involuntary step back as he continued.

'People I didn't know were standing in my room, laughing at me. *Me*. Nicky Simpson, heir to the empire.'

Ellie watched Simpson, noticing the subtle changes in his positioning and facial structure as his jawline hardened. *This* was the Nicky Simpson she knew, and it reminded her of Johnny and Jackie Lucas, the "twins" of the East End. Johnny

Lucas was amiable. Jackie Lucas was the vicious one, however – the "Ronnie Kray" of the twins, so to speak. But everyone knew that for years, Johnny and Jackie had been the same person, with multiple personality disorder, and the problem had always been that when meeting one of them, you never knew which of the "twins" you'd get.

This wasn't anywhere near that level, but Ellie was seeing the same thing here. Nicky Simpson was a definite Jekyll and Hyde right now.

'What. Did. You. Do?' she repeated, emphasising every word.

'I gave him a Chelsea smile,' Simpson replied. 'He was mouthing off, his friends – these absolute strangers – were laughing at me, and I snapped. I pulled the knife from a table. I don't even know why it was there, and started waving it around, mainly to scare him. The others shut the hell up, but he carried on laughing at me.'

He looked at the floor.

'I told him I was sick of his smile, and that if he kept doing it, I'd make it permanent. He goaded me on, and then the next thing I know, he's on the floor, I'm kneeling over him, his friends are screaming and my bodyguard at the time, Saleh, is pulling me backwards, taking the knife from me, telling me I've got to get out of there.'

'Mark?'

'On the floor, with fresh slashes in his cheeks, where I'd placed the blade in his mouth and hammered it home.'

Ellie nodded, not sure what to say. She understood what a "Chelsea smile" was. Also known as a "Glasgow smile" or a "Cheshire grin," it was a vicious wound caused by making a cut from the corners of a victim's mouth up to the ears, leaving a scar in the shape of a smile. Sometimes the perpetrator would only cut a little into the skin, and then kick the victim between the legs to make them scream, the act itself tearing the skin, and sometimes they'd place the blade between the teeth and hammer onto it, forcing it through the cheeks. It was horrible, and unsurprisingly, something Ellie easily believed Nicky Simpson could do without thinking.

'Is that all you did?' Ellie thought it was definitely enough, but knew the man in front of her.

'No,' Simpson shook his head. 'I pulled away from Saleh. I hadn't finished – and crouching down over Mark, I tore his shirt with the blade and then I carved my initials into his chest, one above the other. I told him that I *owned* him now. He was my property.'

Ellie said nothing. It could have been her imagination, but the lockup seemed to have dropped in temperature since he started.

'Anyway,' Simpson replied quite conversationally, 'I stepped back at that point. His friends pulled him away. He was screaming, his face was torn into shreds, his chest a mass of blood. And I told him if I ever saw him south of the river again, I would carve my entire name into him letter by letter.'

He looked away, sadly, but Ellie couldn't work out if this was regret at the action, sadness at the loss of a friend, or annoyance he wasn't able to finish the job.

'I never saw him again,' he said. 'When I last heard his name, he was in Ireland or somewhere like that about four years back. I don't really know. That's the problem with my life, Reckless. There's a lot of people who come into your life and then disappear. And, it was very much a case of out of sight, out of mind.'

'This man knew you from childhood,' Ellie said, appalled. 'And you cast him aside like that?'

'He was being a prick,' Simpson snapped. 'He deserved what he got. If you badmouth the king, you get a smacking.'

'You're the king now?' Ellie laughed.

'I don't like your tone,' Simpson said icily, and Ellie noticed that the jovial banter of the man who'd been with her for the last day or so had gone. She wondered if this was because it was night-time, or because he was going back to see his father. To be honest, there was a whole load of reasons why this could have happened and she couldn't help herself; she kept pressing to see what happened.

'You're a petulant little boy, Simpson,' she said. 'You had a friend who had your back, and rather than bringing him in, you pushed him aside. Of course he was gonna make out he was bigger than he was. People knew he grew up with you. They expected him to be bigger than he was. And all you did was do terrible things to him. No wonder his sister wanted revenge.'

Surprisingly, Nicky Simpson didn't bite, and instead looked away.

'She was like ten, maybe twelve, when I last saw her,' he said. 'Had completely different hair. She was a gangly kid. How the hell was I supposed to recognise her?'

'But you did, didn't you? There was something ... family resemblance perhaps,' Ellie continued. 'Why did she join the health club? There's a million different ways to hurt you. Why this? And why now?'

'Maybe one of your people will work that one out,' Simpson moved towards the door.

'Stop,' Ellie said, nodding at his rear pocket; absent-mindedly or not, he'd picked up the skinning blade and placed it into his pocket.

'It's the gift for Dad,' he said, holding it up. 'I can wrap it if you want, but it's coming with us.'

Ellie considered this and then nodded.

'Okay,' she said. 'You ready?'

'No,' Nicky Simpson admitted. 'But what choice do I have?'

17

THE DRIVER

RAMSEY HADN'T SEEN THE HOUSE WHERE SALEH LIVED UNTIL they arrived, and the choice words he gave upon seeing it pretty much summed up what Tinker had also felt.

'And are we sure he's in there?' he asked, looking up at the building as Tinker buzzed on the intercom.

'Yeah, but I'm not sure if he knows we're the people outside, as his security doesn't have a camera.'

Ramsey was already looking around.

'Where's the car kept?' he asked, and Tinker nodded down the small side road next to the houses.

'Down there,' she said. 'At least that's where the BMW came out.'

Ramsey nodded, already walking down the pathway.

'Hey,' Tinker ran after him. 'Listen, if you're not up for this—'

'Why wouldn't I be up for this?'

Tinker grabbed Ramsey's arm, pausing him.

'Look,' she said, her tone commanding. 'Ellie, Casey,

Robert, they're all muggles, yeah? Normal people. I'm an ex-soldier. I saw bodies up close. I've been where you are. Literally.'

She let go of the arm as Ramsey tensed.

'Look, all I'm saying is what happened today, if you're having problems, it's not a weakness to ask for help.'

Ramsey nodded.

'This helps,' he said, nodding up the path. 'But if I have any issues, Tinkerbelle, I'll definitely clap my hands and call for you.'

Tinker grinned.

'I'll let you have that one,' she said. 'But that's the last time. And it's Tinker Bell you clap for.'

'Not my fault your parents didn't know how to spell,' Ramsey said as he walked up to a double-width garage door. Kneeling down, he examined it.

'Good,' he said, straightening, and reaching into his jacket pocket, pulling out a small white and orange device.

'What's that?' Tinker frowned as Ramsey turned it on. 'It looks like a Tamagotchi from the nineties that started taking steroids.'

Ramsey looked at the screen, considering the description and nodding.

'Flipper zero,' he said, almost proudly. 'Casey got it for me. Said I was spending too much time doing old school things he could do in seconds. It's a hacking device, and can connect to RFID systems, radio systems, anything that uses a remote clicker, basically.'

He pointed at the garage door.

'Like fancy doors that open electronically.'

'This is the toy he mentioned?' Tinker asked as he started clicking through the buttons.

'Yes,' Ramsey replied. 'I realised recently I'm only as useful as my skillset allows. And thieves these days, they're not old school. So, I adapted.'

'So how does this open the door?' Tinker asked.

'Remember when Casey was brought by Saleh to Simpson? The first time?' Ramsey smiled as he clicked into a subsection on the screen. 'He used it to record the frequency of Saleh's clicker. God knows how, probably thought he'd need it to escape. He actually forgot about this when he passed it over, but I remembered. And I've always wanted to try it.'

He pressed the round button to the right of the screen.

'Open sesame,' he said as the garage door slowly rose, to show a garage, a BMW X5 to the right-hand side. 'And I'll bet you the door into Saleh's house from the garage isn't as secure as the one at the front.'

'Jesus,' Tinker exclaimed as they walked into the garage. 'You're like the king of thieves.'

'I've been telling you this for years,' Ramsey smiled as he closed the garage door behind them. 'Not my fault you don't listen.'

He pointed at the floor beside the BMW, where a small puddle of oil was visible.

'Someone needs to fix their car,' he said.

'I think *that* car's now beyond fixing,' Tinker replied.

Ramsey realised what Tinker was saying and nodded.

Walking up to the side door, Tinker tried it carefully, and found it opened into a kitchen at the back of the house. Motioning for Ramsey to keep behind her, but also to keep quiet, ignoring his mocking expression, she made her way through the kitchen, slowly and carefully entering the living room—

To find herself facing Saleh, gun aimed directly at her.

He was tired-looking and bedraggled. If he'd had hair, it would have been uncombed and unkempt. His eyes had dark circles around them, and he was shaking as he held the weapon.

Tinker, unconcerned, stepped forward.

'You'd better put that gun down unless you want to find yourself eating it,' she said sternly. However, at seeing the two arrivals, Saleh had already lowered the gun.

'I thought you were someone else,' he said.

'Someone come to kill you?' Ramsey asked.

Saleh shrugged.

'It's not been the best of weeks, Allen,' he replied. 'You shouldn't be here.'

'Oh, we're getting that,' Tinker said, as Saleh placed the gun on the coffee table, sitting back down in the chair beside him. 'How about you explain to us what's going on?'

Saleh sighed, picking up the vodka he was drinking, downing it in one hard swallow.

'I'm just having a day off,' he said. 'I'm allowed a sick day. I work long—'

'Bullshit,' Tinker snapped. 'You sent a man out to die earlier on. Do you always do that on days off?'

Saleh's eyes widened slightly, as if this was the first time he'd heard of this, and then he shook his head sadly, watching his two trespassers.

'Who sent you?' he asked.

'Well, weirdly, we work for Nicky at the moment,' Tinker smiled. 'So technically, we're on the same team. I think.'

'Yeah, I wouldn't be so sure about that,' Saleh replied. 'You see, there's a lot of teams out there right now.'

He paled slightly.

'Did Nicky send you to kill me?' It was barely a whisper, not the usual level or arrogant tone Tinker had heard from the man before.

'Do you honestly think we're the kind of people who he'd send to kill you?' Tinker laughed. 'Me and Ramsey?'

'Well, he can break in, as he's proven,' Saleh smiled weakly. 'And we all know how much of a psycho you are, Tinkerbelle.'

Tinker let the announcement of her name slip past; Saleh looked stressed. And there were worse things going on right now from the looks of things.

'Saleh, what's going on?' she asked. 'Who told you to stay home? Was it Max Simpson?'

'Was it Paddy Simpson?' Ramsey added.

Saleh pursed his lips together as he thought of his answer.

'Let's just say I was told not to go in today,' he replied carefully. 'There were problems, and wiser heads in Majorca needed to solve them.'

'What kind of problems?'

Saleh leant back, settling into the chair.

'There's been a decision higher up that Nicky is weak, and now he's been outed, there's talk he isn't useful to the family,' he said. His fists on the arms of the chair were clenching and unclenching unconsciously as he spoke.

'And now it's all gone to shit, and he's standing in the middle,' he finished. 'And if he's called you in to help him, then he's really screwed.'

Tinker smiled.

'How did you know?' she asked. 'About this decision from up high? Or have you been working for Max all along?'

Saleh looked as if he really didn't want to answer this question, and almost rose from his chair, before slumping back.

'Look,' he said. 'I didn't mean to send Martinez to his death, okay?'

'Who was he?'

Saleh looked even more uncomfortable, if such a thing was possible.

'A neighbour. He needed money, I gave him some to be me. Anyway, Nicky sent me a text. It was confrontational.'

'I know,' Tinker said. 'Ellie told him to send it – they wanted to bring you out, because you weren't answering your door.'

'Of course I wasn't answering my door!' Saleh retorted angrily. 'I was under the assumption, thanks to your stupid text, that Nicky probably thought I tried to kill him!'

'You started it by apologising,' Tinker added.

Saleh slumped, nodding.

'He sent me a text asking if I was coming in today,' he replied. 'I wanted to reply and tell him he was in danger, but instead, I sent one word. "Sorry." And then his office blew up.'

'Yeah, that does kinda make you look like a suspect.'

'I thought he was dead. No one saw the body. And then … I don't know, I kind of just went into crisis mode, you know? I locked the doors and hunkered down until everything had passed by.'

Ramsey nodded.

'I get that,' he said. 'The problem is, you're not telling us the full story.'

'Which is?'

'You knew they weren't trying to kill Nicky,' Ramsey

replied. 'You knew Max sent one of his old friends, Lawrence Flanagan, to fake Nicky's death and get him out. So why hide?'

Saleh shook his head.

'I didn't know they were blowing up the office, just that I was told to stay home. I assumed they'd just intercept him, you know? Until … well, the boom.'

'So you thought it'd gone wrong?'

'Yeah. Flanagan never misses.'

'Missed, past tense,' Ramsey replied. 'He was shot by armed police a few hours back.'

Saleh nodded.

'I heard,' he said. 'I didn't know about Martinez, but the shootout in Streatham's on the news.'

Ramsey's face darkened at this.

'It wasn't a shootout,' he said, his eyes narrowing. 'It was an execution.'

Saleh didn't look like he wanted to argue this statement, so Tinker stepped in.

'Why would you be listening to orders from Max Simpson?' she asked. 'After all, Max Simpson stepped down a good nine years ago.'

Saleh looked away again, and his expression told the story more than any words could.

'You were Max Simpson's spy, weren't you?' Ramsey replied. 'You'd been telling him everything that his son had been doing, keeping him informed.'

He moved closer, his eyes widening in shock.

'You were doing to him what I'd been made to do for Nicky!' he exclaimed before adding, 'But I bet *you* weren't being blackmailed.'

Saleh shook his head.

'Paddy and Max brought me into the firm when I was a teenager,' he explained. 'I was in my late twenties when Nicky took over. And it wasn't because of anything major, it was because of Parkinson's hitting Max.'

At this, Saleh leant back, puffing out his cheeks.

'He was just building his reputation, he was a good man,' he carried on. 'I promised I'd keep him and his dad in the loop about what was going on. And, as the years went on, I spent more time talking to Majorca than I did Nicky. They knew everything that was going on.'

'So when Nicky sent you a text saying "I know what you did"—'

'Yeah, I thought he'd found this out,' Saleh nodded. 'I thought he was angry I was dealing with his family. So I sent Max a message saying "look, I need to get out of here, Nicky's coming for me." So, Max gave me an address.'

'Max gave you the address to go to?'

'Yes – why?'

Ramsey looked at Tinker.

'The reason someone died in that car wasn't because Lawrence Flanagan blew them up, it was because another assassin was waiting in Kennington,' he said. 'Max sent you there to die. You sent a double out and it was possibly the only thing that saved your life.'

Saleh frowned.

'Why are you talking about Kennington?' he asked. 'Max told me to go to an address near Waterloo.'

Ramsey paused.

'The message sent while your double was in the car,' he said. 'Someone sent one to both of them.'

'Where's your phone?' Tinker asked.

'If you're right and there was a bomb, it'll be in a million pieces, as I sent it with Martinez,' Saleh said. 'I know, I shouldn't have, especially with the messages and photos I had on it. But if you're looking for the texts, it'll be on my iPad, too.'

Picking the tablet up from the coffee table, he brought up the "messages" application.

'Here,' he said, showing the message.

Ramsey read it.

> Go to Donny's under Waterloo bridge. He'll brief you until we sort this.

'Not the same story as Flanagan said,' Ramsey frowned. 'What do those three dots mean?'

'It's syncing,' Tinker replied, leaning closer. 'Pulling from the carrier anything missed while the iPad was offline.'

After a moment, a second message appeared.

> Change of plans. Map attached – go there instead. G-S-D.

Opening the map attached, Ramsey nodded as the location of an all-too-familiar Kennington bridge now appeared.

'Martinez was diverted,' he said. 'Flanagan said the GSD was Max Simpson's code.'

'This was the third text,' she replied.

'I don't get why he'd want me there,' Saleh frowned, confused.

'Because he wanted you there as bait,' Tinker said sadly. 'He wanted Nicky beside you as he died.'

'No, that can't be right, Max would never put a hit on his own son—' Saleh started, but then stopped as some unspoken thought came to him.

'What?' Ramsey insisted.

'He was unhappy with what Nicky was doing, and Paddy was arguing with him,' Saleh said softly, all attempts at caution now gone. 'Max always felt Paddy had overstepped when he put Nicky in, especially as Nicky wasn't supposed to be the one.'

At this, Tinker held up a hand.

'What do you mean?'

Saleh paused, his eyes widening, swallowing, opening and shutting his mouth a couple of times, in realisation he'd given away something he really shouldn't have.

'I spoke out of turn. I meant that Max felt he—'

'Don't lie to me, Saleh.'

Sighing, Saleh took the bottle of vodka, poured a generous measure into a glass and downed it in one.

'Max found out he had Parkinson's,' he said. 'He knew he couldn't last long in this business. He was making mistakes. People could see the shakes. And that was weakness.'

He went to pour another, but thought better of it.

'So, he decided he was going to pass it on to his son – but not Nicky.'

'Nicky Simpson is Max Simpson's only child, though?' Ramsey was confused at the statement.

'Legally, yes, but he's not his only child,' Saleh explained. 'Max, how we say, played away. He had a mistress he'd had a couple of kids with ...'

He trailed off, aware he was treading into dangerous territory.

'You're talking about Mark Mullen, aren't you?' Ramsey shook his head. 'The kid who hung around Nicky Simpson, who thought he was bigger than Nicky Simpson. He knew, didn't he?'

'He knew that his dad was Max Simpson,' Saleh confirmed. 'Max loved him more than his own son because Paddy was doting over *his* own son. Max didn't have a chance with Nicky. Anytime he tried to get close, or suggest something, Paddy would be there. And, the moment Max had his diagnosis, Paddy moved in straight away.'

'He put Nicky in place before Max could recognise Mark?'

'Teenage Nicky was the new heir no matter what was being said, because teenage Nicky was a legitimate Simpson,' Saleh nodded. 'It didn't matter that Mark was Max's flesh and blood.'

'What about Carrie?' Tinker asked. 'Was she Max's daughter?'

Saleh nodded without answering.

'Did Max know you sent a double out?'

Saleh shook his head.

'Then shit,' Tinker whispered, 'I think Max sent you to die, thinking you might have Nicky with you.'

'Max sent Flanagan not to kill him.'

'Not quite,' Tinker said. 'Flanagan was sent to fake Nicky's death. Get Nicky out. Take him somewhere quiet. Where Max could do, well, whatever the hell he wanted to do.'

Saleh continued to shake his head.

'Bullshit,' he said. 'Max is solid.'

'And Nicky? The guy you've been the right-hand man for?'

Saleh's face didn't visibly change, but there were minuscule movements, that tightened it.

'He had his chance,' Saleh said. 'Now it's time for someone new.'

'New like Mark Mullen?'

Saleh laughed.

'No, definitely not Mark,' he replied.

'Then who?' Ramsey insisted.

And, with Tinker and Ramsey leaning in closer, standing in his living room, Saleh told them.

18

MEET THE NEW BOSS

ELLIE STARED UP AT THE RED-AND-WHITE-BRICKED CORNER building across the street from the comfort of her car. It had started to rain, and for the moment she was happy to sit in the dry, waiting for the right moment. It'd gone past six now, and soon they'd need to work out plans for the night. Casey had already returned home to work; the last thing Ellie needed was for him to be grounded right now.

'Is there a reason we're waiting?' Nicky Simpson asked from the seat beside her.

'I'm planning,' she replied, eventually nodding to herself. 'And I've made a decision.'

Simpson didn't reply to this, obviously waiting for the decision.

'You're staying here,' Ellie smiled, opening the door and half-climbing out into the rain. 'Far safer until I know what's going on.'

'What's going on, is you're allowing me to die in your crappy car,' Simpson muttered. 'What's going on is my dad's up there and he can save me.'

'Or he's trying to kill you,' Ellie waggled her hand as she replied. 'Stay until I check it out. Try not to die.'

As Nicky Simpson glared at her, Ellie closed the door and started across the street towards the Red Lion.

Entering, she ignored the patrons of the pub, and headed towards the back, where the stairs to the upstairs function room were. The pub itself was pretty standard, with a burgundy carpet leading to extensive wooden panelling beneath leaded windows.

'We're closed—' the barman started, but Ellie raised a hand to stop him, a single finger in the air.

'Do I look like I don't know where I'm going?' she asked.

The barman considered the question and then returned to pouring the drink he'd paused as Ellie started up the stairs.

Upstairs, the wallpaper changed to a lighter colour as Ellie continued into the upstairs function room. In it, sitting at a table at the end of the bar, a young woman serving, was a man in his fifties, his gunmetal-grey curly hair showing peppers of white throughout it, sipping a pint of lager with a slightly shaking hand. And, beside him were two large men, watching Ellie with interest.

As she walked further in, she saw four more men rise from their seated positions behind her, walking forward, effectively surrounding her.

'You must be Max,' she said with a mock confidence she really didn't feel. 'Nice place. Thought you'd have more of a tan, though.'

'You must be Reckless,' Max replied, a visible twitch of his head bobbing it as his words slightly slurred. 'By name and nature, it seems.'

'I dunno, I think I'm on safe ground here,' Ellie smiled.

At this, Max placed the pint back onto the table and

waved a hand. Instantly, every other man in the room pulled out a gun, aiming it at Ellie's head.

'Want to think that over?' he asked mockingly.

Ellie did a slow circle, checking each of the gunmen in turn.

'No, I'm good,' she said, the smile returning. 'You see, if you know me, you know what I do. I gain favours from criminals. People who need my help, and then agree to give me whatever I want, when I want it.'

She looked back at the man at the table.

'And they will,' she continued. 'Because they all know if they refuse, I'll use a boatload of other favours to destroy them.'

'And why do I care?'

'Because three people in this room owe me favours,' Ellie shrugged. 'And if I say so, they'll turn these guns onto you.'

The room was silent for a moment as the gunmen all looked at each other, weighing up who owed Ellie, and why.

At the table, Max chuckled.

'Okay,' he said, waving his hand again, something that looked harder than it was to do as the gunmen lowered their weapons. 'Where's my son?'

Ellie's mouth shrugged.

'Nearby,' she said. 'I thought I'd check the layout first. After all, you tried to blow him up.'

'You know that's a lie,' Max smiled.

'So Flanagan said, but we'll never know,' Ellie replied, watching Max carefully. 'You did know he's dead, right?'

'I did,' Max nodded, but there was something off with the answer. Ellie went to continue, but stopped as her phone buzzed.

'Hold that thought,' she said, checking the phone. It was a message from Ramsey, and it was eye opening.

Nodding to herself, she looked back at Max.

'You know, I'd have expected more from you,' she said, walking towards the table now. 'I mean, Lawrence Flanagan was your carer for what, ten years? And you just shrug off his death?'

She turned to face the others.

'Imagine how he'll weep when you're all gone.'

'You should be careful who you speak to,' Max was getting angry now, and Ellie turned back to stare at him.

'Why?' she asked innocently. 'I mean, come on, your son's the power in London now, not Max Simpson. He stopped being important about a decade back.'

She threw a hand up to stop Max from replying.

'And before you start your inevitable reply, I just want to explain something.'

'Go on,' Max raised his eyebrows at this response.

Ellie waved around the room.

'All this, it's branding,' she said. 'As bad as Nicky bloody Simpson is at it, too. You, meeting here. With the history behind it, it makes people almost believe.'

'Believe what?'

'That you're Max Simpson,' a fresh voice spoke, and Ellie spun to see Nicky Simpson standing in the doorway to the function room.

'Sorry,' he apologised. 'I got bored, and didn't hear shooting.'

Ellie shrugged, looking back at the older man behind the table.

'It was pretty obvious, to be honest,' she said. 'You're doing your best to fake Parkinson's, but only someone with it can really do it justice. You're just not a good enough actor. That and the lack of a tan.'

The now-outed-as-fake Max glared across the room at them.

'So what do you want?' he asked. 'Mercy?'

'What I'd like you to do is tell me exactly what your plan is here,' Simpson snapped. 'Because right now you're just pissing me off.'

Fake Max smiled, leaning back in his chair.

'You're right. I'm not your dad,' he said. 'But you got to admit, I'm bloody close. Acting aside, I'm almost a double.'

'My dad's still in Majorca, isn't he?'

'As far as I know, he's sitting in a room staring out across the sea, taking as many CBD gummies as he can eat in a handful,' fake Max nodded. 'He's having a good life. You should give him a call sometime. It's been how many years now?'

'What happens between me and my father has nothing to do with you,' Simpson replied. 'What I'd like to know, as I already said, is what the hell's going on here!'

'It's a takeover,' Ellie replied, looking back at him. 'How'd you not realise that?'

'I understand what a takeover looks like, Reckless,' Simpson replied, looking back at fake Max. 'What I'd like to know is who set it up—'

At this point, Ellie simply nodded to the bar, where the woman behind it had been looking away from the action, almost as if by averting her gaze, she wouldn't be associated with it, before she turned back to face them.

'I think this explains it,' Ellie said, as Nicky Simpson looked across to see Carrie Mullen. Or rather, "Carrie Holden," his current receptionist.

'You!' he exclaimed.

Carrie, now exposed, left the bar area and walked over to where fake Max still sat.

'Nicky, I'd like you to meet your half-sister,' Ellie waved her hand over at Carrie.

'My what?'

Ellie nodded.

'It's why Mark always felt he was better than you,' Ellie replied, looking back. 'The text message I just had was Ramsey – he'd just had confirmation of this. Isn't that right, Carrie?'

Carrie, in response, glared furiously at Simpson for a long moment before eventually replying.

'Your dad loved my mum more than he loved yours,' she said. 'He always told us he wanted to leave her, but couldn't because of your family's honour and the arranged marriage he had, all arranged by your granddad.'

Simpson stared, still unable to understand what was going on.

'Mark was my half-brother,' he whispered, more a statement of fact than a question.

'Yeah. And you never wondered, never questioned why Dad was so supportive of him growing up, did you?' Carrie sneered. 'You had the chance to do so many things together. He could have worked with you. You would have been unstoppable.'

Simpson looked back at Ellie.

'You've just found this out? Or you knew this for a while?' he asked. 'Is this one of your sick tricks to get back at me for everything I did?'

Sadly, Ellie shook her head.

'I only found out when Ramsey texted,' she said.

'Although we did have suspicions. Your father wasn't exactly an angel after all, shall we say?'

She looked back at Carrie now.

'And once we realised that she was using a fake name, and that Mark had been spending a lot of time with your family, it made sense. Although keeping the first name was a bold statement.'

'Who told you?' Carrie asked. 'The confirmation Mister Allen sent?'

'Well, first off, that right there was how we worked you out,' Ellie said. 'He never gave his surname to you in Nine Elms.'

'Yeah, I realised that as I left,' Carrie shrugged. 'Assumed he'd be too senile to guess it, to be frank.'

Ellie looked back at Nicky Simpson, watching her emotionlessly. It was a little unnerving, if she admitted it, as for someone to realise they had a secret family, usually there'd be some kind of reaction.

'Saleh knew about it,' she admitted. 'But then he'd been beside Max for a lot of the time that Mark had. He'd have been told, or he'd have worked it out himself.'

'So what, Mark's going to be the new boss of the Simpson empire, is he?' Simpson asked, looking around the room. 'Are we changing the name to Mullen? And are all of you gonna follow him in the same way you followed this imposter five minutes ago?'

There was a genuine uncertainty in the room now, as many of the men there hadn't realised the Max who had been speaking to them hadn't been the real life Max.

Carrie, however, stepped forward.

'My brother's dead,' she said. 'You killed him.'

'No,' Simpson replied now, pulling out the skinning knife,

holding it up like a trophy. 'I think you'll find all I did was carve my name into his chest.'

'No, you carved your initials.' Carrie pulled out a piece of paper. Looking across the room Ellie realised it was an A4 sheet of paper, and on the other side was a printed photo.

She turned it to show Simpson; it was a photo of a man's torso, with words etched into it, the blood flowing from most of them. And, visible to all were two words.

'You didn't finish your name when you did the job,' Carrie explained, tossing it to the floor in front of Nicky Simpson. 'So my brother continued. It became his mantra for the next few years. "*Never Submit*." Never to submit to what you did to him.'

'I didn't mean—'

'He was ostracised, you know. Alone. He didn't realise the power that a man like this could have; scars on his cheeks, letters etched into his chest – they show you've gone through something. Forged yourself in fire.'

Carrie spat to the side.

'He could have been stronger, but he was weak. It made him the man cuckolded by Nicky Simpson. Made into his *bitch*.'

'How did he die?' Simpson asked, still with no emotion in his voice.

'Threw himself off a train bridge three years ago,' Carrie said. 'Funny enough, that was the same moment I decided you had to die. I mean, I didn't like you beforehand, and what you did to my brother? That was arguably worth a battering.'

She looked away; her gaze unfocussing, almost as if she was staring back through time, back at her brother.

'But when Mark died, I knew you were the face he saw before he died—'

'You can't know that!'

'I can!' Carrie almost screamed. 'He told me! You were constantly in his head!'

Gathering her composure, she took a deep breath, letting it go.

'I knew I had to end you,' she continued, far calmer now, matching Simpson for an emotionless state. 'I knew right then that Nicky Simpson, gangland boss, had to die.'

'And of course my dad signed off on this.'

'Oh no,' Carrie smiled darkly, patting fake Max on the shoulder. 'As my friend here said, your dad's been living in his own little bubble for the last ten years. This was all agreed by your dear loving granddad.'

It was almost as if someone opened a window; the temperature in the room dropped by a few degrees, as Ellie turned back to Carrie at this point.

'You're sanctioned by Paddy Simpson?'

'Oh yes,' Carrie smiled, turning from Ellie to Simpson now. 'He's my granddad as much as yours, Nicky. And for years, you were his favourite. Granddad thought you were the best, God knows why. He told my dad that you should be the heir apparent when Parkinson's meant he couldn't work any further. Even though Dad wanted to acknowledge Mark as his son.'

She walked towards Simpson, only a couple of steps, before stopping.

'On paper, Mark was the obvious choice,' she continued. 'He was stronger than you. He was cleverer than you. More liked than you, too, but you were the legitimate Simpson. And Dad couldn't turn around and give it to Mark because he was a Mullen.'

She shook her head sadly.

'Granddad believed at the time you were the future. He thought Mark would work better under your wing, with the two of you eventually becoming a partnership. But Mark, he had issues—'

'You're telling me,' Simpson snapped back. 'He thought he could overtake me; he thought he was better than me.'

'He was better than you!' Carrie screamed back. 'In every way! But when you did what you did to him, it changed him, made him darker – and not in a good way. He wasn't violent to other people, but instead he was violent to himself. And when he died, he was a shadow of the man he was.'

Reaching behind, grabbing something tucked into her belt, she pulled out a pistol, aiming it at Simpson.

'You did this to him, Simpson,' she snarled. 'And I swore right then I would make you a shadow of the man you were!'

'And that's what this is?' Ellie asked. 'All of this?'

'When you were outed,' Carrie continued, 'your grandfather was unhappy. He was a crime lord. He wasn't scared of the press. But you backed away, sent out injunctions. You didn't take it on the chin and acknowledge who you were, you didn't lean into it. You were scared of being announced as being a bad guy in case it hurt your shitty YouTuber brand.'

'And how do you know he was unhappy?'

'Because I went to speak to him,' Carrie's hand was still,

the trigger finger twitching, and Ellie knew she was fighting every instinct she had to not shoot Nicky Simpson in the face right now. 'We'd been talking for years at this point, ever since my other granddad died. He'd even attended Mark's funeral, and you didn't even know he was in the country. Came in under Max's passport, so the police didn't know.'

She straightened, puffing out her chest unconsciously as she continued.

'And he'd realised during the time I was as worthy an heir as you were.'

'And so you convinced him to back your play?' Ellie asked.

'It wasn't difficult after all,' Carrie switched her gaze from Simpson to Ellie, and then back again. 'You've opened yourself up. And then Granddad taught me the secrets about you. How Nicky Simpson, gangland lord, is more of a lie than Nicky Simpson, YouTuber, a puppet for whatever Paddy Simpson wanted to do. He could sit in Majorca and tell you to do things through Saleh, and you'd do them.'

She gave a look of mock surprise.

'Oh, didn't I mention? Saleh works for me, now, technically. I mean, he's always worked for Majorca, for Paddy. Even when doing your laundry.'

'Yeah, you might want to check that,' Ellie muttered.

However, Carrie didn't pay attention to this, the gun still aimed at Nicky Simpson's face.

'And you, dear half-brother? You're going to join my actual brother in the afterlife.'

19

HUNT THE COPPER

CASEY'S MUM HADN'T BEEN HAPPY HE STILL HAD "WORK" TO DO when he got home; she felt the internship he was working through at Finders should have finished months earlier, but at the same time it kept him off the streets, or worse, still, hacking things he shouldn't be. And Robert Lewis, the solicitor who'd employed him, had promised on his word that, during his time with them, he'd not be allowed unmonitored access to any computer network.

Luckily, Casey thought as he turned his main desktop on, *he'd probably crossed his fingers when he promised that, because it's been all I've done since, and they never told her who I'd be working for.*

Sitting in his gamer's chair, he flexed his fingers, linking his hands together and pushing outwards, as he considered his next move.

He didn't need to worry about the hit on Nicky; he knew that would be sorted by the others. And, secretly, he didn't want to be involved in the removal, as he wanted more than anything for Nicky Simpson to be taken out.

After all, that meant someone else would make two million dollars.

Sure, Nicky would be dead, and Ellie wouldn't get closure, but once Nicky was dead, Casey was pretty sure all the secrets would spill out anyway. And even though Nicky had done his best to be nice, all that comics and superhero bollocks in the boxing club had shown him to be a fraud again.

Nicky dying, as far as Casey was concerned, was a win-win situation.

No, Casey wanted to do something more down his street; he wanted to know who owned the phone that sent the messages, and also who was currently taking over the chain of Simpson's Health Spas – mainly because he wanted to shake their hand.

There was also the case of the car Lawrence Flanagan had been driving while in the UK. They'd found, after checking the plates, that it'd been owned by a company in Ireland called Ferdia Holdings, and had been picked up in Gatwick when Flanagan had landed from Majorca. And, with this in mind, Casey had started to drill in on the company.

Ferdia Holdings was an interesting name; he didn't know if it was Italian or maybe something else from Europe. There was a moment, before he started searching where he wondered whether this was Italian, and perhaps that the remaining Lumetta family members had found a way to get their own back on the man who had screwed them over. But, as he continued on, he started finding more.

Ferdia Holdings didn't have a web presence, and seemed to be nothing more than a shell company, which made sense for the type of person they allowed to drive their cars.

He'd found digital paperwork, however, that showed the company had been registered in the Republic of Ireland, with a Dundalk head office. But when he looked on Google Street View to look at the address, the building it showed him – the correct one for the address given on the register – was actually a tiny, weather-beaten, two-door warehouse, which, when he checked further into it, had at least half a dozen different companies, all with different directors based there – which meant it was likely some kind of post-box company house.

This was quite common in the UK, as people creating companies often wanted a desirable postcode, but Casey didn't know if the same was to be said about Dundalk. What was interesting, though, was the searches that came up with "Ferdia" and "Dundalk." Casey had assumed he'd find at the very least some information on the company on some trade site. Instead, he was led to an Irish history page that talked about the hero, Cú Chulainn.

Casey felt a shiver of cold slide down his back as he looked at the name, remembering something Nicky Simpson had said about his grandfather, back in the lockup.

'He always claimed Ireland, and Dundalk, was a spiritual home, especially as Cú Chulainn came from there. He was some kind of mighty hero or something from legend, but I thought it was all fairy stories for kids, so I never bothered looking into it. But this legendary hero had been betrayed by his best friend in the stories, and Granddad had always likened his betrayal to that. I wanted to get back into Ireland, start building places in Dublin, just to show Granddad we could return and make money from it.'

According to the websites showing up because of the search, the name of the friend that had betrayed Cú Chulainn had been named Ferdia.

'There has to be something there,' he muttered to himself as he kept typing, hunting through site after site, looking for something to link to this. He started searching back into Paddy Simpson's history; after all, eighty or so years earlier, he'd been born in Dundalk. Ferdia, according to the legends was Cú Chulainn's best friend who, in their final battle, had sided with the enemy and faced Cú Chulainn across a stream, now known as Ferdia's Ford on the River Dee, a few miles southwest of Dundalk, in Arden. There was even a statue of Cú Chulainn the victor, holding Ferdia in his arms.

There was something about this that drew Casey back. Nicky Simpson had said his grandfather had left Ireland when the boss of their group had screwed him over, someone he'd believed was his best friend.

Was Ferdia Holdings connected to Paddy Simpson? Was this the name of the company he set up there? Or was it a message for Paddy?

Casey noted this down; it was incredibly possible the so-called friend had accepted the role of traitor, especially if he lost everything when the Good Friday Agreement came into force at the turn of the millennium, while Paddy Simpson ruled half of London.

He drilled deeper still, and then leant back in his chair as he struck gold. Ferdia Holdings had a personal interest in destroying the Simpsons – but they were doing it legally. It was visible to see if you had the right brokerage software, and Casey had enough fake accounts to gain one.

A small percentage of shares, freely available in Simpson's Health Spas, had been, over the last year, slowly acquired by subsidiaries of Ferdia Holdings. In fact, as of this moment, they owned fifty-three and a half percent of the stock, which made them the controlling shareholder.

That was why they could freeze Nicky out. Even with his father's shares, he—

Casey stopped.

Max Simpson wasn't a holder of the shares anymore. He'd sold twenty-five percent to Ferdia Holdings three days ago; the same day Lawrence Flanagan had travelled from Majorca to London.

Casey settled back in his games chair as he pondered what he'd found here. Whoever owned Ferdia Holdings had provided a car for Lawrence Flanagan to drive to London in and had effectively bought out Nicky Simpson from his own million-pound business.

Finally, he had a thread to pull, and started following the data from the shares. He knew Ferdia Holdings had been created in the late fifties, and even with this, he still couldn't find anything. It was almost as if someone better than him had scrubbed the internet from anything that could give away the name.

But Casey was better still, and found a scan of an image, an old carbon-copy of a signed agreement on the day Ferdia Holdings was created. Two signatures; the first was illegible on the paper, and the second signature was just as bad, the paper being decades old when scanned, but he could make out the surname, just.

It was Mullen.

'Now you are too much of a coincidence to be anything more,' Casey smiled, leaning closer, flexing his fingers again. 'Especially now we know Carrie Mullen is technically a Simpson.'

'Did you call?' his mother shouted from the next room.

'No, I'm just talking to myself,' Casey yelled back.

'Well, tell yourself to go to bed,' his mother called back out. 'It's late and you've got school tomorrow.'

'It's still a strike day.'

'It might have changed. Bed. Now.'

Casey sighed. He'd faced down some of the biggest criminals in London, but his mother still defeated them all.

He went to turn off the monitor, but paused as he noticed an email.

'I'll stop in five minutes, I promise,' he said as he started reading it, his eyes widening.

Davey had sent him an email with the data she'd found on Seth Taylor's phone, including messages from the same burner phone that had contacted so many other people today.

> Flanagan left before I could stop him. Will sort him later.

> Not to worry, I'll sort it out

Casey stared at the message, frowning. Whoever was making these calls and sending messages was the true organiser here. He needed the calls and messages from this burner phone immediately.

The question was ... how?

ROBERT WAS IN HIS OFFICE WHEN DI MARK WHITEHOUSE appeared in his doorway.

'Bloody hell, you look like the ghost of Christmas future,' he said, leaning back in his chair. Millie, laying in her bed in the corner of the room, looked up, gave the briefest of wags, and then went back to sleep.

'It's been a long day,' Whitehouse said as he slumped into

the chair facing Robert. 'Although I reckon it's been the same for you.'

He looked around.

'Ellie about?'

'Babysitting duties,' Robert replied, closing his laptop. 'Which, as you can guess, she's loving.'

Whitehouse chuckled at this.

'I couldn't believe it when she told me,' he said. 'I mean, come on, we were both there throughout the case. And now they're best mates? Insanity.'

'I wouldn't call them that,' Robert argued. 'It's more a case of he's giving her an option she never expected.'

'Yeah, she told me earlier,' Whitehouse nodded. 'But they're not going to allow her back in, Robert. No matter what happens, you know that as well as I do.'

He looked down at Millie snoring lightly on the bed.

'She was talking about going to Ireland, joining the bloody Garda,' he muttered. 'She'd be homesick in a week. Best she gain closure and move on. Also, these bloody favours could stop, too.'

'I think she likes them, if I'm being honest,' Robert replied. 'Even if she got everything she wanted, she'd still keep on. It's an addiction.'

'Yeah, she always did have an addictive personality,' Whitehouse sighed. 'One that's going to get her killed.'

Robert considered the comment and then nodded, rising from the chair.

'I need to walk Millie,' he said. 'Care to take a stroll?'

His eyes narrowing, Whitehouse stood, nodding.

'Sure,' he said. 'But you can pick up the dogshit.'

THEY'D ONLY WALKED A FEW FEET FROM THE BUILDING BEFORE DI Whitehouse spoke.

'So what's so secret you couldn't talk about it up there?' he asked. 'And don't give me any crap about Millie being desperate. She was asleep.'

Robert nodded.

'I felt bad about bringing it up in such a formal setting,' he replied. 'I thought a walk on a pleasant night might be more, well, candid.'

'Christ, is this about Delgado again?' Whitehouse stopped. 'Robert, please. I hoped you, of all people, would be the rational one.'

'Oh, I am,' Robert nodded again, distracted by Millie as she sniffed the base of a wall. 'But I'm looking into the text messages sent earlier today.'

'That's police work,' Whitehouse replied. 'That's my work.'

'So work with me,' Robert suggested as they walked. 'Look, DC Davey has been working with the coroner—'

'She's been what?'

'It's all legitimate and signed off, so get off your high horse,' Robert smiled. 'You turned a blind eye to Rajesh when he did it.'

'That's because Raj was paying off a debt he believed he owed,' Whitehouse shook his head. 'And he's a serving copper.'

'So's Davey,' Robert snapped, before adding a reluctant, 'well, currently, anyway.'

'I'm guessing she found something, then?'

'Someone sent texts, planning this out,' Robert nodded. 'Someone who's a player here, and currently under the radar.'

Whitehouse was standing in the street now, a narrow side street that was more one of the ancient pathways of London's City than a full-on road.

'We shouldn't be here,' looking around. 'It's exposed. You're playing silly buggers with assassins and dragging me into it?'

'Mark, there's three texts and two calls sent from this phone,' Robert faced him now. 'Texts to Flanagan and Saleh, telling them to meet at a location, while Seth the assassin waited for them. It was a setup and the person with this phone did it. And then—'

'I know, I know,' Whitehouse held up a hand. 'And then they called the armed police, telling them where to find Flanagan, probably knowing he'd end up committing suicide by copper. But that doesn't mean it's Kate.'

'It had a police code,' Robert argued. 'And the phone was in Vauxhall when the call was made, and in Nine Elms when the texts were made.'

'Rough estimates based on cell towers,' Whitehouse said. 'You can't pinpoint a floor or an office. There were dozens of South London coppers at Battersea this morning! Half of them came from my Unit! Any of them could have done it.'

'But only one of them is the god-daughter of Ricky Smith.' Robert pulled out a poo bag, cleaning up after Millie, placing it into a large bin.

'No,' Whitehouse was commanding as he shook his head. 'I'm not having this conversation. You're not going to say my DS is crooked simply because they made a criminal a god-father when she was a bloody baby. If you're basing suspects on past criminal connections, you're bringing in half the sodding force! Including Ellie! Or had you forgotten she came across from Mile End under a DCI known for taking bribes from the Lucas Twins, who was a member of a Glaswegian gang as a teenager?'

'And yet you worked with her.'

'Of course I worked with her! I trusted her with my life! And now I trust Kate with it. You have to, because if you don't, it all falls apart!'

'I have a theory,' Robert said. 'Whoever it was, Delgado, an officer, even you, whoever sent the texts? They had a plan, and it went wrong.'

'How so?'

'They texted Saleh, telling him to go somewhere, but then sent a second message a short while later, changing the meeting to Kennington, before aiming Flanagan there, too,' Robert explained as they continued on. 'I think the plan was to get Flanagan, Saleh and Nicky together by the car, and then for Seth to detonate a device. I think the whole office explosion earlier was to throw guilt onto Flanagan, and when all three were found dead, it'd land on his shoulders.'

'I could see that,' Whitehouse conceded. 'So what went wrong?'

'Saleh sent a double,' Robert shrugged. 'Flanagan saw this, left the scene. Seth, left with one option, decides to change the plan. He texts the burner again, telling them he'll sort Flanagan later. They text back, not to worry, saying *they'll* sort it out.'

'And you know this because Davey's read Seth's texts from the retrieved phone,' Whitehouse nodded. 'Okay, I see that. And our mysterious caller then contacts SCO19 because they know Flanagan's off to a cemetery? How do they know that?'

Robert took a long breath, looking up at the night sky.

'Because Ellie told you, Mark,' he said sadly. 'When she told you Ramsey was checking if someone was dead.'

Whitehouse stared opened mouthed at Robert.

'You think *I* did this?' he whispered. 'Robert, I was the only bloody copper who stood by her through the case! I was the only one who fought to reinstate her!'

'We have more,' Robert continued. 'The phone, the burner? We found the shop it was sold in. We have the time and date on record. It's a five-minute walk from your police unit.'

'Anyone could have done this!' Whitehouse argued, but then stopped.

'Shit,' he muttered, turning away, walking to the side of the road as he spoke. 'I told Kate. About the conversation.'

'She knew Ramsey was at the cemetery?'

'No, well, I said what Ellie said,' Whitehouse leant against the wall now, banging the back of his head against it. 'Bloody fool! How could I be so stupid?'

Robert allowed the moment to pass before continuing.

'It wasn't Kate, Mark,' he said. 'It was you.'

Whitehouse locked eyes with Robert now, staring at him across the street.

'What—'

'We have CCTV from the shop,' Robert explained. 'It shows you buying the phone. They were told to delete it – told by you – but the waste bin on the desktop still had it inside.'

Whitehouse still stared at Robert.

'Why?' Robert asked. 'You're a good copper. As you said, you were the only one siding with Ellie. Why did you do this?'

Whitehouse went to reply, stopped himself and then slumped against the wall.

'I didn't work for Nicky Simpson,' he said. 'I never worked for Nicky Simpson. I swear.'

'Then why this today?'

Whitehouse looked up and down the road, as if expecting police cars to appear.

'My dad,' he eventually replied. 'He was on the take. Paddy Simpson. Not much, but enough to look the other way. I was furious when I found out, I'd only just made DC, but by then Paddy was gone, and everything was fine. But then a few years back, around the time DCI Monroe and Ellie arrived from Mile End, Paddy got in contact.'

'Paddy? Not Max?'

Whitehouse shook his head.

'It was the granddad,' he replied. 'He had papers, proof Dad was corrupt. He was retired now, but he had a police pension. These papers would have sent him straight to prison, don't pass go, don't collect two hundred pounds. So, I started to work for Paddy. And all it consisted of was spying on Nicky. That was it. I swear.'

'Okay, so when did it progress to whatever the hell today was?'

'Bryan Noyce,' Whitehouse slid down the wall, now crouching against it. 'He found discrepancies in the accounts. But rather than going to Max or Paddy, he went to the police. I was told to keep an eye on it, so I volunteered me and Ellie to be the liaisons. And, as Bryan told us things, I passed them on.'

'Were you involved in the death of Bryan Noyce?' Robert asked carefully.

With tears down his face, DI Mark Whitehouse nodded.

'Paddy needed him removed, as Noyce was about to bring

everything down,' he said. 'I was told to let someone know where Noyce would be, and they'd sort it. That's all I did.'

'And who was the someone?'

A delay.

A sniffle.

'Saleh Hussain,' Whitehouse admitted. 'I didn't know they'd kill him, I swear. I thought it was just a smack. And he'd been a prick to Ellie, and I was annoyed.'

'You knew they'd broken up?'

'No,' Whitehouse looked mortified. 'That happened after I gave the information. But when they found the body, I panicked. Ellie had come in with blood on her clothes, from the fight, and I ... I suggested, through a third person, to Rajesh that he should check our clothing too, to remove us from any evidence contamination.'

'Because you knew he'd find the blood, if he did,' Robert's face darkened. 'You son of a bitch, Mark.'

'I know!' Whitehouse pleaded. 'That's why I tried to help clear her! I'd muddied the waters, that was enough. I didn't mean to destroy her career!'

'And was Kate involved at all?'

'No!' Whitehouse exclaimed, before looking around the street. 'You knew all this, didn't you? That's why you wanted a candid conversation.'

'I suspected,' Robert admitted. 'But I'm not a police officer, Mark. You need to tell Ellie this. You need to tell her everything. How Paddy Simpson set up the murder, and how you set up today's attacks.'

He pulled on the lead, stopping Millie from sniffing something rotting in the corner of a trash bin.

'I'll give you until tomorrow morning to make this right,' he said. 'After that? It's on you.'

Whitehouse frowned, his eyes darting around.

'And if I don't?'

Robert pulled out his phone.

'I've recorded the whole thing,' he said. 'Twelve hours, Mark.'

And, this deadline given, Robert shook his head sadly.

'There was no CCTV, by the way, they really did delete it, and wouldn't tell us anything,' he continued. 'I bluffed you. I was confirming a theory.'

'What theory?'

'Ramsey said when he mentioned the conversation you had with Ellie, Delgado was shocked at you, and you said you'd talk later, but this was after Flanagan was killed. There's no way she could have done it.'

He frowned.

'You're not a killer, Mark. I've known you too long to think such a thing. That's why I didn't want to do this inside, I wanted you to feel safe to tell me the truth. Why did you call the club?'

'To let Carrie know Flanagan was there, so she could get him to the stairs,' Whitehouse sighed. 'He really did think he was helping.'

'Make this right, Mark,' Robert said. 'And tell her in person. You owe her that much, at least—'

Robert hadn't seen the extendable baton in Whitehouse's hand, but he felt it as Whitehouse lunged forwards, swinging hard, connecting with the side of Robert's head, sending him to the floor.

'Bastard!' Whitehouse yelled, swinging down with it again, before looking around the street for something bigger. 'Why couldn't you just leave it alone? I thought you'd want him dead!'

Walking over to the trash bin, he picked up a discarded piece of metal. It looked like it was the base of some long-broken light, but it was thicker and heavier than the baton, more a length of vicious-looking metal piping.

'I was doing this for her! Getting rid of Simpson so she could move on!' Whitehouse said, standing over Robert. 'Goddamn you!'

Bleeding badly from a cut on his head, Robert weakly raised a hand to stop him while Millie started barking.

But Whitehouse didn't stop. He brought the pipe down again and again, screaming with rage as he kept striking Robert's body, wiping the splattered blood from his face as he did so. And then, as if realising he was on a public side street, with a barking dog, he picked up Robert's dropped phone, scrolling to the apps, and deleting the voice memo Robert had been recording.

Then, putting it into his pocket, he looked sadly at Millie, still barking, before wiping down the pipe and tossing it back into the bin and, turning once more to stare down at the body of Robert Lewis, he used a handkerchief, spitting on it to wipe his face with, as he realised what he'd done.

And, as Millie barked after him, DI Mark Whitehouse ran from the scene of the crime.

20

PULL THE PIN

'I'D WAIT, IF I WERE YOU.'

Ellie held up her left hand in a warding gesture as Carrie paused, her finger loosening on the trigger as the gun lowered slightly.

'I thought you'd want this,' she said. 'You hate him more than I do.'

'Yeah, well, unfortunately, I also *need* him more than you do right now.'

'Tough shit,' Carrie raised the gun back and, as she motioned with her other hand, the men surrounding them raised theirs again, too.

Actually, Ellie noted, this wasn't quite true, as only three of the men in the room raised their guns. The others, however, didn't.

'You know, Carrie? I'd say you have a problem,' Ellie smiled. 'Because now, the people here understand the truth, realised they've been played, and you're about to discover you're not as popular as you thought.'

Carrie stared around the room.

'Seriously?' she asked. 'You'd do whatever he says without even a check of his passport for confirmation, but when I do it, you back down?'

'Yeah, that's the problem with tradition,' Simpson spoke now. 'It's very hard to go against the established norm, especially when their true boss – me – has walked into the room.'

He glanced at the ones with the guns still raised.

'I recognise you,' he said. 'But I understand. Even I still respect my dad, so I see why you'd come to his aid if called.'

He looked across at the fake Max.

'When I'm done with you—'

'You're not doing anything to anyone,' Ellie, her right hand now in her jacket pocket, looked from Simpson to fake Max. 'Mate? I don't know how much you were paid to do this, but I would suggest you leave now, because it's about to get very messy.'

'Oh, and how's that?' Carrie asked. 'Because all I see here are two people about to be shot in a pub.'

She smiled.

'And, let's be honest, you're not the first to be shot up here.'

Ellie considered this, moving her head from side to side in a rocking motion as she replied.

'True. But I *am* the first to blow the place to hell.'

To emphasise her words, Ellie finally removed her right hand from her jacket pocket, pulling out a grenade.

'This is a little gift from a friend of mine,' said, holding it up for everyone to see. 'She's ex-army, has a few issues, you know, likes to keep souvenirs. Like this. A Mark two, "pineapple" grenade. Also commonly referred to as a "frag" grenade.'

She pointed at a yellow stripe.

'Now, some of these are known as "low explosive," but

when they have the yellow paint? It means they're "high explosive," which means they're filled with lots of nasty, dangerous, fatal shit. I don't even know what's in it. I mean, why would I ask?'

The surrounding men looked nervous as, quickly, she pulled out the ring, holding the pin down with her left hand, while gripping the trigger tightly.

'You kill either of us, you even go to shoot either of us, and I'll drop this in the middle of this fine dining room,' she growled. 'Now, honestly, I'm not sure of what happens next. For example, the blast might not kill you. But I'm pretty sure in a building like this, especially the age it is, you're gonna get caught in a lot of damage. And I'd expect a shit ton of first-degree burns.'

Carrie shook her head.

'You're bluffing,' she chuckled, but the smile quickly faded as Ellie returned her attention to the new gang lord.

'Why would I bluff?' she replied, staring directly at her. 'You're about to kill me. Why does it matter to me whether I die with a bullet or in an explosion? At least this way. I control the story.'

She stepped forward, moving into the middle of the room.

'I wasn't lying when I came in,' she said. 'Several of the people here owe me favours, and I can quite happily tell them the favours are to "get the hell out and leave us be." And you know what? They would.'

There was laughter behind her – Ellie glanced back quickly to see Nicky Simpson chuckling, obviously enjoying the moment.

Probably because he wasn't yet dead.

Ignoring him, she looked back at Carrie.

'And if I let go? Well, then you, and me, and your half-brother here, our story will end and you know what? I'm happy with that.'

Carrie stared impotently at Ellie, aware of the shifting of power in the conversation.

'I'll have everyone you love killed,' she said.

'Wrong threat,' Ellie shook her head. 'You see this prick behind me? The one I'm risking my life for? He's already done that.'

There were a couple of seconds of incredibly awkward silence following this statement, and Ellie allowed it to draw out before continuing.

'There's one thing I need to know, though,' she said. 'Who sent the texts?'

Carrie frowned.

'What texts?'

'The ones to Saleh and to Flanagan, the ones that told them to go to Kennington?' Ellie replied. 'Flanagan thought it was Max, but we've now learned that Max has nothing to do with this. So I'm guessing it was you? After all, they phoned you, too, didn't they?'

'Why do you care about some texts?' Carrie was losing control here, and it was throwing her.

Undaunted, Ellie continued.

'Well, I wouldn't usually, but the problem here for me is the same phone number grassed Flanagan's location to the police,' Ellie explained. 'Interestingly, this, however, had a police requisition code on it, which meant it came from a police officer—'

She leant closer.

'—which meant it has to be one of two people: Mark

Whitehouse or Kate Delgado. Kate Delgado, who is the god-daughter of Ricky Smith.'

'Am I supposed to know who that is?' Carrie shrugged at this. 'Or is this some dusty old gangster shit I don't give a damn about?'

She sighed.

'I didn't arrange the text. Granddad did. But they did call me to get their orders.'

Ignoring the intake of breath behind her, breath that showed Nicky Simpson had finally realised his dear darling granddad was the one who truly hated him, Ellie nodded. She had considered this for a while now. If Paddy Simpson was pulling the strings, then whoever had screwed her over and accused her of murder was probably working for him, which meant they'd been working for the family for a very long time. Possibly even since birth.

Of course, if she went down this line, there was also the possibility that it had been Paddy, not Nicky Simpson, that killed Bryan Noyce – and Nicky had allowed the rumours to float around him purely to gain reputation.

'So what's the plan now?' Carrie nodded at the grenade. 'You looking to blow us all up still?'

'That depends,' Ellie shrugged, holding the grenade up. 'Do you still want to kill me?'

'I never wanted to kill you, it's the bastard behind you I want to shoot,' Carrie replied casually. 'You're, unfortunately, a casualty of war.'

'You think this is a war?' Ellie frowned. 'It's nothing but a long-drawn-out execution.'

'Isn't that what a war is when drilled down to the core?' Carrie smiled. 'I get it, we're in stalemate. You want me to take the hit on Nicky off? You'll need to speak to Paddy Simpson for that. And he's a little busy right now.'

'Oh?' Simpson stepped forward. 'And why's that?'

'He's planning a funeral,' Carrie said, and the smile left her face as she spoke to Simpson. 'Yours.'

Nicky Simpson stared at Carrie Mullen.

'Then why all this?' he waved around. 'Why did Flanagan tell Allen Dad was coming? Why all this bollocks with the double?'

'No idea. Paddy arranged for "Max" to tell Flanagan what to do,' she said. 'I'd been sent into London right after you were outed to start things up, and we knew if I could get reception duties, I could allow Flanagan in to set up the bomb.'

Nicky Simpson nodded at this.

'Saleh,' he said. 'He got you the job, didn't he? He was told to get you in.'

Carrie didn't reply; she didn't need to.

Ellie smiled.

'Well, this has been fun, but as you don't seem to want to debate this, and as we have to go speak to Nicky's grandfather now, I think we need to leave,' she said.

'You think you can just walk out? Even with that grenade?'

Ellie made a point of thinking this over before nodding.

'You know what, I think I do,' she replied merrily. 'So, I suggest you and your fake dad there sit down and make yourself comfortable, because you're not leaving this room for the next fifteen minutes.'

Without looking, she spoke the following.

'Dave? Steve? Adrian? You all know you owe me a favour, right?' She didn't turn, still watching Carrie as three of the men in the room made guttural grunts of agreement. 'Well, my favour now asked of you is to hold the people in this room back from leaving for fifteen minutes.'

Three of the men, the ones apparently named Dave, Steve and Adrian, instantly raised their guns, aiming at Carrie and the others. It was very much a Mexican standoff, with three men facing three others, and Carrie and Ellie facing each other.

'*Now* it's a war,' Ellie smiled, turning to the three men who didn't owe her a favour. 'And you guys. You should consider how far you want to go to bat for this woman. She lied about Max, how do you know she's not lying for Paddy?'

As the three other men looked at each other in concern, Ellie walked backwards, towards the door, still fixated on Carrie.

'You have a nice day now,' she said. 'I'm sure I'll see you again.'

'I'll find you,' Carrie hissed. 'And when I do, my people will end this war.'

'That's the thing about Kings and Queens,' Ellie said from the doorway. 'In plays, they don't tell the audience they're the king or queen. The audience learns it from the way the court acts towards them.'

She looked around the room.

'And currently? Even your court doesn't believe you,' she finished. 'Call us when you've truly taken the crown, yeah?'

Nicky Simpson didn't move, however, staring icily at his half-sister.

'If you are a Simpson, you should know our traditions,' he said.

'Oh yeah? And what's that?'

With a swift movement, Nicky Simpson threw the skinning knife across the room, watching dispassionately as it slammed into the picture of Mark Mullen's damaged torso, pinning it to the floor, effectively stabbed through the heart.

'We always bring gifts,' he said. 'Here, it's yours.'

And with this last gesture made, Ellie pulled Simpson out of the upstairs room.

Running down the stairs, they exited the pub, crossing the street.

'What's gonna happen now?' Simpson asked, still staring at the grenade. 'Where's the ring?'

Ellie glanced at the grenade, still in her hands.

'Ah, shit, I dropped it,' she said, sighing, looking around. They were in the middle of a high street T-junction, and there was nowhere to really throw it.

'Bollocks to it,' she said, opening the car door with her free hand, waving for Simpson to get in. 'Nothing's gonna happen. Your sister's not stupid. She won't have a gun fight up there. There's no need, she knows we're running out the clock, she'll wait her time.'

She smiled.

'Hey, on a plus note, at least we now know who we're fighting,' she said, eventually tossing the grenade into the empty street beside the pub.

Nicky Simpson stared in fascination as the metal pineapple grenade bounced along the pavement, but Ellie had already entered the car as the grenade detonated, releasing flumes of thick, blue smoke into the air. He climbed into the car, confused, staring at Ellie as she started the engine.

'What, you think Tinker would give me a real grenade?' She raised an eyebrow. 'Be serious. It's a practice grenade with the top part painted.'

Pulling out, ignoring the confused expressions from the bystanders, she carried on northwards, towards Elephant and Castle.

'What we need to do now is find a place to stay, while we work out what we've learnt,' she said.

'Do you have one?'

'Yeah.' Ellie replied. 'And you're not going to like it.'

She looked over at him.

'Hey, I'm sorry,' she said. 'If your granddad really is after you and all that.'

Simpson shook his head.

'So many lies, I won't even consider it until I hear from the source,' he replied. 'Now, where are we going?'

'Islington,' Ellie grinned. 'To see an old friend of yours.'

———

THE ROUTE NORTH WAS BUSIER THAN EXPECTED AS THEY attempted to find their way through to Islington, thanks to a mixture of the end of rush hour and the start of the evening theatre crowd in the centre of London. Ellie had tried to avoid it as much as she could, but she was effectively driving from southwest to northeast London and at some point she was destined to hit it.

But, after almost an hour of traffic wrangling, while Nicky Simpson stared out of the passenger window, lost in thought, she eventually found a back road just north of the Angel Underground Station, before pulling up to a stop on a random street.

'We walk from here,' she said, opening the door. 'I don't want to park too near in case they find the car.'

It was another three streets' worth of walking, Ellie in the lead with Simpson grumbling behind her, until she stopped outside a small building. It was industrial, an old warehouse of some kind, but at the same time, it was well secured, with the look of a recent development, a warehouse space turned into living accommodation.

'We'll be staying here tonight,' she smiled, walking up to the door.

'This isn't a house,' Simpson looked around in confusion.

'It is when you're on the run and looking for any inn for the night, because people want to kill you,' Ellie replied, knocking on the door.

'You just want to keep reminding me of that,' Simpson muttered as the door to the warehouse, a thick, red, wooden beast of an entranceway opened and the terrified face of Danny Flynn stared out. His black hair was still in a trendy razor-faded style, and still didn't fit his egg-shaped head, giving him the appearance of a Goth Beaker from the Muppets. He looked as slim as he was before, but his telltale beer belly had slimmed down remarkably.

He actually looked fitter than he had a year earlier.

Ellie smiled.

'Alright Danny?' she said. 'As per the phone call, this is me calling in my favour.'

'I know,' he replied with a smile. 'I've been expecting you.'

'You're kidding me!' Simpson said. 'Danny bloody Flynn is my saviour?'

'I know!' Ellie explained delightedly, walking past Danny and entering the building. 'Isn't it great how life does this sometimes? You must have guessed, you were in the bloody room when he called.'

Grumbling to himself, Simpson stared at Danny, still standing at the door.

'Alright?' he muttered.

'Can't complain,' Danny replied as Simpson walked into the building after Ellie.

The building itself was an industrial warehouse that had been turned into an apartment: downstairs contained what looked like some kind of woodworking shop, while the back led to a covered garage. The walls were brick and painted white, and there was a second door in the wall which, when unlocked, led up some metal stairs into effectively a studio warehouse apartment.

It was nice. Well designed. The walls were white with old brickwork poking out here and there, and the wooden floor was mahogany. It appeared both modern and classic, ignoring the brutalist structure it had been built into, and looking out at giant floor to ceiling windows.

'I thought you lived in Chipping Norton?' Simpson asked. 'If I'd known you owned property here, I would have been asking for this as my debt back then.'

'The house in Chipping Norton is long gone,' Danny said as he walked to the kitchen area. 'Tea? Coffee? I have tap water or La Croix in the fridge, too.'

'After Chantelle screwed him over, Danny divorced her and sold up the house for several million,' Ellie explained, walking over to the fridge. 'Moved here, closer to London.'

'This is stupid,' Nicky muttered, looking over at the windows. 'They're pointless. Anyone could just break them and come through.'

'No,' Danny replied. 'They're lead piped for a start, but also they're bulletproof, solid, tempered glass.'

Ellie passed Simpson a can of La Croix water. It was "pamplemousse" flavour.

'You see, Danny here has a bit of a trust issue. Being almost killed does that to you,' she said.

'Ramsey helped me with the security, "takes a thief" and all that,' Danny explained, like a deranged estate agent. 'The locks are worse, as they're some of the best in the world. You literally can't get into this place. And if you do, I have a shotgun rack in a safe in the gym that'll make you leave pretty soon.'

He waved a hand around the living space.

'It's an armoured panic room made into the shape of a studio apartment. And currently, nobody knows you're here.'

Ellie leant in.

'And let's be frank, Nicky, who in their right mind would believe you'd go to Danny Flynn for help?'

Danny didn't take offence at this, instead pouring himself a beer.

'Hey,' Simpson asked, irritated. 'How come we weren't offered a beer too?'

'First, because it's non-alcoholic. Second, because I don't like you,' Danny sipped at his bottle, removing the froth from the top. 'And right now? You need me.'

Nicky slumped a little, looking around the kitchen.

'How the mighty fall,' he muttered.

Ellie toasted.

'I'll drink to that,' she smiled.

She was about to say something else when her phone went. Pulling it out, she frowned at the unfamiliar number, and answered it.

'Reckless?' she said.

'Um, sorry to bother you, but do you own a dog called Millie?' the voice was female and elderly.

'Yeah, I do,' Ellie replied, confused. 'Sorry, who is this?'

'It's just we found her walking alone on the streets,' the voice continued. 'The name and this number are on her collar.'

'She was alone?' Ellie frowned. 'Okay, thanks, can I come back to you? I'll get someone to call and pick her up.'

'Okay, but we can't wait too long, our train—'

Ellie disconnected the call, phoning Robert.

'Problem?' Simpson, watching her, asked.

'Millie's been found loose.'

'Millie's the dog, right?'

'Yes, Nicky, Millie's the bloody dog,' Ellie snapped, typing out a message to Robert and sending it. 'And Robert was looking after her, but his phone's off, turned to voicemail.'

She stared at the two men facing her.

'Robert's not the sort of person to lose a dog like this, or even turn his phone off,' she said, already texting Tinker. 'I think something bad's happened – I think someone's aiming at my team now.'

21

WAREHOUSED

IT WAS ANOTHER HALF AN HOUR BEFORE TINKER TEXTED TO SAY that Millie had been picked up, was perfectly fine, and that Robert wasn't at the office. Ellie had been trying to contact him for most of that time, but nothing had been heard from him. Ellie had even texted others, including Mark White-house, as Robert had been checking into Kate.

Whitehouse's text came through almost immediately.

> Saw him earlier in office. Still spouting your anti-Kate rhetoric. ;) He said he needed to take dog for walk so we ended then.
> What's up?

Ellie quickly explained Robert was missing and Millie had turned up alone, and then texted her old mentor, Alex Monroe. After all, the Finders' offices were in the City of London, and that was Monroe's remit these days. If he was in the office, and he usually was, he might find out something.

Davey had texted after the news of Millie's adventure came out. She too had chased the City Police she once worked for to learn anything, but for the moment, it looked like Ellie had to wait.

Unfortunately, this meant waiting with Danny Flynn and Nicky Simpson, who still hated each other.

'So who's picking the dog up?' Simpson asked.

'If you mean Millie when you say, "the dog", then it's Tinker.'

Simpson furrowed his eyebrows at this.

'So who's looking after—'

'Probably just Ramsey until she gets back there.'

'Christ, he's screwed,' Simpson replied, but didn't clarify if he meant Saleh or Ramsey in the statement. Eventually, after a moment of being glowered at by Ellie, he turned to Danny.

'I thought you didn't owe her a favour?' he asked as they sat in facing armchairs. 'She used it up getting you to not kill your wife?'

'I felt grateful she did that, so I said the favour could still be granted,' Danny shifted in his seat. 'Lucky me.'

There was a moment or two of uncomfortable silence.

'Where's Saleh?' Danny eventually asked. 'I thought he was surgically attached to your hip?'

'In hiding too,' Simpson replied.

'Is he being targeted too?'

'He thinks so.'

'Wow. Someone really hates you.'

'There's a long list,' Ellie sighed, grabbing the can of sparkling, flavoured water she'd been drinking and then grimacing. 'You don't have anything stronger, do you?'

'Completely dry house,' Danny smiled. 'I'm tee-total since Chantelle went. Thought it was time to change my life.'

'And how's that working for you?' It sounded like a

genuine question from Simpson, but there was a mocking tone to it, that darkened Danny's face.

'I moved back to London and decided to gain my empire back,' he said. 'I've never wanted to be like you, or the Twins; all that upper management shit does my head in. I keep my crew, and I do my jobs. And that gives me this.'

He waved his hands around to make the point.

'In fairness, selling a Chipping Norton Manor House probably helped,' Ellie smiled.

Ignoring her, Danny looked back at Simpson.

'You tried to take everything from me,' he said, his tone darkening as he spoke. You had your claws in Boston, but you wanted more, and you'd have taken all of my connections just to do so. You would have ruined me for your own gain.'

'Nothing personal,' Simpson shrugged.

'Bullshit,' Danny snapped. 'It was always personal for you, you self-centred, trust-fund wanker.'

'Wow,' Ellie raised an eyebrow at this. 'I remember when even the mention of Nicky's name filled you with terror.'

'So do I,' Danny leant forwards, resting his forearms on his lap as he hunched closer. 'But the Simpson I feared wasn't the man I'm looking at right now. This? He's nothing more than a nobody. A yesterday's news.'

'You'd better be careful,' Simpson hissed. 'This will get fixed, one way or the other, and I'll be back. And I'll remember this.'

'Yeah? Then remember this,' Danny sneered. 'I only helped you because I owed her a favour. If I hadn't, I would have let you die. Hell, I'd have gained the money for myself and shot you in the face when you knocked at my door. Just like every other cold-hearted bastard you thought was your friend.'

Simpson rose at this, walking to the window.

'I deserve that,' he said.

'You what?' Danny looked incredulously at Ellie. 'Is he on drugs?'

'He's been on a bit of a journey of self-discovery,' Ellie said. 'Especially since he learnt his granddad probably put the hit on him.'

'Well, that makes sense, especially with his dad ...' Danny stopped as Nicky Simpson spun around.

'With my dad *what?*' he hissed.

Danny rose now, facing Simpson, but gone were the bluster and the arrogance.

'I thought you knew,' he said. 'Your dad went into intensive care about three days back. Stroke. He's on life support, but they don't expect him to wake up.'

'Bullshit!' Simpson replied. 'I'd know if this was true!'

'Not if your grandfather is the one who'd tell you,' Ellie said, looking back at Danny. 'How do you know this?'

'The Balearics have a lot of ex-pat criminals over there,' Danny replied, his whole demeanour changing, returning to the one Ellie recognised from before. 'One of them has been a friend for years. Went in for a hernia operation, saw them wheeling Max in. They were keeping it quiet, like, but the nurse hadn't been given the memo, and told him. And he, well, he knew how I disliked you, so he called to let me know.'

Ellie looked back at Simpson.

'It matches the timeline,' she said. 'The hit goes on you yesterday; Flanagan, possibly one of the few people to truly follow Max is sent over here; Paddy has free rein.'

Nicky Simpson stared at them both.

'The place is soundproofed, so if you want to scream, you

know, go ahead?' Danny suggested. 'I mean, personally, I'd be wanting to scream. And gain revenge on the people who lied to you.'

'How do you mean?'

Danny shrugged.

'Your dad went into hospital three days ago, there's no way people didn't know,' he said. 'The hit only went out on you last night. That's two days where nobody told you. And I know Saleh knew.'

'Again, how do you know that?' Ellie asked.

'Because the same people I know, they know him, and bad news always travels fast,' Danny replied coldly. 'Your man knew, and two days later this happens? Not a coincidence.'

Simpson took in the news and softly shook his head, looking Danny up and down.

'You look better than you did before,' he said, changing the subject, his voice level and calm. 'Working out?'

'Yeah.'

'Public gym or one here?'

'I have one downstairs, in the back half of the warehouse,' Danny beamed. 'State-of-the art. Puts your shit to shame.'

'With a gun rack,' Ellie mocked.

'Looking at putting a shooting range in the basement and the stairs are there.'

Nicky Simpson considered this.

'Could I use it?' he asked, almost nervously. 'The gym? I could really do with a session right now. I always think straighter when I do a session.'

'Sure, it's down there, second left, down the stairs,' Danny pointed down a corridor leading from the main living space. 'Light is motion detected, so it'll go on when you arrive.'

Simpson nodded his thanks and, with a brief glance at Ellie, walked off.

'Jesus,' Danny muttered once he was sure Simpson was out of earshot. 'How the mighty fall.'

'I'd be a little careful there,' Ellie suggested. 'It could happen to any of us.'

Danny reluctantly nodded at this and then looked back at the corridor.

'He's a mess,' he said. 'I thought I'd feel better about it, but I don't.'

'That's a good thing,' Ellie said as her phone buzzed. It was Tinker again.

Robert found.

That was it; nothing more. Ellie wanted to scream, to shout. Instead, she dialled a number and waited.

After a second, Tinker answered. There was noise in the background, and she sounded like she was in a car, driving.

'What's going on?' Ellie asked.

'Didn't want to worry you while you were dealing with Simpson,' Tinker replied.

'Are you in the jeep?'

'Yeah. And don't worry about Millie, I dropped him with Casey. His mum loves Spaniels.'

'Why have you dropped Millie off?' Ellie felt a cold sliver of ice slide down her back. 'Where was Robert found?'

There was a pause on the end of the line before Tinker replied.

'Ellie, sit down,' she said.

'Tinker, just tell me—'

'They found him in an alleyway,' Tinker said. 'Dead. Well,

they thought he was, but he was still breathing. Just. He's lost a ton of blood, and he's had the shit beaten out of him. He's on his way to the hospital now, but they don't even know if he'll make it.'

Ellie couldn't help herself; her legs gave way, and she stumbled back into the armchair.

'Who—'

'No idea,' Tinker's voice was tight, holding her emotions in check. 'Current suggestion is he walked Millie and someone attacked him. Police think it's a mugging, but that's bullshit. His phone was gone, but his wallet was on him, with a couple of hundred in it. Wasn't touched—get out of the way, you prick!'

'Which hospital?' Ellie asked, rising. 'I'm coming.'

'Don't be an idiot,' Tinker replied over the noise. 'You'd have to bring Nicky, and that's what they could have hoped for. If he doesn't make it, then you don't help by being there. And even if he does, he's not gonna be in any state to do or say anything for a while.'

There was a screech of brakes, another expletive, and then Tinker spoke again, softer.

'Ellie, he's in a bad state,' she said. 'I saw people nowhere near as bad as him go down in battle, and they didn't make it. You need to prepare yourself for the worst.'

Ellie felt the room spinning around her. Danny walked up with a glass, passing it to her. She took a mouthful; it was neat whisky.

'I thought—'

'I wasn't giving *him* my finest malts,' Danny said, almost sadly. 'You, however ...'

Ellie nodded gratefully. Danny couldn't hear the conversation, but just by watching her, he'd seen it was something bad.

'I need to be there, Tink,' she almost pleaded. 'When we were in the crash, he stayed there all night while I was in a coma—'

'It's the Royal London Hospital in Whitechapel,' Tinker said. 'He'll be safe. And I'll be there beside him and keep you updated. He stayed beside me, too, remember?'

Ellie, returning briefly to the present, paused.

'Where's Ramsey?' she asked.

'With Saleh,' Tinker replied. 'Bloody man won't leave his house. Thinks he's safe there, even though we got into it in like ten seconds.'

'Get Casey looking into Robert's phone's location.'

'Ellie, it's late, and he's—'

'I don't care!' Ellie snapped. 'Get it done, Tink, please! This is Robert we're talking about!'

The line went dead; Tinker was never one for goodbyes.

Ellie stared at the phone, speechless, hoping she hadn't crossed the line with her outburst.

'Should you be using phones?' Danny asked. 'Can't they, like, find you through cell towers and shit?'

'It's a spare,' Ellie said absently. 'Only known by my team, and trusted people.'

'And me,' Danny smiled, 'I'm guessing you called me from it, so I have the number too.'

'As I said,' Ellie replied, watching him. 'Trusted people.'

Danny almost blushed at this.

'I appreciate that,' he said. 'Can I ask what happened?'

'Robert, the guy you met when you came to Finders—'

'Solicitor bloke? He seemed solid. Didn't stare at Chantelle's tits once, so I knew he was a good one.'

'Yeah, well, someone attacked him, beat him badly and left him for dead,' Ellie replied angrily. 'It's a message.'

'Or a murder attempt,' Danny suggested. 'Maybe he'd found something out? Maybe someone couldn't have it revealed? Think how Chantelle screwed with your brakes? She thought it'd kill you, but it didn't, so maybe this was more than a message.'

'Robert was looking into something,' Ellie nodded slowly at this. Danny Flynn made sense. 'It could have blown up in his face.'

She stopped, looking down at the phone, going through the texts again, reading Whitehouse's text once more.

Then, dialling a number, she held it to her ear again.

'Ellie?' Whitehouse was surprised to hear from her. 'It's late. Do you need something?'

'When you spoke to Robert, was there anything off?' Ellie asked. 'Like anyone hanging around the offices?'

There was a pause as Whitehouse considered the question.

'No, not that I can remember,' he replied. 'Why?'

'They found Robert. In an alley.'

There was another pause, but this one felt different, as if Whitehouse didn't know what to say.

'Oh, Ellie, I'm so sorry.'

'He's on his way to The Royal London,' Ellie continued.

'He's alive?' Whitehouse sounded stunned. 'Sorry, you made it sound like he was gone.'

'Only just,' Ellie said. 'But someone did this deliberately, Mark. Someone was waiting.'

'I'll look through CCTV,' Whitehouse offered. 'See if I can find something.'

'Anything you can do,' Ellie said. 'Please.'

Disconnecting the call, she rose again, walking to the corridor.

'I'd better check on Simpson,' she said, but stopped at the top of the stairs.

'You said the light was motion activated, right?'

'Yeah.'

'Well, it's not on. Nicky?' Ellie called down. 'You okay?'

At no answer, she walked downstairs, into the gym, but as the light turned on, she saw there was nobody there.

'Ah, shit,' she said, running back up. 'Nicky?'

Danny was at the top of the stairs.

'He's gone, hasn't he?' he asked.

'Where did you say that shotgun rack was?' Ellie was already heading down the stairs, walking into a state-of-the-art gym, with an expensive shotgun and rifle case at the end. It was unlocked, the doors open, cartridges and rifles strewn on the floor.

'You didn't lock it?' she asked as Danny joined her.

'I thought you were in danger, so it'd be better for quick access,' Danny walked over, picking up and replacing a shotgun as he looked around. 'He's taken the Mossberg 20 gauge Hushpower, and a box of shells.'

'A Mossberg is a ...?'

'A pump-action shotgun, Ellie,' Danny said, looking over at the window. It was currently open. 'A pretty vicious one.'

Ellie walked to the window as well, looking out. It was open, the chilly night air blowing in, and was an easy exit onto the main street.

'Damn,' she said. 'Looks like Nicky Simpson's going into business for himself.'

'Shame.'

She looked back at Danny.

'You did this,' she said, putting the pieces together. 'You deliberately aimed Nicky at Saleh.'

'Dunno what you mean,' Danny squared his shoulders up. 'I think you've been watching for shadows so long—'

'Don't give me that!' Ellie snapped. 'I know you didn't want him here. I get that. But you told him where the weapons were. You even left the rack open. Is his father even dying?'

'Everyone's dying, Reckless,' Danny smiled darkly. 'Maybe my source wasn't a hundred percent correct?'

Ellie stared, horrified, at Danny. Suddenly, everything was falling into place.

'What did you do?' she whispered.

'I fulfilled my favour,' Danny replied, walking back up the stairs, Ellie following. 'You needed a place to hide. I gave it to you.'

He stopped at the front door to his warehouse apartment, opening it.

'But now he's gone, and my debt to you is complete,' he said. 'You can leave, too.'

Ellie stared at Danny.

'From the start,' she said. 'From your call earlier today, offering help, all the way until now, you planned it all, didn't you?'

'I had help,' Danny shrugged. 'There was always a game-play, Reckless. You never saw it, as you were too close to the ball.'

'Does the shotgun even have shells?'

Danny nodded.

'Oh, they're in it, but whether he'll have a chance to use it … that's a different matter.'

'Wow,' was all she could say. 'I thought you'd changed

since Chantelle tried to kill you.'

Danny said nothing else, simply standing in the doorway.

'You have a revenge-filled Influencer to find,' he said. 'Chop, chop, Reckless.'

Ellie, straightening, walked out of the doorway, and into the night.

Danny, almost as if feeling sorry, stood watching her at the door.

'One thing,' he said, stopping her in her tracks. 'I don't know if it helps. First off, I am sorry for your solicitor friend. That's shit. But second, I wasn't lying when I said I have a bloody good network of people out there. And they tell me things. Simpson is over from Majorca.'

'I've heard that already,' Ellie snapped. 'And he isn't. There's a pretend Max walking around.'

'I don't mean Max,' Danny said. 'I mean Paddy Simpson is back in town, and has been since this whole bloody thing started. And, having spoken to him earlier today, I can vouch for that. Goodnight, Ellie.' He closed the door behind her.

Now alone in the street, Ellie stared back at the closed door.

Finally, the pieces were fitting together, but there was something, a small part of the plot she not only knew she was missing, but that she knew without a doubt she'd already been given.

But that could wait, because first, she needed to find the homicidal Nicky Simpson. And her car was three sodding streets away.

Walking to where she'd parked up and pulling out her phone, she made plans.

22

VIGIL

TINKER WAS SITTING IN THE WAITING ROOM OF THE ROYAL London when Mark Whitehouse arrived.

'What the hell are you doing here?' she asked as she rose. 'Look, if you're looking to arrest me or Robert, it's a shit time—'

'Ellie told me,' Whitehouse said, holding up a hand. 'I come in peace. Look, no Delgado.'

Tinker relaxed slightly as Whitehouse sat down on one of the cold, plastic chairs.

'Have they said anything?' he asked.

'No,' Tinker grumbled. 'They said something about "severe traumatic brain injuries," and I heard "intra-parenchymal bleed" and "intercranial haemorrhage" being bounced about, so it's not good. I think he had a stroke on the way here, too. Although I might have misheard that.'

'Damn,' Whitehouse said, looking away. 'Did they give any indication if he'll make it?'

Tinker glared back at Whitehouse.

'Dude, they're stunned he's still alive,' she said. 'Apparently, he was literally dead in the ambulance for twenty seconds. Like clinically gone.'

Whitehouse nodded at this, and Tinker watched him, frowning. It was as if he was simply going through the motions, nodding because he felt he had to, not really listening to the words being spoken.

He acted like a man in shock.

'You okay?' she asked.

'I was with him,' he replied, still staring off. 'I was ... I might have been the last person to speak to him.'

'Hey,' Tinker said, grabbing his arm, pulling him out of whatever trance he was in, turning him to face her. 'Stop that. He's not dead. He'll get better.'

'Will he?' Whitehouse rose. 'I'll see if I can find out anything else.'

'And what makes you think you can do better—' Tinker stopped herself with a weak smile. 'Warrant card. Of course.'

As Whitehouse walked off to speak to the doctors, Tinker felt her phone buzz. Looking at it, she let out an audible groan.

> Simpson on loose. Has shotgun. Danny screwed us. Need to find him before Paddy Simpson, apparently in London, does first.

Tinker whistled. *It never got any easier.* She checked the clock on the wall – it was gone ten pm now. Would Casey still be up?

Of course he is. The boy's sixteen, not twelve, she thought to herself as she dialled his number. *And you texted him ten minutes ago when Ellie had her meltdown.*

He answered on the third ring.

'Tinker?' he asked. 'You checking in on Millie? She's fine.

Mum's made up a little bed for her and she's eating boiled eggs. I never even knew dogs liked boiled eggs.'

'Are you with your mum?' Tinker asked, carefully.

'Yeah, I …' Casey's voice stopped as he realised why Tinker was asking this.

'Mum, I'm just going to take this in my room,' Casey continued, off the phone. 'Tinker needs something I have on the laptop.'

'Didn't she just text you?'

'She's old, like you. She forgets things.'

'Just remember, it's a school night.'

'Mum, there's a strike.'

There was a pause in the conversation, presumably as Casey walked to his room.

'Will your mum mind you working?' Tinker asked.

'Nah, she's playing with Millie,' Casey replied. 'Dad was never really a dog person. Mum always wanted a German Shepherd, so she's loving having a Spaniel in the house. What's up?'

Quickly, and keeping her voice low, Tinker brought Casey up to speed with what had happened that evening; the attack on Robert, carefully avoided while passing Millie to Casey's mum earlier, the information Ellie had sent her about the pub meeting, and the recent news that Nicky Simpson was now AWOL, with a shotgun, and possibly hunting Paddy Simpson, now a piece on the board as well.

In return, Casey told her what he'd found; that the person texting Flanagan and Saleh had also texted the assassin, and that Ferdia Holdings owned the stock to Simpson's Health Clubs, thanks to a donation of stocks by Max Simpson a couple of days earlier, as well as owning cars that both Flanagan, and the tanned assassin who came for them at the boxing club had used. He also gave an update on the hunt for Robert's phone – as yet, nothing had been found, although he was close to logging in to Robert's cloud account, and when that happened, he might be able to work out what happened immediately before the attack.

Once they'd both caught each other up, there was a moment of contemplation.

'Shit,' Tinker muttered. 'This is way more than we thought.'

'What do you need from me?' Casey asked.

'I need you for something else. Something I think you did in the lockup.'

There was an uncertain pause on the end of Casey's line.

'I've done nothing wrong,' he said.

'Interesting. You immediately think that you're to blame,' Tinker smiled. 'Look, kid. I know you don't like Nicky. And I remember when we were in the car, before we went to the lockup and when you realised he was being tracked, you seemed to have some kind of idea, something about tracking before we left the car, and I wanted to know if you continued on with it.'

There was a moment's silence, and Casey sighed down the phone.

'I realised if Nicky was being tracked, it was a good idea to track him ourselves,' he said. 'That way, if something happened, we'd know where he was. And to be honest, I didn't trust him at that point. Still don't. And I thought, if I could track him, then if he attacked you, or Ellie, or whatever, we'd know what was going on.'

'So did you place a tracker on him?'

'Who do you think I am? MI5?' Casey laughed. 'Nah, I didn't place a tracker on him. I just had what I had to hand, which wasn't much considering the fact we were, well, in a lockup. But I had an AirTag in my rucksack. And I took it out and slipped it into his hoodie before he went.'

'And he didn't see this?'

'There was a slight tear in it, so I was able to place it into the lining under the seam,' Casey explained. 'I don't think he even realised what was going on.'

'Okay,' Tinker said. 'So he has an Apple AirTag in his jumper, which we know he's still wearing. How does that help us?'

'Well, an AirTag sends out a secure Bluetooth signal, of a range of about thirty feet, that can be detected by nearby devices on Apple's network. So iPads, Macs, iPhones, all of those. These devices use their own Wi-Fi or carrier network to send the location of the AirTag to your iCloud, where you can then see it on a map,' Casey explained. 'The entire process is anonymous and encrypted to protect your privacy, but it means any time my AirTag goes near an iPhone, it pings, which means I can get a pretty good, real-time estimate of where it is. And being in London, there's a lot of iPhones.'

'Okay,' Tinker replied. 'Where is he now?'

She could hear a tapping down the phone as Casey started checking.

'Last time I have a ping is fifteen minutes ago,' he said. 'It looks like he was heading towards Angel Islington Station.'

'The underground,' Tinker nodded to herself. 'Fifteen minutes is a long time, though. How come you don't have a more recent ping?'

'You have to be near a Wi-Fi signal and by a phone,' Casey continued typing as he spoke. 'And unfortunately, the underground cuts both off, so if he's on a train, we won't know exactly where he is until he pops up again on the surface.'

'And you're sure he's on a train?'

'God no,' Casey replied. 'But what I can tell you is that somewhere like Angel, filled full of people and at this time at night? Place would be packed – he would have pinged a dozen times by now. The fact he hasn't must mean he's gone on the underground.'

'Angel Islington is a Northern Line train,' Tinker was working this through in her head. 'It goes north up to Camden, where you can get either of the two lines north, and is the right-hand-side line outwards, through Liverpool Street, London Bridge and ...'

She trailed off.

'That line leads to Elephant and Castle,' Casey helpfully finished the sentence. 'Do you think he's got unfinished business there?'

'Could be,' Tinker said. The Red Lion was less than a mile's walk from the station.

'Hold on,' Casey suddenly said, typing. 'I just had a reply to something.'

'I can't really hold on—' Tinker started, but looked across the waiting room. Mark Whitehouse was showing a nurse his warrant card, probably trying to gain information on Robert's status.

What are you saying? the voice in her head replied. *You've all the time in the world to hold on.*

'Take your time,' she added.

Annoyingly, Casey did.

'Tell me about Danny Flynn,' he eventually said.

'I already have,' Tinker frowned. 'She burnt a favour, he let them in, Nicky left with one of his shotguns.'

'After he wound him up and watched him go?' Casey asked.

'Yeah,' Tinker replied. 'Told Ellie after the fact he'd said it deliberately. Got him angry, told him where the guns were, even gave him a way out …'

'Why would he help him?'

'I don't think he intended to help him,' Tinker said. 'I think he intended to watch him do something stupid.'

'Well, I have an answer to why Danny wants to get rid of Nicky Simpson,' Casey said. 'Ferdia Holdings.'

'The company behind Flanagan's car?'

'Yeah. I was looking into them tonight,' Casey explained. 'I started looking into their trading deals.'

'And how do you do this?' Tinker asked, surprised. 'Or shouldn't I know?'

'I have a brokerage account,' Casey replied, and Tinker could almost hear the smile on his lips. 'But this was done through the corporate account I have at the health clubs. These accounts have the right to check the company accounts, and as Simpson Health Spa is a publicly traded company, has been for about five years, this includes who owns what. And that's where this gets interesting.'

'Only the son of an accountant could think this is interesting.'

Casey ignored the jibe.

'When it started, Nicky Simpson had sixty percent of all shares, his father had twenty-five percent, and his grandfather, Paddy, had ten.'

'That's ninety-five.'

'Don't spoil my punchline, Tinker.'

'Okay, so far I understand this. Carry on.'

'Two days ago, maybe three now – I've lost track of where we are, Max Simpson sold his shares to Ferdia Holdings.'

'Which we've heard of before.'

'Ferdia Holdings was created in the late fifties, and was a joint company. The signatories were Fergus Mullen, and after screwing around with a ton of image fixing AI stuff, Paddy Simpson.'

'Fergus Mullen?'

'Yeah, looks like Paddy and his then-boss needed a legitimate entity,' Casey replied. 'Stopped trading when he left for London and was forgotten for decades – until about six months back.'

'What happened then?'

'Paddy Simpson took it out of mothballs and put all of his share holdings into it,' Casey replied. 'Including his ten percent. And Ferdia Holdings has also been buying up shares in Simpson's Health Spas, whenever Nicky let some go onto the market, small amounts here and there, eight percent in total.'

There was a pause, probably from Casey smiling triumphantly and fist pumping, showing he was clever or something down the line.

'Currently, Ferdia Holdings have just under fifty-three percent of the shares in Simpson's health clubs,' he said. 'Five percent of which were given to them, as controlling options, by the owner of the shares, Danny Flynn.'

'Danny Flynn owns shares in Nicky Simpson's health clubs?' Tinker was stunned by this.

'Yep, looks like he bought them six months back too, probably around the same time as he sold his house and bought this Fort Knox Ellie thought would save them.'

Tinker looked around the waiting room as she considered this.

'Danny Flynn buys five percent of the shares and passes them to Ferdia Holdings, which is owned by Paddy Simpson. At the same time, Paddy puts his shares across, and then Max sells his shares, which makes forty percent, as well as around eight other shares picked up on the stock exchange. That's only forty-eight,' she argued. 'You're five short—oh. This is your punchline, isn't it?'

'Saleh Hussain had five percent of the shares as well given to him, probably by Nicky when he started the clubs.'

'Let me guess. Two days ago, Saleh sold his shares to Ferdia Holdings.'

'Yeah,' Casey said. 'Saleh's known about this from the start. And I've got something else on Saleh.'

'Please don't tell me he's another illegitimate bloody grandson of Paddy Simpson.'

'No. But he is a liar. He didn't answer when you went to knock on the door, right?'

'Yeah.'

'There was a reason he didn't – he wasn't at the house.'

Tinker stared at the phone.

'Okay, you have to explain that one.'

'Saleh's phone shows he was at the house, and you saw his BMW leave, right?'

'Right.'

'Back when I first met him, he took Ellie and me to see Simpson,' Casey explained. 'I used the BMWs Wi-Fi to hack into the health club's security, with the help of Nicky's password, because the BMW that Saleh was driving had an internet connection, you know, so it could download updated travel information and things like that.'

There was a pause, possibly for deliberate dramatic intent.

'But Davey sent me the details on the car that exploded, the one you followed ... it wasn't the same BMW.'

'I know this, because Ramsey used your little thingie to open the garage door,' Tinker replied, crushing Casey's moment. 'So what?'

Tinker thought back to when they entered the house. It had been a double garage Ramsey had opened, but there had been a second BMW, an X5 SUV Hybrid, in there.

'Anyway, the original BMW, the one I was in, its Wi-Fi pinged this morning.' Not realising Tinker was deep in thought, Casey continued. 'It pinged at Nine Elms, around the same time the explosion went off. Which means Saleh had driven there in the spare car.'

'Or, Saleh had someone drive it, like he had someone drive the other.'

'True, but the talk about the Tesla made me wonder,' Casey replied. 'It's not as easy to hack one of those as people seem to think from the movies. To do it, you need access. A key, card, the app, whatever. You need to be verified. And the only other person verified was Saleh.'

'He did it to make Nicky think he was being targeted,' Tinker realised now. 'He saw Nicky was going for the car, but needed him scared.'

'I think Saleh was working with somebody else to make sure that Nicky was taken out,' Casey said slowly. 'I think Flanagan genuinely believed he was helping Nicky, but all he was doing was helping the narrative Paddy Simpson wanted.'

'And the hit?'

'That's the thing,' Casey added. 'I've trawled the dark web, the UK sites. There's talk of a hit, but no actual details.

Enough to get the word out, but even when it's two million, nobody does it unless they know for sure they get the money. It's not true. So, anyone who talks about it as if it is? Probably involved.'

'Ramsey's alone with Saleh,' Tinker wanted to curse and swear. She'd completely fallen for the belief Saleh was as innocent a victim as Nicky was.

'The AirTag just appeared,' Casey said, typing. 'London Bridge.'

'Why would he be there?' Tinker asked.

'Maybe there's enough signal to appear?' Casey said. 'Or, he's changing trains.'

Tinker pulled up a London tube map on her phone.

'London Bridge links with Network Rail, Thameslink, the Jubilee Line ...'

She stopped.

'Shit, we have a coin toss,' she said. 'He's either carrying on to the Red Lion, and his half-sister, or he's diverted and he's off to Bermondsey and Saleh.'

'With a shotgun.'

'Well, it's probably hidden, but yeah,' Tinker replied. 'Tell Ellie to go to the Red Lion – if he goes there, we have a gang war happening.'

'What will you do?'

'Warn Ramsey and try to stop him if he turns up for vengeance,' Tinker said, disconnecting the call. Looking around, she couldn't see Whitehouse – the chances were he was calling in, or being told the details by the nurse elsewhere.

There was one face she recognised, though, entering the main waiting room area.

'What are you doing here?' she asked Joanne Davey.

'Done everything I can, heard about Robert, came as fast as I could,' Davey replied. 'Also, he's my boss and only hired me today, so I kinda feel I should be here.'

'Good, I need you to keep an eye on him,' Tinker pulled her jacket on. 'I need to go stop Nicky Simpson from killing someone.'

'Of course you do,' Davey replied. 'What do we know here?'

'Nothing much, he's under the knife right now,' Tinker explained, pointing at the side door. 'Mark Whitehouse just went through there,'

'DI Whitehouse is here?' Davey was surprised.

'He's using his police ID to get information,' Tinker said. 'But there's something off. I'd appreciate it if you used your police ID to get in and watch him.'

'Will do,' Davey smiled. 'And don't worry about anyone coming in, I know this place well. I once pushed my old boss through the back corridors as hitmen came to kill him.'

'Well, aren't you lucky,' Tinker smiled, patting Davey on the shoulder. 'Looks like you get to do that again.'

23

PULLING THE CORDS

THE *ADULT CRITICAL CARE UNIT*, WAS ON THE FOURTH FLOOR of the South Tower, and after Davey had shown the nurse her own warrant card, and been allowed through the doors to find her way to it, she found herself experiencing a rather strange sense of déjà vu.

She hadn't lied when she talked about the last time she'd been here; she really had been running for her life, using back corridors as ways to escape. And this gave her a little more caution as she entered through a door to the right that led into a bridge corridor, the windows that showed the outside world ignored as she continued through a set of double doors.

She was now in a corridor with two options; one was to Ward 4E on the right, and on the opposite side, around a corner to the left, was Ward 4F.

The nurse had told her the ward number, and she continued around to the right now, continuing through the central area until she reached a room at the end, where, inside, she found Mark Whitehouse standing there, staring at the bed.

'How is he?' Davey asked. 'Did the nurse say anything?

Surprised at the voice, Whitehouse spun around, looking back.

'I'm sorry, what?' seeing Davey, he frowned. 'DC Davey? What are you doing here?'

'Tinker asked me to check in,' Davey replied. 'You'd used your badge to get through, so I thought I'd do the same.'

She nodded at the empty bed.

'I assume he's still in surgery?'

Whitehouse nodded.

'Probably for a few more hours,' he said, and his face paled a little as he spoke. 'So I think he'll be there for quite a while.'

As if realising why she was there, Whitehouse forced a smile.

'You don't have to wait, you know,' he said. 'You didn't know him that well.'

'I didn't get the impression you were that close, either?' Davey asked.

'No, but he helped Ellie, and Ellie's a friend,' Whitehouse was staring at the empty bed still, his vision locked onto it, but his mind obviously far away. 'I feel I should be here.'

'I get what you mean,' Davey leant against the wall of the room. 'As of this morning, Robert Lewis is my boss, and I kinda hope he doesn't die, because if he does, then I have to find a new job.'

Davey held up a hand before Whitehouse could reply.

'Sorry, gallows humour,' she continued. 'I can't help myself, it's my defence mechanism.'

'It's okay, I get that,' Whitehouse smiled in return.

'No Delgado?'

'I didn't think she'd enjoy this.'

Davey nodded at this, understanding before her attention was diverted.

'You've changed your suit,' she said, changing the subject.

'What?'

'Your suit,' Davey repeated. 'You've changed it since I saw you this morning.'

'Yeah, so what?'

'Nothing, really,' Davey smiled. 'It's just having worked with a lot of male detectives over the years, I don't often see them change their "job" suits unless something bad has happened.'

She leant in.

'So, what did you spill on it? Chocolate? Mayonnaise? Whisky?'

'Why I changed my suit is none of your business,' Whitehouse said, unconsciously pulling at his shirt cuffs as he stepped back. 'And I'd appreciate it if you didn't treat me like your friend.'

Davey frowned at this.

'I'm sorry, have I pissed you off or something in the past?' she asked. 'I don't seem to recall kicking off with you.'

'Let's just say I'm not a massive fan of your mentor.'

'Doctor Markos?'

'No. DCI Monroe.'

At this, Davey laughed.

'Yeah, he's definitely not my mentor,' she said, shaking her head. She stared at Whitehouse's sleeves for a moment, but then turned away, walking over to the room's window and looking out of it.

'Did he say anything before you saw him leave?' she asked.

'Robert? No,' Whitehouse said.

'Why did he call you in?'

Whitehouse watched Davey for a moment and then smiled.

'You know damn well why he called me in,' he said. 'You sent him information about the text messages and the phone call. He thought it was Delgado. He's still pushing the fact that she's guilty of these things. I didn't believe it.'

'You don't?'

'No I bloody well don't!' Whitehouse exploded. 'She's been my partner ever since they kicked Ellie out. And throughout that time she's been solid beside me. I can't believe she'd do this.'

'But what about Ricky Smith?'

'Ricky Smith is an old school gangster. And, as I said to Robert, every single one of us has got a background, a history that could get us kicked off the force. Christ, you even acted on it, so don't give me the high horse speech here!'

Davey narrowed her eyes, and her lips thinned as she spoke.

'Don't for one second think I'm like one of your coppers,' she growled. 'I've done things I regret. But if I had that chance, I'd do them all over again.'

She paced around the room as she continued.

'I understand what it's like to have a history,' she said. 'And I understand what it's like to have revenge. I'm here today because the man in the operating theatre right now offered me a lifeline, and I'll do whatever it takes to prove myself ... even if it involves finding the man who did this to him.'

Whitehouse went to reply, but then stopped.

'Man? You don't think this was more than one person?'

Davey shrugged.

'I didn't see the wounds yet,' she said. 'I've seen some photos that were taken at the scene, but we're still early days.'

Whitehouse smiled at this; he didn't need to ask how Davey had seen the pictures as the City of London was Davey's old stomping ground.

'So, I'm guessing Monroe and his team are checking into it?'

'I called in a favour,' Davey nodded. 'I understand that's the done thing around here.'

She stepped closer.

'Trust me, the best investigators known to man are checking this out at the moment. And don't get me wrong, Mark – I can call you Mark, right? We *will* find out who did this.'

Whitehouse smiled, but it didn't reach his eyes, which narrowed at Davey's words.

'I think I need to make a call,' he said. 'I don't think Robert's going to be back for a while, and I need to let the office know that—'

'Why do you need to let the office know anything?' Davey interrupted. 'You're off the clock now. You could leave now, there's no real reason for you to be here. Unless you feel there *is* a reason.'

She moved closer still.

'So tell me, Mark, why do you have such a belief that you need to be here right now? Is it because you want to be here when he wakes up? Or is it because you *don't* want him to wake up?'

At this, Whitehouse straightened.

'What in God's name gives you the right to—'

'I can tell you right now what gives me the right,' Davey interrupted again, her voice darkening as she pointed at his cuffs. 'The bloodstains on your shirt. When you hit someone, beat someone even, blood spatter lands on you, often enough to force you to, say, change your suit, make sure no one sees the blood, sees what you did. But the one thing people always forget is the shirt underneath.'

Whitehouse looked at his cuff, noticing for the first time the specks of blood on it.

'I bet you cut yourself shaving, right?' Davey smiled. 'I bet there are a dozen innocent reasons why you've got blood on your shirt cuff. I get that.'

Whitehouse didn't reply as Davey started towards the door.

'So let's just cut to the chase,' she said. 'I'll go get something to check it with. We'll do a little DNA test, yeah? We'll just make sure this isn't the blood of Robert Lewis.'

Whitehouse glared at Davey.

'You have no idea what you're stepping into,' he said.

'No, I don't,' Davey replied. 'But you know what? I face down serial killers and gangsters, corrupt cartels and mercenaries daily, and a bent copper is nothing compared to them.'

Whitehouse sighed, before reluctantly pulling out a gun from his waistband.

'Well, now we'll see how I compare, shall we?' he asked, aiming it at her.

'Oh, please, you're not going to kill me in here,' Davey smiled, almost amused at the scene. 'We're in a hospital.'

'It's the night shift, and I'm a copper, while you're pretty much as blacklisted as Ellie is,' Whitehouse replied. 'So while I work out what to do next, and we wait to see if Robert lives or dies, just sit down and get comfy, because we're here for a while.'

WHEN CASEY WAS TEN, HIS FATHER HAD BOUGHT A COMPUTER.

His mum had wanted him to be more sporty, but his father never really was the sporty type himself, and had always been a proponent of brains over brawn. After all, he was an accountant and worked his entire life surrounded by numbers. And Casey, for most of his life, had followed his father's career, finding a similar love in numbers that his father had.

He never went into sports, unless they were extreme, like skateboarding. And his mum, although a little disappointed, never complained.

And, as he grew up, Casey found his aptitude for numbers turned into *coding*. And from coding, Casey moved into the next logical position, and became a hacker.

Amusingly, this was something his father hadn't been too happy about. He'd understood Casey needed to go through it, and kept telling Casey's mum it was likely a rebellious phase, and he'd always been sure that Casey would grow out of it.

He hadn't encouraged Casey, but Casey had known from the start of this phase of his life, there was a subtle understanding – or at the very least, a quiet approval of him doing this.

Of course, at the time Casey hadn't known that his father had been working for gangland bosses, or that he was organising laundered money for the Simpsons. He also didn't know that his father had been having an affair with one of the police detectives that he'd been working with; that was all something to come up down the line.

Casey's father had died before Casey could show him what he could do. He'd always been too scared to tell him, in case his father disapproved, but after his death, Casey had berated himself constantly, convinced this was something that, if he'd just come clean, he could have helped stop. It was something he could have used to save his father's life.

But he hadn't.

However, after years of working behind the computer keyboard, Casey's abilities had led him here, to the end of a very long road.

It hadn't taken Casey long to break into the Finders' system network. Robert's laptop had been left on in his office when Robert had taken Millie for a walk, and because it was linked to the network, Casey could remotely connect into the server, something he had made sure he could do from the moment he began working for the company, and once he was in the laptop, he found it far easier to remote unlock the phone from the password and user ID saved in the browser. The phone itself was turned off, but Casey knew better than anybody that the phone was simply a physical manifestation of the data inside; the data was the important part, and the data was something Casey knew he could find.

All phones these days uploaded to a cloud network. Apple had iCloud. Android had Google. Every phone had its own cloud system. And, once Casey had logged into the one Robert used, whatever had happened on his phone – the numbers he'd called or texted, the photos he had taken – everything was still available.

He'd spent ten or so minutes going through the cloud server, looking for anything that could give him a clue about what Robert was doing shortly before his attack, but after nothing came up out of the ordinary, Casey tried a different approach, and looked into the deleted folders file.

This was the problem with cloud drives; you could delete a photo, or a voicemail, or half a dozen other things off your phone. But if you were connected to the cloud system, the cloud would back it up for you, just in case you'd made a mistake, and this was an accidental deletion. Most times, this was a Godsend for people who'd accidentally deleted a photo when they wanted to keep it, and the deleted file system would hold anything removed for as long as a month, sometimes longer.

Unless the deleted file itself was re-deleted from that folder a second time, to ensure it was gone for good.

Casey discovered, while searching, that a recently deleted file, currently sitting in the folder hadn't had a chance to be secondary deleted and, pulling across to his own laptop, he opened it up ...

So, he sat and listened to Robert Lewis's last conversation before his attack.

And, as he heard the words, the confession of Mark Whitehouse, his face darkened as he realised what this meant.

When the audio file finished, Casey stared at his computer.

There were options.

First off, he could tell Ellie, although currently, Ellie had her own problems. Second, he could do something about this himself. Or third, he could fix this from his bedroom, like a good hacker would.

And so, taking the file, compressing it down to fit onto an email, he addressed it to a particular email address and pressed "send." This done, he typed a message into his phone and sent it, before walking over to his backpack, the one he'd been carrying all day, and opened it up.

Inside it, half hidden at the bottom, was an unfamiliar item to him, something he'd picked up from a drawer while they waited in the lockup, pulling it out of the backpack and holding it in his hands. He turned it around in them slowly, checking it over before removing the clip, checking the bullets inside.

Happy the gun was loaded, he then placed it into the back of his belt, grabbed his jacket and his skateboard, and climbed out of his bedroom window.

Mark Whitehouse was guilty of many things, but in his admission to Robert, the admission Robert had wisely recorded, he admitted he hadn't killed Casey's father.

But Casey now knew who did ...

And it was time for Casey to get back some justice of his own.

24

CONFRONTATIONS

RAMSEY ALLEN HAD BEEN SITTING ON THE SOFA IN SALEH'S house, watching the bald man as he paced around the living room nervously.

'I'm sure it's all fine,' he said. 'Can I do anything to help?'

'You can find out why your muscle decided to leave me to die,' Saleh snapped. 'Or why nobody seems to know where Nicky is?'

'You sure he wants to speak to you?' Ramsey smiled.

At this, Saleh muttered to himself and, grabbing his glass of vodka, walked out of the room, heading to the kitchen.

'If you're making a tea, I'll have one,' Ramsey shouted out after him. He was going to continue, give his milk and sugar request, but there was a flash of light to his side.

On the armchair beside him and on silent, a message had flashed up on Saleh's phone.

Ramsey couldn't help himself, he leant closer, peeking down at it.

FROM: SHARETRAKKER

Your trade of 300 SHSP shares has gone
through to Ferdia Holdings. Funds have now
been unlocked.

Ramsey stared at the message, confused. But, returning to his seat, he opened up his own phone, searching for an online stock tracker. Once there, he typed in SHSP to see what it was.

```
SHSP — Simpson's Health Spa (All Sessions)
```

He didn't need to know what the other text meant; he recognised the name. Both names, in fact. And, as Saleh walked in, ice now in his vodka, Ramsey looked up at him.

'You okay?' Saleh asked, instantly suspicious.

'No,' Ramsey lied. 'I had a message from my broker. He's lost me money in bloody shares. That's my pension buggered.'

'You don't need a broker,' Saleh said, walking over to the window, staring out. 'You can do it yourself.'

'Yeah, if you have a bloody degree or something,' Ramsey laughed.

'No, I'm serious,' Saleh replied as he looked back. 'There are apps out there which can help you.'

'The thing I always get confused about is the money,' Ramsey added, leading Saleh in the direction he needed. 'Like, say I sell some shares in Amazon.'

'You have Amazon shares?'

'No idea. The broker does it,' Ramsey found the lie coming easy now. 'But say I sell, maybe a grand or two's worth. If it was crypto, I could send that back to my bank pretty much immediately. But with stocks, it takes bloody ages.'

'Ah, that's the big problem with trading,' Saleh raised a glass. 'When selling equities on a share dealing or ISA account—'

'Already lost me.'

Saleh sighed, holding his frustration in check.

'When selling shares, there's a "settlement period" of two or three days before your funds become available to withdraw,' he replied. 'It's so the platform or company you use can exchange, clear, and settle your trade. It's a rule, I'm afraid.'

Ramsey smiled in thanks at this, while secretly he worked the trade days backwards.

Saleh sold his shares in Simpson's Health Spas around three days ago, around the same time Max Simpson did, if Casey's earlier message was correct. Which pretty much meant Saleh wasn't as squeaky clean as he was claiming.

'You should go,' Saleh said abruptly. 'I don't want you getting into any kind of danger. Your friend already bailed, just leave, I won't hold it against you.'

'You trying to get me out of here?' Ramsey enquired politely. 'Sounds like you're trying to get rid of me.'

'I'm trying to save your bloody life,' Saleh muttered, sipping his vodka.

Ramsey kept quiet, watching him for a few seconds.

'Saleh, how long have we known each other?' he eventually asked.

The bald driver considered the question for a moment.

'That's a tough question to answer,' he replied. 'I mean, you were around a lot, yeah? You were a face on the London scene since I was a teenager. But I don't think I really knew you. I don't think *anyone* really knows you. Especially the people you work with now.'

He took a sip of his drink.

'I'd say I only really got to "see" you properly a couple of years back, when Nicky started using you.'

Ramsey bristled at the word "using" but nodded.

'And, in all that time, have I ever given you the appearance of being an idiot?'

'You've been a grass, a scorpion, a snake and a real bastard,' Saleh smiled. 'But no, I don't think you've ever been that.'

Ramsey took a deep breath, rolling the dice in his head and tossing them onto the craps table.

'Then why treat me as one?' he asked calmly, watching Saleh. 'Because over the years I've "seen" you too, and not once have you struck me as a coward.'

At the term, Saleh's eyes glittered in anger.

'You dare—'

'Yes, I sodding well dare,' Ramsey replied, rising to face Saleh now. 'I don't know what game you're playing here, but while Nicky's been running all over the place, you've sat here in one, easy to find location. You've sent people out to die dressed as you, and to be honest, I'm not even sure you even cared about them, either.'

'You think I want to be here?' Saleh raised his voice, but Ramsey could see the expression of outrage on his face didn't match it.

'Yes, actually, I do,' he replied. 'I think this serves your purposes fine. I think it serves things better if I'm not here, although you probably need a witness for whatever you've got planned. And I also don't think you were here when the poor bastard drove out to his death.'

'Oh?' Saleh raised an eyebrow. 'So where was I then?'

'Probably near to Nicky,' Ramsey considered his state-ment. 'Yes, I really think so. I don't know how, maybe you were in the other BMW in the garage, and we didn't check, so we can't prove this, but you've always given the impression of a man who wants to be where the action is.'

Saleh went to reply to this, to give more indignance to the situation, but stopped and chuckled.

'Ramsey Allen, too intelligent for his own good,' he said. 'Your boss knows this?'

'Considering I only just realised, probably not,' Ramsey tipped an imaginary hat to him. 'But she's not stupid, Saleh. None of them are. They'll work things out. They'll know you sold your soul to Ferdia.'

Saleh was genuinely surprised at Ramsey's utterance of the name, but before he could reply, his phone, on the chair between them and easily seen by either party, pinged.

FROM: DANNY FLYNN

He's coming to you. Has the package. Hold him for the old man.

Ramsey watched Saleh with interest.

'Now that's interesting,' he said. 'You know Nicky's out there, you know he's pissed at you and has a shotgun, and then this mysterious message comes through, from a man I thought you hated, and you don't bat an eyelash. What's the package? The shotgun? And who's the old man? What do you know I don't? '

'Many things, Granddad,' Saleh walked to the phone, picking it up and placing it in his pocket, away from Ramsey's watchful gaze. 'So, as it looks like my end is near, feel free to piss off.'

Ramsey thought back to what they knew about Ferdia Holdings: the ownership, and the history. For Saleh to sell to the company, meant he had either been told to, or he did so out of loyalty.

Which meant …

'No, I'm fine,' he said, rolling those imaginary dice again. 'I know Nicky hasn't got a problem with me. So I'll wait and say hi to Paddy before I go.'

'Paddy?'

'The old man,' Ramsey replied. 'I think this is the plan, isn't it? Nicky has a shotgun, but what, it's not loaded? Danny Flynn was always a devious prick, and I saw his gun case when I did his locks. Which means Nicky walks in, believing you're the devil, realises he's screwed, you hold him here until Paddy turns up and – well, I don't know what happens there, all I care about is Paddy.'

'You think he'll want to speak to you?'

Ramsey shrugged.

'I see it like this,' he replied. 'Nicky's been paying the costs of my mum's housing in a rather nice old people's home. If he's removed from power, which looks to be soon, he won't be doing that anymore, will he? So, I thought I'd wait to see the new boss, or the old boss, rather, and see if I can get the same deal.'

'You'd turn on your friends? Work for Paddy?'

Ramsey considered the question, and then picked up Saleh's discarded and half-full glass of vodka, downing it before replying.

'Why not?' he asked. 'It's what you did, isn't it?'

ELLIE WAS IN HER CAR, PULLING UP OUTSIDE THE RED LION, when the message came through from Tinker.

> Casey just texted. AirTag heading to Red
> Lion.

Ellie looked up from the phone; it looked like Nicky wasn't as quick as he'd thought, and even though he'd gone by train, she'd managed to beat him there.

Or he'd already turned up and killed everyone.

No, then there would be police everywhere.

Looking behind her through the car's back window, she couldn't see Nicky approaching, so he must still be en route. Which gave her a minute or two's worth of time.

And so, for a moment, Ellie sat in the car, trying to plan her next move. Things were moving in a direction she hadn't considered, and she was furious she'd been played by Danny Flynn.

She should have been aware of what he would do.

The moment he had called offering his services she knew in her heart it was too convenient. And even though they had done their best not to use him, the fact he'd been there waiting, offering weapons that could kill people and defences to save them, while at the same time talking about hits, solidifying the threat while giving the information that Nicky needed to take revenge, was actually quite clever for the man – which made Ellie wonder whether it'd truly been Danny who had planned this.

Staring up at the pub, she wondered if fake Max and Carrie were still there. And, as she considered this, Danny Flynn's last line came back to mind.

'Paddy Simpson is back in town, and has been since this whole

bloody thing started. And, having spoken to him earlier today, I can vouch for that.'

There was every chance Carrie was working for Paddy, which meant there was every chance Paddy was up there, too. She needed to play clever here; she was entering a scenario which could end really badly.

Opening up her phone, she scrolled through her Cloud files and downloaded a particular document hidden deep within a series of sub-folders. Written months earlier, just before the Lumetta case, in fact, it was a single line, a command, followed by a list of numbers and names. It wasn't every person who owed her a favour, but it was a fair few, possibly even half. At the top of the list was an email for the command to be sent to, another favour to be burnt, and with a nod, she sent it by email to the unnamed source, with a request to wait for her next message before enacting. After all, if she was about to find herself in a terrible situation, she'd need every advantage she could find.

The message sent, she climbed out of the car and walked into the Red Lion Pub. It looked the same as it had earlier on that night, apart from the fact that there were fewer people there. It was late in the evening though, and the pub was looking to close.

The barman, looking up and seeing her, shook his head.

'They've gone,' he said. 'After you and your boyfriend left a few hours back, they spent a while arguing, then half an hour back, some old geezer turned up. Ten minutes later, they all left, almost like he walked in and said, "the party's over," you know?'

Ellie felt a sliver of ice slide down her back. The "old geezer" was most likely Paddy Simpson.

'Did they say where they were going?' she asked.

'Not really. It was quite recent, and I was serving,' the barman shook his head, before pausing. 'No, wait. Someone was asking about traffic. Said something about Jamaica Road if that helps?'

It was a vague clue; Jamaica Road ran through Bermondsey, which meant there was every chance they were heading to Saleh. She nodded, thanking the barman and left the pub, hastening to the car.

Staring out of the windscreen, Ellie planned out what to do next.

They were going to Bermondsey, but Nicky was coming here. Or was he?

Logic suggested that Nicky Simpson was going to have a faceoff with Saleh, with a shotgun that was likely doctored by Danny Flynn. The chances were that Tinker wouldn't get there in time, and Ramsey wouldn't be able to stop them from fighting. And when Paddy Simpson and his granddaughter Carrie arrived, Nicky would be taken, possibly even killed.

Casey lied to me.

Swearing, she turned the engine on, pausing as her phone rang.

It was a familiar number, one she had in her contacts, but hadn't seen for a long time.

Bryan Noyce – Home

Ignoring the spike of adrenaline that surged seeing Bryan's name, Ellie pressed the button to answer the call.

'It's Ellie,' she said. 'Is Millie okay?'

It wasn't a strange question; Ellie knew Millie had been brought to Casey and his mum by Tinker when she headed to the hospital. And the first thought she had was maybe the Cocker Spaniel had done something bad, maybe even destroyed Casey's house while waiting for her "mummy" to return.

However, the voice that spoke at the end of the phone was nervous and a little scared.

'Reckless,' Casey's mum replied. 'It's Pauline. Sorry to call, but I don't know who else to contact.'

'What's going on?' Ellie asked, realising this was way larger than just a dog.

'It's Casey,' Pauline Noyce replied. 'He went upstairs to sort something out for the woman who brought the dog here, Tinker. And I was playing with Millie – she's a beautiful dog, by the way – and I lost track of time. But after half an hour I hadn't heard from him, and I worried he'd, you know, fallen down a rabbit hole on the internet like he does.'

Ellie smiled at this; Pauline had no idea how deep Casey could fall into an internet rabbit hole. If anything, she believed he was just a slightly more intense gamer, rather than a hacker.

'What happened?' she pressed.

'I went up to ask if he wanted a cup of tea. But there's nobody here,' Pauline explained. 'There's an audio recording on his computer. File named "Lewis recording" I think.'

At this, Ellie shivered. *Casey hacked Robert's phone and found something. A recording from before he was attacked, perhaps?*

'I turned it on,' Pauline continued down the line. 'The recording is two men talking. I don't recognise the voices. But they talk about my husband's death. They talk about who did it.'

'Wait, hold on,' Ellie felt the world spinning around her for a moment. 'You have a recording saying *who killed Bryan?*'

Pauline's voice was tight at this point.

'You have to know I'm the last person who would talk to you about this,' she said. 'I still blame you for what happened, and I know the two of you were screwing. But I knew he'd grow out of it. You were just something new and exciting, something to give him distance from his life.'

She paused, gathering her composure before continuing.

'I also know because Casey told me that the two of you had broken it off when he died.'

Ellie wanted to push past this moment of guilt and regret, but she knew this was something that she had to go through.

'Casey told you this?' she asked.

'Casey tells me everything,' Pauline replied, and once more Ellie was forced to hold back a laugh. 'I know you were just a fling. And I knew Bryan. I knew he was a charmer, and I know these things can happen.'

'Please,' Ellie whispered. 'I get you need to have this conversation, and we can have this as long as you want later. After we've found Casey.'

There was a pause, and then a reluctant mutter of agreement from Pauline.

'Who is on the audio?'

'I don't know. But they said that the murderer was a man named Sally—'

Ellie's world imploded at the name of the name, and she found herself short of breath, clutching her chest, feeling her heart hammering, ready to explode.

'Saleh,' she said.

'Could have been, I don't know.'

Ellie leant back in the car seat. Casey had broken into

Robert's phone and had found an audio of someone confessing to his dad's death. And in the confession, they had named Saleh as the murderer.

And right now, at this very moment, Casey knew where Saleh was.

'Okay,' Ellie straightened, trying to slow her heart rate as it hammered against her chest. 'I'll see what I can find out. He can't be far.'

'Ellie, there's something else,' Pauline said, and the urgency in her voice scared Ellie. 'When I came in to find him, the audio was still playing on a loop, but he was gone, the window open. And on the floor, I found a bullet.'

'A bullet?'

'Yes,' and Pauline's voice was hardening. 'Did you give my son a gun?'

'Of course I haven't given him a bloody gun!' Ellie snapped back. 'I don't even carry a gun.'

But as she spoke the line, Ellie knew she was wrong. There was a moment in the lockup where Casey had been ferreting around in the corners, and had looked guilty when he was called back to task.

Could he have picked up a gun then? One that was once used by the owner of the lockup?

'Look,' Ellie said. 'Trust me – and I know that's difficult for you – but trust me to find him and sort this out. If Casey has found the man he believes killed his father, and he has a gun, then he's gone to find revenge. But I know the person he's aiming for, and I know there's people there already who can stop this.'

She looked in the rear-view mirror, seeing a set of car lights pulling up behind her.

'Your son will be safe, I promise—'

'You promise,' Pauline replied tonelessly. 'You promised you'd keep Bryan alive. You promised you'd make sure everything was fine for the family. And what did you do? You tried to take him from me. And you killed him.'

Ellie knew she couldn't reply to this. She knew Casey's mum had every right to say this. But it wasn't the time.

'I'll find your son,' she said quickly, disconnecting the call before anything else could be said and gripping onto the steering wheel with both hands, waiting for the wave to hit – and hit her it did.

The tears came faster.

And she started to cry.

Not sad tears, but ugly, racking sobs of pain and agony that coursed through her system. Every moment of the trial, every moment of the court case hit her like a hammer. She had seen Saleh countless times over the last couple of months, years even. And all that time she'd faced this monster, this killer of the man she loved, without even realising it.

When everything faded, Ellie sat back. She was suddenly clear-headed and knew what needed to be done. Casey was heading for Saleh, where Ramsey was, and he needed to be stopped. But before that, there was something else to sort out.

Climbing out of the car, she faced the car behind her, the lights still on.

'What the hell are you doing here?' she asked, as Tinker climbed out.

'Casey texted me,' Tinker replied. 'Said Nicky was here.'

She frowned.

'Are you telling me he's not?'

'Shit,' Ellie hissed. 'He's in Bermondsey.'

'Then why would Casey send us both here?'

'Because he has proof Saleh killed his dad,' Ellie replied, holding up her hand. 'And no, we don't have time to go into all of it. Just know we need to get to Bermondsey before Nicky tries to kill Saleh, Casey succeeds, and Paddy Simpson kills everyone.'

'How would Casey succeed—'

'He has a gun, Tink. God knows how.'

Tinker stared at Ellie for a long moment.

'I was only driving for twenty minutes,' she grumbled. 'Only twenty minutes, and the entire world's fallen apart.'

She climbed back into her Land Rover Defender.

'Come with me, or go in both cars?'

'Go,' Ellie waved. 'I have something quick to do first. But I'll catch up with that hunk of junk before you even reach the end of the road.'

'You wish,' Tinker smiled, but Ellie could see the concern in her eyes as she started the car and, with a squeal of rubber, performed an illegal U-turn, heading north.

Ellie climbed back into the car, and once more alone, the mask she'd forced herself to wear fell off Ellie's face, washed away by new tears.

All she wanted to do right now was throw it all away. Walk away from this argument, go to the hospital, and stand beside Robert, wait for him to get better.

She thought back to a moment, in a room a few weeks earlier, hiding from Lorenzo Lamas, Robert and Ellie forced to lie on top of each other, behind the sofa. There'd been a feeling, a moment, that something important could have happened there. But like usual, she'd pushed it to the side.

Angry at herself, angry at the world, angry at Nicky Simpson even, but furious at herself for what had happened,

Ellie picked up her phone again, and sent one last email to
the unknown address.

> Do it now. I'll give the countdown soon.

This done, she pushed the car's gear into drive, did a
second illegal U-turn, and headed after Tinker to
Bermondsey.

25

LATE NIGHT VISITORS

When the buzzer went off, Ramsey didn't know whether it was Nicky Simpson or his granddad who'd be there, and Saleh, with a little more nervousness than his bravado probably allowed, walked to the wall and clicked the intercom.

'Yes?'

'Saleh,' the voice of Nicky Simpson echoed through the intercom's tinny speaker. 'I think we need to talk.'

'Who is this?' Saleh asked, warming up now, relaxing thanks to the vodka, and seemingly enjoying the moment.

There was no reply, and Ramsey sighed.

'You should have one in-built with a camera,' he said.

'Where's the fun in that?' Saleh asked as he buzzed the gate open. 'Could you be a dear and open the door for him?'

Ramsey, sighing, walked over to the door to the house, opening it, staring out into the London night.

Nicky Simpson, in the same clothes he'd worn earlier, stood facing him with what looked to be a pool-cue bag over his shoulder.

'You,' he said, part in surprise and part in some kind of betrayal.

'Of course me,' Ramsey muttered. 'You were there when Ellie told Tinker and me to come here.'

Nicky Simpson nodded at this.

'You protecting him?'

'That depends,' Ramsey replied. 'You here to attack him?'

'Attack, no,' Simpson stated as he walked into the hallway, past Ramsey. 'Kill? Hell yes.'

As Ramsey went to reply, Simpson shrugged off the case, holding a pump-action shotgun in his hands.

'You might want to leave now,' he said.

Ramsey, however, shook his head.

'We told you at the start, we weren't going to allow you to take things into your own hands,' he growled. 'It's not too late to walk away, Nicholas. It's not. Too. Late.'

Even though he'd emphasised the words, they were ignored as Simpson pushed past him, walking into the living space, Saleh now sitting in an armchair.

'Hi boss,' Saleh lounged. 'I quit.'

'You can't quit when you've been fired,' Simpson said, patting the barrel of the rifle. 'And I have your severance package right here.'

'That's Danny Flynn's shotgun?' Saleh rose from the chair now, reaching behind his jacket, to something tucked into the back of his waistband.

'Don't!' Simpson snapped, the barrel of the shotgun rising. 'Hands where I can see it.'

'Or what you'll shoot? Oh, piss off,' Saleh laughed.

The echo of the shotgun blast almost deafened Ramsey.

Saleh staggered back, clutching his chest — before laughing, removing his hands to reveal no blood.

'As I said, that's Danny Flynn's shotgun, you pathetic little meathead,' Saleh pulled his own gun out now from his waistband. 'He's been part of this for weeks.'

Nicky Simpson stared in horror at the shotgun, pulling out the box of shells and letting them drop to the floor. Then, gripping it like a club, he—

'Nu-huh, don't you dare,' Saleh shook his head. 'Your granddad doesn't want you dead.'

He glanced at Ramsey.

'Well, not until he's here, at least.'

'My grandfather ...' Nicky frowned, then shook his head. 'Or is this like my dad supposedly being here? Only to be revealed as some fake-ass prick?'

'That fake was there to legitimise your sister before you crashed the party—'

'Half-sister.'

'Whatever,' Saleh waved for Simpson to sit on the sofa, texting Ellie as he did so. 'Take a seat. We've got someone else arriving soon, and then we're all set for a pleasant little family reunion.'

'When did he start working for my granddad?' Simpson asked Ramsey, but it was Saleh who answered.

'I think you'll find—'

'I didn't ask you!' Simpson screamed. 'I asked the man in here whose opinion I trust!'

'You think Ramsey Allen has your back?' Saleh tutted as he shook his head. 'He's only here to make a deal with Paddy to keep his mum in that nice new home you put her in.'

Ramsey shrugged, giving a weak smile in response.

'You know me,' he said. 'I'm nothing more than a tick on a shaggy dog.'

If Simpson caught the reference to their earlier conversation, he didn't acknowledge it, his eyes narrowing ever so slightly.

Ramsey hoped he'd realised the context; that Ramsey did this only when it helped the team.

Basically, *hold tight – help will come.*

'Danny … he set me up,' Simpson shook his head, chuckling now. 'When did that prick grow a pair?'

'Probably when he got rid of Chantelle,' Ramsey suggested. 'But he always was a devious bastard if we're being honest.'

'And when did you decide working for me was a bind?' Simpson turned to Saleh again.

'Oh, I can tell you that,' Ramsey smiled. 'He's never truly worked for you, he's been Paddy's bitch. Even sold him his five percent of shares.'

At this, Simpson glared at Saleh.

'Turncoat bastard,' he said. 'Was Danny lying about Max?'

Saleh's mouth shrugged.

'I don't know what he said,' he replied. 'I mean, if he said Max is munching a tub of CBD gummies a day, then sure.'

His eyes narrowed wolfishly.

'But, if he's telling you he knows first-hand that Daddy's on a ventilator …'

'This was all for me, wasn't it?' Simpson sighed. 'To get me here? I'm honoured. So now what?'

'Now?' Saleh raised the gun again. 'I aim this at you until Paddy turns up. Then he decides if I get to kill you or not.'

'I have a better idea,' a new voice spoke, as Casey emerged from the back of the room, from the same door Ramsey had entered through earlier, a Glock 17 in his hand, completely calm, as he aimed the gun at Saleh's head. 'How about you give me a reason not to blow your head off?'

'The brat,' Saleh muttered without looking. 'Go away, boy, I've got no time for you.'

There was an audible click as Casey cocked the pistol.

'Make time,' he said.

Saleh lowered the gun slightly as he looked at Casey.

'Is it "bring your toy gun to school" day today?' he mocked. 'What's your problem with me, anyway? It's him you're supposed to hate.'

'I do hate him,' Casey replied, his voice still ice cold. 'But he didn't kill my dad. You did.'

The room went silent as Ramsey watched both Simpson and Saleh.

'And how would you know that?'

Casey pulled out his phone, eyes locked on Saleh, as he pressed the screen. The sound of an audio recording echoed through the speaker.

'*Were you involved in the death of Bryan Noyce?*' The familiar voice of Robert Lewis said.

'*Paddy needed him removed, as Noyce was about to bring everything down,*' the voice of Whitehouse replied. '*I was told to let someone know where Noyce would be, and they'd sort it. That's all I did.*'

'*And who was the someone?*'

'*Saleh. I didn't know they'd kill him, I swear. I thought it was just a smack. And he'd been a prick to Ellie, and I was annoyed.*'

Casey turned off the recording.

'You believe that?' Saleh half laughed. 'The word of a—'

'Shut up!' Casey screamed. 'Just be a man and admit it!'

Ramsey stepped forward.

'Casey, now's really not the time,' he said. 'Ellie and Tinker will soon—'

'Ellie and Tinker aren't coming,' Casey said, eyes still locked on Saleh. 'I sent them to Camberwell. I couldn't have them stop me.'

Nicky Simpson folded his arms.

'I won't be stopping you,' he said, a slight smile on his lips, triumph at the change of positions.

Saleh had now turned the gun on Casey.

'Who knows about this?' he asked.

'By now? Not that many,' Casey replied. 'But Whitehouse is about to have a really bad day.'

'And why's that?'

'Because I sent the cavalry,' Casey smiled. 'And while Ellie's away, I'm going to do to you what you did to my dad—'

'I don't think that'll be happening today,' a new, older voice said, as a thin, almost skeletal man with a long-term suntan walked into the room, Carrie Mullen behind him, and a cutdown shotgun in his hands. 'Drop the gun, kid, I need him alive, while you … not so much.'

As Casey, realising he was in deep shit, lowered the gun, dropping it onto the floor, Ramsey walked over, stepping in front of him.

'He has a right to vengeance for his anger, Mister Simpson,' he said. 'And I won't let you kill him.'

'Bloody Nora, Ramsey Allen being heroic? Gotta be some kind of angle,' Paddy Simpson smiled. 'The kid can stay if he stops being a bloody drama queen.'

He turned to face Simpson.

'I'm only here to kill my grandson, anyway,' he said, cocking the shotgun and aiming it at Nicky's face.

'STOP BLOODY SMILING.'

DI Mark Whitehouse paced back and forth in the ward-room; the place was almost empty, the only other patient at the other end, and as such, the nurses had left the two police officers alone, unaware of the standoff inside.

Davey had taken the empty bed, laying on it, hands behind her head.

'Why?' she asked politely. 'Surely if I think it's funny, I'm allowed to smile?'

'It's not!' Whitehouse snapped.

'How do you see this going?' Davey asked, finally sitting up. 'Even if Robert doesn't remember, you'll never know if it'll stay forgotten. And I know. And I'm sure by now others know.'

'And how would that happen?' Whitehouse sneered. 'I deleted it from the phone.'

'Yeah, but did you delete it from the cloud?' Davey shook her head as she saw the realisation on Whitehouse's face. 'This is the problem with you Met types. You always think by one problem at a time. By now Ellie's computer kid has probably hacked the phone, and sent it to bloody well everyone.'

'That's not possible—' Whitehouse rummaged in his coat for the phone, and that single moment of distraction was all Davey needed, as she grabbed and threw a metal tray at Whitehouse's head, using his motion of swatting it away to dive forward, grabbing at the gun in his hand.

Whitehouse was stronger, but Davey was more agile, and not averse to fighting dirty, kneeing him in the groin as she pulled the gun up, the weapon firing into the ceiling, the faint sounds of screams heard outside the room, as the nurses and patients in the central ward area realised the two officers inside it weren't just playing cards while they waited.

He didn't let go, so she kneed again, even harder, and with a whimper, he fell to his knees. Stepping back and wheezing, her heart pounding in her chest, Davey aimed the gun at him.

'You utter prick,' she muttered.

There was more noise now; people running down the corridor, and Davey backed away, against the wall now as the door smashed open and DS Kate Delgado stood in the doorway.

'Get back!' Davey cried, the gun now aimed up at her. 'I've kicked the shit out of one corrupt, murdering bastard today, I can do two!'

'Stand down,' a gruff Scottish voice said, the tone gentle and parental, and Davey almost wept as the familiar form of DCI Alex Monroe emerged into the room behind Delgado. 'She's with me.'

Lowering the gun, allowing it to drop to the floor, Davey gathered her breath as two officers ran in, grabbing Whitehouse, pulling him, complaining and still clutching between his legs, to his feet.

Delgado stared at Whitehouse as he looked away from her piercing gaze.

'We got a recording,' she said. 'Sent by one of Reckless's team. It's you and the lawyer currently in surgery. You confess everything.'

'It's not true!' Whitehouse whined. 'It's AI tech! That kid's setting me up!'

'If he is, we'll know soon enough, laddie,' Monroe added. 'Your man Lewis is just out of surgery. Coming back right now. And they reckon he'll be making a full recovery.'

Whitehouse paled as he looked around.

'I want to make a deal,' he said. 'I can give you Paddy Simpson. He's in town too, so you can get him before he goes.'

Delgado couldn't help herself; she punched DI Mark Whitehouse fully on the nose, drawing blood as he fell back.

'That's for making me believe Reckless was a murderer,' she snarled.

'And corrupt?' Monroe suggested.

Delgado turned to look at him, her eyes cold and emotionless.

'I'll settle for murderer to be struck off the list right now,' she said as the officers led the handcuffed Mark Whitehouse out of the wardroom. 'The jury's still out on the rest. She learned under you, after all.'

And, this stated, she nodded to one officer to bag up the gun before storming out of the room.

'You know, I don't know if she's joking or serious,' Monroe mused.

'She's serious,' Davey replied, gathering her things together. 'Thanks for coming. And bringing her, I suppose.'

'I had to,' Monroe smiled. 'Delgado's south of the river. Needed a local guide and all that.'

He patted her on the shoulder.

'Besides, if my team learnt that everyone who leaves gets shot and killed, none of the wee buggers would leave, so I had to keep you safe.'

He stopped the smiling act though, as genuine concern came over his face.

'You can come back anytime,' he said. 'The Last Chance Saloon is there for you.'

'I appreciate it,' Davey looked back at the bed. 'But, right now, I think I have a new team to check out.'

Monroe nodded at this as the two of them left the ward.

'Always check your pockets after sitting with Ramsey Allen,' he said, his voice fading as they walked away. 'Never call Tinker by her real name, don't piss the child off as he can do terrible things to you online, and always tell Reckless's bloody dog she's a good girl ...'

TO NICKY SIMPSON'S CREDIT, HE DIDN'T FLINCH WHEN THE shotgun was aimed at him.

'Before you kill me, you could at least explain why,' he said. 'I was your choice! You picked me over Dad!'

'I picked you because the option was a twitching mess of a man who couldn't form sentences!' Paddy shouted. 'You were only marginally better! If I'd known I had other grandchildren, things would have been different!'

'So that's it?' Simpson looked around. 'Basically, because I was outed on a sodding livestream, you took over my health clubs and now you intend to kill me?'

'Oh no, you're going on a "spiritual pilgrimage" somewhere,' Carrie replied sarcastically. 'You'll not, of course, be doing that, but nobody will know, and you'll quickly be forgotten.'

'I have over a million Instagram followers,' Simpson snapped back. 'They won't forget me.'

'They already have,' Carrie smiled.

'It wasn't just being outed,' Paddy continued. 'It was the fact you were ashamed of it! You tried to take it down! You were so scared of losing this persona you'd created, you made me and your father, your legacy, look weak!'

'My legacy?' Simpson looked back at his grandfather now. 'My "legacy" only started because you lucked in when the Richardsons got too violent for their own good and were banged away! I built my empire with my own two hands!'

'And with the money you gained from illegal activities,' Ramsey said. 'Sorry, just stating facts.'

'You left the world you were groomed for long ago,' Saleh said now. 'I did everything, not you. And now Carrie and I will do everything while you piss off into obscurity.'

'And us?' Ramsey asked, still shielding Casey. 'Because we'd really like to live.'

'Ramsey Allen, you always were a snivelling little shit,' Paddy muttered. 'Even when you were screwing the Lumetta bitch, we all knew you were bad news. So no, you'll be going on holiday too.'

He looked back at Nicky. 'Maybe we'll kill the kid and make it look like you did things to him first? Let's really kill your legacy.'

'It's a "Hashtag me too" moment,' Carrie smiled.

'Aw, that sucks. You see, I really wanted to see you kill Nicky,' a new female voice spoke now, and Ellie walked into the room, flanked by Tinker, a gun in her hand. 'But when you threaten my team, you take all the fun out of a good old gangster face off.'

She looked at Saleh.

'Did you know your garage door's wide open?' she enquired with a smile. 'You really ought to do something about that. Some kids are taking the wheels off your BMW.'

She now turned her gaze back to Paddy and Carrie.

'Literally anyone can get in,' she said.

'I had guards outside,' Carrie snarled. 'They had orders—'

'Yeah, about your guards,' Tinker said, clicking her neck muscles as she stretched. 'If you want to be some kind of female kingpin here, you'll need better ones, as I'm afraid I broke them. And the tanned prick you had pretend to be a hitman at the gym? He just ran off like a girl.'

'So what's the deal here?' Paddy Simpson asked. 'Why has the great Ellie Reckless turned up? Surely not to save the man who killed her true love?'

'Nice try, but we all know now who really killed Bryan,' Ellie said, nodding at Casey. 'Thanks to him finding the recording where Whitehouse confesses.'

She glanced back at Saleh.

'That sabbatical you were all just talking about? You might want to consider it yourself.'

She looked at Casey.

'Your mum's worried about you, and it was a dick move sending me to Camberwell.'

'Well, I didn't want you stopping me from killing my dad's murderer,' Casey muttered. 'Which I would have done if Captain Ancient here hadn't stopped me.'

'So what do you want?' Paddy, ignoring the insult, asked.

'Well, Paddy, it's your lucky day,' Ellie smiled now. 'Because I've got favours to burn and I'm feeling generous. You like to deal, right? So, let's deal.'

26

MEXICAN WAVING

'You've got guts,' Paddy Simpson said, stepping forward. 'I've wanted to meet you for a while, you know, ever since Bryan Noyce.'

Ellie kept all of her emotions from her face as Paddy continued.

'Ellie Reckless, the copper for criminals, always there to help, if you give her a favour,' he sneered. 'How does it feel? Spending all this time building these favours to find out who killed your boyfriend, or should I say your lover? The man you broke a contract with God over, only to find that the person you believed killed him, was too much of a pussy to even try to do it?'

Paddy paused as he considered a second point.

'You lost your marriage as well, didn't you?' he asked. 'Court case too much for him, perhaps, hearing all about your infidelities?'

Ellie walked across to the bar, picked up the bottle of vodka, and poured out a glass.

'You don't mind, do you?' she asked Saleh. 'It's just it's

been a bit of a long day. What with having to keep *that* prick alive.'

She motioned at Nicky, currently standing in anger, staring at her.

'You know a lot about me, good for you,' she said to Paddy now, sipping the vodka. 'I'll be honest, I know sod all about you. I know you were Billy big-balls while I was a kid, but by the time I was old enough to give a shit, you'd run off to Majorca like a coward, leaving the firm to your son.'

She frowned as she said this.

'I suppose you only become one of the "great" gangsters, like Billy Hill, the Krays, even the Richardsons ... if you get nicked, or do something of note. You, Paddy, did neither.'

'This is an interesting way to negotiate,' Paddy growled, angering.

In response, Ellie shrugged.

'As I said, it's been a long day keeping your grandson alive, and I'm tired of bullshit,' she said. 'Although we weren't trying to keep him alive, were we? This whole thing has been smoke and mirrors, theatre, just to have a little fun at his expense.'

'What's that supposed to mean?' Nicky now asked, looking around. 'I've got a two million pound hit on me.'

'Yeah, about that,' Ellie replied. 'You don't. Does he, Paddy?'

Paddy Simpson didn't reply, instead just giving a hapless shrug, smiling as he watched Ellie walk around the room.

'I couldn't work out what was going on at first,' she said. 'Too many things weren't striking true. First off, we have Nicky having the explosion at his office. Then we have his Tesla turning on and revving up when he's walking towards it. Things that would make him think he'd managed some kind of near-miss escape. Things that kept him running.'

She waved around the room with her drinking hand, spilling the vodka slightly.

'He knew he couldn't go to the police, and so he came to me. You *aimed* him at me, in fact, and at the same time, you decided you were going to aim other people at me – people that I thought were there to help. People like Danny Flynn, for example.'

'Danny,' Nicky answered irritably. 'That scroat's got a lot to answer for.'

'I agree,' Ellie smiled. 'I will say, however, that the monster he is right now was created by you. When you bullied him for his contacts in Boston, or when you forced him to pay his debt, you changed him, made him someone who'd do anything to see you fail.'

She looked back at Paddy now.

'And so, Danny, once he was away from Chantelle, he looked for new allies – "enemy of my enemy" – and all that. And guess what he found? Nicky's dear darling granddad. Danny told me as much when we spoke today. He said he had friends in the Balearics, people he spent a lot of time with. And it's true. Danny had spent a lot of time in Majorca over the years. A lot of his father's old friends lived there in the Costa del Crime. And over the years he met Max, and maybe even you, Paddy – getting annoyed with how your grandson was running things.'

She walked over to Nicky Simpson now, patting him on the back.

'He really hated you. And I get that, because I'm not a fan of you either, but at least I don't want you dead,' she said.

'It's a start,' Nicky, unsure what else to say, smiled.

Ellie looked back at Paddy Simpson.

'I'm guessing you knew Danny,' she said. 'After all, you probably hung around with Danny's father back in the day. And this would have given you some kind of relationship to build from. And then you've got Carrie returning to the family, the granddaughter you never really knew. I don't know if it was Danny, or Carrie, that reminded you about Ferdia Holdings, but I'm guessing it's the latter.'

She turned her attention back to Carrie now.

'Your grandfather and Paddy set it up together in the fifties. And for the last few decades it's sat fallow, doing nothing. Perfect for some kind of shell company to do things off books, especially as it was done when there was less of a digital footprint to worry about.'

She looked back at Nicky.

'If I'm right, the plan was simple, to start with,' she explained. 'They wanted to take away this world that you'd built, this legitimate world, and force you to become the Simpson your grandfather wanted. He didn't give a shit about your fame, your celebrity, he saw this as a weakness. "Old school" in mindset, and convinced you'd end up giving away everything to the people he spent decades crushing down. So, according to Ramsey, who sent me a very interesting text while chatting to Saleh, Danny started buying shares in your publicly funded company, and Ferdia Holdings started doing the same. But as time went on, things changed. For a start, Matteo Lumetta outed you to the world. And you didn't react how a gangster would. Paddy would have started a bloody gang war, whereas you sent your lawyers in. That wasn't something Granddad wanted to see.'

Nicky nodded.

'I'm aware of that,' he said, glowering at Paddy.

'So, at this point, Paddy's got Carrie whispering in his ear, a woman who wants bloody revenge. He's got Danny pointing out you're last year's news, nothing but a joke here now, and he realises it's time for a succession. Maybe he comes back and takes the reins again. Maybe his grand-daughter has a chance, as she's been pampering his ego, convincing him she's a chip off the old block. Either way, you're out. And so they work out a way to take your eye off the ball long enough for them to do what they need to do.'

'The hit?' Nicky asked.

'There is no hit,' Ellie replied. 'We thought there was, because we'd been given the impression there was.'

She looked around the room again.

'Saleh informs Max there's a hit on Nicky. Max is suggested, in his drugged state, to send Flanagan to get him back. Flanagan is old school, but Flanagan is also loyal to Max and, therefore, Nicky.'

She smiled at Paddy.

'You needed him gone if you wanted to take over properly. Max would never let anybody touch his son, even family. And so Flanagan's given a car and told what to do. Fake a murder. Get Nicky out.'

She pointed at Carrie now.

'You've joined the club by this point, but you weren't aware Nicky recognised you, were you? At least enough to know that something is wrong. And while watching you, he realised that the alarms have been cut to his room. Which means he isn't there when the explosion goes off, which causes a problem with the plan, because Flanagan had arranged a webcam to pass a message to Nicky. Who didn't see it. And, when he gets down to the basement, Saleh, realising he's going to get in his car and drive away, remote turns it on with his own key.'

Ellie looked back at Saleh.

'You were there, weren't you?' she asked, waiting for the nod before turning back.

'But because Saleh couldn't be there and have an alibi, he convinced a neighbour to shave his head and pretend to be him if anybody called. And in the chaos, Nicky Simpson was guided to us; the only people that he knew had no skin in this game.'

She paused, looking back at Paddy.

'It was a good plan. Get Nicky to us. Have us look after him and then follow Nicky based on the tracker in his watch, bastardising something Max did to keep his son safe. And it would have worked if we weren't so good at our job.'

She turned to the group again.

'The problem was, Danny was too good at convincing us everybody was after Nicky,' she continued. 'So, when we hid out in a boxing club, you sent some of your own men to pretend to be assassins.'

'And just so I know, how'd you know they weren't real assassins?' Paddy asked curiously.

'Assassins don't stand outside the door and demand you bring someone out.' It was Tinker who replied to this. 'Assassins don't offer ten grand when they don't have it. Assassins will just enter. Those guys had enough firepower to walk into that boxing club and subdue everybody without a problem. But they all turned up at the same entrance and made enough noise to let us get out the back. It was purely to keep us moving. Same with the cars. Always moving, never thinking. And the fact the leader had a tan and drove a car owned by your company was a big bloody clue.'

'Because at this point, your plan had gone wrong,' Ellie added. 'Because somebody had gotten a little carried away.'

She glanced at Carrie.

'The original plan was a backup "murder." If Nicky escaped without being picked up by Flanagan, then you had a second location. A place you could fix things – but there was someone else waiting there. Seth Taylor.'

'I don't know a Seth Taylor,' Paddy complained.

'That's because you didn't hire him. She did,' Ellie pointed at Carrie. 'In her mind, it was a chance to actually kill Nicky once and for all. She didn't care about Saleh. She didn't care about who had sent us a distraction. All she cared about was that if Nicky walked over to Saleh to speak to him, she could take him out with an explosion, even taking Flanagan out at the same time, giving it all a nice, neat bow. The problem was, she hadn't banked on Flanagan being more aware of what was going on when Seth killed fake Saleh, realising that he was being set up himself.'

'How would you know I did this?' Carrie scoffed.

'Phone numbers,' Casey now spoke. 'The burner being used by Whitehouse, the one that sent everyone the location texts and later called the armed police on Flanagan.'

'He also made a phone call to the club, ten minutes before everything kicked off,' Tinker replied now, nodding at Carrie. 'It would have been answered by reception, where that bitch was working.'

'Chances are Whitehouse was calling Carrie to tell him what was happening, or asking for his orders. Probably the latter, because by that point Flanagan would have been in position. And by then, Whitehouse would have already sent Saleh the meetup location – Carrie changing the address for her own reasons, and getting Whitehouse to do it is why

Saleh's phone had two different ones,' Ellie continued. 'We know he worked for you, Paddy, so he was working for her too by default, and probably thought this was agreed upon from on high. And he knew of Seth, because his dad, who worked for you arrested him, and then let him go free about twenty years back.'

Carrie chuckled.

'Your team's good,' she said. 'Shame they have to die at some point.'

'If we die, it won't be today and it won't be by you,' Tinker said, gripping the gun tighter, as Ellie, watching, shrugged.

'Flanagan died because you needed to have him removed. If he started telling people the truth, then everyone would know what was going on. We were still on the run and by now, the tracker had been removed. You had no way of finding him, and this was a problem. You realised you needed to bring us to you instead. So, you told people Max was in town. After all, Paddy was using a fake ID to get into the UK, under Max's name, so the flight logs matched up if anyone looked. But when we met fake Max, you hadn't realised the men you'd bought with you *weren't* as loyal as you thought they were.'

Paddy went to reply, but Ellie waggled a "nuh-uh" finger at him.

'And then you aimed us at Danny Flynn – Danny who, when we arrived, gave us a story of how Max had been put in some kind of coma by Paddy, and how Paddy was in town. He led Nicky down the garden path, even showing him where the shotguns were, so Nicky could go off on his own little revenge spree.'

She glanced at Simpson now.

'Every button pressed, Nicky was primed and ready to go,

but then there were more problems now. Mark Whitehouse had been outed by Robert Lewis, one of our team, and after confessing on tape, he beat Robert to within an inch of his life, leaving him in a critical condition, which threw the team into disarray. Tinker went to the hospital. Whitehouse, realising Robert was still alive, also went there to see what he could do to stop the message getting out. We took our eye off the ball.'

'How did you know I was here?' Nicky now asked.

'Casey placed a tracker on you,' Tinker nodded at Casey, who shrugged.

'You didn't think Ramsey would realise Saleh was working for you,' Ellie's voice was darkening now as she continued. 'You didn't think we'd work out you took Max's shares, as well as buying Saleh's and Danny's to gain a controlling interest in the company. You underestimated us from the very beginning.'

'It's a great story,' Paddy eventually spoke. 'But where does it leave you right now? It leaves you standing in a room of gangsters, having a bit of a family squabble. Nothing more.'

He pointed at Tinker.

'Your woman has a gun, but we have two. Saleh? He makes three. You might think you're controlling the situation, but as you said, I used to deal with things a little differently back in my day. And I don't care if I have bodies lying on the floor. After all, when this is all said and done, Carrie, who's just a receptionist at Nicky's health club, will tell a story of how the terrible Nicky Simpson had a fatal gunfight with the woman who had been hunting him for ages. Fatal for all of you, I'm afraid.'

27

BURN THE FAVOURS

For a few seconds, nothing more was said in the room.

And then, before Ellie could reply to this, there was a movement from behind Ellie, and as she spun, she saw more men entering, guns in hand, one of whom was the rather pissed off, tanned "assassin" from earlier.

'Oh dear,' Paddy sighed theatrically, hands now out in mock surrender. 'It looks like my friends have arrived. That could be a problem for you. What are you going to do now?'

Ellie shrugged.

'To be honest, I just want to make a deal,' she replied. 'I'm not the police anymore. Mark Whitehouse has been taken. He'll be confessing everything to get some kind of deal for himself, anyway. But I was tasked with doing two things. Save Nicky Simpson's life and find out who did this. That's all I need to do.'

She looked back at Nicky.

'I've almost completed the job,' she smiled.

Nicky looked at the guns and then turned back to Ellie.

'I'm not sure "almost" is something I would say here,' he replied.

Ellie shrugged, checking her watch before looking back at Paddy and Carrie.

'So, now it's time to negotiate,' she said.

At this, Paddy laughed loudly.

'How the hell do you think this is a negotiation still?' he asked.

'Because, as I said before, I have cards I haven't yet played,' Ellie explained. 'The deal's very simple. You don't want Nicky running your criminal empire, you want Carrie running it. That's fine by me. I couldn't give a shit. Take the empire. Bring back the days you used to love. Teach your granddaughter the ways of being a leader. Great. Wonderful. But give Nicky Simpson back his clubs.'

'You what?'

'You heard me. You give Nicky back the shares you've taken from him. His dad can keep his ones, as I feel he was probably conned out of those without realising what he was doing. But the rest goes back to Nicky, and he becomes the owner once more of Simpson's Health Spas.'

'Say I do this,' Paddy narrowed his eyes, holding a hand up to stop Carrie's protest. 'And then what?'

'Then you leave him alone. Nicky Simpson walks away from this side of the business, is excommunicated from the Simpson family, bar maybe his dad, and carries on being the man he claims he is, the YouTuber with the TikTok following, and the health spas, and the macro smoothies, and whatever bollocks he's going to create this week. The two of you go your separate ways.'

Nicky Simpson looked at Saleh.

'I don't want him as my driver either,' he said.

Saleh, looking back, shook his head, confused.

'I've always worked for Paddy Simpson,' he replied. 'You were just an arrogant prick I had to look after.'

'Good. You're still fired,' Nicky nodded.

Ellie, realising she was losing control of the conversation, raised her hand.

'We don't want bloodshed. We just want stability. Give Nicky back his life and let him walk away from the criminal side. You can have it. We're all more than happy for you to be the new head of the underworld.'

'I prefer the idea of just killing him,' Paddy replied, shaking his head.

'And that's your option,' Ellie replied. 'But you still haven't heard my counter offer.'

She walked into the middle of the room now, finishing the glass of vodka before carrying on.

'It's very simple,' she explained. 'I'm the cop for criminals who gains favours, and I've used a lot over my time. I've had favours burned to bring me dog food. A lift for an old woman I met on a street once. I've had experts help me in my cases. I've had people fix my cars, and I had a drug dealer kneecapped on a roof once. My favours are varied. But they were all for one reason – to find out who killed Bryan Noyce, and who ordered the hit.'

She stared at Paddy now, and the room's temperature seemed to lower at the gaze.

'And thanks to this case, the information *has* come out. And, thanks to a police officer now in custody, who's spilling his guts out probably by now, I know Saleh killed Bryan and you ordered it, Mister Simpson.'

'Bold words. But can you prove it?'

'I don't need to. Remember, that's not my job anymore.

I've told you, my job is to keep my client alive and find out who did this. I have the latter, I just need to fix the former. That's why I've offered you a deal that makes everybody happy. And that's why, if you decide not to go for it – I will *burn every single favour I have to destroy you.*'

At this, Paddy Simpson laughed.

'And how do you destroy a gang lord?' he chuckled, looking around.

'By cutting off his air supply,' Ellie said. 'If you can't operate, you're no use. You're weak. And the vultures come in.'

She checked her watch again, smiling.

As she did this, Paddy's phone buzzed with a text.

Picking it up, he stared in confusion at the message.

'What did you do?' he asked, looking up at Ellie in a mixture of surprise and shock, as his phone buzzed again.

And again.

And then it rang. He answered.

'This is Paddy – Dave, look – no, listen—'

Paddy Simpson disconnected the call and stared back at Ellie.

'What did you do?' he asked, his face expressionless.

'I knew you'd say no,' Ellie shrugged, looking around the room. 'And so I made sure I had a backup plan. A lot of the people who owe me favours are quite high in the criminal underworld. My deal is always the same. A favour given freely no matter what it is, but something they can always do.'

She held her own phone up now.

'I sent a message out today to a large chunk of these favours, telling them that if I hadn't called a particular source by—' she looked at her watch '—five minutes ago, they were to cease all ties with the Simpson organisation with immediate effect.'

'That's not you anymore, by the way,' she looked back at Nicky. 'It's all your granddad's again, because he wanted it back.'

She looked at Paddy.

'I'm sure down the line you'll be able to get these arrangements back. But right now, you are friendless. You are powerless.'

She looked back at the men who had arrived.

'Is there a word for "ally-less?"' she asked, as one by one, each of the men received a text message, read it, and then looked at Paddy apologetically before placing the guns away and leaving. Even the tanned assassin guy shook his head sadly before walking out silently.

'You should have known I'd do this when we faced off in the pub,' Ellie said to Carrie. 'You knew back then I had a longer reach than people expected. But I banked on your inexperience to ignore it. Looks like I was right. So here's the deal, Paddy. Let your grandson free and in exactly thirty days, once he's free of all ties to you, I'll make sure that every single person who backed away from you tonight is given the option to freely come back if they wish.'

She walked closer now, pushing the end of Paddy's sawn-off shotgun aside as she stared at him.

'But if you don't, you're nothing more than a sad old man, with delusions of grandeur and a criminal empire that no longer exists.'

Surprisingly, Paddy laughed, clapping his hands.

'You're good,' he said. 'I almost wish you were on a different side of the table. I'd love to have had you as my right-hand man, back in the day.'

'I was trained by the best,' Ellie said, spitting into her palm and holding it out. 'Do we have a deal?'

There was nothing else that Paddy Simpson could do. He spat on his own palm, and shook Ellie's hand.

'Deal is made,' he said, ignoring Carrie's yelp of anger. 'My grandson can go free. We won't cause any more problems. And by tomorrow, we'll transfer the stocks back into his account. He can have his little toy health club back.'

Nicky grinned, looking at Carrie.

'You're fired too, by the way. Just so you know.'

'Got a new job,' she hissed. 'Yours.'

'Good luck with that,' Ellie said as she walked backwards, motioning for her team to join her.

One person didn't.

Casey, standing still, stared at Saleh, fury in his expression and tears of rage building in his eyes.

'He killed my dad,' he whispered. 'He needs to die.'

He looked back at Ellie.

'Why didn't your deal include him dying?'

'Because that's not how things work,' Ellie replied sadly. 'We know he killed Bryan. But it needs to be proven in a court of law,'

'So you can get your life back,' Casey muttered. 'Is that all you cared about?'

'I don't want him dead,' Ellie snapped. 'That's too quick. I want him found guilty. I want him banged up and I want him remembering, every single day of his miserable life, that he was taken down by us.'

In the background, they could hear the faint sounds of police sirens. Paddy raised an eyebrow.

'You grassed us up?' he asked, genuinely mortified.

'I'm not one of you,' Ellie replied angrily. 'I never was.

And yeah, of course I grassed you up the moment they found Whitehouse. They're here to take down the man who killed two people today, based on their orders. A man who started a wave of terror, blowing up a health club.'

She smiled at Paddy.

'The man who is currently head of the Simpson criminal organisation.'

As blue lights flashed through the window, and the sounds of car doors slamming could be heard from outside, Paddy simply laughed.

'That's some grand playing, there, Reckless,' he hand clapped. 'Now we'll leave it in the hands of our solicitors.'

EPILOGUE

THE POLICE, LED BY KATE DELGADO, HAD TAKEN PADDY, Carrie, Saleh and Nicky into custody, but, on Delgado's orders, had let Ellie, Casey, Tinker and Ramsey go, even though she knew Tinker held a firearm. Ellie assumed it was Kate's way of apologising, but considering the fact Delgado didn't speak a word to her while they took the protesting Simpsons and associates away, she wasn't sure.

After that she took Casey back home to a distraught mother, playing down what happened, but pointing out that Casey had helped in a police sting that likely brought to justice her husband's killer. After taking back Millie, Pauline made it perfectly clear to Ellie that she wasn't welcome there anymore, and so she left, taking Millie away from Casey's house.

They didn't allow dogs in the hospital, so Ellie left Millie in Ramsey's care. She didn't know if Ramsey was happy about this, but she'd burnt enough favours for the night and, to be honest, she thought that with the horrors Ramsey had seen that day, having a dog that just wanted treats and snuggles would probably help him. And, this done, and with Tinker promising to check in later, Ellie went to the ACCU ward to check in on Robert.

Davey had been there; she'd stayed even after White-house was arrested, and claimed it was purely because Robert had hired her that morning and she felt it was bad luck to walk out on a boss the same day, and also gave Ellie a message from Alex Monroe, asking her to contact him some time for a chat. With the shift effectively changed, Davey went home for a well-earned sleep, while Ellie sat down in the chair beside the sleeping Robert.

He was bruised and battered, his head shaved on the right-hand side, with ugly-looking staples holding the skin together, and his left arm was in a full cast. The doctors had said he was lucky, and that with rest and recovery, he should return to almost a hundred percent.

It was the "almost" in their words that worried Ellie. They'd also explained he'd had what was literally the equivalent to a stroke, brain trauma wise, and she should prepare for anything.

On day two, the police had released Nicky from custody; his solicitors had pointed out clearly that Paddy Simpson had obviously been the force here, claiming his old stomping ground for his granddaughter, while Nicky, the only legitimate member of the family, had tried, heroically, to stop it.

Ellie had laughed when she read that report, passed across by Davey.

Meanwhile Paddy, now in custody was having thirty years of crimes thrown at him, crimes he'd escaped while in Majorca, his expensive solicitors arguing each one and likely to get away with it, too, while Saleh was charged as an associate, a case now being opened by Delgado on whether he, not Ellie, had killed accountant Bryan Noyce.

It wasn't vindication, but after the court case, it would be, even if Paddy Simpson walked. And, if he did, Ellie knew exactly who she'd be throwing every favour she still had owed to her at.

As for Whitehouse, he'd been released on bail on day three, shown to be nothing but a lackey. He'd disappeared the moment he left the station, probably whisked away to a safe house while he completed his side of whatever deal he'd made. Ellie wondered if she'd ever see him again, or, rather, what she'd do if she did.

She didn't know, and that scared her a little.

———

It was three more days before Robert awoke from his coma.

During that time, apart from showering, eating and checking in on Millie, who seemed to gain weight because of a lot of treats being passed on by a guilty-looking Ramsey, Ellie had spent every waking moment at his bedside, talking, reading, even singing to the unconscious Robert. At one point, shortly before evening drew in she'd even snapped, shouting at him, telling him he was a coward for taking the easy way out.

That he couldn't leave.

That she needed him.

It was around lunchtime when his eyes finally opened, and he stared up at Ellie, leaning over him, nurses and doctors beside her. It hadn't been by chance; he'd started showing micro movements for about half an hour, and everyone had been waiting for this. And, after five minutes of poking and prodding, the medical staff left, leaving Robert and Ellie alone.

'Mark ...' Robert whispered.

'We know,' Ellie reassured him. 'We got the recording you made. He's gone, Robert. He'll never bother you or us again.'

'Nicky ...'

'Again, all sorted,' Ellie smiled. 'I won't bore you right now, but when you get better, we'll go into it in detail. Okay?'

Robert made the slightest of head motions, as if barely nodding.

'Date ...'

Ellie looked at her watch.

'It's Wednesday the—'

'No ...' Robert whispered, stopping her. 'Date. You. Me ...'

Ellie smiled.

'Let's talk about that when you're better,' she said, but stopped as she realised Robert was snoring.

Laughing to herself, she sat back down on the chair.

He wouldn't even remember he asked the question.

But she would.

IT WAS ANOTHER TWO WEEKS BEFORE LIFE STARTED TO GET BACK to normal; Ramsey had been removed from dog sitting duty when Millie had been found to have gained almost a kilo in weight, which Tinker claimed was purely from sausages, while Robert got better every day. He was slower in his thoughts, and more wary of speaking, as if he knew something still wasn't right, but it was progressing the right way.

And, as he was moved from ACCU and into a regular room, Ellie had started to plan for the future of the team.

She'd done what she needed, and she'd answered the questions she needed explained. The police, after the trial, would exonerate her completely, and her life was her own once more.

But what would she do with it?

The answers, strangely, came from a sixteen-year-old boy.

She'd not seen Casey for a couple of weeks by this point; Pauline had made sure he wasn't involved with Finders anymore, and with the teacher strikes over, Casey was back in school. But, on a Saturday morning, he met with Ellie in the same booth they always met in, in Caesar's Diner.

'Mum's banned me from working with you,' he said. 'And that sucks.'

'It's probably for the best,' Ellie smiled. 'God knows what would have happened if you'd stayed with us.'

'We'd have done good things,' Casey shrugged. 'Helped people.'

Ellie shook her head.

'My work here is done,' she said, if a little melodramatically. 'I found what I needed. Took down who I wanted.'

'Yeah, but that doesn't mean you stop, right?' Casey's eyes widened. 'You can't!'

Ellie leant back in the chair.

'Robert's still in recovery,' she said. 'He's there because of me. Ramsey was beaten badly by the Lumettas. Tinker was in a car crash—'

'With you.'

Ellie accepted this.

'True, but what I'm trying to say is these people suffered because of me. Because of my crusade.'

'What about the people you saved?' Casey asked. 'You removed the Lumettas. You saved Danny Flynn—'

'And what good did *that* do me?'

'You still saved him, Ellie. What he did after that is his own concern,' Casey sucked on his milkshake straw for a moment. 'What about the dead you gained justice for? Natalie, the painter's assistant, or Paulo Moretti?'

'That's the police's work,' Ellie replied.

'That'll be the same police that employed Whitehouse, right?'

Ellie nodded, raising her mug of coffee.

'Touché,' she said.

'What I'm trying to say is that even without me, you do good,' Casey continued. 'You still have a ton of favours owed. You can't just walk away.'

Ellie sighed. She wanted nothing more than to walk away, but she also knew without a doubt that she'd never be allowed back into the force now. Not only would the officers who accused her have issues, she'd also taken down one of their own.

All she had left was Finders.

'And besides, Davey only just started,' Casey smiled. 'Be real harsh to start a new job and lose it on the same day.'

There was a motion at the door to the diner as it opened, and Pauline Noyce walked in. Slim, blonde and wearing a denim jacket even though it was raining outside, she nodded to Casey.

'Time for you to say goodbye,' she said, 'while I have a word with Miss Reckless.'

Casey looked as if he wanted to speak, but then nodded, looking back at Ellie.

'I'll be in touch,' he said as he left.

'No, he won't,' Pauline replied as she took his place in the booth, facing Ellie, who was watching a reluctant Casey nod at her through the window, before skateboarding off.

'Drink?' Sandra the waitress asked, appearing like a ghost beside them.

'No thanks,' Pauline said.

'Just the bill,' Ellie replied, passing her card across. With a nod, sensing something bad was about to happen, Sandra left, leaving Ellie and Pauline in an awkward silence.

'You almost killed him.'

The accusation was blunt and to the point.

'I know,' Ellie replied. 'It was never my intent. I even turned his help down at the start. But Casey can be ... quite persuasive.'

'I don't want him working with you.'

Ellie's face tightened.

'With all due respect, Pauline, we both know you and Bryan weren't happy together,' she said. 'God knows I wasn't happy with Nathan. If it hadn't been me, it would have been someone else, as well you bloody know, so while I understand why I'm painted as the villain here, I'm getting a little sick of it.'

She leant closer.

'It takes two to have an affair, and I didn't lead Bryan astray. We were both as guilty as each other. And I think it's pretty shitty of you to take it out on his son.'

Pauline stared in shock at Ellie, and Ellie realised she probably expected some kind of contrite apology.

'I *am* sorry,' she added, even if the contrition was lacking. 'But your son's ability, his expertise, it saved a lot of people, whether or not he worked for me. And he found your husband's murderer before I did – and I'm ... I was ... a bloody good copper.'

Pauline looked away.

'He's too much like his father,' she whispered. 'And that worries me. He won't listen to me.'

'He's a teenager,' Ellie replied. They don't. Do you remember when you were his age? What were you doing?'

Pauline nodded.

'If he returns to your company, it's during holidays and breaks,' she said. 'And he gets double pay. He's starting his A Levels next year and needs the money for Uni.'

'Understood,' Ellie replied, deciding not to mention that after the Lumetta case, Casey took several thousand pounds' worth of gold home. 'To be honest, Pauline, I don't even know what I'll be doing, let alone what the team will do.'

'You'll be doing this,' Pauline rose from the seat now. 'You're good at it. And you'll do it for Bryan. For his memory.'

She actually smiled at this point.

'And if Millie needs a dog sitter, I'm sure I can help. It'll be hard to start, but I'll do my best.'

Ellie rose to face Pauline, holding out her hand.

'I really am sorry,' she said. 'Bryan was a hell of a guy. And I – we – shouldn't have ...'

'Yes, he was,' Pauline replied, ignoring the offered hand. 'And you're right. If it wasn't you, it'd have been someone else.'

And, before she could say anything else, her lip quivering, Pauline turned and left the diner.

Ellie moved back to the booth seat, moving Millie out of the way. She didn't know what she intended to do next, and that scared her. She didn't even know what to do the moment she left the diner.

Sandra, ever the cheerful waitress, walked over with the card reader, a frown on her face.

'Your card isn't working,' she said. 'Tried it three times.'

Ellie took the card reader, checking the screen and smiling.

SO AM I IN? Y/N

Laughing, Ellie pressed Y, and the screen suddenly changed to TRANSACTION APPROVED. It was the same trick Casey had used to get on to the team, and strangely, this singular, nostalgic act filled her with a little hope for the future. She passed it back to Sandra who, after looking surprised at this, passed the card back to Ellie and tore off the receipt, giving this to her as well, before leaving her alone at the booth.

Rising, allowing Millie to jump off the seat as she clipped the lead on, Ellie paused as she reached the door.

Nicky Simpson was there.

'I hoped to catch you,' he said.

'I'm walking the dog,' Ellie replied, indicating for him to move out of the way. 'You can walk with me.'

OUTSIDE CAESAR'S, THE LONDON STREETS WERE QUIET; THE City was always more silent when it wasn't a weekday.

'Didn't think I'd see you again,' Ellie said as they walked. 'Saw you did a tell-all in *The Sun*.'

'Felt like the best way to distance myself,' Simpson replied, stepping to the side as Millie found an interesting sniff at his feet.

'Saw you've sorted care for your dad.'

'The least I could do.'

'And you're still paying for Ramsey's mum.'

'Well, technically that's from a slush fund Paddy never knew about, and as he's technically the boss, until someone realises, then Paddy's paying it,' Simpson said, running a hand through his deliberately messy hair. 'I-I wanted to thank you, Reckless.'

'Just remember you owe me a favour at some point,' Ellie shrugged. 'At least I know now why you could never tell me which of Delgado or Whitehouse worked for you.'

'Neither,' Simpson smiled. 'And Paddy always kept his cards close.'

'Have you been to see them?' Ellie asked. 'Paddy or Carrie?'

Simpson shook his head, and for a moment, the darkness in his eyes returned.

'My family's dead,' he said coldly. 'I'm just me now.'

Ellie nodded, stopping in the street.

'What is it?' she muttered, looking around. 'This isn't enough for a personal visit. What aren't you telling me?'

Nicky Simpson looked out across the road.

'You've made a sea change in London gangs with this,' he said. 'South London's up for grabs with Granddad gone. Rumours are Jimmy Tsang is pushing his way in.'

'They won't accept Tsang.'

'True, but he's working with locals,' Simpson sighed. 'Danny Flynn, for a start.'

Ellie nodded.

'Good for him. Maybe I'll use the favour Kenny Tsang owes me after all.'

'He's also pissed at you. Big time. Something about a

game of chess?' Nicky Simpson actually laughed at this. 'You know what, Reckless, I underestimated you. You're more fun to be around than I expected. Perhaps—'

'Goodbye, Nicky,' Ellie replied flatly. 'When I need a favour, I'll call.'

Slightly startled by the coldness of the response, but understanding it better than Ellie realised, Simpson went to reply, nodded, then turned away.

'Finders have a free corporate membership,' he said. 'Any time.'

And, with that said, Nicky Simpson walked back to his Tesla, illegally parked across the road and drove off, leaving Ellie and Millie alone on the street.

———

SHE HADN'T MEANT TO GO TO FINDERS, BUT THE WALK HAD taken her close by, and so she took the opportunity to pop up to her office and get some admin done – after all, if she was going to carry on, she needed to do it with a clean slate.

There was nobody at reception; that wasn't a surprise for a weekend. But, as she walked towards her glass-walled office, she could hear voices in the boardroom.

Opening the door, she looked into the room and scowled.

'What the bloody hell are you doing in?' she asked.

Tinker, Ramsey, and Davey looked up at her.

'We're just waiting for our next job,' Tinker smiled.

'We knew you'd be in, as you're a workaholic and you have no life,' Ramsey added. 'And Casey put a tracker in Millie's collar when I looked after her.'

'I don't know you well enough to make a disparaging

comment, boss, but I saw Robert last night, and he said you need a fresh case to get your teeth into,' Davey offered.

She picked up a folder.

'And we've been passed one,' she said. 'That is, if you're still in the business of finding things, solving crimes and helping people?'

Letting Millie off her lead, allowing her to go to her bed in the corner, Ellie sat at the head of the boardroom table.

'So, what do you have for us next?' she asked.

Ellie Reckless and her team
will return in their next thriller

Released November 2023

Gain up-to-the-moment information on the release by
signing up to the Jack Gatland VIP Reader's Club!

Join at www.subscribepage.com/jackgatland

ACKNOWLEDGEMENTS

When you write a series of books, you find that there are a ton of people out there who help you, sometimes without even realising, and so I wanted to say thanks.

There are people I need to thank, and they know who they are, including my brother Chris Lee, who I truly believe could make a fortune as a post-retirement copy editor, if not a solid writing career of his own, Jacqueline Beard MBE, who has copyedited all my books since the very beginning, and editor Sian Phillips, all of whom have made my books way better than they have every right to be.

Also, I couldn't have done this without my growing army of ARC and beta readers, who not only show me where I falter, but also raise awareness of me in the social media world, ensuring that other people learn of my books.

But mainly, I tip my hat and thank you. *The reader.* Who once took a chance on an unknown author in a pile of Kindle books, thought you'd give them a go, and who has carried on this far with them, as well as the spin off books I now release.

I write these books for you. And with luck, I'll keep on writing them for a very long time.

Jack Gatland / Tony Lee,
London, May 2023

ABOUT THE AUTHOR

Jack Gatland is the pen name of *#1 New York Times Bestselling Author* Tony Lee, who has been writing in all media for thirty-five years, including comics, graphic novels, middle grade books, audio drama, TV and film for *DC Comics, Marvel, BBC, ITV, Random House, Penguin USA, Hachette* and a ton of other publishers and broadcasters.

These have included licenses such as *Doctor Who, Spider Man, X-Men, Star Trek, Battlestar Galactica, MacGyver,* BBC's *Doctors, Wallace and Gromit* and *Shrek*, as well as work created with musicians such as *Ozzy Osbourne, Joe Satriani, Beartooth* and *Megadeth.*

As Tony, he's toured the world talking to reluctant readers with his 'Change The Channel' school tours, and lectures on screenwriting and comic scripting for *Raindance* in London.

As Jack, he's written several book series now - a police procedural featuring *DI Declan Walsh and the officers of the Temple Inn Crime Unit*, a spinoff featuring "cop for criminals" *Ellie Reckless and her team,* and a second espionage spinoff series featuring burnt MI5 agent *Tom Marlowe*, an action adventure series featuring conman-turned-treasure hunter *Damian Lucas*, and a standalone novel set in a New York boardroom.

An introvert West Londoner by heart, he lives with his wife Tracy and dog Fosco, just outside London.

Feel free to follow Jack on all his social media by clicking on the links below. Over time these can be places where we can engage, discuss Declan, Ellie, Tom and others, and put the world to rights.

www.jackgatland.com
www.hoodemanmedia.com

Visit my Reader's Group Page
(Mainly for fans to discuss my books):
https://www.facebook.com/groups/jackgatland

Subscribe to my Readers List:
www.subscribepage.com/jackgatland

www.facebook.com/jackgatlandbooks
www.twitter.com/jackgatlandbook
ww.instagram.com/jackgatland

Want more books by Jack Gatland?

Turn the page...

LETTER FROM THE DEAD

"BY THE TIME YOU READ THIS, I WILL BE DEAD..."

A TWENTY YEAR OLD MURDER...
A PRIME MINISTER LEADERSHIP BATTLE...
A PARANOID, HOMELESS EX-MINISTER...
AN EVANGELICAL PREACHER WITH A SECRET...

DI DECLAN WALSH HAS HAD BETTER FIRST DAYS...

AVAILABLE ON AMAZON / KINDLEUNLIMITED

THEY TRIED TO KILL HIM...
NOW HE'S OUT FOR **REVENGE.**

NEW YORK TIMES #1 BESTSELLER **TONY LEE** WRITING AS

JACK GATLAND

THE MURDER OF AN **MI5 AGENT**...
A BURNED SPY **ON THE RUN** FROM HIS OWN PEOPLE...
AN ENEMY OUT TO **STOP HIM** AT ANY COST...
AND A **PRESIDENT** ABOUT TO BE **ASSASSINATED**...

SLEEPING
SOLDIERS

A **TOM MARLOWE** THRILLER

BOOK 1 IN A NEW SERIES OF THRILLERS IN THE STYLE OF
JASON BOURNE, JOHN MILTON OR **BURN NOTICE,** AND
SPINNING OUT OF THE **DECLAN WALSH** SERIES OF BOOKS

AVAILABLE ON AMAZON / KINDLE UNLIMITED

JACK GATLAND

THE LIONHEART CURSE

HUNT THE GREATEST TREASURES
PAY THE GREATEST PRICE

BOOK 1 IN A NEW SERIES OF ADVENTURES
IN THE STYLE OF 'THE DA VINCI CODE'
FROM THE CREATOR OF DECLAN WALSH

AVAILABLE ON AMAZON / KINDLEUNLIMITED

EIGHT PEOPLE. EIGHT SECRETS.
ONE SNIPER.

THE
BOARD
ROOM

HOW FAR WOULD YOU GO TO GAIN JUSTICE?

NEW YORK TIMES #1 BESTSELLER TONY LEE WRITING AS

JACK GATLAND

A NEW STANDALONE THRILLER WITH
A TWIST - FROM THE CREATOR OF THE
BESTSELLING 'DI DECLAN WALSH' SERIES

AVAILABLE ON AMAZON / KINDLE UNLIMITED

Printed in Great Britain
by Amazon